ALSO BY KEVIN ROBERT ALDRICH

Mysteries & Thrillers

CAMERON HAUK MYSTERIES

Eyes in the Dark

Key Witness

Scale of Justice

Tête A Tête

~

Romance

Flames of Freedom

Bare Trap

Spellbound

Racing Hearts

Alli & Ollie

SCALE OF JUSTICE

KEVIN ROBERT ALDRICH

SCALE OF JUSTICE

For Holly, Jayda, and Taegon

1

THE HALLS of the Department of Justice building were dark and silent as Cameron Hauk padded their marbled lengths. The air cooled his cheeks, the temperature in the building set low for the long end-of-year holiday break. A time for the men and women of the DOJ to enjoy their families, to think back on another year of working to protect the citizens of the United States, to feel good about themselves and their mission.

And a time for Cam to rob their workplace while they nodded off on the couch at home with glasses of rum-spiked eggnog tipping in their sleepy hands.

Cam wore stretchy black jeans, a black long-sleeved t-shirt, and a black pullover with a high collar that covered his neck. Add in the black sneakers and a black beanie and he wore the traditional garb of a thief in the night. Not very original, perhaps, but the outfit was a classic for a reason. Stealth, movement, disguise. The clothing suited the purpose. He would blend into the deep shadows, hiding his body shape from the security cameras. If he spotted a security guard, the dark clothing would prevent a flash of light or color from catching the corner of the guard's eye.

The fact that the outfit was warm and comfy as hell was just a bonus.

This was not Cam's first time inside the historic Robert F. Kennedy Department of Justice building. He'd been through it several times before—always during the day, of course—on tours, both with the public and with his classmates. But he never ceased to be awed by the marble floors, the limestone walls, the aluminum leaf on the barreled ceilings.

And the artwork. Even deep in the night, Cam could still see the artwork throughout the building, illuminated by spotlights that served to provide security lighting, but also to accentuate the beauty of the work spread throughout the massive building. Murals, statues, paintings, frescoes, friezes. Art was everywhere, and not just on the walls. Detailed, ornate marquetry adorned the columns and pilasters throughout the building, and even the elevator doors shone with inlaid aluminum designs.

President Roosevelt had used the construction of the building during the depression in the 1930s as an opportunity to provide work for unemployed artists. It was a shrewd use of the government during an impossible time for its citizens, and a shrewd political move for FDR, as well. But it always made Cam proud to think that his country considered art in the same breath, in the same physical space, that it considered justice. Art is about empathy, mercy. Justice cannot live without art. Without empathy or mercy, justice is merely state-sanctioned oppression.

The fact that he had snuck into the building to steal from justice did nothing to reduce his pride in the system. We all play our roles. Justice wouldn't exist without criminals to probe and define the boundaries. Like white-hat hackers in the tech world, criminals like Cam helped to make the justice system stronger.

Not that Cam actually thought of himself that way. But it was a good story to tell in class to see if he could get a rise out of his professors. And like any good story, there was a grain of truth to it.

He carried a key card that would grant him access to most of the building. He'd stolen it from Vernon Stratham, the reedy, bespectacled campaign finance manager for the Attorney General himself. It seemed a little odd to Cam that Attorney General Jenkins would have an office for his campaign manager in the building where he worked. He was a political appointee, not an elected official. It seemed an improper use of taxpayer resources to house someone working on his presidential campaign in the Department of Justice building. But who was Cam to judge? A little bend in the rules, a willingness to look the other way to serve himself once in a while would only play to Cam's advantage in the endgame.

Cam had lifted Stratham's key card from his laptop case almost by accident months earlier during a donor event on a megayacht in the Santa Monica Bay, but he hadn't used it yet. Like most government buildings, the DOJ was old and massive. It was kept in remarkably good shape and had been modernized many times over the years, but with a building that old and that large, there were always physical vulnerabilities somewhere. A broken camera, a loose window, an old access corridor that had been bricked up and forgotten over time. It was Cam's job to find and exploit those vulnerabilities. When he was done, the police would figure out how he'd done it and plug the hole in their security. A win-win for everyone.

Cam's hat wasn't white. It was definitely black. But there was the odd grey thread here and there.

He hadn't used the key card because he knew when he did, the clock would start ticking. Some security monitor somewhere would get an alert that Vernon Stratham was in the building after hours. A guard would come checking, doing his due diligence, just making sure that Mr. Stratham was okay—and letting Stratham know that his presence had not gone undetected.

But Cam wanted to go undetected for as long as possible. Forever, if he did his job right.

And Cam always did his job right. He didn't always get the outcome he wanted. Plans were made to fail, after all. But his parents had taught him well. They'd brought him on jobs with them before he knew how to walk. He could pick pockets before he could do long division, could scout a location's security weaknesses before he could ride a bike. Before his voice had broken, he could hack into the video feed of a bank and swap the live view for a recorded loop of an uncompromised vault. He wasn't a master thief. Not yet. But he was damn good, if he did say so himself.

He kept the key card in his pocket. He'd use it when he needed it, not before.

Until then, he exploited the vulnerabilities. He crept through the dark halls, keeping both ears open, one eye looking out for security while the other enjoyed the artwork, and made his way to Stratham's office, two floors down from the office of the esteemed Attorney General William Jenkins.

Presidential hopeful and Democratic frontrunner, Bill Jenkins was a man with much to lose.

And much to hide. Or so Cam hoped.

2

JUST STEPS AWAY from the famous law library with its twenty-foot ceilings and gorgeous murals from artist Maurice Sterne depicting man's "Struggle for Justice", the Attorney General's office was on the fifth floor, the top floor of the building. Cam didn't need to go that far. Not yet, anyway.

He made his way without a sound and without incident to the third floor instead. To Stratham's office. Perhaps it was a nod to the impropriety of an appointed official housing their political campaign finance manager in a public building, but AG Jenkins had chosen not to keep Stratham close at hand on the fifth floor. Stratham's office squatted amongst the rank-and-file DOJ employees. He still had an office, with a door and a window, but it was not in a position of glory or honor.

Knowing Stratham, he wouldn't care. He would have his eyes on a bigger prize. Chief of staff, maybe? No, the campaign manager would seize that plum first. Secretary of Commerce, then. SEC commissioner, perhaps. Someplace Stratham could enrich himself for life, no doubt.

That was another reason Cam had no qualms whatsoever about breaking into the DOJ building and stealing from Stratham. There are as many criminals on the so-called "right"

5

side of the law as there are on the "wrong" side. Right and wrong, after all, are just a matter of perspective.

As he crept through the building, Cam scanned the area through the high-tech augmented reality glasses he wore. The spoils of another heist the Christmas prior, the glasses were the last prototype built by tech billionaire and certified genius Dr. Christopher Nestrom, founder and former owner of Nestech, Inc. His tech hardware had already changed the world twice, and these glasses would have done it a third time if the man's own family hadn't offed him first.

From the reports Cam read in the news, that family was now embroiled in a bitter internecine struggle for control of Nestrom's company. Their insults and condemnation had spilled into the press. They seemed to be too busy bickering to bring the glasses to market. Ironic, because if they did, they'd make a fortune for themselves, enough money to forget all about petty squabbles for power. Their riches would buy each of them all the power they wanted.

But Cam wasn't at all sure it was a good idea to sell the glasses as-is to the general population. The glasses were powerful, and therefore dangerous. The prototype he wore had immediate face recognition and biographical information pulled from the internet. It synced with any cameras in the area—in any area, really, since it could connect to any camera in the world—to show the locations and identities of any individuals around the wearer. It let you see in the dark, magnified objects and text from long distances, and identified weapons and threats to physical safety. And it even looked kind of cool, in a nerdy, tech-bro way. There were a thousand other capabilities, too, and Cam had only scratched the surface. He often wished there had been an owner's manual he could have stolen with the glasses. But he muddled through in his spare time and found out the capabilities of the glasses through trial and error.

The glasses were powerful, and that was dangerous. But they

were even more dangerous because that power was addictive. If released, they would not only destroy what vestiges of personal privacy still existed, they would probably result in a populace who spent all their time fiddling with their hardware, spying on each other, and watching cat videos and porn, and no time doing anything useful at all. Society had not shown a penchant for restraint or common sense in recent years. This kind of technology could be used for good. It could change the world for the better. But, given human nature and the manipulations of corporate ad-mongers and the media, it probably wouldn't.

Cam, however, was definitely putting them to good use. He might not know everything about the glasses, but he knew enough, and what he did know gave him a huge advantage in his work. With the glasses, he didn't need any light at all to move through buildings at night. He could move as quickly and as safely in the pitch dark as he could in broad daylight. And he could clearly see the locations and movements of all security staff, including the seven guards who were working in the DOJ building that night.

He'd done his homework, of course. Part of his parents' training. He knew the shift schedule, patrol routes, command structure, and even the names and faces of every guard on staff, not just the seven working that night. Unless he lost focus or stopped paying attention, there was no way Cam could be surprised by a security guard while he was wearing the glasses.

And as he'd been prepping for this job, he'd found one other capability the glasses had: a cloaking device.

Okay, not really a cloaking device. Cam just liked to think of it that way. The glasses didn't make him invisible to a person looking at him. But they emitted some kind of beam or ray that confounded any cameras, making Cam appear as a fuzzy black spot in the image. Anyone watching would be able to see that something was there, that something weird was happening. But instead of seeing a thief sneaking around the building, they'd see a shadowy smudge moving across the screen. More than likely, they'd waste time thinking it was some kind of glitch in the system or something smeared on the camera lens before they'd think to come investigate. And by the time they did, Cam would have moved on. No detection, and no photographic evidence of his presence left behind.

The glasses really were amazing. Cam readjusted them on his face and tugged his black beanie down tighter over his ears as he slipped through a doorway from the main central hall on the third floor.

Contrary to the grandeur of the hall, he found himself in a stuffy room with high-walled fabric cubicles packed tightly into clusters, separated by narrow aisles barely wide enough for Cam's shoulders. Where the hall outside had been lit by spotlights spilling over the artwork adorning the wall, Cam's glasses let him see that this space was lit by fluorescent light fixtures, their bulbs shadowed and stained with age, tacked to the stained ceiling tiles. Where the hall outside had marble floors that gleamed in the reflected glow of the spotlights, this room had carpet that once may have been plush, but now was threadbare and pressed thin from decades of trampling by scores of mid-level government workers. Where the view in the hall had extended from one side of the building to the other, giving a sense of the long sweep of the eye of justice, the high walls of the cubicles in this room blocked Cam from seeing more than a few feet ahead. Out there, his heart soared. In here, he was a rat in a government maze. If he weren't wearing his glasses, he wouldn't have even been able to see the windows, wouldn't have even known there were any.

Thankfully, his glasses let him see everything. They provided Cam with a perfect floor plan for that room, the adjoining rooms, even the floors above and below him. An incredible density of information was cleverly arranged in his visual field in such a way as to be completely intuitive. The glasses provided not just a map, but a sense of movement around him that was as subconscious as when you walked into a dark room and felt the presence of someone waiting in the shadows. Only, with the help of the glasses, that person might be three rooms behind you and two floors up.

Cam had already entered his destination into the glasses. It overlayed a subtle route onto his view, a series of soft green lines showing him several paths to Stratham's office, with the most direct route a little brighter than the others. A good thing, too. Without that help, he might have gotten lost in the cubicle maze and not been found again until next Christmas.

He wound left and right and left again until he emerged before a row of doors against an exterior wall. Cam followed his map to his right, to the second-to-last door. Vernon Stratham's name was etched in white capital letters onto a small, black plastic plaque stuck to the center of a wooden door. The door seemed to be made of thin laminate, probably hollow, undeniably cheap. Cam could see that just by looking at it. And the plaque was as cheap as the door. It curved out on one side, the adhesive coming loose beneath it. These areas were not on the public tour, and the government had clearly spared every expense in maintaining them over the years. AG Jenkins may be inappropriately devoting taxpayer resources to housing his campaign finance manager, but at least he wasn't devoting much of them.

The only thing that seemed like it might have been updated during this century was the key card reader. It wasn't modern or state-of-the-art by any stretch, but it was a step up from a physical lock and key. Cam pulled Stratham's key card from his pocket. As soon as he swiped that card, that clock would start ticking. He would have to get inside, get into Stratham's computer, and find something he could use before the guards came to check up on him.

But Cam couldn't worry about that. He had to get in. Time

was running out. He would graduate in May, just five months away, and he had to be ready when he did. He had until then to get some information he could use to blackmail the AG. His mother's release from prison depended on it. The rest of her life —and his—depended on it.

Cam pulled in a deep breath and reached out with the key card.

As he did, alarms began to sound.

3

THE ALARM WAS an assault on Cam's senses. A blaring klaxon set a throbbing pulse beneath a wail that swooped up in pitch and back down again. It was like the two most annoying car alarms imaginable, set on top of each other and cranked up to eleven in volume. Along with that, security lights set at intervals throughout the building strobed in a rhythm that did not match the beat of the klaxon. The visual rhythm clashed with the auditory rhythm in a way that would drive Cam mad if he had to endure it for long.

It was ingenious, really. The guards were probably trained for it, but the intense and sudden sensory overload might help to slow or disorient a criminal long enough to prevent their escape.

Not Cam, naturally, but a lesser criminal, perhaps. One without Cam's training, or his glasses.

As he instinctively ran for the exit, following the floor plan on his viewscreen, Cam's first thought was that he'd set off the alarms when he brought the key card near the card reader. That Stratham had reported it stolen or lost and they'd set up a trap to trigger the alarm as soon as the key card was used.

Then Cam's rational mind kicked in and overrode his

instinctive fear. Stratham had surely reported the card as missing, but it was highly unlikely the DOJ would go to all that trouble for a lost key card. At worst, its use would trigger an alert in their security system that the key card had been used. They'd then rely on camera footage and the security guards to catch the user. They wouldn't trigger a building-wide alarm.

Cam ran out the door and down the marble hallway toward the stairwell, ignoring the artwork this time. The spotlights were still shining, but the flashing lights gave the long, empty hall a strobing, horror-movie feel. All that was missing was thunder and the sudden appearance of Count Dracula in the hallway between strobes.

The alarms couldn't be Cam's fault. He hadn't even swiped the card. He'd started to. He'd reached out, but the alarm had sounded before he got close enough to the reader.

Cam swung to his left and through the stairwell door, careful even in his haste to minimize the sound of the door handle, catching the swinging door before it could slam into the wall behind it. He could see in the glasses that there were no security guards nearby, but habits were habits, and he didn't want to become complacent. He'd brought the glasses on every job since he'd stolen them, but there might come a time when he had left them behind or they stopped working for some reason. And the last thing you wanted to do when fleeing a crime scene was to make a bunch of noise to draw attention to yourself.

He checked again the locations of the guards in the viewscreen of his glasses. All seven were moving quickly, but none of them were in or approaching his stairwell. They seemed to be converging toward a location above him and on the other side of the building, in or below the law library. Cam was in the clear.

He closed the door softly behind him. As he turned and stepped onto the landing, something came down the stairs to his right and knocked into him. Before he could even react, Cam was tumbling down the marble steps. They were bowed in the center and worn smooth from a hundred years of use, but every single tread still battered Cam's body as he slid, rolled, and bounced down the stairs. He tucked his arms over his ears. It exposed his torso to more punishment, but his arms would protect his head as he fell.

A weight rode him down, making each jab of the stairs even worse. Someone else's body on top of his. They crumpled in a heap on the landing below. As luck would have it, Cam wound up on the bottom and absorbed the shock of not only his own weight, but the weight of the other person as they hit the floor.

Despite the protection of his arms, Cam's head snapped back on impact and banged hard against the cold marble. His glasses came loose, kept from flying off only by one earpiece tucked under his beanie. The world around him turned black, punched through by flashes of red.

He could taste hot metal in his mouth. He must have bitten his tongue. The thought came faint and distant.

Cam could feel the pain blooming in head, his back, and his hips. His breath had been knocked out of him when he hit the floor. He sucked in a deep breath to replace it and caught a faint scent of lilac and lavender. Not a perfume, but a faint and subtle smell, like scented soap.

Adrenaline coursed through his blood and pushed away the pain in his back and hips. It pushed back the red flashes behind his eyes. The darkness remained, but now it was punctuated by flashes of white.

The security lights.

The sound of the klaxons was duller, quieter. Cam wasn't sure if that was because there were no speakers in the stairwell or because he'd damaged his hearing when he fell.

Cam had landed flat on his back. The other person splayed on top of him. He bunched his muscles to buck them off. Cam could feel their form pressed flat against his. He could feel their shape.

The shape. The scent.

The person on top of him was a woman.

Before Cam could push her off, she pushed herself up over him, straddling his hips. She pinned his arms with her hands and hooked her feet inside his crotch to pin his legs. Heavy boots dug into Cam's thighs.

She wore a mask, a black nylon balaclava that covered everything but her eyes. A black baseball cap was pulled over it, the bill twisted to one side from the fall.

She leaned over him, staring down at him with suspicion. The security lights strobed behind her and above her, each flash backlighting her, keeping her masked face shrouded. Cam desperately wanted to reposition his glasses so he could see the woman clearly, but they were askew on his face, and she had his arms pinned hard.

She examined him for a moment, then pulled his arms down to his sides and pinned them with her knees, freeing her black-gloved hands. Her knees dug into Cam's forearms, twisting his skin, searing them with pain.

She straightened the bill of her ball cap and pulled it down tight, then sat back on her heels. Her hip bones ground against Cam's, sending a flash of heat through his body. He ignored it.

She bent over him again, her face still hidden in shadow, and tilted her head. "Nice glasses."

Her voice was low and smooth and resonant. It flowed into Cam's mind like a balm. He closed his eyes and shivered as a flush of warmth washed over him from head to toe.

She pulled his glasses off, sliding the earpiece from under his beanie, and examined them. Cam's heart froze in his chest. She tilted her head back to let the strobing light fall on the glasses. In that flash, Cam could see her eyes, sea-green and limpid. Beautiful. Calculating. And curious.

And then she was gone. She pushed off of him and sprinted down the stairs, kicking one boot hard into his left thigh as she did. Cam groaned in pain, then sat up and watched her run between flashes. She took the stairs two at a time, and he could only see her from behind. Tall, slender, agile. Like him, she wore all black, with black work pants and those thick boots, and a black jacket.

Cam struggled to his feet, tried to run down the stairs after her, but pain bloomed in his leg. It wasn't broken, but he'd have a hell of a bruise in the morning. He limped down the stairs after her as quickly as he could, swinging himself with his arms on the rails, but he knew he wouldn't catch her.

By instinct, he reached for his glasses. If he couldn't catch her, at least he could watch her, see which way she went. He reached for his glasses, and found nothing.

She'd taken them.

The woman had stolen his glasses.

Cam stopped dead on the stairs, nearly fell down again. He backtracked to the landing, searched in the strobing light in case they'd been dropped.

Nothing.

How could he get the information he needed now? How could he free his mother? He needed those glasses. And he'd lost them.

The strobing of the lights and the clanging of the alarm finally broke through Cam's stunned mind, snapping him back to reality.

No, he hadn't lost them. That woman had stolen them.

Now Cam would have to steal them back.

The darkness felt so foreign he had to fight his own fear and disorientation to keep going, using the glimpses of his surroundings provided by the strobe to limp his way through the building. He could no longer locate the security guards, but he'd last seen them headed to the other part of the building. Whatever had happened there, they'd soon be searching for whoever had done it.

And with as fast as the security guards had been running, Cam guessed that the police would soon be arriving to help.

He moved as quickly as his lame leg would allow, opening his senses as best he could. That was another feature of the alarms and the strobes. They made it difficult for a criminal to see or hear if anyone was coming for them.

Swinging his leg and hopping down the halls, keeping one hand on the walls for support, Cam made his way down the stairs to the basement, past the klaxons and the strobes, and out the way he'd come in.

The silence of the cold night air wrapped him like a warm blanket. He retuned his hearing. Sounds of car engines, cross-walk signs, the freeway in the distance, moving fast this late at night. He could hear police sirens, faint. Getting closer.

Cam moved through the streets, away from the sound. He pulled off his beanie and tucked it in his pocket, shoved both hands in his jacket pockets, let the cold air cool him and the silence envelop him, calm him. He pulled in long, slow breaths, slowing his heart rate, slowing his pace to minimize his limp. A limp would attract attention. A man moving down a well-lit sidewalk on a cold evening wouldn't.

He hoped.

When a cop car careened around the corner and headed toward him, sirens wailing and lights flashing, all the breathing in the world couldn't stop his heart rate from spiking. But when the car screamed past without slowing, Cam knew he was in the clear.

He had a long walk home, longer thanks to his injury. But the time would pass quickly. He had a lot to think about.

Someone had taken something from him, something very important. He had to figure out who.

And get it back.
Soon.

4

THE CRIMINOLOGY PROGRAM at McFadden University in Washington, D.C. was a great program, but it wasn't the best in the nation. U Maryland at College Park usually took that honor, followed by ASU. But McFadden was consistently in a group of four or five schools vying for the third spot each year.

Cam didn't care about rankings or prestige at all. He didn't even care about criminology when he'd joined the Master's program two years earlier. Under a false identity, of course. The son of a convicted felon would raise more than a few eyebrows in a graduate school for criminology. But Sam Davis, a hard-working, genial young man from a small town in Indiana, joining the program to try to make a difference in the world, didn't even earn a second thought.

The only reason Cam enrolled at the school was because the valedictorian each year earned a private audience with the school's main benefactor and most distinguished alum, none other than Attorney General William Jenkins himself. Cam would grit his teeth, study his ass off, earn that top spot, and use his private audience to blackmail the AG into arranging for his mother to be released from prison.

That was the plan. For fifteen years, he'd been trying to get

18

his mother out. A prison break wouldn't do. His mother didn't want to be a fugitive for the rest of her life. A criminal, maybe. A fugitive, no. Cam had tried one plan after another, failing each time. He'd earned a law degree in the process, hoping he could find a legal path to release. He'd briefly taken a job at a prison, studying the system from the inside, looking for an angle. He'd even completed an online program for computer science, low-level OS skills that he hoped would allow him to hack into the system and finagle his mother's release through a computer glitch. None of those plans had worked. He'd learned a lot, but it had all been a waste of time.

And while he flailed around trying to free her, his mother was stuck in a six-by-nine cell in Taconic Correctional Facility.

They'd concocted this latest scheme together years earlier. Cam had spent that night building a fake backstory online for Sam Davis—fake transcripts, fake work history, fake identity—then applied to McFadden the next day. He'd prepared himself for the grind of appearing to be a model student, but had been surprised to discover that he actually found the subjects interesting and the work engaging.

Since then, he'd worked his ass off. The school was demanding and his classmates were driven and smart. School came easily to Cam. It always had. But it was clear that it came just as easily for his fellow students. Cam had to study hard to beat them, because his plan only worked if he finished the program at the top of his class. The top five students would be rewarded with an intimate group dinner with the AG, but only the valedictorian got the private one-on-one time.

For a typical student, it was a rare opportunity to get on the fast track in the justice system or in politics. A powerful mentor could mean the difference between decades of struggle or a rocket ride to the top of the power structure in the US justice system. Truly a great reward and a huge draw for applicants to McFadden.

For Cam, it was nothing more than an opportunity to free his mother, but it would only work if he was alone with the AG. He didn't want to make a scene, some kind of public situation that would back Jenkins into a corner. But, the man was very busy and very prominent. It was practically impossible for a nobody like Cam to schedule alone time with him. And with Jenkins' rapid rise to fame and his recent turn toward politics, there had been more than one threat to his life. His security detail was top-notch. Not only the personal guards, but the tech systems they'd installed everywhere in the AG's personal life. Cam wouldn't be able to sneak up on Jenkins. His defenses were impenetrable, even with Nestech glasses.

And Cam didn't even have those anymore.

He ground his back teeth as he rounded the corner of the Jenkins Center for Society and Law, a stately building with an endless grand staircase leading to a Corinthian portico supporting a triangular pediment. Cam glanced up as he always did at the peak of the triangle high above him, framed this morning against a chill sky dotted with thick clouds. The building was modeled after the august government buildings just a few miles east and had been built around the same time. The building had once been called simply SocLaw, but was now reverently referred to as the Jenkins Center, ever since Jenkins had diverted some charitable donation or another to the school. He'd chosen the building specifically, no doubt to serve as the perfect backdrop for his congratulatory press conference each year. Setting his image as the statesman, the guardian of the people, his feet firmly planted in "the grandeur and history of this great nation", etc. etc. spin spin spin.

For Cam, Jenkins' grandeur was a pain in his ass each morning. The long, steep staircase left even the strongest students puffing at least a little bit when they reached the top. Normally, Cam would jog up the wide steps just for the exercise, and as a meaningless fuck-you to the AG. If he was going to be puffing at the top anyway, he might as well get it over with quickly. Today, with his thigh already on fire from his encounter with the mysterious thief at the DOJ building a few nights earlier, he took the steps at a slow but steady pace, staying close to the handrails. He blended into a stream of hundreds of other students headed for their first class after the winter break.

Cam unzipped his jacket just a bit to let the heat of exertion out and the cold January air in. As he climbed, he repeated a mantra in his mind.

I am Sam Davis.

I am Sam Davis.

I am Sam Davis.

With each repetition, he slipped further into his alter ego. After nearly three years, Sam Davis was as comfortable as a well-worn pair of jeans. In some ways, there was little difference between Sam and Cam. The details of the biography varied widely—one an unassuming Midwest man, the other a lifelong thief from a family of thieves. But the important parts, the values and the ideals, those were more or less the same for both.

I am Sam Davis.

I am Sam Davis.

He let the mantra fade into the back of his mind as he donned his character completely. The ache in his thigh, burning with each broad stair he climbed, didn't help. A slip on a patch of ice, a fall down the short stairs in front of his apartment building in Rosslyn. Easy cover story.

But each burning twinge reminded him of what he'd lost, and what he still had to lose.

5

Sᴀᴍ ᴇɴᴛᴇʀᴇᴅ the classroom from the back and looked down over the huge bowl of the lecture room. The auditorium held at least five hundred students, and it was standing room only for every one of Professor Oweli's lectures.

As more students filed through the doors behind him and down the steep aisles, Sam scanned the seats. He caught a raised, waving hand from the corner of his eye. With a lift of his chin and a small smile, Sam moved toward it.

He heaved himself down into the folding seat. The burning in his thigh flared when he sat, but then eased into a throb that gave Sam more relief than he was willing to admit. Not for the first time, he was grateful that McFadden had thought to upgrade the auditorium seating when Jenkins made his bequest. The seat cushions and seat backs were soft and thick and comfortable enough to soothe a sore thigh through a three-hour seminar.

"Barely made it," said Jem, his friend who sat beside him.

Having a friend who wasn't in on the con was dangerous in any job. They were too likely to inadvertently attract attention or become suspicious. But in a long con like this one, it was more suspicious not to have at least one friend. In his early thirties,

Sam was on the older end of the student age spectrum, and that gave him some cover for being less social than a typical student. His work ethic and high marks gave him more. But it made sense for him to have at least one close friend. And he and Jem had hit it off on their first day in Professor Slader's quant methods class. Jem was a computer geek like Sam. They bonded over analytics modules and plotting techniques in Python, sharing code and methodologies like a pair of seven-year-old boys would share their Pokémon card collections, and had been friends ever since.

"Woke up late," muttered Sam. He centered his backpack on the floor between his feet, pulled out his laptop, and slid the bag beneath his chair.

"Is that all?"

Sam opened his laptop and logged in. He'd carefully partitioned the hard drive into two logins. One login was for innocuous things like schoolwork, web browsing, media consumption, and the like. Another login, well-hidden and accessible only from the system's back end, was for his other work. Unless they knew exactly where to look, only a government-grade hacker would even find the hidden login. And even then, it would take a good deal of time, patience, and ingenuity to get through Sam's security and decrypt the data.

Sam frowned at Jem. "What else would there be?"

Jem nodded solemnly, but his eyes shone with mischievousness. "So you haven't seen it yet."

"Seen wha—?"

"Good morning, class," boomed Professor Oweli in his deep bass voice. Despite a head gone bald and a full-white, carefully trimmed beard, with his tall, muscular build and the pregnant energy of a dammed river, Oweli gave the impression of a man in his twenties. He was also a world-renowned genius in geopolitics, social justice, and criminal law, with an encyclopedic recall of facts, a photographic memory, and a deft mind capable of teasing out the subtlest nuances in any argument. His personal history only augmented his already impressive bona fides. As a young boy, Oweli and his family had fled a corrupt and oppressive regime in his home country after being targeted for political persecution. He grew up with a keen interest in justice, power, and politics, and had become the world's foremost thinker in the intersection of those disciplines.

That fact made him an impressive professor. What made him a popular one was the way he lectured. He spoke with palpable passion, filling his lectures with stories that engaged as much as they educated. And he did it all with a voice that made James Earl Jones sound like the fourth Powerpuff Girl.

The three-hour lecture passed in the blink of an eye. As Oweli bid them a good afternoon, Sam looked down at pages of notes on his computer, surprised to see them, surprised to see that it was already after noon. He had been so engaged in the lecture, he didn't remember taking notes at all.

As he and Jem packed up and joined the queue of students filtering up the stairs and out the back of the auditorium, he remembered what they'd been talking about before the lecture had begun.

"What was it I hadn't seen?" he asked Jem.

"Hmm?" Jem replied.

Sam smiled faintly. Jem was playing coy.

"You said before the lecture that there was something I hadn't seen yet."

"Did I?"

Sam smiled wider. Two could play that game. Jem liked having a juicy secret, but he liked sharing it even more.

"I thought you did," Sam shrugged, "but maybe I was wrong. Wanna hit Dover's for lunch?"

Jem reached the top of the stairs, stopping Sam just behind and below, and leaned down toward him, holding up two fingers. "I have two words for you, Davis. Reggie. Moon."

"That's more like one word and a proper noun," said Sam as Jem turned back and they resumed their exodus from the lecture hall.

"It's your personal armageddon, is what it is," Jem replied.

"Reggie Moon is my personal armageddon?" said Sam. "I thought the four horsemen would have more exotic-sounding names."

"You think the four horsemen would come down just for you?" said Jem. He shook his head at Sam. "You'd be lucky to get a cherub on a donkey."

Sam chuckled. "So what makes this so personal?"

"You've already got the rest of us beat, so we don't care. We just get to enjoy watching you squirm."

"What do you mean I've got—?" Sam furrowed his brow. The only way he had anyone beat was in their grades. Jem was third in their class, narrowly trailing Sarah Fulkins, whose GPA was a full two-tenths of a point behind Sam. Not insurmountable, but Sam would need to stumble badly for Sarah to catch up. There were two others, Annie and Motsu, clustered just behind Jem. Together, the five of them were far and away the front-runners for the AG dinner, and with only one semester left to go, barring something catastrophic, Sam was a lock for the top spot.

Unless he wasn't.

Sam stopped in his tracks for a moment. Students muttered behind him as they jerked to avoid running into Sam's back.

No. He shook his head and continued walking. There was no one who could possibly have caught him. He had last checked the rankings during the winter break. There had been no classes since then, no assignments or grades. There was no way someone could have dethroned him in the last week. Could there?

Jem just shrugged at the question, a sly smile on his face. He put his arm around Sam and patted his shoulder, shaking his head. "You know, Sam, winning isn't everything." He squeezed

Sam in a sidelong hug, then pulled him forward. "I had leftover Dover's for breakfast. Let's get burritos."

Sam followed Jem, but he had lost his appetite. *Winning isn't everything.* Generally, Sam would agree with that sentiment.

But this time, Jem was wrong. To Sam, winning this particular contest was the only thing.

6

THE SIZZLE OF THE GRILL, the rich scent of the carne asada, the din and jostle of the crowd in the tiny space of their favorite Mexican place, Los Bandidos, were like sepia photographs hung on distant walls in the background of Sam's mind. His burrito grew cold on the table in front of him, neglected on its foil wrapper, only one bite taken from the corner. He rested his chin in one hand, elbow propped on the table.

"Who the fuck is this Reggie guy?" he said.

"Transfer student," said Sarah around a bite of quesadilla. "From somewhere out west."

Sarah swung her neck to the side to whip her sleek blonde hair over one shoulder, narrowly avoiding the long cable of melted cheese that hung between her mouth and her quesadilla. She and Annie had already been in line when Sam and Jem had walked in. As Sam sulked and stared into space, the three others chewed their food and shared exultant looks around the high-top table, clearly enjoying Sam's distress.

"Stanford, I heard," added Annie. Annie stood at the tall table, as usual, refusing to sit down. She rocked from foot to foot as she ate. Annie rarely sat still, constantly moving her body or her hands, fidgeting. Her body reflected her mind, which moved at lightning speed, never stopping or slowing for a moment. She was crazy smart, but riddled with anxiety. Sam didn't know how she could sleep at night. To hear her tell it, she didn't. Not for long, anyway.

Jem shook his head. "UC Irvine." He wiped a piece of cilantro from his cheek. "Someone I know knows someone who works part-time in admissions and saw the transfer form."

"How can someone transfer in as a third-year with only one semester left?" Sam's blood was as hot as his food was cold. He pushed the burrito away and leaned his elbows on the table, pulling both hands through his hair. He did his best to reel his anger back, to hide the anxiety that drove it. He'd cultivated the persona of a hard-worker, but a laid-back one, espousing the attitude that he would do his best and let fate decide who took the top spot in the academic rankings.

But that was his outward persona. In most cases, it would have been accurate. But in this case, inwardly, he would outwork anyone to take the top spot. He would stop at nothing to free his mother from prison. He certainly wouldn't let some stupid college grades hold him back.

His studiousness didn't stop with the schoolwork itself. He'd studied the personal histories of every professor in the criminology program at McFadden, read every work they'd published, hacked into their records at their graduate schools, undergraduate schools, even high schools to glean some insight into their personalities. Were they sticklers for rules or looser in their approach to them? Had they been disciplined students or were they gifted with talent, or both? Had they always driven toward their chosen profession or had they come to it after much trial and error? Sam knew if they were straight or gay, fashion-conscious or mismatched and rumpled, had children, wanted children, or avoided them at all costs. All of these factors and more dictated Sam's approach to each class, to each professor, all in order to ingratiate himself with them to curry the highest possible grade.

He had to back it up with exemplary work, of course. But college, especially graduate school, was as much about interpersonal politics as it was about academic achievement. Sam had to play the whole game, and play it better than anyone else.

Which he'd done for two and a half years already. The finish line was in sight. Fifteen years after being arrested with Sam's father dying in her arms, his mother's freedom was within reach.

Until Reggie Moon.

Sam pulled his hands from his hair and curled them around his bottle of cold black tea on the table, felt the sweat on the bottle cool the heat in his skin.

Reggie Moon's GPA was now three one-thousandths of a point in front of Sam's in the class rankings. 0.003. A whisper. An afterthought. The breadth of an eyelash.

And enough to ruin Sam's plan entirely.

Sam spun the bottle between his hands, over and over, a soft warbling sound with each spin.

He had fallen into second place.

Warble. Warble.

Second place would not earn him a private audience with the Attorney General.

Warble.

Without a private audience, Sam could not blackmail the AG unless he did it in front of others.

Warble. Warble. Warble.

In front of others, the AG would be forced to grandstand or lie or, worse, admit the truth in order to save face, save his political career. Sam didn't want that. He wanted the AG to capitulate to the blackmail in the hope that whatever dirt Sam would have dug up would stay hidden.

Warble. Warble.

Sam needed to have the man alone so he could convince him to commute his mother's sentence.

Warb-

Jem stopped the bottle with his hand. "The question, Davis," he said around a bite of burrito tucked into his cheek, "isn't how Reggie Moon transferred in." He chewed the rest of his bite with a smug smile and swallowed. "The question is what you're going to do about it."

"I say you kneecap him." Motsu strode up to the table and threw his backpack underneath. "You gonna eat that?" he said, pointing to Sam's burrito. "Or were you saving it for me?"

The burrito was halfway to Motsu's mouth before Sam even opened his own to respond.

"It's probably cold," Sam muttered.

"It is cold," Motsu replied, his voice muffled by the massive bite of burrito he'd taken. "What the fuck, Davis? You couldn't keep it wrapped for me?" He took another bite. "What do you think I am, some kind of animal?"

Motsu was one of those people who made you wonder why the hell they were doing whatever mundane job they had instead of being a movie star or a model or a rock star some- where. He had long, sleek jet-black hair down to his shoulders. His lanky body was chiseled and covered in colorful tattoos, which he showed off at every opportunity. In the muggy D.C. fall or the first warm day of spring, Motsu would pull his shirt off as they left their last class, causing more than one of the female students to blush and look away or lick their lips and come closer, depending on how bold they were. Motsu had the face and body of an anime action hero, and the brash confidence to match.

And he was one of the smartest people Sam knew. His only weakness was his work ethic. He just didn't want to work that hard. He wanted to enjoy his life while he could. The fact that he was still fifth in the rankings—sixth, now that Reggie Moon had butted in—was a testament to his ability. If he ever decided to apply himself, Sam's plan would be in serious trouble.

Fortunately, Motsu had zero interest in doing that. And it was too late for him to catch up, anyway. No, the race was down to Sam... and Reggie Moon.

Motsu carried the burrito around to the other side of the table and shifted Annie's chair to the side. "Move over, Fulkins."

"Fuck off," said Sarah, not budging. "I need my space. Make the skinny girl move."

"I'm not skinny," said Annie. "I have a—"

"—high metabolism," said the others in unison.

Annie pressed her lips. "It's true," she mumbled.

Everyone adjusted their chairs to make room for Motsu.

"You want to know your problem, Sam?" Motsu said.

"*I* do," said Jem.

"You're going to tell me whether I wan—"

"Your problem is that you care too much." Motsu took another bite and nodded sagely at Sam as he chewed it. "So some prick from California swooped in and took your spot in the rankings. So what? You'll still graduate. You'll still get your pick of jobs. What's the big deal?"

"He won't get alone time with the AG," said Sarah. "Duh."

"Pffft," said Motsu. "Fuck the AG."

"The AG is going to be the president in a couple of years."

"Okay, fuck the soon-to-be president, then. Why does it matter if you get a couple hours alone with him? You think Jenkins will make or break your career?"

"He could," said Annie, chewing on one thumbnail and rocking from foot to foot.

"He's done it before," said Jem. "Look at Ben Conway. Assistant DA for the State of New York, and he only graduated two years ago."

"Yeah, but he's not the DA."

"He will be soon." Jem said. "Bulger's going to retire any day."

"You think Jenkins has anything to do with that?"

"You don't?" said Sarah. "The man has his hands on everything and everyone in the criminal justice system."

"You think you don't need to care because you're not a lawyer," said Annie to Motsu. "But Jenkins can help you, too. He can get you a profiling job in a heartbeat."

Motsu took another bite and grinned at Annie as he chewed. "I don't need him for that. I'll get in on my own." He stared at Annie and grinned harder, squishing bits of mushed burrito onto his lips. The others groaned at the display.

"You think the FBI will hire you?," said Sarah, handing Motsu a napkin. "You're barely housebroken."

Sam shook his head. They all wanted Jenkins to help them get a head start in their careers. But Sam didn't *want* Jenkins. He needed Jenkins, and for something far more important than a career boost.

"It doesn't matter," Sam said. The others looked at him. He slapped his hand on the table. "It doesn't matter, because I'm not going to lose."

Jem raised his eyebrows, a slow smile growing.

"Whoever this Reggie Moon guy is, I'm going to beat him."

Around the table, the others watched Sam. No cheers, no murmurs of encouragement, no attaboys. Just curiosity. They were all friends, but friends born of competition. Their first instincts were to beat the others. Since that was no longer a possibility, they were reduced to being interested observers. But they knew Sam. They didn't know Reggie Moon. And because of that, they were on Sam's side. He could feel their quiet support.

He felt it, but he didn't need it. Whether he had their support or not, Sam had no choice. He had to win. His mother's freedom was riding on it.

The first thing he had to do was to find out as much as he could about Reggie Moon.

7

Sam didn't have class that afternoon. He left the others outside the restaurant and trudged home on foot. The air was cold, but the sun was shining. The morning clouds had scampered off, leaving a bright, painfully beautiful blue sky behind. The icy air, the bright sun, and the blue sky would normally lift Sam's mood. It was his favorite kind of weather, cool and picturesque. But today, it didn't help.

He shoved his hands into his jacket pockets and strode through the streets, easing into a rhythm of long, loping strides. He would usually take the metro from school back to his apartment in Rosslyn. The ride was only twenty minutes. Walking took nearly an hour. But today, Sam needed the time, the movement. He needed to heat and stretch his aching thigh. And he needed to calm down, let his fears and anxieties fall away as he walked, and leave behind a mind as cool and objective as the air around him. He needed to focus on finding a solution.

More than one solution. Sam's problems were adding up. Reggie Moon was only one of them. His operation in the DOJ building the other night had been a bust. He'd failed to even get into Stratham's office, let alone find any useful information. He had to find an appropriate night to rectify that unfortunate error. It would be harder now that the holidays were over and all the employees would be back at work. Despite their reputation, Sam knew that government workers, especially at the DOJ, worked just as hard as those in the private sector. There would be plenty of people burning the midnight oil at the office after hours. Sam would have to negotiate around them.

And worse, he'd have to do it without his Nestech glasses. Sam clenched his hands into fists in his pockets. Losing the glasses was a major blow. He couldn't decide if he was angrier for the loss of the glasses or for becoming so reliant on them. He'd only had them for a year. He'd done hundreds of jobs in his life without super-tech glasses, and only a handful with them. Why did he feel such a gnawing emptiness in the pit of his stomach at the thought of sneaking into the DOJ building with no glasses in his toolbox? Sure, it would be a hell of a lot easier to avoid detection if he had the glasses, but he could still do the job without them.

He shook his head as he turned to walk down Constitution Avenue. Those damn glasses were addictive, all right. Dangerously addictive.

Cam let his Sam Davis persona drop away as he passed the Supreme Court building and entered the mall. After nearly three years, he could pull Sam Davis on and off like a favorite t-shirt. And he never wanted to lose sight of himself, his true self. He had to drop the fake identity once in a while.

And if he were being honest, he wasn't as focused at that moment as he normally would be. His thigh was already starting to burn—another painful reminder of his failings—and his irritation was burning even more.

Did the woman who stole the glasses realize yet how addictive they were? Was she stuck in a room somewhere, already lost down the rabbit hole, watching the world through the glasses and forgetting all of the skills that had brought them to her? Cam doubted it. Whoever she was, that woman was a pro.

Smart, quick, strong. She'd gotten the drop on him, and he'd been wearing the glasses at the time.

That thought stopped him short. A man in a long, black overcoat and black leather gloves, holding a cell phone to his cheek, muttered something unprofessional as he dodged around Cam from behind. Cam started walking again, glancing around to see if anyone else had noticed his sudden stop.

The woman had gotten the drop on him. In the stairwell, in the dark, Cam hadn't seen her coming. Didn't even know she was there.

How was that possible? The glasses showed him everyone. They showed the location of the guards at the other end of the building and three floors above. How could he not have noticed a person coming down the stairs right in front of him?

Because she wasn't there. She was there in real life, but she hadn't appeared on the glasses. Cam had no idea how, but something about that woman—her clothes, her mask, something— caused her not to register on the glasses.

They were just a prototype. Could have been a glitch. But if so, it was the first glitch Cam had found in over a year of using the glasses.

No, something else was going on. That woman must have had tech of her own, tech that jammed Cam's glasses. She wouldn't have done that on purpose, of course. Very few people in the world even knew the Nestech glasses existed. But she had some kind of jamming tech, and it was even more effective than she probably knew. Who could have tech that powerful? Who the fuck was that person he'd run into that night?

Cam strode down the wide sidewalks in the bright, cool air. He passed Senate Park on his right, the Capitol building across the street to his left. In summer, the view would be obstructed by the leaves on the trees. Today, Cam could see the columns of the Senate chamber, the trees mostly denuded. Staffers and senators in scarves and overcoats streamed up and down the steps like ants trooping to and from the hill with food.

Cam strode on, past a phalanx of motorcycle cops stationed at a street corner, past the Department of Labor, the National Gallery, the Archives Museum. His breath plumed in front of him. Despite the sunshine, the air had turned colder. But Cam felt uncomfortably warm. He stopped, careful to step to the side of the walkway so as not to bump into anyone, opened his collar to let some cold air in.

He looked up and saw that he had stopped directly in front of the Department of Justice building.

He knew he shouldn't be there. Shouldn't call any attention to himself. Shouldn't provide any evidence of his existence, let alone his existence in proximity to the DOJ building. Odds were very slim that any connection would be made, but fate was a bitch who didn't take kindly to being tempted.

Yet Cam couldn't move. He stared at the building, his thigh on fire, heat and pressure welling behind his eyes. Instead of a historic structure, he saw only failure and frustration. He felt his face flush. He unzipped his jacket completely, fanned it open. His body practically steamed in the cold air. He pulled one hand through his hair. It came back damp with sweat.

Two squat, round-bellied guards stood chatting in front of the building, bright yellow vests over dark blue jackets, peaked caps pulled low. Lopez and Markinson, if Cam's memory served. Markinson laughed at something Lopez had said, glanced at Cam, then glanced back, her body language stiffening. The smile dropped from her face as she took one slow step toward him. Cam made a show of pulling out his phone and pretending he was lost, looking down at the screen and turning in place as if to get his bearings. From the corner of his eye, he saw Markinson stop, relax, and go back to chatting with Lopez.

Move your ass, he ordered himself. He forced his feet to walk, one foot in front of the other. Like the fucking Sasquatch in that Christmas show. Cam nearly laughed out loud at the random memory, choked it back. The last thing he needed was to be giggling like a maniac beside the National Mall, calling even more attention to himself. If he was lucky, Markinson wouldn't think twice about the moment, wouldn't think to include it in her daily report. If he was lucky. But Cam wasn't in the habit of relying on luck. Not when it came to a job.

He put his phone back in his pocket and focused his eyes straight ahead, down the long, straight, flat path of Constitution Avenue. It ran the length of the National Mall, past the Smithsonian museums, between the Washington Monument and the White House, past the memorials and the reflecting pools. So much history. So much war and death. And pain, most of it unwritten. History is written by the victors, after all. And in their own stories, the victors are always heroes, never villains.

And at the end of the road, more than a mile in the distance, the Potomac River. Washing clean the sins of the Founding Fathers. Washing the ton. Absolving them of their guilt and shame, or so they hoped.

On the other side of that Rubicon was Cam's apartment, his home.

So near he could feel it. So far, it felt like his steps brought him no closer at all.

He shook his head as he worked back into his stride, willing his thigh to relax, to loosen. He couldn't let himself fall into a negative mindset. Pessimism was just as foolish as optimism. What was needed was realism, with a healthy dose of creative problem-solving. See the problem clearly, then believe that you could resolve it. That's what his parents had taught him.

See the problem clearly. That was the realism part. Cam's problems were already clear. First, he needed proof of wrongdoing on the part of the AG. Or, if not wrongdoing, something that would make him look very bad, something that would convict him in the court of public opinion. He figured taking massive contributions from someone he knew to be an international arms dealer, the late Devin Minsk, would do the job.

Second, Cam needed to find a way to get that proof. The glasses weren't the issue. That was a distraction. A nagging, unfortunate distraction, but not a problem that Cam needed to solve. He just needed to get back into the DOJ building, get into Stratham's office, and get the data he needed.

Third, he needed to get the Attorney General Jenkins alone so he could blackmail him into releasing his mother. To do that, he needed to finish at the top of his class. What had been a cakewalk a week ago was Cam's biggest problem now.

Those were the problems. Now he needed to believe he could find a solution to them.

Reggie Moon. He needed to find out all he could about Reggie Moon.

His strides grew longer, his pace quicker as he loped along the length of the mall. He drove his thigh past the point of pain to the point of numbness. By the time he crossed Roosevelt Bridge, with the river on his right as he strode up Mount Vernon Trail, his mind finally began to focus.

That focus shattered in an instant when he found a package on his doorstep. A black box with a pink bow and a card on top.

Addressed to Cameron Hauk.

8

Cam stood, arms crossed, and stared down at the box where it sat on the coffee table in front of the futon couch in his living room. He tugged his lip between thumb and forefinger. A knocking sound beat at his head like a woodpecker on a tree. Were the neighbors hanging pictures? Building something?

He realized the sound was coming from himself, from his boot tapping the wood floor like a jackhammer cranked up to eleven. His anxiety didn't lessen at the realization, but something in him deflated, like the puffed top of a hot air balloon falling in on itself as the air rushed out. He hadn't felt this keyed up in a long time. Whoever this woman was, she was fucking with him, trying to get into Cam's head. And she was succeeding.

He forced himself to sit on the couch, to set his arms on his knees and fold his hands together. That stopped him from twisting a hole in his lip, but it didn't stop his foot from tapping.

Why would she even care about Cam? They'd run into each other under odd circumstances, sure. Maybe she just wanted to know who he was and why he'd been there. Professional curiosity. Or maybe she recognized the value of the glasses she'd stolen and was playing an angle, hoping to extort some cash from Cam in return for the glasses.

Or maybe she was just bored and enjoyed fucking with people. Cam shook his head and sighed in irritation. Idle speculation wasn't going to get him anywhere.

He pushed himself up with his arms and folded his legs beneath him on the couch. He felt a searing pain in his left thigh at the movement, slowed down and eased it into the stretch, then forced himself to recline against the tall cushion of the couch back, stretching the thigh even more. He had a hell of a bruise on his thigh, yellow and purple and black and all sorts of colors he never expected to see on his own body, but nothing seemed broken. Just a bad muscle contusion. As he stretched, pulling fresh blood into the wounded area, he clenched his hands together against the pain until the knuckles went white.

The first thing he'd done when he got inside his apartment with the box was to check the recordings from the full-color, high-resolution security camera he'd installed above the front door. A woman dressed all in black—high-collared black jacket, black work pants, black gloves, and thick black boots—had dropped off the box about an hour before Cam had returned. Only one hour, and no one else had approached the box or even passed the doorway, let alone stopped for a closer look.

Cam's real name, then, was safe. Around here, Cameron Hauk didn't exist. Around here, he was Sam Davis, and he wanted to keep it that way. He could have played off the incident. Wrong address, old friend, whatever. But he preferred to keep Cameron Hauk out of the minds of the people around him altogether. Don't even run the risk of someone putting two and two together. For now, no one knew who he really was.

Except the woman.

After checking the recording from his own camera, Cam had checked the apartment's camera feeds to study the woman's approach to his door. Cam's apartment complex had been built fairly recently, four floors high, with stylish appointments aimed at the twenty-something crowd, including a pool and hot tub that was open year-round, a courtyard designed for parties, and open-air walkways lined with textured concrete and thick wrought-iron rails, giving the complex a feeling of effortless cool that would probably feel hopelessly dated in a few decades, but that worked well enough for now. The complex was full, with a long waiting list, and the courtyard was lively at night, especially on the weekends.

The walkways of the complex were named for streets in downtown D.C.—Pennsylvania, Constitution, Massachusetts, etc. Cam had chosen a unit on K Street, one of the interior corridors, which afforded more privacy than the others. He had no idea if this was a subtle dig at the lobbyists on the real K street, or the often unsavory connections to them that most politicians preferred to keep hidden, but he liked to think so. More importantly for Cam, the front doors of the apartments on K Street were well hidden from both the street and the courtyard.

Aside from this fact and its relative proximity to McFadden, one reason Cam had chosen this particular apartment complex was for its security considerations. There was a gate with a card reader at the front entrance and at each landing in the stairwells, another required to use the elevator, and cameras covering every inch of exterior space, including along the sidewalks that bordered the complex. The gates and card readers served as deterrents. The cameras gave Cam visibility, once he'd hacked into them. That process had been easier than Cam had hoped it would be, but, then again, he was very good at hacking, so he couldn't begrudge the security team at the apartment complex too much. Their security was better than most.

And that security had allowed Cam to follow the woman from the front sidewalk all the way to his doorstep. She wore the same black baseball cap she'd worn the other night, with a black hoodie pulled up over it, hiding her face in shadow. She entered from the street, rode the elevator to Cam's floor, and came down the walkway.

She'd had no trouble gaining access to the front gate or the elevator. She hadn't waited for a resident so she could follow them in or sweet-talked someone into using their card for her. She'd had her own key card. And it was clear from the way she approached, from the way she moved, that she knew exactly where the cameras were, knew exactly how to keep herself hidden from them. The woman was a pro. She had known she was being recorded, and she knew Cam would watch the recordings. She was showing Cam how easily she could get to him.

The box tucked under one arm, she had walked casually, completely relaxed, like she belonged there. She even nodded to a neighbor as she passed, the neighbor smiling back. Who the hell smiles at a hooded figure in all black carrying a box through an apartment complex in Rosslyn? The neighbor should have called Homeland Security, or at least the apartment's security office. Cam recognized the neighbor, a man he'd seen before but didn't know by name. He lived somewhere on Cam's floor. Cam made a mental note to research the guy later, maybe ask him what he could remember about the woman.

The woman had kept her face hidden from every camera—no easy feat, given the number of cameras in the complex—and walked straight to Cam's door without breaking stride, without hesitation or uncertainty. In the view from the apartment feeds, Cam could see the woman in profile from both sides, the hoodie shielding her face as she stood in front of his apartment door. In the view from his own camera, he saw the top of her head as she looked down at Cam's doormat, a recycled polyester mat woven with the image of a sunrise over fields of grain waving in the wind. Brown on beige.

The woman regarded the doormat for a moment, then squatted down with the box. She placed it carefully, then regarded it for another moment and tilted the box at a slight angle across the mat. Not square to the sides, but at a slight angle, perhaps ten degrees from the horizontal. Cam had no idea if that detail was significant, but his mind was racing, on high alert, scouring the images for even the tiniest clue that would help him figure out who this woman was.

She stayed squatted, sitting on her heels for a moment, regarding the tableau she'd created, then stood. And then she turned her head up, looking square into the camera above Cam's door. After all that work avoiding her face being caught on camera, now she looked dead center into the lens.

The camera Cam had installed above his front door was well-hidden and tiny, barely as big as the first knuckle on Cam's index finger. Tiny enough to be difficult to notice even when you knew it was there. And yet the woman had turned her head up and looked right down the barrel of the lens in one smooth, unhesitating motion.

Again, she was telling Cam that she was a pro, that she had done her research, and that she knew all about Cam's security measures.

And she showed him her face. Sort of. The hoodie and the ball cap blocked her head and hair, and she wore huge sunglasses that went from halfway up her forehead to halfway down her cheeks, blocking the top half of her face. Between the glasses, the hoodie, the hat, and the high collar of her jacket, Cam could really only see the woman's lips and the shape of her jawline. With as loose as her clothes were, he couldn't even make out the shape of her figure.

But this was still more information than he'd had before. He'd seen her eyes in the stairwell of the DOJ building, brilliant sea-green eyes that were hard to miss, and even harder to mistake. Now he could add full, pink lips to the picture. She wore no lipstick, no makeup of any kind, as far as he could tell. Her skin was clear and creamy white, but not pale. Her jaw swept in a smooth, deep curve to a rounded chin.

Given the green eyes and the light skin, Cam guessed she could have the classic Irish red hair, which might be why she would be so careful to wear a hoodie over it. Not definitive, but it did make sense. The other night, she'd worn a balaclava which had also covered her hair. He hadn't noticed if the balaclava was bunched up or puffed out in places, so he couldn't be sure if she wore her hair short or long.

Aside from the hair, the curve of her jaw suggested a triangular shape to her face. Her collar was too high for him to see her neck, so he couldn't guess at her weight, but her cheeks were not over-full, so he guessed she probably wasn't heavy-set. Plus, the feel of her body against his on the landing of the stairwell the other night had given the impression of a lean and muscular figure beneath the loose, black clothing.

A warm shiver ran through Cam's body at the memory. He ignored it.

After a long look into his camera lens, the woman had given the camera a sly smile. No teeth—that would have been another clue—but a long look and a knowing smile.

She was definitely fucking with Cam.

And then she'd left the same way she'd come in—quickly, easily, and without showing her face to a single camera. She encountered no one as she went to the elevator. She shoved her hands in her jacket pockets as she rode down, rocking back and forth on her feet, head tilted down, away from the camera. The elevator camera glitched briefly on the way down, but only for a second. When she reached the bottom floor, she left the complex, walked to the corner, and crossed the street like any other resident off for a trip to the Target two blocks over to pick up some toilet paper or a twelve-pack of White Claw.

Cam quickly pulled up the feeds from the city cameras— another easy hack—that he kept on his own hard drive. He kept recordings of the last twenty-four hours from each of the seventeen cameras in the immediate vicinity. Overkill? Probably. But server space was cheap, and a little extra caution didn't hurt anybody. Usually.

He watched the woman leave the view of the apartment's sidewalk camera and enter the view of the city camera on the corner, looking across the intersection toward the woman. She waited on the sidewalk for the lights, head down, hands in her pockets. When the lights changed, she stepped off the curb and lifted one hand to pull back her hood. Cam leaned toward the screen. Finally, he would get to see the woman's face.

And then she disappeared.

The people around her were still there, crossing the intersection normally, unaware that a woman had just evaporated from the space beside them. Cam pulled up the feeds of the adjoining cameras. There was no trace of the woman. She had simply vanished.

As he leaned back on the futon couch, feeling the searing burn in his left thigh slowly ease into an ache, Cam thought about what he'd learned. The woman knew who he was and where he lived, obviously. She knew the entire security setup around him, not only bypassing the card readers, but identifying the location of every apartment camera. She knew that Cam had his own security rig, separate from the apartment complex. She had shown her face to Cam's camera, but not to any of the cameras that belonged to the apartment complex. She'd deliberately chosen to show herself to him, and only to him.

But she'd only shown her cheeks, lips, and mouth. Given how meticulous she was in every other aspect, Cam had to assume that decision, too, was deliberate. She'd worn the clothes from the other night, as well, or something very like them. She wanted Cam to know she was the same person, and she wanted to give him another clue to her identity.

She'd covered her departure, somehow evading the street cameras so he had no idea which way she'd gone. She could have crossed the street and walked to Rosslyn station. She could have doubled back the way she'd come. She could have climbed into an Uber and driven anywhere.

She wanted him to find her. She wouldn't have shown her face, otherwise. She wouldn't have come at all. But she didn't want to make it easy.

She wasn't fucking with him. She was playing with him, playing a game of catch-me-if-you-can.

Another warm shiver coursed through Cam's body, down to his toes and all the way back up his neck to tingle his scalp.

She'd thrown down the gauntlet. With a grim smile, Cam decided to pick it up.

9

CAM LEANED FORWARD, cross-legged on the futon couch, stretching his sore thigh. This time, he relished the spears of pain. He leaned into them even more, letting the pain fuel his focus. He then directed that focus at the box sitting on the coffee table in front of him.

Despite his shock at seeing the box on his doorstep, Cam had regained enough of his wits in the moment to look left and right down the walkway to make sure no one was coming, then to open the door and step past the box without moving it. He returned quickly, pulling on a pair of latex gloves, documented the scene from every conceivable angle with his cell phone camera, then examined the box closely. He saw no evidence of explosives that might be triggered by pressure pads or trip wires, no sounds of ticking from inside the box. He couldn't be one-hundred percent sure from a quick external visual examination, but his gut told him not to worry, not about explosives, at least. And he usually trusted his gut.

In a perfect world, he would have reviewed the video from his door camera before moving the box, but he didn't want to risk a neighbor walking by and seeing the name on the card under the bow on the box. His gut told him the box was safe to move, and leaving the box exposed on the doorstep had seemed the greater evil. Cam had cleared off his coffee table, brought the box inside, and set it down before turning to his examination of the video feeds.

Now, alone in the relative safety of his own apartment, having learned what he could from the video, he peered more closely at the box itself. He pulled over two bright desk lamps, setting them up on either side of the box for more light, and began a slow, meticulous examination. If this woman wanted to play games with Cam, he'd show her just how well he could play.

Cam's cursory examination on the doorstep had shown a matte black cardboard box about five inches wide by seven inches long and three inches tall, with a pink ribbon and bow tied around it. The card with Cam's name on it was slid under the bow.

Upon closer inspection, Cam saw that the matte black cardboard was actually some kind of black crepe paper that had been fused to the surface of the cardboard, maybe with papier mâché paste or something like that. It gave the box an elegant, unique texture that scattered the light, deflected it away from itself at odd angles, making it difficult to see the surface clearly, but lending the box an aura of stately, mysterious elegance.

From a distance, the ribbon had looked like a normal pink ribbon made of cheap polyester satin with a stick-on bow. But closer inspection revealed a kind of gauzy fabric with silken golden strands woven throughout. Without untying it, Cam could see that the pink ribbon and bow were all one piece. At various points along the ribbon, the strands coalesced into interesting geometric designs before splitting apart again. Like the box, the material was unique and elegant. It definitely didn't look like the kind of ribbon you'd find at your local Walmart.

Just by visual inspection under the lights, Cam could see that the card was equally elegant. It was made of textured, cream-colored paper with small flecks of blue and yellow and dark brown throughout, with a border like a red-wine stain, but faded to a pale pink that matched the ribbon. The only text on the card was Cam's name. The ink was black, but not uniform, which suggested it had been hand-written, not typed. In addition, there were slight variations in the letter 'a' in *Cam* and *Hauk*. Those variations would not have been there if the font were computer-generated, unless the author were being very clever and had introduced the variation on purpose. Cam had no doubt this woman could be that clever, but he didn't think she had done that in this case. The lettering was definitely hand-written. He turned his attention to the handwriting itself.

Cam was no handwriting analyst, but the strokes seemed sure and confident. He opened the magnifier app on his phone and inspected it more closely. The ink soaked into the texture of the thick paper differently at different points, giving Cam clues about how the pen was wielded when the words were written. He saw no evidence of hesitation mid-stroke, no blobs of ink or disruptions in the gradient of the ink that moved from darker to lighter along the length of each stroke. The writer had been relaxed, comfortable, confident.

And artistic. The strokes were aesthetically gorgeous, with an elegant but playful hand. And the thickness of the strokes varied, too. Again, Cam was no expert, but he knew his way around a sketch book. The strokes on the card looked like they could have been made with a calligraphy brush or a Copic sketch marker, or at least a high-quality fountain pen. It certainly wasn't written with a cheap Bic ball-point pen.

Cam lifted the box, careful to hold it level, and examined it from underneath. More black crepe and the cross of the ribbon, slightly off-center. He set the box down again.

He pulled in a deep breath and let it out. Time to start taking things apart.

He removed the card first. It slid easily from under the bow.

Cam held it up to the light. The translucence of the light was brighter in some spots, indicating that the paper was thicker in some places than in others. The card stock was thick and stiff and gave a satisfying thock when Cam flicked it off of his gloved finger. But the texture of the paper and the flecks of colors throughout made it seem almost handmade. Cam had once seen someone make their own paper by ripping bits of other kinds of paper—all kinds, any kinds—that had been shredded into small pieces, soak them in water and blend them together, then dry them on a screen to form sheets of thick paper with unusual colors and textures. The paper on this card was of a much higher quality than the homemade paper Cam had seen, but it was similar in texture and uniqueness.

He flipped the card over to look at the back. Dead center on the back of the card were two words. Where the front of the card had been beautifully hand-written, these words were undoubtedly printed from a computer. In all lower-case letters in a tiny font, barely large enough for Cam to read without magnification, it said:

threee-three

Cam frowned at the card as he held it in his hand under the light of the desk lamps. He had no idea what that could mean. Three-three? Was it a date? March third? Or was it a number, the number thirty-three? Maybe thirty-three days to figure out who the woman was before she did something to Cam? Maybe it was a timer, a countdown. Three days and three hours until the next contact. Three weeks and three days until something happened. Or maybe it was a scoreboard. Cam and the woman were tied, three to three, using some scoring system Cam hadn't discovered yet. Cam shook his head. None of these ideas made sense, and nothing more concrete came immediately to his mind. He set the card down and turned his attention back to the box.

The ribbon was expertly wrapped, its lines perfectly parallel to the sides of the box, pressed flat and tight against it. The twists in the ribbon were hidden underneath the bow. For its part, the bow carried the same artistic ease as the handwriting on the card. The entire bow was offset to the upper left quadrant of the rectangular box. It wasn't a poofy, frilly circular bow like the stick-on bows sold by the bag at drug stores at Christmastime. Nor was it a drab bolo-style with flat, dull loops and long, stringy ends. This bow had personality. It was alive somehow, leaping off the box at Cam, vibrant without being ostentatious. The loops were transverse, but doubled and separated on each side in a shallow X pattern. Two short tails fell from them, each cut into a sharp point, offset to one side of each tail. The way they curled down from the bow and came to points, the tails looked like vampire fangs.

Cam pulled on one fang and untied the bow slowly, tugged the ribbon loose and slid it off the box, cringing backward as he did so, half expecting the box to pop open and some explosive device to detonate or a clown on a spring to pop up and cackle at him. Instead, the ribbon slid off the box with a quiet sigh. Cam pulled it through his fingers once, feeling the rough texture of the gauze, contraposed to its delicate beauty. In the bright lamp light, the silky strands gleamed gold along the ribbon's length, coming together into abstract patterns and separating again. Several small notches were cut in the sides of the ribbon at various points along its length, but the ribbon was otherwise intact. Beautiful, but uninteresting. Cam coiled it around his fingers and set it on the table beside the card. Time to examine the box.

Cam studied the box under the light, looking for a seam. Unless he was meant to cut the box open, there had to be a seam somewhere on the box, a place where the lid separated from the bottom. But he couldn't see one. He pulled the lamp closer. Even with a bright light at close range, the bumps and ridges of the crepe paper made it difficult to see the surface clearly. Cam looked for a seam in the paper itself, thinking perhaps the crepe paper had covered the box like wrapping paper. But still he found nothing.

Finally he thought of those boxes, like the one his iPhone had come in, with tops that go all the way down the side and are fitted so tightly to the bottom box that the pieces are almost suctioned together. Cam gripped the top of the box, holding the long edges lightly in his hand, and hovered it a few inches over the table. He gave it a subtle, gentle shake.

There was a weight to the box that he hadn't noticed when he moved it. It wasn't heavy by any means, but it was sturdy. Slowly, slowly as he held it up, the bottom began to move, to slip, then to slide out from the lid. Cam lifted the box higher. The bottom slid faster. Cam lay his other hand flat beneath it and the bottom dropped gently into his palm with a tiny pop as it finally released from the lid.

Cam turned the lid over in his hand, examined the inside. It was made of flat, smooth black cardboard. No texture. Nothing written inside. He set it down, then took the bottom of the box in both hands and lowered it gently to the table again.

A solid piece of black foam filled the box from edge to edge. Cam pulled some metal shims from a toolkit in his closet and slid them carefully around the sides of the foam, looking for any tension, any subtle tug on the shim that might indicate a trip-wire or trap of some kind. Finding none, he used the shims to pincer the foam up far enough for him to take it with his hands and pull it out the rest of the way.

What he saw underneath, laying on another bed of foam that matched the one he'd just removed, nearly took his breath away.

The Nestech glasses.

The woman who'd stolen the glasses had just returned them.

10

CAM FELL BACK in shock against the futon couch. The black crepe box sat, innocuous and coy, on the coffee table in front of him. Resting patiently, innocently, on the carved black foam block inside, the Nestech glasses reflected the glare of the desk lamps in its crystal clear lenses.

Cam had been neat and methodical in his work, and the coffee table showed it. The card sat in one corner, its edges aligned with the edges of the table. Beside it, the pink and gold ribbon sat in a tidy coil. Above them both, the box top and foam, placed with care. Everything was ordered and orderly, allowing Cam's mind to focus.

But his mind was anything but focused now. Now, his mind reeled.

Cam didn't know who the woman was, but he knew she was no fool. The way she handled herself in the DOJ building that night was enough to tell him that. The way she negotiated his apartment complex to deliver the box and leave without a trace confirmed it. So why would she have returned the Nestech glasses she'd stolen from him? Surely she would have recognized their value.

Unless she hadn't bothered to put them on. Maybe she was

some kind of Luddite who was afraid of new technology, one of those 5G conspiracists afraid the radiation would melt her brain.

No, that seemed unlikely. Aside from the dubious science behind the conspiracy theories, the woman had negotiated the apartment complex without showing her face to a single camera, and she'd managed to mock up a key card to get through the gates. Sure, she could have lifted someone else's card, but Cam had checked the security system and seen no record of any key cards reported stolen by any tenants. Maybe she'd taken one and returned it, or maybe it hadn't been reported yet. Both were possible, but it seemed more likely that she'd figured out how to fake her own card instead.

No, this woman had no fear of technology. She seemed to embrace it. So why would she return the most valuable piece of personal tech hardware Cam had ever seen, less than a week after stealing it from him?

Cam examined the foam around and beneath the glasses, even pulled out his magnifier app to scrutinize every millimeter. He found no tricks, no traps. He set his phone down on the couch beside him, took a deep breath, and picked up the glasses.

Nothing exploded. No clowns popped up at him. The glasses did not break or disintegrate into ash at his touch.

They were just his glasses, resting in his hands. Returned safely to him.

He examined the glasses as closely as he had the foam beneath them, but found no evidence of tampering. No scuffs or scratches on the lenses or the frame. No cracks where the woman might have tried to reverse-engineer the design. Everything seemed perfectly in order.

With just a moment's hesitation, Cam put on the glasses and powered them up.

The familiar Nestech logo, a floating blue letter N, appeared in his viewscreen for a few moments. Behind it, his apartment layout appeared in chalky white lines against a blue background, like a blueprint, then resolved into crisp, clear, sharp lines and colors. Futon couch and coffee table in front of him, desk and chair by the window, cabinet in the corner. Minimal furniture, lots of open space. All appeared in a natural light and perspective, as if Cam had put on a normal pair of eyeglasses and was seeing the room with his own eyes.

Then something happened that wasn't normal at all.

A voice greeted Cam.

There had never been a voice greeting Cam before.

It could be that there was some setting, some toggle in the configuration for the glasses that Cam had never discovered, but the woman had. A setting that she'd flipped on and left on. There was so much capability in the glasses that, even after a year of owning and exploring them, Cam felt he'd barely scratched the surface. It was startling, but it wasn't surprising that the woman might have found a new feature.

And if the voice had been the voice of Nestrom's late wife, which he'd used as the voice assistant in the workshop where Cam had found the glasses, or the voice of Nestech himself, or even a cheerfully dull AI voice like Siri or Alexa, Cam wouldn't have thought twice about it.

But this voice wasn't any of those. This voice was low and smooth and resonant. It flowed into Cam's mind like a balm. He closed his eyes and shivered as a flush of warmth washed over him from head to toe, just as it had the last time he'd heard that voice. Which was also the first time he'd heard it, in the stairwell of the DOJ building.

It was the woman's voice. Sultry and close. Intimate.

The fact that the voice was even there was disturbing enough. How had the woman managed to get her own voice into the glasses? She'd only had them a week, and Cam had seen no evidence of tampering. In just one week, how could she have hacked into a prototype made by the foremost technical genius of a generation, maybe of all time?

That was disturbing. But what the voice actually said was even worse.

It greeted Cam, said, "Hello, Cameron Hauk." Cheeky, but not upsetting.

But the sound panned in Cam's ears. The word "Hello" was directly ahead of Cam in the spatial field, as if the speaker were standing in front of him. Then there was a pause, brief enough to still sound natural, long enough to prick the listener's attention. When the woman's voice spoke again, it said "Cameron Hauk", the sound panned to his left as if the woman were suddenly speaking in his left ear.

Again, interesting, but not upsetting. What upset him was what the voice whispered at the same time in the other ear.

As it said "Cameron Hauk" in his left ear, it whispered, "Sam Davis" in his right.

The woman had not only surprised him at the DOJ building and stolen his glasses. She had not only figured out his real name and his home address. She had not only hacked through the apartment security, Cam's security, and the operating system for the glasses. But she'd figured out Cam's cover identity, the name he'd been using for his long con for the last three years.

Cam knew what he was doing. He was no slouch when it came to hacking or digital security. He knew how to fake a paper trail that even the FBI couldn't follow. The only person who'd ever connected his alter ego to his real name was Dr. Christopher Nestech, the tech deity himself. And now, in just one week, this woman had done the same.

Cam looked through his glasses at the apartment around him and sighed. The afternoon light that had been bright white through the cracks of his plantation shutters was dull and pale yellow now. The tension he'd carried during the investigation of the box drained from Cam. He'd been at it for hours, and he was tired.

Whoever this woman was, she wasn't just good. She was

incredible, a hell of a lot better than Cam. Fortunately, now that he had his glasses back, he could let bygones be bygones and just stay out of her way.

But as he looked at the empty crepe paper box, at the pink ribbon and the handmade card with its mysterious message on the back, something told Cam the woman wasn't done playing with him yet.

11

Celina Maxwell looked out the window of her Uber as she passed the Washington Monument, the spotlights just starting to flicker to life in the fading daylight. She'd visited D.C. before, but this was the first time she could call herself a resident, even if it was only for a few months. The city had a great history, and the politics were notorious, of course, as was the inequality, the congestion, and the crime, at various points in its history. And not just the white-collar political kind.

But what tended to get lost in the stereotypes about the city was its beauty. Especially at dusk on a clear, cold January day, when the lights are coming on and the sun is going out, the city takes on an impressionistic glow. The stonework on the monuments loses the harsh bleaching of daylight, the unforgiving eye that reveals every chip, every scuff, every sign of wear earned over hundreds of years. The view from the lidded eye of the setting sun, filled in by the soft yellow glow of the spotlights, brings the monuments to life in the same way dim house lights and vibrant stage lights bring out the magic in a nightclub. Lincoln in his grand La-Z-Boy suddenly seems amused, not stern. When the sun goes down, he and Jefferson shake their heads over a beer and chuckle together at their tangled history and that of the nation they helped to build, the nation whose cracks seemed like chasms in the hard light of day. At night, the Washington Monument transforms from a lonely spire to a towering beacon, the White House from a Southern plantation house to a global symbol of hope.

As the Uber passed the Capitol building, gilded with the last of the sun's rays and come alive with light from within, its dome looked to Celina like an enduring symbol of statesmanship and the promise of a great experiment in government. During the day, it looked like a fucking butt plug. Lately, there was little doubt which was a more accurate metaphor for business-as-usual in Washington politics.

Celina's phone buzzed in her hand, a staccato triplet pattern she'd coded herself. She didn't bother to look down at the screen. She knew what the alert meant.

It meant Cameron Hauk had finally put on the glasses.

She eyed the setting sun as it slid beneath the horizon for the night, and snorted a quick, quiet laugh to herself.

Game on.

Jesus, it fucking took him long enough.

12

SAM JERKED AWAKE, opened his eyes wide, and sucked in a breath as the students around him stood from their chairs. Sudden panic combined with the soft thunder of lecture hall seats folding and the rustle and scrape of backpacks zipping to shove away the boozy half-dreams lingering in Sam's mind.

That day's LCJ lecture had been brutal, long and dull. In general, Sam had been surprised at how much he liked his studies, and he normally enjoyed the seminar on topics in Law, Crime, and Justice, one of the few courses that spanned both semesters of Sam's final year.

But he hadn't slept well the night before, rolling in his bed all night. Every time he closed his eyes, he saw the woman sneaking soundlessly to stand by his bed in the dark in her ball cap and balaclava, watching him. Sometimes she slid into bed and pressed her body over his. Sometimes she stabbed him in the heart with a dagger made from homemade paper. Sometimes her long red hair curled in waves over her naked breasts. Sometimes it hooded her face as she pointed a gun at his heart and pulled the trigger. Sometimes she just stood there, watching him, waiting, her green eyes glowing in the dark. When his phone alarm had finally ended his torment, Sam's bed sheets had been as tangled as his mind.

He'd dragged himself into class five minutes late and immediately regretted it. Professor Thompson had been called away due to a family emergency, and one of his teaching assistants was lecturing. Unlike Professor Thompson, the TA was more interested in the obscure academic minutia of that day's topic than he was in its practical applications. On top of that, despite having a body like a banana leaf, the man had a low, mellow voice that would have made millions if he'd left academia behind and started a YouTube channel to help people fall asleep. All he had to do was talk, and he'd have a gazillion subscribers looking for a surefire way to combat their insomnia.

Even four hastily chugged shots of espresso didn't help after the night Sam had. Jem had spent most of the three-hour lecture elbowing him awake. From his seat, Sam looked up at his friend, who had stood to stretch. By the sound of his groans as he did so, Sam figured Jem had succumbed to sleep himself for the last bit of the lecture. Looking around at the other students rubbing their faces, staring dully into space, or still sleeping in their chairs, Sam could see that he and Jem weren't the only ones.

Jem slapped shut his laptop and turned to stuff it into his bag. "Any new intel on Reggie Moon?"

Sam stood and slung his backpack over one shoulder. He hadn't even bothered to unpack his laptop when he'd arrived. "Nothing new," he said. "You?"

"I know he's not in our LCJ section." Sam's leg burned as they filed in with the other students and climbed the steep stairs out of the lecture hall. "If he'd been in that class, he'd be transferring back to Arizona State by now."

"I thought he was from UC Irvine."

Jem shook his head. "ASU. The Irvine thing was a red herring."

"A red herring? What is this, an Agatha Christie novel? Don't you mean that your friend of a friend of a friend fucked up?"

"He claims the transfer form he saw was planted to throw him off."

Sam scoffed, too tired even to tease Jem.

"Well, I haven't found any new clues, Monsieur Poirot," he said. "Sorry to disappoint you."

The truth was that Sam hadn't even bothered to look. It had been three days since he'd found the box with the Nestech glasses on his doorstep, and he'd been unable to focus on anything since then. The woman wasn't just haunting his dreams. She was behind his eyes every waking moment. He caught himself snapping his head around in hallways or sidewalks, sure he'd just seen her from the corner of his eye. There was never anyone there, nothing but a growing unease and a feeling that Sam was going crazy.

He was going to have to get a handle on this, and fast. Reggie Moon might be 0.003 points ahead of Sam in the race for top of the class, but he'd win by a much wider margin if Sam couldn't focus on his schoolwork for the last semester.

The others already had a table at a burger place nearby, outside in a courtyard in the back. During the warmer months, wisteria and climbing roses bloomed on a pergola overhead and local bands played live music from a stage in one corner. In summer, each step on the gravel-covered ground sounded like ice pouring into a glass. But in January, even on a bright, blue, relatively warm day, the courtyard was spare and stark. The wisteria and roses wrapped their skeletal limbs around the thin, weather-cracked beams of the pergola. In winter, each step on the gravel sounded like thin ice cracking over a frozen pond.

Still, the tables inside were all taken, and the day was warm enough that Sam couldn't quite see his own breath. Besides, standing over his food in the cool air helped him stay awake.

"No one has seen him," said Sarah around a mouthful of bacon cheeseburger. "I don't think he's even attending class."

"He has to attend class," said Annie, rocking from one foot to the other as she ate. "How can he keep the top spot if he doesn't even go to class?"

"You don't need to be in class to learn," said Motsu. It was exactly the kind of thing Motsu would say, and not without reason. He was fifth—now sixth, Sam corrected himself—in the class, and he barely attended half of the lectures. "We'll spend most of our careers learning outside of the classroom. Why not start now?"

"Because some of us want to graduate," Annie grumbled.

"I'll graduate," said Motsu. He shoved a handful of fries in his mouth and winked at Annie. Her rocking stuttered and her cheeks blushed red.

She shook her head and muttered, "We're not all lazy, beautiful geniuses."

Motsu put a coquettish hand to his chest, raised his eyebrows, and dipped his chin toward her. "You think I'm... beautiful?" He fluttered his eyes.

Annie rolled hers. "Beautiful mind, maybe." She said it with disdain, but she smiled behind the burger she brought to her mouth.

The server came to the table with the food Jem and Sam had ordered. Jem tore into his burger, but Sam eyed his plate warily, trying to decide if the twinge in his stomach meant he needed to eat or that he would immediately hurl up anything he swallowed.

"If we're going to figure out who the hell this guy is," Jem said as he chewed, "we need a plan." He shook his head. "We're about to graduate with degrees in criminology. We should be able to figure out who someone is by now."

"We're about to graduate," said Sarah, "but we haven't graduated. And we don't have jobs, which means we have no authority. No one's going to run a background check for us, and we can't access the systems to run one ourselves."

"Not without a warrant," said Annie.

"Which we can't get," Sarah said, "because—wait for it—*we haven't graduated yet.*"

"Not to mention that Reggie Moon hasn't broken any laws," said Motsu. "Unless being a pain in the ass is against the law."

"Believe me," said Jem, "if it were, you'd have been locked up years ago."

Motsu grinned at Jem around a mouthful of fries, then chewed with his mouth very wide open. The table collectively groaned in disgust.

"Is he in the school directory?" asked Annie.

"No room, no phone number," Jem replied.

"Ask your friend in admissions to get a copy of his class schedule," said Sarah to Jem.

"I did," Jem replied. "He can't access them, and they wouldn't let him print it out, even if he could. Those are considered private information."

"A fucking class schedule is private information?" scoffed Motsu. "That's ridiculous."

"You wouldn't want anyone to know you're taking remedial English, would you?"

"Teaching it, you mean. And why would I care if they did?" he replied, then snapped his fingers. "Because there'd be a stampede to sign up for my class. Good point." He nodded solemnly, then shrugged. "Well, that's what wait lists are for."

"What about you, Sam?" said Sarah, ignoring Motsu entirely. "You're awful quiet over there, and you're the one with the most to lose. Any bright ideas?"

Sam had been staring glumly at the burger in his hand, trimming bits of lettuce and melted cheese off the sides with sullen indifference. He had lots of ideas, but none of them had anything to do with Reggie Moon. They were all focused on a stranger dressed in black. Her brilliant green eyes floated in front of him, superimposed on the real life around him, watching him watch the world. As he moved through the day, he could feel the press of her body against his, like he had in the stairwell at the DOJ building.

He was obsessing, falling down the rabbit hole without a trail of bread crumbs to bring him home. A part of his brain knew that the woman wasn't important. She was a side show. A distraction. A tantalizing one, but a distraction, all the same. He needed to focus on Reggie Moon. He needed to focus on finishing first in his class.

And he needed to focus on getting the information from the DOJ building so that, when he did have his private meeting with Attorney General Jenkins, he'd have something real to use against him. If Sam stood there with Jenkins and tried to bluff his way through, he'd fail. He knew it in his bones. Jenkins was smart, smarter than most people, let alone most politicians.

Vernon Stratham was smart, too, and he was a puppet master. But Jenkins was no puppet. Jenkins had a plan, and he had the drive, the resources, and—Sam was banking on this part —the arrogance to pull it off.

Sam shook his head. Every time he tried to focus on what was important, those green eyes swam into focus in front of him, like the damn Cheshire cat. They now had a grin to match.

"Nothing?" said Sarah. "Really?"

"You can torture that burger all you want," said Motsu with a wry smile. "It'll die before it'll talk to the likes of you."

Jem frowned at Sam, then glanced around the table at the others. Sam was staring down at his burger, but he could feel the raised eyebrows and shrugged shoulders that responded to Jem's look.

"It's okay, Sam," Jem said. "We'll meet Reggie Moon, eventual-ly." He clapped a hand on Sam's shoulder. When Sam looked up,

Jem grinned at him, eyebrows raised. "He'll be the one giving the valedictory speech."

Sam clenched his jaw and sighed hard through his nose. Ignoring the sea-green eyes and the grinning cat that now seemed to be laughing at him, he tore a bite from his burger.

13

ALONE IN HIS APARTMENT, Cam stared at his laptop screen. The plantation shutters were closed, as they usually were, but not to block the sunlight. The sun had set hours earlier. Cam kept the shutters closed at all times for privacy. It set the apartment into a permanent cave-like darkness, but he didn't mind the darkness. Preferred it, really. He'd chosen plantation shutters for that reason. Aside from a bit of light leaking through the cracks, they blocked even the brightest sun, leaving the room dark, still, peaceful. And they blocked any prying eyes just as well.

Cam preferred to create his own lighting. He favored soft, yellow-hued lights in the corners and on desks. Calm on the eyes and on the mind. No harsh overheads for him. A calm home creates a calm mind, and you can carry that calm mind with you when you leave. Cam could always return home in his mind to find peace when he needed it.

Usually, anyway. Lately, that peace had been shattered by a woman in black and her all-seeing green eyes.

Cam curled his hand around the tumbler of whiskey on the desk beside his laptop, spun the glass idly in circles between his thumb and two fingers. The ice had melted, and even the condensation on the glass had dried hours ago, though the expensive Scotch inside had not gone down at all.

He'd made similar progress on his computer. He had two windows open. One was a paper he was writing for his Theories of Punishment seminar. That was a topic rich in ideas for Cam, ideas that drove deep into his beliefs, into his childhood. It was a topic that set Cameron Hauk and Sam Davis at odds with one another. This was the first paper of the semester in that class, and Cam was struggling to reconcile his two personas. In the past, he'd sided with Sam Davis every time. Cameron Hauk wasn't getting a degree in criminology. Sam Davis was. And Sam Davis hadn't been raised by thieves. Sam Davis couldn't pick a lock in under three seconds or steal a gold watch from a woman's arm while he looked her in the eye and carried on a pleasant conversation. Sam Davis didn't have a mother serving a forty-year prison sentence because his father died in her arms outside a botched bank robbery that they weren't a part of.

That was real punishment. Cruel *and* unusual. His parents had done hundreds of jobs in their lives, bringing Cam along on dozens of them by that time. In all those jobs, they'd never hurt a soul, never carried a weapon, never even raised their voices. They were your friendly neighborhood thieves, stealing with the cleverness of their minds, the boldness of their spirit, and the genius of their planning. Violence was failure, in their view.

So when the family went to the city for lunch one day and Cam's father parked on the curb, stepped out of the car, and caught a bullet fired by some smash-and-grab asshole fleeing the scene on foot amid a gunfight with the police after a bank job gone bad, yeah, that punishment had been cruel. When he staggered around the still-hot hood of the car, fell into Cam's mother's arms, and died on the curb while Cam, fifteen years old, stunned immobile, watched through the car window, that punishment had been unusual.

That he'd been shot through the heart and died in the arms

of the love of his life, watched by a son who idolized and adored him, that was just fate being a dick.

Cruel and unusual punishment was unconstitutional. But the government had no jurisdiction over fate. And yet they still felt it appropriate to arrest Cam's mother while his father's body was still warm, his blood still hot on her hands, her tears still fresh on her cheeks. They felt it appropriate to drag her away without even letting Cam say goodbye. They felt it appropriate to leave a fifteen-year-old boy to fend for himself. Old enough, the judge said. *Consider yourself lucky not to be incarcerated, too, young man*, he had said.

So yeah, Cam had some theories about punishment in the criminal justice system. But Sam Davis would have other thoughts. Normally, Cam could blend the two just enough to give Sam an edge. His professors said Sam thought "outside the box", with "fresh, innovative ideas" that were exactly what the justice system needed to move forward. Little did they know that the secret to innovation was to ask the criminals to help reform the system.

But that night, Cam couldn't focus on what Sam's thoughts might be. He stared at the blank screen on his laptop, stared at the blinking cursor. The blank, mindless repetition of that flashing vertical line seemed a perfect metaphor for the state of his mind in that moment.

No, actually it didn't. His mind wasn't blank. Not at all. He wished it were. Instead, his mind was full of images, thoughts, feelings, all in a tangle, running around his head like frenzied toddlers released for pre-school recess. He couldn't focus, couldn't bring any order to them. He couldn't find the threads to pull, the incentive to wrangle those screaming toddlers into line. He'd been sitting at his desk in the dark for hours trying, but hadn't put one single word on the screen. With every flash of the cursor, his memories flashed in his mind. His father on the side-walk. His mother behind bars. Those damn Cheshire cat eyes.

Jenkins behind the microphone at a press conference. And fucking Reggie Moon.

The other window on his screen was in a similar state to the first, though this one didn't carry the baggage of Cam's alter ego. This screen was for code. He had a notion to hack into the school's system to find out who Reggie Moon really was, once and for all. But he was conflicted there, too. For two and a half years, he'd deliberately avoided hacking into anything remotely associated with the school. He was a great hacker, and he knew it. Not the best in the world, but a great hacker. But he also knew that arrogance was the thing that most often brought down the best people, criminal or not. He was not willing to jeopardize the plan, to risk his mother's freedom, on the assumption that he was good enough to cover his tracks if he hacked into the school's systems. They would boot him in a heartbeat if they caught him meddling in their databases. It would jeopardize the integrity of all the work Sam Davis had done.

And yet he had to get a bead on Moon. He had to know who he was dealing with. What were Moon's weaknesses? What were his strengths? How could he be beaten? There was only one semester left before graduation. Moon was ahead in the class rankings, but not by much. Sam Davis could catch him, but he only had one shot at this. He had to get it right. Cam's mother's freedom was riding on it.

Cam flipped to the coding window. It might be too risky to hack into McFadden's systems, but that didn't mean he couldn't hack into the systems of other schools. No one seemed to know where Reggie Moon had come from. Stanford, UC Irvine, Arizona State. They'd all been mentioned as possibilities. So Cam would hack them all. Hell, he'd hack every college in the country to find Moon, if he had to.

He started the way any such hack would start, with a simple Google search. Why go to the trouble of hacking when you could find what you needed legally? Criminal risk brought an adrenaline rush, sure, but unnecessary criminal risk was just stupid.

The search returned a real estate agent in the northwest, a friendly-looking guy with grey hair and a grey goatee. Probably not the same Reggie Moon. Neither was the mixed-media artist in Tribeca, the twelve-year-old boy with the Twitch account in Modesto, or the bulldog from England. An actual dog with a first name, a last name, and an Instagram account. With over a hundred posts. Some people had a lot of free time.

Unfortunately, Google was suspiciously silent on the subject of Reggie Moon, criminology student. Seemed odd for a twenty-something grad student to have zero social media presence. Even Sam Davis had enough presence for him to claim that he wasn't interested in social media. A smattering of haphazard posts displayed indifference. No posts anywhere at all, ever, aroused suspicion. For Cam, anyway.

But maybe Reggie Moon was unusually driven, dedicated to being the best criminal justice student in the history of mankind. Or, more likely, maybe he was determined to be a politician, become president one day, just like Attorney General Jenkins. Maybe Jenkins was his idol, and he wanted Jenkins to become his mentor. So he'd get top of the class and meet the man himself, face to face, to win him over. For someone aspiring to politics, going dark on social media wasn't just a good idea, these days it was practically essential. Might make it hard to win the younger vote, but it eliminated the risk of compromising images torpedoing the campaign before it even started. Moon could find other ways to woo the youth voters when the time came.

With no luck on Google, Cam turned to the universities. He set up a program that would route his traffic through a randomized server path around the globe that would shift ten times every second, using multiple threads so Cam wouldn't notice any disruptions on his end. He had already partitioned his hard drive into Sam stuff and Cam stuff, but he partitioned the Cam side even further to wall off his hacking activity from the rest of his computer. No way to trace the outbound traffic, no way to infect the computer with an inbound virus or tracking software if something went wrong and Cam's snooping was detected.

He started with Arizona State University, since that was the last school that Jem had suggested Moon might have come from. Site security was token, and Cam was inside within minutes. No record of a Reggie Moon there. He switched to Irvine. Similarly lax security. There he found a Reginald Moon, but he was an adjunct professor of classical studies in the music department, specializing in the Baroque period. Not the guy Cam was looking for.

Cam tried Stanford next. Their network was a bit harder to crack. The administration probably had to beef up their systems not to keep out the criminals, but to keep out their own students. They'd probably been burned too many times by computer science whiz kids too smart for their own good, too young to know better, and too full of themselves, dreaming of owning the world one day. It wasn't overly difficult for Cam to hack, but it did require a bit more time and attention than the other schools. Instead of minutes, it took Cam about an hour to get through the layers of authentication and security. After the effort, though, Stanford yielded nothing but frustration.

He tried more schools, running through every criminology program he could think of, then Googling to find more. No record of Reggie Moon at any of them.

By the time he looked up from his screen—his leg stiff, his neck and shoulders sore from hunching over his laptop, his eyes dry and aching—thin white lines lit the cracks in his plantation shutters. Cam glanced at the clock in the corner of his computer screen. It was already seven in the morning. He'd worked through the night and had nothing to show for it. No paper for his class, and nothing on Reggie Moon.

He had class in one hour, but decided to skip it. He'd be worthless, anyway, if he didn't get some sleep. Besides, the class was statistics. Both Cam and Sam Davis could do that in their sleep, so he might as well sleep through it. Annie was in the same class, so he could check with her to make sure he didn't miss anything important.

He glanced back at his screen, at the flashing vertical line of the cursor in the coding window, and clenched his teeth. Before he hit the sack, he might as well try a few more schools.

14

SAM SLAMMED his hand down on the wooden table between Jem and Annie, rattling the plastic cups filled with water and cola and a milkshake. Jem startled, and Annie nearly jumped out of her skin. Sarah just raised an eyebrow and kept on chewing her bite of what looked like a pulled pork sandwich, the rich scent of barbecue sauce teasing Sam's nostrils. Motsu had seen Sam coming and laughed at the reaction of the others.

"Fresno," said Sam, triumphant. He still hadn't had a moment of sleep, but he'd finally found Reggie Moon. At Cal State in Fresno, of all places.

"Fresno?" said Sarah.

"Is that where you've been?" said Jem, turning and leaning back in his chair to get a look at Sam. "You look like you've been to Fresno and back. When's the last time you slept?"

"When's the last time you showered? " said Motsu. "You stink."

Sam frowned. Did he stink? He'd showered the day before and had barely left his desk since, let alone his apartment. Hadn't even touched his Scotch.

"You don't stink," said Jem.

Sam scowled at Motsu, who grinned in response.

"What about Fresno?" asked Sarah.

Sam pulled a chair from another table and sat down. "That's where Reggie Moon came from."

"No," said Jem around a bite of food, "he's from Indiana State. My old roommate is dating a guy whose sister works in the registrar's office."

"I thought you said she was from the West coast," said Annie.

"Close enough."

"Indiana is not—"

"It's Fresno," said Sam. The smell of the food all around him was making his stomach clench tight and growl like a trapped bear. Light-headed and disoriented, like he was walking through a dream, he glanced over his shoulder, half expecting to see a woman dressed all in black standing there, watching. He tugged his hands through his hair, trying to pull his mind back to some semblance of coherent thought. "I found the records myself."

Sarah swallowed her food with a gulp. "How?"

"Online." Sam waved his hands in a vaguely dismissive gesture, hoping to avoid any further questions about his methods. His friends knew Sam Davis was good with computers, just like Jem. They did not know he was a first-rate hacker, and they didn't need to know. "The records are incomplete. There's no picture, no high school transcript, no undergrad. But there are graduate courses and grades and record of a transfer to McFadden University last month."

"Online?" said Sarah, skeptical.

"Sounds like our guy," said Jem.

"No picture?" said Annie. "How are we supposed to find him if we don't even know what he looks like?"

Motsu slapped the table. "We should set up a meet," he said. "Like in a spy movie. A dead drop. Send him an email and tell him to meet us in the park by the oak tree near the fountain."

"There is no fountain in the park," said Sarah.

"You know what I mean."

"And that's not what a dead drop is," Sarah continued. "You have to drop something for it to be a dead drop."

"Why would I drop something?" said Motsu. "I'm the one calling for the dead drop."

"They have to drop something. Otherwise... it's just dead."

"What if they drop dead? Then is it a drop dead drop?"

Everyone groaned. Sarah's eyes narrowed, and she punched Motsu in the arm. "You should be shot dead for that joke," she said, a laugh escaping at the end of her words. "Your dad jokes are cruel and unusual punishment."

Sam flinched at the phrase.

"If I drop the dad jokes," said Motsu, "would that be a dad drop?"

"Whether he drops something or not," asked Annie, her voice loud enough and pointed enough to change the subject, "how can we email him? Do we have his email address?"

"Wouldn't it be reggie.moon@mcfadden.edu?" said Motsu with a shrug.

"Maybe," said Annie, "but not necessarily. Mine isn't annie dot xi. They don't always use your nickname or your preferred name."

"What's your email, then?"

"It's not a bad idea, actually," said Jem. "Try to lure him to us instead of us trying to find him."

"But even if we did lure him," said Sam, "how would we know it was him?"

"What's your email, Annie?"

"If we lured him to a more private location," said Annie, ignoring Motsu, "we'd know. He'd be the only one there besides us."

"Could work," mused Sam, "but we'd need to find a good reason for him to come to us."

"Something about school," said Jem. "A study group."

"Why would he join?" said Sarah. "He's top of the class. He doesn't need the help."

"Hey, Annie," said Motsu, "there's something I need to send to you. Could you give me your email?"

Annie smiled softly, but purposely avoided looking at Motsu.

Jem shook his head. "Maybe he likes helping others."

"Doubt it." Sarah took another bite of her sandwich.

Sam's stomach growled so loud at the sight, both Annie and Jem turned their heads. Without a word, Annie slid the second half of her turkey club in front of him. With a slump-shouldered sigh and a grateful glance, Sam shoved the sandwich in his mouth. A turkey club had never tasted so good. He took the huge half-sandwich down in three bites.

"Jesus, remind me not to get my hands too close to your mouth," said Motsu.

"Sorry," said Sam, "I haven't eaten since lunch."

"This is lunch," Motsu replied.

"Yesterday's lunch."

Jem slid what remained of his burger toward Sam at the same moment that both Motsu and Sarah slid their remaining fries toward him. Sam laughed out loud.

"Thanks, guys," he said. He took a handful of fries and pushed the plastic baskets into the center of the table for everyone to share, then dug into Jem's burger. The blue cheese bacon burger at Cole's was the best in town. Even though there were only two bites left in Jem's, it tasted like heaven.

"What if we fake an email from the professor?" said Annie. "Say he needs to meet Reggie, asks him to stay after class. Then we watch to see who hangs back."

"Which professor?" said Jem. "And which class? We don't know Reggie's schedule."

"You said you found transcripts," said Sarah. "Can you figure out which classes he needs to graduate?"

"Maybe," Sam nodded. "I'll give it a try."

Luring Moon out with a fake email was a good idea, but weak. It was too easy for Reggie to see through it. He might just ignore it and not show up. He might send someone else in his place. Impersonating a professor was better, but they'd have to spoof the return address, and if Reggie got any whiff of suspicion and knew even the most basic information about email protocols, it was too easy to check. They'd have to hack the system to pull off the spoof properly, and Sam didn't want to do that. Not unless he absolutely had to.

"How else can we flush Moon out?" he asked. "Other than email."

"Did you get an address?" asked Jem.

"No," Sam said, "but I didn't really try."

"If he's living on campus, he won't have one," Annie said. "Just a mailbox number."

"Why would he live on campus?" asked Motsu.

"We can't all afford to live in swanky brownstones in Georgetown," said Sarah.

"It's a shame." Motsu shook his head in mock sorrow. "They're really nice."

Sarah picked a fry from the basket in the center of the table and flung it at Motsu's face. With startling reaction time, Motsu opened his mouth wide and caught the fry. He flung his arms up in triumph as he chewed. Sarah picked up another fry and bounced it off his nose while he was looking away.

"Still, it's worth looking into," said Sam. "I'll see what I can dig up. Maybe he'll show up on Google."

Sam doubted it. He'd already tried Google. But it was worth a shot. He hadn't been looking for an address that time, so he might have better luck with a more focused search. And if didn't find one on Google, he might be able to hack around to find an address somewhere else.

"Well, folks," said Motsu, wiping his face with a napkin, "as much as I enjoy hatching top-secret spy schemes in the middle of a crowded barbecue restaurant," he wadded the napkin and threw it onto the table, "I need to go to class."

"You're actually going to class?" said Annie, eyes wide with incredulity.

"Wait," said Jem. Motsu glanced at him. "Courts and Sentencing? Professor Smythe?"

Motsu grinned, his eyes shining. The man grinned more than anyone Sam had ever met, but he could see why. When he grinned like that, the heavens sang and even the angels couldn't help falling in love. He had no idea why Motsu even bothered with criminology. He could make a fortune in Hollywood.

"I'm in her class, too," said Jem, standing and grabbing his jacket from the back of his chair. "I'll walk with you."

"Who's Professor Smythe?" asked Annie.

"Rich, young, and hot," said Jem as he slid into his coat. "That's who Professor Smythe is."

"I'll send you her picture," said Motsu to Annie. "Just give me your email."

Annie rolled her eyes. Sam could hear Motsu laughing all the way to the door.

Sam and Sarah watched Annie in silence. She stared down at her hands folded on the table, the fingers of her top hand riffling against her bottom hand again and again. Her face worked through contortions in response to her emotions. First gleeful, then tortured, then self-recriminating. Annie was an open book. You could practically narrate her thoughts just by watching her face. She'd make a terrible poker player, but she was a good friend.

She looked up, finally noticing the silence. "What?" she said.

Sam and Sarah exchanged a look. There was an undeniable tension between Annie and Motsu. For Annie, who showed no romantic interest whatsoever in anyone else, it was clear she liked Motsu. Motsu's intentions, on the other hand, were not as clear, and no one wanted to see Annie get hurt, let alone by a member of their friend group. Let alone by Motsu, whose past was littered with the shards of shattered hearts.

Sarah glanced again at Sam, took a slurp from the straw of her milkshake, and shook her head. "Nothing at all, honey. Nothing at all."

Sam stuffed one more handful of fries in his mouth, then said his goodbyes. He had work to do, both for that Theories of Punishment paper, and to find out more about Reggie Moon.

And he needed a shower. He sniffed his pits as subtly as he could while weaving through the crowded tables toward the door. Motsu was right. He did stink.

15

EVEN THOUGH HE hadn't slept in more than thirty hours, adrenaline and optimism counteracted Cam's sleep deprivation. Yet as much as Cam wanted to start looking right away for Reggie Moon's address, he forced himself to focus. And to shower.

He cleaned up and dressed, then sat down and wrote his entire paper for his Theories of Punishment class. He managed to find Sam Davis' voice and construct an essay that pushed the boundaries of contemporary opinions without coming completely out of left field or looking so pro-criminal that his professor would laugh him out of her class or, worse, wonder who this Sam Davis kid really was. He found and walked the same line he'd been walking for two and a half years, the line of a brilliant, promising criminology student who would one day become a leader in the criminal justice community.

By the time that was done, the sun had set. Even though he kept the shutters closed and the interior lights on all the time when he was awake, Cam could see a subtle difference in the quality of the light inside the apartment when the sun was up. During the day, with just a little bit of natural light seeping through the shutters, the room felt more complex, somehow. Like the new water bounces among the older water in a tide pool between waves, swirling it with foam and oxygen, the rays of white daylight leaking through the shutters would mingle with the yellow lamplight. But when the sun was down, the room was pure lamplight, soft and warm and simple. More relaxing. At night, alone in his apartment, Cam felt like he was tucked in with a blanket and a good book.

With his paper written and out of the way and a box of mac and cheese in his stomach, fatigue pulled on Cam, like huge, gentle hands enveloping him, urging him to lie down in his bed and sleep. But he resisted. Sleep could come later. Right now he had work to do. He thought about Reggie Moon and called up that adrenaline again, made himself a mug of strong coffee, and drank half of it in one swallow. He sat on his futon couch, put his feet on the coffee table and his laptop in his lap, and opened up his browser window.

For a moment, he stared past the screen at his feet. Or, more specifically, at the spot where his feet rested on the table. It was the same spot where he'd examined the box the woman had left on his doorstep a few days earlier. His eyes flicked to a cabinet in the corner. The box and the glasses were locked in a drawer inside.

He hadn't forgotten about the woman. It was all he could do to focus on anything else. She still plagued his dreams, woke him with a start in the middle of the night, sweat beaded on his bare chest. Those green eyes hovered and watched him, shrouded by blood-red hair. Sometimes he woke in fear, sometimes in arousal, sometimes in anger or frustration or a confused sense of loss.

Whatever feeling it was that woke him, he would sit up and stare into a darkness so dense and complete, he couldn't tell if he was awake or still dreaming. The closed bedroom door blocked the faint lights on his computer and his shutters blocked any light from outside. Normally, Cam loved the darkness and the quiet. He felt safe in it, hidden. He and his family owned the darkness, used it like a trusted member of their crew. But after all the broken sleep he'd been getting, Cam was considering buying a night light just so he wouldn't have to look into that fathomless nothing anymore.

He pushed aside those thoughts. He had even more work to do to find that woman, work that needed to be done. But she could wait. Reggie Moon was the more pressing issue.

He started simple. He'd already looked for Moon on social media and come up empty. Now, he tried a reverse address lookup site. He found a Reginald Moon in Hyattsville, Maryland, but the man was in his sixties. Another one lived in Virginia. Close enough to commute, but a quick search showed that he was a forty-year-old corporate development analyst with a wife and two kids. Not the Reggie Moon Cam was looking for.

The third entry was promising. Showed an R. X. Moon who was a college student in DC. Cam clicked on the entry, then pulled his legs down and sat up straight on the couch, wincing only a bit when his left leg twinged.

The detail page showed that this Moon was a grad student in criminology at McFadden University. This was the guy. Cam clicked to reveal the address.

A chill ran down his spine, and a flush of adrenaline made the rest of his coffee completely unnecessary.

Reggie Moon's address was in Cam's apartment complex. 45 Pennsylvania. Just two corridors over and a floor above where Cam was sitting at that very moment. For all he knew, Cam could have walked by Reggie Moon a dozen times, could have shared an elevator or held a door open for him.

Reggie Moon had been right under Cam's nose this entire time.

He checked the clock on his computer. Ten in the evening on a Thursday was probably too late for a visit from a random stranger. Sam had class at nine the next morning. He could pay Reggie a visit around eight. Might not get an answer, but at least it wouldn't attract undue attention, wouldn't be considered rude.

Cam slapped the laptop shut, set it on the table, and stood up with his coffee cup. He ran one hand through his hair and walked to the kitchen, dumped the rest of the coffee in the sink and poured two fingers of Scotch into the same cup, threw it back in one swallow, and poured two fingers more.

He ran one hand along the counter, checked the lid on the bottle of Scotch, and set it back in the cupboard. He went back to the couch, sat down, then stood and again downed the Scotch in one swallow. He set the mug in the sink in the kitchen. Went back to the coffee table, picked up the laptop and set it on the desk. Went back to the kitchen, to the sink, rinsed the empty coffee mug, set it in the top rack of the dishwasher. Ran his hands through his hair again and blew out a long breath he hadn't realized he'd been holding. Went back to the desk, picked up the laptop again, then stood there, laptop drooping in his hand, paralyzed between the desk, the kitchen, and the couch.

His chest was tight and his stomach burned. Between the adrenaline, the black coffee, and the Scotch, his stomach acid would probably melt steel. He wanted to go to Moon's apartment right then, but he couldn't do that, not until the morning. But he had to do something.

He thought back to what Sarah had suggested at lunch. He could check Reggie Moon's transcript, see if he could figure out what classes Moon would be in. Cam set the laptop back on the desk and flipped it open.

He opened the window he used for hacking and started typing, then slammed the laptop shut and shot to his feet again, again pulling his hands through his hair. He completed the movement before his conscious mind even realized it. He was surprised to find himself standing in the center of the apartment again. He turned in a bewildered circle, chest even tighter, stomach burning even more.

Was he nervous? Excited? Excited. That had to be it. He'd just found Reggie Moon. The mystery man. The cause of so much trouble, for Sam Davis and for Cam. He wanted to pound on the door of 45 Pennsylvania Ave and finally put a face to a name, to meet the man that was jeopardizing his mother's freedom.

And then what? Ask him to stop? To throw a test or skip an assignment? Would he break cover, tell Reggie Moon all about Cameron Hauk and his alter ego, Sam Davis? Tell him about his mother and blackmailing the AG? Would he tell him about stealing the Nestech glasses, or about pretending to be a wealthy investor to sneak aboard a luxury yacht in Southern California to steal incriminating evidence? How about the two murders he knew about and helped cover up? Would he tell Reggie Moon about those, too?

Cam pulled in a long breath, long enough and deep enough to expand his chest, to spread his rib cage until he felt the stretch in his sternum, felt the tightness there pulled apart. He blew out the breath completely, fully, slumping his shoulders, dangling his arms limp, softening his knees, letting that tension flow out with the breath. He did it again, and a third time, until he was slightly lightheaded, but his mind had settled and his nervous excitement had abated.

He'd found Reggie Moon. Probably. Maybe. He wouldn't know for sure until he confronted the man. But that wouldn't be until tomorrow. Between now and then, Cam could do nothing but wait. And, hopefully, sleep.

But sleep wouldn't come for a few hours yet. Deep breaths or not, Cam could tell that much. He pulled the coffee mug back out of the dishwasher and poured one more finger of Scotch. Self-medicating was a bad idea. Yo-yo-ing back and forth between stimulants and depressants while working on zero sleep in the last day and a half was an even worse idea. But Cam had already come this far. He'd sleep in an hour or two.

He sat down at the desk and opened the laptop once more. If Cam was going to meet Reggie Moon in the morning, he might as well learn as much about the guy as he possibly could before then.

16

CAM WALKED through the open-air corridors of his apartment complex. It was still deep night, and a thick fog had rolled in. The security lamps which normally lit the corridors with bright white light were transformed by the fog into pale, ghostly pearls hovering in the darkness, illuminating only a few feet around them, leaving the rest of the walkway shrouded and opaque.

Cam's feet were bare, ice-cold against the floor, the texture of the concrete rough against his numb soles. He wore dark sweatpants and a thin white t-shirt. Even though the air was cold enough for him to see his breath, he was sweating like he'd just run a marathon, his shirt sticking to his chest, so damp he could see his skin through it.

The air carried the smell of sweat and chemicals, a plastic scent, faint and dull, and the fog seemed to swallow every sound. The soft pad of his footfalls were dull thumps, like punching a stack of pillows. Cam could hear nothing else. The fog seemed to seep through his ears into his brain, dulling his senses.

He didn't know where he was in the apartment complex, or where he was going. There were no doors on either wall as he walked. He came to an intersection and looked at the signs, white letters on green rectangles, fashioned to look like the street signs in downtown Washington. PENNSYLVANIA and MASSACHUSETTS, they said. Two streets that never meet in the real Washington, but which intersected in the apartment complex.

Pennsylvania. 45 Pennsylvania. Reggie Moon's apartment.

Cam turned right onto Pennsylvania and counted down the apartment doors as he passed them. Forty-nine. Forty-eight.

The doors seemed to emerge from the fog, then fade into it again as Cam passed, as if the only doors that existed were the ones directly beside him. With no sound from his footsteps, it seemed almost as if he were standing still and the doors were moving past him.

Forty-seven.

An involuntary shiver shook Cam's whole body. He folded his arms over his chest for warmth.

Forty-six.

The hair on Cam's bare arms stood on end.

Apartment forty-five.

He stopped in front of the door, raised his fist to knock.

A figure emerged from the fog to his left. Hooded, dark. Eyes glowing green, red hair flowing around her face, streaming from the recesses of her deep cowl like a headdress made of snakes. A Medusa in the night.

Cam tried to run. He tried to scream. He tried to pound the apartment door. He couldn't move, couldn't speak. Those green eyes trapped him, held him in their thrall, gorgeous and frightening, as the figure came closer.

Slowly. Inexorably.

The eyes grew larger, filled his vision, pulled him into their depths, so beautiful Cam's chest ached. He fell headfirst into those eyes, falling, falling...

Cam jerked awake. His head lay flat on something. He stared slant-wise at the futon couch across from him.

The green eyes were gone. The light in the room was soft and yellow. Warm and welcoming.

No fog. No cold clouds of breath.

No green-eyed, red-haired Medusa dressed in black.

He lifted his head and immediately regretted it. His left cheek peeled away from the laptop keyboard, and spears of pain ran up his stiff neck and back. He ran his hand over his cheek and felt the square indentations of the keys pressed into his skin.

He'd fallen asleep at his desk, slumped over his laptop. The screen sprang to life when he moved. Cam checked the clock. 2 AM.

The screen was a mess of gibberish typing and random windows that Cam's cheek had opened while he slept. Whatever he'd been working on was probably gone forever, but it didn't matter. Aside from the address, Cam hadn't found squat on Reggie Moon.

He stood, his thigh adding to the complaints from his neck and back, and stretched gingerly. He ran his hands over his chest and found his shirt drenched in sweat, just like in his dream. He shut his laptop and turned out the lights, then peeled off his shirt and dropped it on the floor as he stumbled to the bedroom in the dark.

Six hours later, bleary-eyed but feeling more human, driven by some real sleep beneath his adrenaline, Cam walked down the same apartment corridors he'd walked in his dream. Instead of fog shrouding everything, the sun was up and the sky was clear, blue and beautiful.

Cam took the stairs up one level and stopped in front of the door to 45 Pennsylvania. He ignored the shiver up his spine as he lifted his fist to knock, resisted the nearly overwhelming urge to look to his left to be sure there wasn't a hooded figure stalking toward him. He took a deep breath, then rapped lightly on the door.

He shifted his backpack on his shoulders and waited for a

few seconds, listening. Hearing nothing, he lifted his hand to knock again. As he did so, the door swung open, leaving him with his hand in the air like a kindergarten student asking a question.

A woman stood before him. Long, straight black hair, dark sunglasses with tortoise-shell frames, a leather messenger bag slung over one shoulder and across her body. She was trim and tall, wearing a stylish dark-grey wool jacket over jeans that hugged every curve down to her black leather boots.

"Hi," was all she said. She stood, one hand holding the door, waiting for Cam to respond. No anxiety, no surprise. She was calm and cool. Cam's gaze fell to her lips, full and pink against her clear, pale skin.

For some reason, he found himself tongue-tied. He was expecting Reggie Moon to answer the door, not a gorgeous woman. "Um, hi," he replied.

They stared at each other in silence for a long, awkward moment.

"Okay, nice talk," she said. She pushed past Cam, pulled the door shut behind her, and turned to lock it.

"I'm looking for Reggie," Cam finally managed to stammer. "Reggie Moon. Is he here?"

The woman slipped her keys into her bag and stared at Cam. Even though he couldn't see her eyes through her sunglasses, Cam could feel the intensity of her stare.

"Who's asking?"

"I'm Sam Davis," said Cam. "Reggie and I go to school together."

"Is that right?" She smiled, a broad smile that lit her face and made Cam's heart flip in his suddenly tight chest. "Well, that means you and I go to school together."

"You go to the same school as Reggie?"

The woman stared at Cam for a long moment, then turned without speaking and walked down the hallway.

"Wait," Cam called after her. "Is Reggie here?"

"Just me," called the woman over her shoulder, "and I've got to get to class."

Cam jogged to catch up to her. "I'm going to class, too," he said. "I'll walk with you." The woman didn't turn, didn't slow down. "If that's okay with you," Cam added hastily.

The woman stepped into the elevator, but held the door for Cam. He took that to mean it was okay for him to walk with her. He stood beside her in the elevator and she punched the button for the ground floor.

"What class do you have this morning?" Cam asked. He might not have found Reggie Moon, but he found someone who knew him. She must have been his roommate. Or his girlfriend, though Moon had only transferred a few weeks ago. If this woman was his girlfriend, Moon worked awfully fast. Especially since she already had keys to his apartment. And with as good-looking as this woman was, Reggie Moon must be some kind of Adonis.

"Theories of Punishment," she replied.

"With Professor Riskin?" It was the same class Cam had. "Did you finish your paper?"

She glanced at Cam with a sly smile. "You're in the same class?" She turned to face forward again. "What a coincidence."

The elevator dinged, the door slid open, and the woman strode out. Cam had to hustle to keep up with her. He'd made a personal connection, something he and the woman had in common. If he could play off of that, maybe he could get her to tell him more about Moon.

"I wrote about appeal to authority," Cam offered. The paper had been about logical fallacies in criminal judgement. They were to choose from a list of logical fallacies and write ten pages about how that type of error in logic could lead to unjust punishments for criminals.

"Just because it's the law, doesn't mean it's just?" asked the woman, raising one eyebrow. "Bold premise for a graduate degree in upholding and defending the law."

They walked out the front gate and down to the corner. The light changed and they crossed the street together. The woman was shorter than Cam by a few inches, but she walked so quickly he could barely stay with her.

"No better way to fix the system than from within," said Cam.

The conversation and the brisk walk helped Cam slip into his Sam Davis persona. Cameron Hauk preferred to stay outside the system altogether, taking advantage of its inconsistencies, the logical fallacies rife within it. These were the chinks in the armor of the criminal justice system. A society needed clear rules to exist and to grow, standards of behavior for people to follow. But for any given individual within that society, those rules were subject to interpretation, given the specifics of a situation. That was Cameron Hauk's mentality, the mentality of an anarchist—and a professional criminal.

Sam Davis, on the other hand, believed firmly in supporting the system, working to fill those chinks in the armor with better logic, clearer thinking, and just a little bit of creativity. It would never work, since the weakness in the criminal justice system came from the weaknesses of the people who ran it, but it was a good cover story, all the same.

"Is that right?" said the woman. "Funny, you don't seem like a 'fix from within' kind of guy to me."

She hustled down the staircase from the street to the Rosslyn Metro station. The woman was taking them one step at a time, but Sam had to practically jump down them to keep pace, taking every other step in long, clomping leaps. The staircase was a long one. By the last leap or two, he was afraid his left leg would give out.

"What kind of guy do I seem like?" Sam said, breathless, his left thigh burning, as he caught up to her on the platform where she waited for the train to arrive.

The woman smiled to herself as the dim twin lights of the train appeared in the tunnel in the distance. The squeal of the brakes and the rush of the train car made further conversation impossible for the moment. The train pushed a gust of warm, fecund air at them, blowing the woman's hair around her face like a dark halo.

As the doors opened, a line of people pushed off of the train while Sam and the woman joined another line pushing its way on. Everyone's face bore the same grim, robotic expression. They all just wanted to get where they had to be and get through the day so they could finally enjoy their weekend.

They got separated in the crush, but Sam fought his way back to the woman's side. The train started with a jerk and he fell into her. She caught him in steady hands and set him right. She wasn't holding on to anything, just standing in the aisle, yet she hadn't wavered an inch when the train jerked into motion. Hadn't even shifted her feet when she caught Sam. The woman was as steady as a rock.

After he regained his balance, Sam stood for a long moment, inches from the woman, her hands still on his chest. Again, his gaze fell to those full, pink lips.

The lips twisted into a wry smile. "You seem to me," she said, "like the kind of guy who hasn't quite figured out what the problem is yet." She tilted her head at him. "Let alone how to fix it."

Sam opened his mouth to speak, then realized he had no idea how to respond. She was right, of course. He'd just never heard anyone say that to him before, let alone say it so clearly.

And they'd only met ten minutes earlier. Was it really that obvious?

And if so, why did he feel so surprised?

17

THE THEORIES of Punishment seminar was a smaller class than the others Sam was taking that year. Where the others filled lecture halls, this one had only thirty students or so. They met in a classroom with three long, concentric, semicircular tables arranged on shallow risers, facing a desk in the center and a massive whiteboard on the wall. It was a lecture hall in miniature, with thin grey carpet instead of concrete and marble.

Jem caught Sam's eye with a raised hand as Sam followed the woman through a door in the front of the classroom. He tapped the woman on the shoulder.

"Why don't you sit with us today?" he said. "I'll introduce you to my friend."

The woman raised an eyebrow at him, then shrugged and stepped aside to let Sam lead the way.

"Let's get started, please," called Professor Riskin as she strode in from a side door.

Riskin was an older woman, nearly seventy, but she looked like she wasn't a day over fifty. And her energy levels were off the chart, making Sam feel like a crotchety old man. When Riskin asked a question and fixed her eyes on you, the intensity of her look nearly burned holes in your skull. She'd been a federal prosecutor, then a federal judge, and in her retirement had become one of the most feared and respected criminology professors in the nation. She was genius-level smart, took no bullshit from anyone, and had a caustic sense of humor that could skewer the most arrogant student in a heartbeat. Sam had seen it happen in his first year, back when Riskin still taught Criminology Theory. He didn't even want to imagine what it must have been like to face her across a courtroom.

Sam and the woman hustled to their seats beside Jem without another word, not wanting to be caught out by Riskin's gaze or her sharp tongue. Jem raised his eyebrows at Sam in question about the woman, but Sam just smiled and shook his head. He would worry about the introductions later.

Riskin moved at her usual blistering pace through the class, throwing out references that Sam had never seen and insights that blew his mind, three steps of inference or deduction beyond where Sam would have stopped. He took careful notes, but he would have to work extra hard to chase down all the references. Most of them weren't in the assigned reading for the class, which Sam had already finished for the semester. He liked to be prepared, and being prepared meant working ahead. When it came to Riskin, being prepared meant scrambling to keep up instead of falling hopelessly behind.

The woman beside him didn't take any notes at all. She didn't even take her laptop out of her bag. She just leaned on her elbows on the desk, chin in one hand, and listened to Riskin speak as if she were having a conversation with a friend at a coffee shop.

His own computer on his lap as he reclined in his chair, Sam could only see the woman in profile from behind. She had set her sunglasses on the desk and shrugged off her jacket. Her black hair shone in the overhead lights, spilled down to her shoulder blades over the light sweater she wore. A pale brown sweater. Cashmere, from the look of it, probably as soft and silky as her hair seemed to be. He could see the line of her long neck arcing up to a smooth angle of cream skin along her jawline, her cheek. He thought of her full lips. Were they as soft as her hair and her sweater? He bit his own lip in response to the thought. He needed to focus.

The woman didn't have a laptop, didn't use her phone for recording or notes, didn't even have a paper and pencil. Sam wondered how she'd made it to her third year, since she didn't seem to have much of a work ethic. She could be some kind of savant, but even a savant had to take notes once in a while, didn't they? He hadn't gotten the slacker vibe from her during their walk, but they hadn't had a lot of time to get to know each other. And when it came to beautiful women, history proved that Sam wasn't the best judge of character.

He shook his head and refocused on the lecture, and over the next two hours, he lost himself in it. Riskin's genius extended beyond her subject-matter expertise. She was one of the most engaging lecturers Sam had ever seen. The knife edge to her voice, the intensity of her mind, the storytelling aspect to her delivery, raising questions and then leaving you dangling before answering them. Riskin made it hard for Sam to take notes. He kept getting swept up in her arguments, her examples, her stories. He had to force himself to remember to jot things down. Maybe that's why the woman didn't bother. She just let herself get swept away.

That seemed to Sam like a good way to get a bad grade. But, then again, not everyone cared about finishing at the top of their class. Sam did, and he had extra incentive for it. He focused even more on his note-taking.

Riskin finished the lecture and called for everyone to drop their papers in a basket on the central desk in front on their way out of the lecture room. She announced that she'd created a semester-long project, one that they would complete in groups.

As third-year students, she said, they would soon be in the real world, where individuals had to work together to accomplish their tasks. Once they had jobs in the industry, they would have to work together, even while they were competing with each other for promotions, choice assignments, and the like. To that end, she paired each student with one other student in the class. The pairings were made in order of class rank, so that you were paired with your closest competition, and would be posted on the class website within the hour. Each pair would complete their assignment together and hand it in at the end of the semester. The project would constitute half of their grade in the course.

It wasn't the first group assignment Sam had gotten during his three years at McFadden, but he hoped it would be the last. He hated working in a group.

Ironic for someone who had grown up trained to work with a crew of thieves. But on a job, every member of the crew was carefully and intentionally chosen not just for their particular expertise, but for their character, their reliability and their motivation. On a job, if someone slacked off, everyone was at risk of imprisonment or even death.

In a school assignment, all that was at risk was a grade. Inevitably, someone in the group would slack off and the others —meaning Sam—would have to cover for them. For group assignments, it came down to one simple rule: whoever cared the most, did the most work. And since Sam cared more than anyone, he had come to approach every group assignment as an individual assignment where he would do all the work and everyone else would share in his A+ grade.

Riskin's method of pairing students was an interesting twist. Since their friend Sarah wasn't in that class, Sam figured he'd be paired with Jem, who was next in line in the class rankings. That was some comfort. Sam still would have preferred to work alone, but at least he knew his partner wouldn't be a slacker. Jem was a hard worker like Sam, and he cared about his grades almost as much.

The class rose with a thundering of sliding chairs and shuffling bags and footsteps on the risers. Sam snapped his laptop shut and stuffed it in his backpack, pulling his paper out to drop in the basket on the way out of class. He followed the woman down the aisle and through the line of students that snaked from the seats to the basket. She dropped her paper in just ahead of Sam. He took a quick moment to glance at the cover sheet. She hadn't told him what her paper was about. Hell, they'd rode the Metro into class together and he hadn't even gotten the woman's name.

The cover sheet didn't help in that regard. Her name wasn't on it, just the title and the class information. The title was *Begging the Question: Implicit Assumptions and the Compromise of Justice.* Sounded intriguing. Sam was surprised. Maybe the woman wasn't such a slacker after all. Slacker or not, she was definitely interesting.

He reached to check the second page for a name, but Jem nudged him from behind. A glance over his shoulder showed Sam he was holding up the line. He dropped his paper on top of the woman's and followed her into the hallway.

He and Jem had to hustle. She was halfway down the stairs before they caught up to her.

"You hungry?" Sam asked her. "Jem and I are meeting some friends for lunch."

The woman turned her head, that same enigmatic smile on her face. She'd put her sunglasses on already, so Sam couldn't see her eyes, couldn't read the smile more clearly. She lifted her chin and regarded them both for a moment.

"Sure," she said. "Why not?"

18

THEY CHATTED AS THEY WALKED, talking about Riskin and the project and the pairings. The air was cold, but the sun warmed their faces. The sky was so blue, the sun so bright, that everything around them leapt into vivid color. Even the tired granite facades seemed to gain a level of roguish mystery in their crooks and shadows.

Lunch that day was at a Japanese food truck called Taberu. The truck used to move around town, following the government workers out for their lunch breaks. Then it got so popular that they leased a small building, but kept the truck. They parked it out front, cooked and sold the food from there, like they always did, and used the building as a pavilion for people to eat in when the weather was snowy or inclement in the winter or too hot and muggy in the summer to be comfortable outside.

Jem ordered his usual pork belly okonomiyaki and Sam opted for yakisoba noodles with grilled chicken. The woman spoke quietly to the man taking the orders, the son of the owner, and ordered something called umeboshi onigiri. Sam didn't see it on the menu, but the man smiled when he saw her and nodded at her order.

"You some kind of regular here?" asked Jem.

"No," she said, "but I've been a few times. Tashi and I hit it off when we met. He and his family are from Asakusa, in Tokyo. I spent a month or so there one summer as a kid when my dad was in Japan for work."

"What was that thing you ordered?"

The woman smiled that damn enigmatic smile of hers. "Secret menu," she said. "Very hush-hush."

"You could tell us, but you'd have to kill us?" said Jem.

"Something like that."

The orders came up quickly, one of the hallmarks of Taberu's reputation. Sam looked at the woman's plate. Three triangular balls of rice wrapped in seaweed with some kind of chunky purple stuff in the center. He'd never seen it before in his life.

They found Sarah and Annie already seated inside, scooted chairs around to make room. Sam introduced Sarah and Annie to the woman.

"I'm sorry," he said when the moment came to tell the others her name. "We've been hanging out all morning and I never even caught your name."

The woman slid out of her jacket and slung it over her chair back. She smiled and pulled off her sunglasses. A beam of sunlight came through a skylight and fell over her face.

Sam felt like he'd been knocked in the head. The woman's eyes were straight out of his dreams. His nightmares. They were the same glowing green that he saw every night, that each night woke him in a sweat.

The woman squinted and shifted her chair to one side to escape the ray of bright sun. The glowing green of her eyes faded to a more natural color. Still green, an intense dusky green, and gorgeous, but no longer glowing, no longer the eyes that haunted Sam's dreams. He stared more closely at them. These eyes had flecks of blue and orange.

The woman caught him staring and raised an eyebrow at

him. Her favorite thing to do, apparently, and an effective gesture for all kinds of situations. Sam looked away and cleared his throat. He was still rattled by the sudden vision, but he had to pull his shit together. His dreams were starting to invade his reality, starting to affect his mind.

The woman settled in her chair and looked around the table. "I'm—"

"Absolutely stunning is what you are." Motsu emerged from out of nowhere, grabbed a chair from a nearby table, and slid in beside the woman like he'd ridden in on greased rails, his voice and his smile as smooth as his movements. He hung one arm over the back of the woman's chair. "How is it we've never met before?"

A lock of long black hair fell over one eye, magnifying the charm of Motsu's smile and good looks. The guy was undeniably beautiful. If Motsu looked at him the way he was looking at the woman, even Sam would have fucked him.

Motsu looked down at the woman's plate. His slick smile dropped, replaced by a look of amazement, like Motsu was a kid on Christmas morning. "No fucking way," he said. "Is that umeboshi onigiri?" He helped himself to one of the triangles from the woman's plate and took a huge bite. His eyes rolled back in his head, he slumped back in the chair, and he moaned like a man dying of heat who was finally slipping into a cool bath. "Oh my god, I haven't had this in so fucking long. My sobo used to make this when I was little. Haven't had it since the last time I was in Tokyo."

"Help yourself," said the woman with a good-natured laugh. She looked around the table. "Would anyone else like to try some?"

"That's Motsu," said Sarah in reply, jerking a thumb toward him. "He's a dick."

"A beautiful dick," said Motsu around a mouthful of rice.

"If you say so," muttered Annie. Her eyes moved back and

forth between Motsu and the woman, eyed her with suspicion, suspicion that Sam noticed had only started when Motsu arrived. He glanced at Sarah, who had noticed, too. She made a resigned face that was the equivalent of a shrug, a sigh, and an *oh well.*

"If you're looking for proof, Annie, just say the word." Motsu took his arm off the woman's chair, set the onigiri back on her plate, and slid his chair to Annie's side, now resting his arm on the back of Annie's chair. He leaned into her, grinning and squishing rice through his teeth. Annie laughed and pushed him away in disgust, but Sam could see that her whole demeanor had brightened again.

"I'll try a bite," said Sarah. The woman handed the onigiri Motsu had bitten to her. Sarah's brow furrowed as she nodded in appreciation at the taste. "Oh my god. What is that? Sweet pickles?"

Jem took the piece from Sarah, looked down at it. "Purple pickles?"

"It's umeboshi, you American philistines," said Motsu.

"Pickled ume," said the woman. "Kind of like a sour plum."

"Fucking hell," said Jem around a mouthful. He held the rice ball out to Sam. "Sam, you have to try this."

Sam took it with a laugh. "Since we're all eating your lunch for you, maybe you could tell us your name, so we can thank you for it?"

He bit into the rice ball as the woman answered. The rice was sticky and chewy and delicious. The plum was tart and salty and sweet all at once. The combination was bewildering and unusual and unexpected and absolutely amazing.

The woman laughed. "It's no problem," she said, "and it's nice to meet you all." She focused her gorgeous green eyes squarely on Sam, whose mouth was full of onigiri. With that sly smile of hers, she said, "My name is Regina, but everyone calls me Reggie."

<h1 style="text-align:center">19</h1>

SAM INHALED in surprise and sucked in a lungful of onigiri rice. His head was practically exploding already from the woman's revelation. The coughing fit that followed finished the job. Sam doubled over in his chair as he hacked away.

Jem's distracted backslaps thumped through Sam's chest, not helping his cough or his head. But Jem wasn't even looking at Sam. He and the others were staring slack-jawed at the wom—at Reggie.

"Reggie... Moon?" asked Sarah.

"Yeah, that's right," said Reggie. "How did you know?"

"Fucking hell," said Motsu. "Hot, loves umeboshi, *and* smart as fuck? You're my dream girl."

Sam recovered enough to glance at the storm cloud that covered Annie's face. He saw that Sarah had noticed it, too.

"You've been something of a topic of conversation for us for the last week or so," said Jem. "Tell me something." He leaned toward Reggie conspiratorially. "Did you transfer from UC Irvine or Indiana State?"

Reggie frowned at him. "Fresno."

"Damn it," Jem swore under his breath. "Well, it's nice to finally meet you." He slapped Sam on the back again as Sam gave one final hacking cough. "Look, Sam," Jem said. "It's your competition."

Sam's head still felt like it was going to explode, but at least he could breathe again. Sarah pushed her cup of water to him and Sam sucked down a huge sip. His face was probably as red as a tomato. If so, it wasn't just from the coughing fit. He couldn't believe the thought had never even occurred to him that Reggie Moon might be a woman. He was an idiot for missing that possibility. A sexist idiot.

"You and I are one and two in the school rankings," said Sam, finally recovering the power of speech, trying to explain Jem's statement.

"I know," said Reggie, giving Sam a cartoonish frown, the real-life equivalent of a frowning emoji. "Sorry about that."

"Are you?" asked Motsu.

"Not really." Reggie smiled, wide and bright, and Sam found himself not the least bit upset with her. "But I do feel for you."

"It's okay." Sam shrugged, trying to play it cool, even though he had been anything but for the last week.

"Now it's suddenly okay?" said Jem.

"Because you've been kinda freaking out all week," said Annie.

"Yes." Sam gritted his teeth and glared at them. "It's okay." He smiled at Reggie. "I don't mind some competition."

Sarah scoffed. "We'll see about that," she muttered.

"I guess you two will be paired together for Riskin's project, then," said Jem with a sigh, "which means I'll be stuck with some slacker, probably." He pulled out his phone and went to the class website.

Sam thought back to Riskin's class, where Reggie had been sitting there, taking no notes, calmly absorbing the lecture *au naturel*. If she was that good, that smart, how could be possibly beat her? Sarah might be right. Sam didn't mind a challenge, but this might be more of a brick wall than a friendly rivalry.

"Yep," said Jem. "You two are Group One, and I'm in Group Two with... Carly Berenski." He frowned. "Who the fuck is Carly Berenski?"

"She's been in at least three classes with us," said Annie. "She sat two seats away from you for all of P and P."

"Huh," said Jem. "I don't remember her at all."

"Policies and Practices is pretty riveting," said Sarah, her voice drenched in sarcasm. "I can see how you'd be distracted."

"We even went to a party at her house last year," Annie continued.

"The one in Penrose?" asked Jem.

"No, in Foxhall."

"When we got there," said Sam, "you called it a bourgeois palais and said you should have worn brocaded heels and a wig."

"Oh, yeah." Jem scrunched his face. "That place was ridiculous. Even the homeless people had Gucci bags."

"But the catering was incredible," said Sarah.

Motsu chimed in. "Oh, those little meatball things with the—"

"The green sauce on top?" said Sarah. "Fucking amazing."

"Motsu stayed the night," said Annie darkly.

"Did I?" Motsu frowned, as if trying to remember. Then his face lit up. "Yes," he grinned and wagged his eyebrows. "I definitely did."

"Got it," said Jem. "Rich Carly Berenski, from Foxhall."

"Ask her for some meatballs when you see her," said Motsu.

"I definitely won't," replied Jem.

They finished their food in amiable fashion, talking about classes and professors and Fresno and why Reggie would transfer so close to the end of term. She said she had already completed enough coursework at Fresno to graduate, but there were a few required courses she didn't care to take. She transferred to McFadden because she knew she could graduate in one more semester without those classes, and she wanted the chance to meet District Attorney Jenkins in person. Plus, she wanted to see what Washington was all about.

"You wanted to be where the real action is?" said Jem.

"More action than Fresno, anyway," Reggie smiled.

Seemed like weak reasons to move across the country so close to the end of a degree, but Reggie was smart. Maybe genius-level smart. Sam had known one or two geniuses before. They seemed to operate on a different wavelength from everyone else. Their choices made no sense to normal folk, but the outcome was always astounding.

"Well, it's nice to have you," Jem said. He clapped Sam on the shoulder. "Even if you did bump old Sam here out of the top spot."

"Not for long," said Sam.

"Is that a challenge?" said Reggie. That one eyebrow arched again.

The others ooohed dramatically.

Sam stared hard at Reggie. If she really approached every class with the casualness she had shown in Riskin's lecture, and still managed such a high GPA, then Sam was fucked. It's tough to compete with an actual genius.

But, 0.003 points was a slim margin to make up. And if Sam had any advantage at all, it was that he had one thing Reggie probably didn't have: a powerful motivation.

A slight smile played at the corners of his mouth. "It's not a challenge," he said. "It's a promise."

The others ooohed again, louder.

Reggie's other eyebrow arched, joining the first. A sparkle crept into her beautiful green eyes, like emeralds under bright light.

Reggie held out her hand. "Fair and square."

Sam took it. Her skin was soft and cool, but her grip was firm. "Of course," he said.

They shook. Reggie tightened her grip and grinned at Sam.

She leaned forward slightly, bringing her face back into that beam of sunlight. Her smile gleamed, her face lit as if from within, and her green eyes glowed. But this time, instead of being reminded of his fear, Sam saw only the beauty. Reggie Moon was a genius, she was gorgeous, and her eyes were absolutely captivating. Sam felt the world around him fading as he fell into them.

Reggie gripped his hand harder and pulled him closer. "May the best woman win," she said, and released him.

Sarah and Annie cheered and pointed fingers at Jem, Sam, and Motsu, talking shit. Reggie leaned back out of the light and laughed with them as Sam fell back against his chair.

He swallowed hard. He'd only met Reggie Moon a few hours before, and already he was spinning out over her. And not only was she smart as hell and already ahead in the class rankings, now they were partnered together for a project that was half of their grade in one of their three classes.

He swallowed hard again, his throat suddenly parched.

He had to win. He had to come in first in his class so he could bargain for his mother's freedom.

To make that happen, Sam would need to focus, push aside the feelings stirring deep inside him, and focus.

Reggie grinned at him again, those green eyes flashing in the sunlight.

Sam had some serious work to do.

20

CELINA SAT in the back seat of her Uber and watched Cameron Hauk walk down the sidewalk away from the Japanese restaurant where he'd eaten lunch. He seemed frazzled, upset about something. His hands were stuffed in his pockets and his shoulders were slumped together as if he were walking through a biting wind, but the weather was unusually sunny and warm for January in Washington. His hunched shoulders were due to something else.

Celina had a hunch of her own about what it might be.

She signaled to her driver that he could move on, then watched Cameron as they pulled away from the curb and slid past him. He stared at his feet, not looking up as he walked, his brow furrowed, deep in troubled thought.

Cameron was headed in the direction of his apartment, but his friends had gone the other way. Maybe back to another class or to their own homes. Celina wondered what Cameron had told them about her. If he'd told them anything at all.

Probably not. He used an alias at his school, and he referred to himself with that alias in front of the others. Didn't seem like the kind of thing someone would do if they liked to share things with their friends.

Why would he do that? What was he hiding, and who was he hiding from? His friends? From the school? What was so important, so awful, or so secret that he felt the need to construct and maintain an alias for three full years while he earned a degree, and in criminology of all things?

The more she learned about Cameron Hauk, the more curious she became. He was smart. She'd hacked into the administration servers at the school and seen his transcript. And he seemed to have earned those grades the old-fashioned way, without any manual adjustment of his own. He had the hacking skills to do it, she was sure, and yet Cameron Hauk had chosen not to doctor his own grades. Celina didn't know whether to admire him for his honesty or deride him for the wasted effort. She was fairly certain he didn't give a shit about criminology. Maybe the subject, but certainly not the degree. He wasn't looking for a government job any more than he'd gone to law school to become a lawyer.

No, Cameron Hauk had something else planned.

She hadn't really started digging into his background yet. The AR glasses had been a treat. Classic work from Dr. Nestrom. Had all the hallmarks of his style and wit, though it was obvious that he hadn't yet added the guardrails he would always apply before releasing the hardware to the public. The glasses were still far too powerful for casual use. Nestrom was no fool. He would pare back the power significantly before letting the criminals and the criminally stupid—most of the population—have access to them.

Celina didn't know how Cameron Hauk had wound up with the glasses in his possession, but she'd been sad to learn of Dr. Nestrom's passing two Christmases earlier. She'd been reading the Christmas card he sent to her when she saw the news of his death crawl across the bottom of her television screen. The whole scene had suddenly felt eerie, like the card was a missive from beyond the grave.

The glasses were probably the last thing he'd been working on. Since Celina hadn't seen any news of a new product from Nestech, she guessed that Nestrom hadn't yet involved the company in the development process. Again, classic Nestrom. He would work out every last detail, then drop it on his company for production and distribution, like manna from heaven.

And it was exactly that. The people at Nestech, from the CEO to the janitorial staff, had all become wealthy, to varying degrees, thanks to the genius of Dr. Christopher Nestrom. They were good at what they did—supply chain, marketing, retail. But the technical genius of that company was contained in one man, Dr. Nestrom. He dropped the next big thing in their laps, and they all rode it to the bank.

Only this time, he must have died before the drop. And they were all probably scrambling—and squabbling—trying to figure out what to do with the prototypes they found.

But how had one of those prototypes ended up on Cameron Hauk's face in a dark stairwell in the Department of Justice building one night during the holiday? And what did he plan to do with them?

Celina smiled. The sun shone through the heavy tint of the back window, reflecting her smile back at her, the monuments of the mall visible in the distance as the car worked onto the freeway.

Most people were as dull as fake grass. They might look good from a distance, might even feel good against your bare feet once in a while, but no one spent hours laying on fake grass and staring up at the clouds.

But Cameron Hauk might be different. If nothing else, he raised a lot of questions that she had yet to answer. That, by itself, was a hell of a lot more than most people could do.

She sat back against the cool leather of the car seat as the city flicked by outside the window. Cameron—Sam Davis—

hadn't reacted to Reggie Moon the way Celina had expected. She'd been watching carefully at the Japanese restaurant, expecting him to react with anger, competitiveness, even cold, murderous intent. Cameron may have tried to hide it, but Celina would have seen it.

Except she hadn't. Nothing of the sort. Cameron had shown surprise. Hadn't even tried to hide that. Practically passed out from surprise. He'd shown what looked to be disgust, but at himself, for some reason. And then he'd shown something Celina absolutely had not expected to see. Admiration. Admiration for Reggie Moon, the woman who'd unseated Hauk from the top of the class rankings.

That reaction had surprised Celina. And she wasn't surprised often.

Maybe the school rankings weren't as important to Cameron as she'd thought. Maybe he knew he could always hack in and change them, if need be, even if he hadn't done it before. Maybe he really did love a challenge and felt confident he could beat Reggie Moon in the end.

Or maybe the class rankings weren't the end game. Celina already knew he didn't care about the degree. So why would he get so worked up over the rankings?

She was already intrigued by the simple fact that she'd been watching Cameron this long and still didn't know what he was up to. That was a very unusual feeling for her, one that was both intriguing and mildly irritating.

But she knew he had something else planned, and she would find out what it was. There was no doubt in her mind about that. And Celina would start by answering one simple question: who the fuck was Cameron Hauk?

21

It was mid-afternoon on Saturday, but Cam had already been working for hours. He woke in his bed in the early light, not covered in sweat this time, thankfully. The only green eyes plaguing his thoughts were Reggie Moon's, green with flecks of blue and orange in a ray of sunlight.

What woke him was not fear, but anxiety. Not arousal, but determination. He had hoped that once he put a face to the name, Reggie Moon would cease to be a worry, just some hot shot transfer student that Sam Davis would roll through to regain the top spot in the class rankings.

But the real Reggie Moon was not someone who would be steamrolled. Cam knew from just one morning with her that she was a force to be reckoned with. Something about the way she carried herself, with an easy confidence, one born not from self-affirmations or social status but from actual achievement, from struggling to overcome obstacles and succeeding on her own merits, her own hard work and intelligence. Reggie Moon believed in herself. You could see it in her eyes, in those gorgeous green eyes.

And that was one more obstacle. After thirty-three years, Cam finally knew himself well enough to know that he had a weakness for beautiful women. For some reason, his judgment tended to go out the window around them. He couldn't let that happen this time. He couldn't go to his mother at the end of the school year and tell her she had to spend the rest of her life in prison because Cam had been dazzled by yet another beautiful woman.

And so he'd gotten up before the sun had cleared the horizon. He'd made a pot of coffee and started working through the syllabi for his courses for the year. By the time he brewed his second pot of coffee, the sun was halfway to its peak and Cam had worked through the readings for the next month for all of his classes.

His plan was to do all of the readings and all of the assignments for every class for the rest of the semester, and to do it all that weekend, if he could. That way, the only thing that would be left to do would be the group project he had been assigned to work on with Reggie. He could tweak and adjust the other assignments as the semester wore on, revising them to work in new ideas or things discussed in class that might up his chances of a higher grade. But he knew that Reggie and their joint project would become a massive distraction, and he wanted to clear out as much of the other work as he could before that distraction became too great.

Not to mention the other distractions, which weren't distractions at all, but the main objective. He still needed to get into the DOJ, collect the evidence he needed from Stratham's office, and use it to blackmail the Attorney General into setting his mother free.

And then there was that woman, the mystery woman in black. Another gorgeous woman, with another set of beguiling green eyes. Another potential obstacle to his mother's freedom.

Cam sighed as he stood to fill his coffee mug for the umpteenth time. One green-eyed beauty plaguing Sam Davis at school, that one with dark hair. Another green-eyed beauty plaguing Cameron Hauk outside of school, that one with red hair. Both of them brilliant. The black and the red. It was like playing a game of high-stakes poker against the two best players in the world. Only the pot wasn't a million dollars. It was his mother's freedom.

Cam set his mug down too hard on the counter. The crack of the ceramic made him jump. Nothing happened. Cam examined the mug. It hadn't even chipped. But panic crawled up his throat anyway, tightening it, a lump forming in the center that made it hard for him to swallow.

Too much damn coffee.

Focus. You're close. After all this time, you're close. Break the problem down and focus on one task at a time.

Cam rinsed out the coffee mug and filled it with water this time, drank it all, then filled it again.

He pulled in a long breath, held it, then blew it out slowly. Focus. Don't get overwhelmed. Just do the next task.

He stood at the sink, staring at the whitewashed cupboards, seeing nothing, coffee mug hanging precariously from his fingers.

His parents had taught him that, taught him how to handle himself in a crisis, when all the plans had been shot to hell and all hell was breaking loose around him. Take deep breaths. Slow down your movements. Focus on the task in front of you. He'd had lots of practice with that technique. Just about every job he'd ever been on had fallen apart at one point or another. That was the nature of plans. They all fell apart eventually.

He walked to the window and scissored open the slats in the shutter with his fingers, peering through the narrow space at the world outside his apartment. He could see the back of the apartments on the corridor beside his, the freeway in the distance through the gaps. Overhead, a bank of grey clouds was chasing the sun across the sky.

Weather was coming in. A snowstorm, Cam assumed. The

return of winter after more than a week of unseasonable warmth. The storm would bring stiff winds, slippery sidewalks, wet snow in his face when he walked. People would move more quickly, would retreat into themselves as protection against the weather, seeking shelter in their own safe harbors.

Cam loved a good snowstorm. Not that he would get to see it. He closed the blinds again and turned back to his work. One month's worth of assignments down, three more to go.

He dozed on the couch when he needed to, but never for more than an hour at a time. His anxiety was his alarm clock, determination his drug of choice. And caffeine. Far too much caffeine. By the end of the weekend, he would have the adrenals of an eighty-year-old man, but he would be done with his coursework, come rise or ruin. Or green-eyed devils.

He worked through the night and well into the next morning. He'd finished two more months' worth of readings and papers and assignments, leaving just one month of work left to complete. The snowstorm had come while he worked. When he peered out the slats in the shutters, the trees that had been narrow brown scratches against the blue sky were now thick white lines against a grey-white background. The walkways of the apartment complex were a sodden dark grey, scraped mostly clean by the diligent staff, but dusted between passes by the inexorable storm. The traffic light on the corner, usually visible in the distance, had become a pale tint behind a wall of white, shifting from green to yellow to red, again and again.

Cam checked the weather app on his phone, saw bright yellow warning icons. *Winter Storm Warning in effect in your area.* It was a bad one, apparently, and scheduled to continue at least through the rest of the day. If it had been a weekday, traffic would be snarled all over the city. Being a Sunday, most people seemed to be staying at home, watching the playoffs on TV or curling up by the fire with a good book or whatever.

Cam heard the scrape of a shovel outside his window, flicked open the blinds to see the bent back of one of the apartment staff, bundled against the snow, pushing an ever-growing mound of white down the walk, leaving a dark trail behind, like the slimy trail of a slug.

He shut the blinds and turned back to the desk, blew out a deep breath. One more month's worth of work. A few hours to go and he'd have one item checked off his list.

He heard a knock on his door, three sharp, businesslike raps. Cam frowned. He'd been going for twenty-eight hours straight, with only a few scattered hours of sleep. Too much caffeine had laced that sleep like a moth. The thought of interacting with another human in that moment caused a shift in Cam that brought his mental house of cards tumbling down. The weight of his fatigue fell on him like a guillotine. He could power through a few more hours of schoolwork. He was already in that mindset. But he could not survive an interaction with another person, friend or not. He just didn't have the energy. Whoever was at his door, he would have to get them to leave.

He pulled open the door without even checking the camera or the peephole. That's how tired he was. So he was completely unprepared for who he saw standing on his doorstep.

"Reggie," Cam mumbled. "What are you doing here?"

"Hi... Sam," said Reggie. Her green eyes flashed. She wore lined duck boots and a thin wool jacket with the collar pulled up, but no hat or gloves. Snow dusted her black hair, and her arms were folded for warmth. Her cheeks were flushed red with the cold, and snow had melted on them, making her look like she'd been out jogging. "I figured, since the storm has shut every-thing down anyway, we might as well start working on our project."

Cam was still drinking in the sight of her, still processing the incongruity of Reggie Moon, the mystery man who was actually a woman, standing on his doorstep. His one-track mind was struggling to slow his train of thought, to turn it around.

Reggie tilted her head, a questioning expression on her face. "I know it's early," she said. She checked her watch. "Early-ish." Cam cleared his throat. He knew she was being kind. It was already after ten. "And I know we've got all semester to work on it," Reggie continued. "But I like to get things done early when I can. I figured maybe you did, too?"

Cam's gaze roamed over Reggie's face before finally fixing on her eyes. That proved to be a mistake. What had been fatigued befuddlement became fixated incoherence. Those damn green eyes. He was such a sucker. He fell into them like falling into his bed—cool pillow, warm blankets, blissful sleep.

Sleep. He needed sleep.

"Sam?"

He snapped to his senses. Had she called him Cam? His eyes focused, saw Reggie staring at him, head tilted again, that sly smile on her lips.

She had beautiful lips.

No, she must have said Sam. His tired mind was playing tricks on him.

"Can I come in?" Reggie said.

Cam had to get her to leave. He needed to get back to work for a few more hours, then get to bed.

So naturally, he let her in.

22

REGGIE BRUSHED the snow off of her hair and her jacket before she came in. The scent of her perfume drifted by Sam as she passed, a mix of lavender and fresh country rain that made him feel giddy and light for a moment, like his head was filled with helium. All at once, he was elated to have her there and cursing himself for letting her in.

Sam shut the door behind her. What's done was done. They would work on the project for an hour or two, she would go home, and he would finish his schoolwork and get to bed early. No big deal.

"Nice place," she said, surveying the room.

"You sound surprised."

She smiled at him, not the sly, mysterious smile she'd given him all morning the other day, but a full, natural smile that turned Sam's heart in his chest. "I suppose was expecting more of a Goodwill chic vibe."

"And what would you call this?"

She examined the room again as she shrugged out of her jacket and slipped off her boots by the door. As he reached for her wool coat, Sam's eyes swept from her thick, cozy black socks up her black leggings. A long-sleeved white t-shirt rose from below her hips and hugged the curve of her torso before opening into a wide V-neck. A pendant in the shape of a crescent moon hung from a silver chain and nestled in the hollow of her throat.

His gaze traced the long line of her neck, the angle of her jaw. When it finally made it over Reggie's full pink lips and back to her green eyes, Sam found them watching him. Examining him. That damn eyebrow was arched once more. Only this time, Reggie wasn't smiling. Sam could feel heat rush to his cheeks. Had he really just done a full body scan on this woman? What was his problem? It had to be disorientation from lack of sleep. He was clearly delirious, out of his mind.

For a long moment, they both held the jacket between them. Sam couldn't read her eyes, couldn't tell if she was angry or just annoyed. He was usually fairly good at reading people, but in that moment Reggie Moon was inscrutable.

What he could feel was her intensity. She stared at him as if she were cataloguing his soul. He wanted to look away, close his eyes, to blink, even, but was caught in her gaze like being caught in a rip current.

"It's a step or two above Ikea," she said at last, releasing the jacket and looking back toward Sam's apartment, "but quite a few steps below Restoration Hardware. And surprisingly minimalist."

It took Sam a moment to catch up, to remember what they'd been discussing before he had ensnared himself in her stare. He hung her jacket on a hanger in the coat closet.

"Maybe... Pottery Barn meets Jim Jarmusch?" she said.

Sam laughed as he closed the door, surprised at the feeling of genuine amusement.

"Pottery Barmusch?" he said.

Reggie laughed then, too. "Yeah, that's about right."

He invited her in, offered her something to drink. She

initially accepted coffee, then declined when she saw his coffee maker.

"No Nespresso?" She clucked her tongue. "Moka pot? Not even a French press?"

"There's a Starbucks on the corner," Sam said drily. "Would you like me to run and get you something?"

"Starbucks." She made a disgusted face. "I know I'm your competition, Sam, but you don't need to poison me. Water will be fine, thank you."

He refilled his mug with water and filled a glass for Reggie. They settled on opposite sides of the couch.

"You didn't bring any books or a laptop or anything," Sam said. "I thought you wanted to start working on the project."

"I do." She smirked at him. "I don't need a laptop to start talking about a topic. Do you?"

Though his competitive juices spiked at the comment, Sam didn't take the bait. "If I want to take notes, a laptop can be very helpful."

Reggie gestured toward the laptop on Sam's desk. "Please, don't let me stop you."

Sam opened his computer, pulled up the assignment sheet for the project, and read it out loud. They debated which topics to address, how to approach the assignment, how to twist it to bring it up to a higher level than Professor Riskin would be expecting.

It didn't take long for Sam to see what he'd already surmised: Reggie was smart as hell and an outstanding student. And even more impressive, it was clear from the way she spoke that she not only knew the subject, but she knew how to get inside the professor's head, to anticipate the grading rubric and use that to her advantage to secure the highest possible grade. All the tricks that Sam had been using for the last three years, Reggie seemed to know instinctively.

And from the way she talked, Sam could tell she'd already

learned the material for the rest of the semester. Sam still had a month's worth of work to do, but Reggie seemed to already have done it. A part of Sam despaired, seeing how talented this woman, his competition, was. Another part of him was exhilarated by the conversation. Reggie's mind was quick and agile, and she viewed the topics from the same slantwise point of view as Sam. She even edged further than Sam, toward the angle that Cam really took on these subjects, the point of view of a criminal. Reggie was truly unique. Sam almost felt bad for wanting to take the top spot from her. She deserved to be first in the class. Sam Davis wasn't a student. He was just a role, a means to an end. Reggie was the real deal, someone hoping to start a long and promising career.

But she didn't have a mother in prison. And her career would still be long and promising, Sam was sure.

He had intended to let Reggie stay for only an hour or two, but the time passed in a blur. When Sam glanced at the clock for the first time since Reggie had arrived, it was already evening. He got up from the couch, his left thigh stiff from sitting for so long, and looked out the window. The walkways were still clear—the apartment staff was working hard—but snow was piled heavy on the roofs and on the tree limbs. Full dark had fallen, and through the pale glow of the lights above the walkways and the streetlamps in the distance, Sam could see that the snow was still coming down, even thicker than before.

"You hungry?" Sam asked over his shoulder.

"Yes," said Reggie, standing, "but if your fridge looks anything like your coffee maker, we should eat at my place."

"I have mac and cheese." Sam opened the refrigerator. "I also have sliced deli turkey." He pulled out a jar and turned it to examine the label. "And some mustard."

"I'm sure your mustard turkey mac and cheese is incredible," said Reggie, moving to the coat closet to pull out her wool jacket, "but let me make you something for dinner. It's the least I can do for you letting me barge in on you all afternoon."

A few minutes later, they were at Reggie's place. Her apartment was the opposite of Sam's in every way. Where his furniture was limited to a few pieces, tasteful but spare, hers was filled with a couch, love seat, armchair, side tables, buffet and more. Where Sam's apartment had only two pillows, both on his bed, Reggie's had an array of throw pillows in a variety of shapes, colors, and textures. She had a blanket seemingly on every sittable surface, gorgeous colorful artwork on the walls, framed photos on the tables, a large flat-screen TV on the wall. She had lamps everywhere, casting the room in a soft multi-hued glow, and even candles burning here and there, the scent of sweet apples and spice filling the room. A pale blue rug in the center of the room was so fluffy, Sam wanted nothing more than to peel off his socks and run his toes through it.

It was an explosion of color, shape, and texture, yet somehow it all came together in an eclectic, elegant whole. Reggie's apartment was refined and lively, but also warm and welcoming, like the embrace of an old friend. And not at all what Sam expected.

Reggie's kitchen was more of the same. A bar ran across the front of a deep galley kitchen, fully stocked and well-appointed with a row of copper pots hanging above the stove, a block of knives, a bowl of fruit, and various kitchen gadgets on the pristine white stone counters, and a Nespresso machine in the corner for making Reggie-approved coffee.

When she opened her refrigerator, Sam's eyes popped wide. It was overflowing with food, mostly produce, in a riot of green leaves and bright orange carrots and deep red radishes and onions. Most students Sam knew subsisted on takeout or dinners that came with instructions on the box. Reggie was definitely not like most students Sam knew.

"You some kind of chef?" he asked, taking a seat on a high stool at the bar.

"No," said Reggie, pulling an armful of vegetables from the kitchen and setting them on the counter by the sink before turning back for more. "I'm a human being. I eat food. It's kind of what we do."

"I'll have to try that sometime."

"You'll be trying it in about forty-five minutes," Reggie said. "Now come over here and chop these veggies. You don't eat for free in my house."

"I thought you were thanking me for letting you barge in on me all afternoon."

"That was just a ruse to lure you to my apartment."

She gave him that sly smile he'd gotten used to. He almost told her she didn't need a ruse to lure him, that he'd follow that smile anywhere, but he managed to keep that thought to himself.

Dinner turned out to be baked chicken, caramelized carrots, and a dressed green salad that Sam made himself, albeit with the help of detailed instructions from Reggie. The meal was simple, elegant, and absolutely delicious.

They chatted and laughed throughout, talking about Sam's friends and Reggie's apartment. Reggie was careful, it seemed, not to ask much about Sam's past, so Sam returned the favor. Some people took longer to open up than others, and Sam would respect that. Besides, the last thing he needed was a long heart-to-heart talk about each other's childhood. The more he got to know Reggie, the more he genuinely liked her. He would still take her down in the class standings, but he liked her. And he didn't want to have to lie to her.

Sam helped with the washing up, then glanced at the clock.

"Holy hell, is it that late already?" He'd only gotten a handful of hours of sleep in the last two days. By this time of night, he'd planned to be fast asleep. But somehow, he hadn't felt remotely tired until that moment, when he looked at the time.

"You've got something early in the morning?" Reggie asked.

"Oweli," Sam said, drying his hands and hanging the towel on the handle of the stove.

"No shit," said Reggie. "I used to watch his classes on YouTube just to listen to that voice."

She dried a mixing bowl, the last of the cleanup, and set it in a cupboard, then waved Sam after her down the hallway toward the front door.

She opened the closet and handed him his coat. "How's your leg, by the way?" she asked as he pulled it on.

Sam startled so badly his arm missed the hole in his jacket and he stumbled forward, nearly knocking himself over. Ironically, he felt a twinge of pain in his left thigh as a result.

"My leg?" he asked, trying to make his voice sound natural. How could she possibly know about that?

Reggie leaned on her hand on the door handle and stared at Sam. She gave a slight smile.

"I saw you limping the other day, last week," she said. "Followed you out the gate one morning." Her smile broadened. "Didn't even know it was you."

"Oh." Of course. Sam finally got his jacket on, shook his head more at himself than anything, and returned Reggie's smile. She had a good eye. Sam had thought he'd hidden his pain well. Not even his friends had noticed him limping. "I'm fine."

"What'd you do to it?"

"Just banged it on something. The corner of my coffee table, I think." He shrugged. "Tripped in the dark and landed on it. Stupid."

"Must have banged it pretty hard." Reggie stared at him for a long moment, that enigmatic smile lingering on her lips, then pulled open the door for him. The air that swept in was cold, but the snow seemed to have stopped falling.

"Thanks for dinner," Sam said.

"You're welcome. Next one's on you." She held up a finger. "Human food."

Sam laughed. "Right. Got it."

He stuffed his hands in his pockets, tucked his head against the cold, and started down the walkway toward his apartment.

"Watch out for those dark landings," Reggie called after him. "You don't want to hurt your leg again."

Sam waved without looking back. It took another moment for Reggie's words to sink in, for Sam to parse them. Dark landing? Hadn't he said he'd banged his leg on the coffee table?

When he turned back toward Reggie, her apartment door was already closed.

23

A CYCLE of storms settled in for the next few weeks. Sam trudged to class alone, but ran into Reggie so often that they fell into the habit of walking together. One of them would greet the other at their apartment door in the morning bearing travel mugs filled with coffee. Sam even bought a Nespresso machine of his own so he could bring Reggie her coffee the way she liked it: double espresso, one scoop of sugar and a dollop of steamed milk, all in a tiny travel mug that was only half full. A macchiato, she called it, but not the sugary abominations—her words—served up by Starbucks under the same name. This, she claimed, was the true Italian technique. *Macchiato* was apparently Italian for "stained", as in a cup of coffee stained white with a few drops of milk. As long as she was happy, Sam didn't care what she called it.

They met two or three times a week to work on their project, ending each session with dinner. The first time Sam had tried to pull together a decent dinner, Reggie had laughed at what he served and they ordered takeout. The next time it was Sam's turn to cook, Reggie had arrived with one of those folding canvas beach wagons filled with spices, kitchen tools, and fresh vegetables. Where she managed to find such bright, fresh vegetables in the middle of January in Washington, Sam had no idea. But with every bite, he was grateful.

Once he was properly stocked and equipped, Sam's cooking rose to the occasion, helped by a little friendly competition and several cookbooks he'd ordered online. He and Reggie quickly fell into a comfortable routine together, but they still somehow avoided any real discussion of each other's past. At first, Sam was grateful for the omission. But after a while spending so much time together, it began to feel odd. He decided to broach the subject himself.

He set a plate of homemade turkey ragout served over creamy parmesan polenta before her at the small table outside his kitchen.

Reggie set her napkin on her lap and drew in a deep breath through her nose, savoring the rich scent of the ragout. "Very nice, Mr. Davis," she said. She dug in with relish, then nodded and made happy, moaning sounds at the first bite. Sam felt a flush of pleasure at seeing her enjoying his cooking. He wasn't sure if it was the joy of succeeding at their cooking competition or simply the joy of pleasing his new friend.

For she was a friend now. Still his competition in school. Still someone he intended to beat, someone he absolutely had to beat. But a friend, too. And their friendship had formed faster and stronger than he ever would have expected.

Sam poured red wine into her glass, a nice Cabernet that he had also used to make the ragout. An extravagance, using a forty-dollar bottle of wine to make a tomato sauce, but Sam wanted Reggie to like the food. He poured some wine in his own glass, then set the bottle in the center of the table and sat down to his own plate.

"What made you want to study criminology?" Sam asked casually between bites.

Fork halfway to her mouth, Reggie hesitated for a fraction of a second, then took her bite and chewed it slowly before answering.

"My father," she said simply.

"Oh, yeah? Does he work for the FBI? A judge?"

"He was killed," she said in a light, conversational tone, then took a long drink of her wine.

Sam immediately felt like shit. He set down the forkful of food he'd been about to eat. "I'm so sorry, Reggie," he said. "I didn't mean to—"

"It's no problem." She waved him off. "Please don't feel bad for asking. I don't mind talking about it."

"How long ago did he die?"

"He didn't die," she said, staring down at her plate, fork held in her fist like a switchblade. "He was killed." Her words were sharp, sharper than Sam had ever heard from her before.

"Right," he said softly. "Sorry."

"It'll be five years in May," she said. "Five years on graduation day, as it turns out."

Sam nodded. "And you went into criminology to try to stop criminals from doing to others what they did to you and your father?"

Reggie took another bite, took a long time to chew and swallow. Her eyes stared at the bottle of wine in the center of the table, unfocused. "For justice," she said, then looked up at Sam. "I'm doing this for justice."

Her green eyes were so vivid, Sam felt a flush of energy wash through him. Maybe tears had sprung up, just a little, just a few. Enough to draw out the color of her eyes, make them shine in the light cast by the chandelier over the table. Whatever the cause, Sam felt an unnerving and intoxicating mix of awe, attraction, and fear. Awe at the gorgeous, intense color of Reggie's eyes. Attraction to their beauty, to her vulnerability, and to her passion. And fear at how they echoed another green-eyed woman, this one with red hair, who hadn't haunted Sam's dreams lately, but still prowled the shadows of his mind.

He pulled his thoughts away from the woman, thought about Reggie and her father's murder. How many people enter careers in criminal justice because they've been scarred by injustice themselves? Medicine seemed the same way, with people whose loved ones get sick or who get sick themselves and go on to become doctors. Sam had met a lot of people in school who had loved ones who had been wrongly accused or arrested or otherwise treated badly by the system. As a result, those people had been moved to dedicate their lives to changing the system from within. Good people trying to improve a flawed system.

But every system has flaws. Fixing one flaw usually just creates another one somewhere else. Still, Sam supposed it was better than doing nothing. Better than becoming bitter and angry. Better than resorting to violence, or worse, murder or vigilantism.

"What about you?" Reggie asked. "Why are you here?"

Sam had expected the turnabout. "Same as you," he said without hesitation. "I'm doing this for justice."

She waited, watching him. When he didn't elaborate, she lifted one eyebrow.

Sam sighed. How could he give her more information about himself without lying to her?

"My father was killed, too," he said. He held up a hand to stop the inevitable mumbled expressions of sorrow, the same kind he'd just offered to Reggie. "A long time ago, when I was sixteen."

Reggie nodded slowly.

"We were in the wrong place at the wrong time," Sam said. "He got caught in a crossfire between the cops and a guy who had just robbed a bank and was running down the sidewalk, trying to get away."

"The police killed your father?"

Sam wondered how that might have changed things. If a police bullet had severed his father's aorta instead of a criminal's bullet, maybe his mother wouldn't be in prison. Maybe they would have struck some kind of deal with his family to avoid an embarrassing lawsuit.

Or maybe they would have concocted some cover story to defend themselves, claimed Sam's father was involved in the robbery somehow, and given themselves medals while still throwing his mother in jail.

"No, the bullet came from the bank robber's gun."

"How do you know that?"

That gave Sam pause. He knew that because that's what the police told him and his mother. The officers had been firing 9mm Glocks. The bullet taken from his father's chest was a .357, and ballistic forensics had proven that it had come from the robber's gun.

Or so they claimed. But maybe that was the cover story. Sam shook his head. He could hack into the police department to pull up the files, try to find the truth, if it was in there. But to what end? He'd just drive himself crazy, and his mother would still be in prison. That way lay madness.

"So, what," said Reggie when Sam didn't respond, "you got into criminology to keep those kinds of criminals off the streets?"

That wasn't it at all, of course. Sam shrugged. "Something like that."

"Why did you wait so long?"

"What do you mean?"

"I mean, you're how old now? Thirty-something? And you've been in this program for three years. Yet your father was killed when you were sixteen. Why did it take you so long to decide to get into criminology?"

Sam frowned down at his plate. The meaty red ragout had seeped into the creamy yellow polenta, staining it red. Sam swirled it with his fork, swirled it into one of those old spiral patterns that mesmerized characters in the old cartoons. As if a simple spinning image were enough to induce a hypnotic state. He swirled it around even more.

He was uncomfortable with the question, even a little angry, but he couldn't figure out why. Reggie's tone was merely curious, not accusatory. Her question was innocent enough. He might have wondered the same thing.

"I studied law first," he explained as he tried to sort through the emotions swirling inside himself, "after undergrad." His undergrad degree had been falsified, of course, to get into law school, but he'd learned enough just by his own study and curiosity to earn a dozen undergraduate degrees. "I guess it just took me a while to find my path."

Reggie's question still irked him. Maybe because it called out how much time he'd wasted on fruitless attempts to free his mother. Seventeen years now. Seventeen years where his mother had been confined to a six by eight prison cell, with nothing but grey walls and a square of sky through a barred window to look at. Sure, she'd made a lot of friendships while in prison, with guards and fellow inmates, but that was his mother. Her spirit was indomitable and her compassion knew no bounds. That love for life and for people poured out of her. People couldn't help but love her. And yet, for seventeen years that spirit and that compassion had been locked in a closet, all because fate had taken her husband from her in the cruelest possible way.

The scrape of the fork against the plate grew louder as Sam swirled his ragout and polenta. His other hand formed a fist on the table beside the plate. He wanted to smash the plate against the wall, to punch a hole in the table. He wanted to march into the Attorney General's office and beat him senseless until he gave up and released his mother.

But he knew his anger was useless. It always was. His parents had taught him that.

And they'd taught him that violence was equally useless.

Violence led only to more violence, more pain. It never led to a solution, no matter how much it seemed like it should. He forced himself to release his fist. The muscles of his hand were stiff as he stretched his fingers open. He forced himself to set down his fork. He wiped his mouth with the napkin on his lap and glanced up at Reggie.

She was watching him very closely, those green eyes focused and intense. Sam had the odd feeling in that moment that she was seeing a lot more than just some guy scraping the hell out of his plate.

She stared at him for a moment longer with that same intensity. Then, like the bright orange of a stove burner darkening as soon as you turn it off, she switched off the intensity of her gaze, replaced it instead with that characteristic look she had, the one with the sly, subtle smile. It never failed to send butterflies fluttering in Sam's stomach.

"Sometimes," she said mildly, swirling her own polenta slowly, "it takes us a while to find what we really want."

She said it mildly, but Reggie's words felt like they carried the weight of a thousand worlds. There was some deeper meaning to what she said.

As Sam watched her swirl her food, he wished he knew what it was.

24

CAM RETURNED to his apartment and quickly shut the door behind him. The wind was howling that day, the sky carrying both the color and the oppressive weight of concrete. The people on the sidewalks strode with purpose, their shoulders folded in around their heads, their collars pulled up around their necks, their gloved hands holding them closed as tight as possible to keep out the wind and the cold.

He stowed his things in the closet and used his coffee maker to boil a pot of water for tea. Even through his gloves, the air outside had frozen his fingers to popsicles. They were numb and stiff as he clenched and unclenched them, trying to force his blood to flow. Cam was grateful he didn't have to do anything finer than pouring water and punching a button. In that state, his frozen fingers couldn't handle much more.

With his schoolwork done for the semester and the project with Reggie well in hand, Cam turned his attention back to his other tasks. The Attorney General wasn't going to blackmail himself, after all. He needed to get into Stratham's computer and get the info he needed. And with the AG's presidential campaign heating up, Stratham would be traveling all over the country, maybe even all over the world, drumming up financing. If Cam wanted to catch him in Washington, he'd have to get ahold of Stratham's schedule and be ready to act fast when the opportunity came.

He'd tried hacking into Stratham's computer remotely, but Stratham never connected to the DOJ network. Hacking into a wi-fi network was easy, but Stratham did everything on his laptop, and he'd either installed a cellular modem into the laptop itself or he consistently used his cellphone as a hotspot to connect to the internet. Either way, Cam had been unable to isolate the signal. If he wanted to get Stratham's data, he'd have to gain access to the laptop itself.

He cursed himself for not being bolder on the yacht the previous summer. He'd gone to a fundraiser on a megayacht in Santa Monica to break into the files of a major donor, Devin Minsk, thinking he'd find information there to incriminate the Attorney General. That didn't work out as planned. Stratham had been running the fundraiser and had been in on a plot to kill Devin Minsk, a plot that had been successful.

Though it wasn't Stratham that was responsible in the end— that honor fell on yet another beautiful woman, yet another of Cam's bad choices—Stratham had been there, and so had his laptop. Cam had even been looking at the screen at one point. At the end of the night, he'd tried to grab it, but he'd been too timid, unwilling to attract attention. He should have just knocked Stratham out and stolen the computer.

But that would have been the kind of smash-and-grab job his parents despised and had taught Cam to reject. No originality, no creativity, no respect for the people involved. And not just their fellow criminals, but the bystanders and the people whose possessions were being stolen. They were human beings like everyone else, worthy of a basic respect for life.

His parents had taught him never to lose sight of what was truly important: life and love. They loved each other, madly and deeply, and they loved the life they had built together, the life they had welcomed Cam into when he was born. A life of love and learning.

And, yes, a life of thievery, what any one of Sam Davis' classmates would call crime. But for Cam and his parents, it wasn't crime. It was art. Picking a pocket without being detected was as deft and intricate as the greatest magic trick ever done. Planning a heist required the creativity and imagination of the greatest novelist. Executing that plan required the awareness and sensitivity of the greatest jazz musician playing live in front of an audience.

They stole from people or institutions who could afford the loss, the kind of people who would most likely find a way to come out better off. Rich people with insurance policies or banks backstopped by the federal government. And Cam's parents never hurt anyone. Ever. No physical harm at all, but not even emotional harm from threats of violence. And certainly no murder.

Their philosophy—now Cam's philosophy—was a noble one. But it did make things harder sometimes. Violence seemed an easy solution when the pressure was on or when time was too short for a proper plan. Cam had resisted violence on the yacht. He was glad of that, but his life was more difficult now. He would have to rely on the creativity his parents prized so much to come up with a way to achieve his goal.

He stalked around the main room of his apartment as his water boiled, unsure where to start. His laptop sat, closed and quiet, on his desk. As they thawed in the warmth of the apartment, the skin of his fingers itched, as if they, too, were ready to make some progress toward the goal. Time was running out.

Usually, his parents weren't on a timeline. Once the job began, they would have to work quickly, sure. But they had all the time they needed to plan the job before then, to use their creativity to identify and solve as many problems as they could foresee. They would take months to plan a job, and only pull off two or three each year, making sure each would pay off enough to support them at least until the next job.

Cam, in this particular situation, was working against a deadline. It was already mid-February. Graduation was in May, which meant that the dinner and alone time with Attorney General Jenkins was only three months away. Not much time to complete a plan to blackmail someone who most pollsters assumed was going to be the most powerful person in the world in a year or so. As President of the United States, Jenkins could exact whatever revenge he wanted on Cam and his mother. If Cam didn't pull off this job in just the right way, both his life and his mother's life could be ruined, even if he did manage to secure her release. In order to work for the long-term, with no threat of retribution, the job would require just the right combination of firmness and delicacy, threat and obeisance.

But first it required hard evidence. Unlike most politicians, Jenkins was no fool. And Cam, despite all of his fake identities, was no actor. Jenkins would see right through Cam if he made threats without the evidence to back them up. Cam had to get real information, damning information. Information that, if leaked to the press or the public, would wreck Jenkins' political aspirations forever.

After what he'd witnessed on the yacht, Cam was sure he could find what he needed. Even if Jenkins claimed he didn't know what Stratham was up to, the taint of having a murderer—whether he bloodied his own hands or paid someone else to do it—in such a prominent position on his campaign team would scuttle Jenkins' ambitions for the presidency. Cam had seen some of Stratham's records and felt confident he could find enough information to build a case strong enough that Jenkins would give in to Cam's demands.

But first he had to get that information.

The water in the coffee maker was starting to gurgle. Cam glanced again at the laptop on his desk as he paced back and forth. Stratham's laptop still eluded his hacking skills, but he had successfully hacked into the systems for Jenkins' campaign. Jenkins hadn't officially announced his candidacy, but he'd formed an exploratory committee and everyone assumed an official declaration would come in the next month or two.

After a few minutes of digging around in their systems, Cam had found a shared document with a fundraising schedule. Stratham, as Jenkins' campaign finance manager, would no doubt be at all the high-profile fundraisers. Checking the document, Cam saw that he was currently on a west coast swing and wouldn't be back until the third week of March. He was out glad-handing the Hollywood elite and the nouveau riche in Silicon Valley and Seattle, going back to that bottomless well once again.

That gave Cam a little more than a month to prepare for another run at Stratham's office. At some point, once he declared, Jenkins would rent office space for an official campaign headquarters and Stratham would move to that location. That would undoubtedly be easier to infiltrate than the Department of Justice building. But Cam didn't know when that would be. The rumors were that an announcement was imminent, but those were only rumors. As the presumptive nominee, Jenkins could afford to take his time, but Cam couldn't afford to wait. Besides, he'd already infiltrated the DOJ building once. Doing it again wouldn't be so hard, would it?

He wasn't the only one who'd infiltrated the building, either. The woman in black, the green-eyed, red-haired woman who lurked in the back of Cam's mind day and night, had done it, too. Thankfully, she'd returned Cam's Nestech glasses. Those would make the job a hell of a lot easier.

Cam heard the hot water pouring into the pot in the kitchen, and the itching in his fingers had subsided. He finally felt like he could use his hands again. He pulled the Nestech glasses out of the cabinet where he kept them locked up. They were still in the box that the woman in black had returned them in. He ran his hand over the black crepe paper, then set the box on the coffee table and opened it. The glasses were nestled inside, along with the note the woman had left him and the ribbon she'd used to tie a bow on the box.

He pulled out the note. Unique card stock, thick and flecked with different colors of paper. His name handwritten on the front in artistic strokes. On the back, typewritten, the enigmatic phrase *threee-three*. What the hell did that mean?

He checked his phone. March 3 was a Saturday, less than two weeks away. Maybe something significant would happen. Maybe the woman in black would return to Cam's apartment and reveal herself. Maybe she'd bring him another cryptic package. Or maybe she'd try to kill him or frame him or otherwise try to hurt him.

Cam knew almost nothing about this woman. He didn't know why he'd run into her at the DOJ building that night, didn't know why she'd returned his glasses or even how she'd learned his real name or his address, which was registered under Sam Davis. He didn't know if she was a friend—she'd returned his glasses, after all—or a threat—she had stolen them in the first place—or just fucking with him—the packages and the mysterious notes and so on.

She could be any or all of those things. Cam didn't know, and he wouldn't know until he figured out who the woman was. And since she seemed to be able to get in and out of the DOJ building just as easily as Cam, she could interfere with his plans at any time. If she meant to hurt him or fuck with him, she could.

Cam pressed his lips together and blew a heavy breath through his nose. He was going to have to solve the riddle of this woman in black before he could safely pursue the information he needed from Stratham. That was going to take time, time that

Cam didn't have. But if he didn't do it, he risked squandering what could be his last chance to free his mother from prison.

Cam put the note back into the box and set the box on the table in his kitchen. Stratham would be back in a little over a month. The woman might try something else in a little less than two weeks. Those were his deadlines.

He poured hot water over a tea bag and settled down to study the clues he'd been given.

25

CAM SET the contents of the box on the table before him, piece by piece. When he was finished, he had a carefully laid tableau consisting of an empty box, two pieces of black foam, a note card, and a ribbon. Each piece, Cam felt, contained a clue that could lead him to the location and identity of the woman in black.

The box, in two pieces, top and bottom, wrapped in black crepe paper. Where had the paper been purchased? How had it been glued so seamlessly to the box itself?

Two pieces of black foam cut to the exact dimensions of the box on the outside and the exact shape of the Nestech glasses on the inside. How had the woman formed the foam so expertly? It had to have been cut by a laser or some kind of computer-guided knife. Where would she have access to such tools?

The note card, made from card stock that seemed home-made. The writing on the front, in confident, artistic strokes. What did that tell him about the woman? The writing on the back, typed, some kind of cypher. What did it mean?

And the ribbon. Silken gold strands running its length, forming odd patterns, then breaking apart into individual strands again. Notches cut along its length in various shapes and sizes. Tips which had been cut into sharp points. Where had the ribbon come from? It didn't seem like your average gift ribbon. Maybe Cam could track it down, trace its origin to a particular store. Maybe that store would give him a clue to the woman's location.

Four clues for Cam to track down.

He put the card and the ribbon back inside the box and set it to one side. He would research those later. There had to be a craft store nearby. If he could find a good one, not one of the big box stores, there was a chance the owner might be able to identify either the crepe paper, the card stock, or the ribbon. But Cam's fingers had just unfrozen, and he didn't look forward to going back out into the frigid weather. The craft store could wait. He had other clues he could start with.

The foam seemed more promising. The cut of it definitely seemed unique. He brought his laptop into the kitchen and began searching for types of foam, techniques for cutting and shaping it, and tools needed to get the work done. He found a surprising amount of information about foam wrap rolls, foam sheets, foam pouches and tubes and blocks. There were foam liners with an egg-carton shape and pick-and-pull grids that let you pull out rectangular sections to form little pockets in which to nestle whatever possessions you wanted to protect.

He found information about different materials from which foam could be made: polystyrene, polyethylene, polyurethane, and even charcoal. Foam made from polyethylene came in two types, cross-linked and non-cross-linked. Cross-linked polyethylene was denser and stronger. It, too, came in two types, one with physical cross-links and one with chemical cross-links, where heat, pressure, or chemical additives caused the molecules to make chemical bonds instead of or in addition to physical bonds, resulting in an even denser, stronger foam.

Some foams were rigid, others more flexible. Some foams had electrostatic properties, resisting the buildup of static charges that could damage sensitive electronic devices. Cam learned more about foam in an hour on the internet than he'd ever wanted to know in his whole life.

But he managed to learn what he did want to know. He was pretty sure the foam in his box was cross-linked polyethylene, probably chemically cross-linked. Unfortunately, that was an incredibly common type of foam, available just about anywhere.

The carving inside the foam, on the other hand, was more unique. The foam was split into two halves, and the carving crossed the two, like a mold made for casting. Whoever made this foam had carved half of the shape of the Nestech glasses into one half of the foam and the other half of the shape of the glasses into the other half of the foam, and had done it in a way that the two halves matched up absolutely perfectly.

This was not a rudimentary pick-and-pull rectangle shape. The lines of the shape carved into the foam matched the shape of the glasses so well, Cam could easily see exactly what part of the glasses went where, and in which specific orientation. The glasses only fit into the foam in one specific way, and when he set them into it, they fit like the foam had been molded around the glasses themselves.

This was no kitchen table hobby project. This was an expert job, done by someone who knew what they were doing and had the tools at their disposal to do it.

Cam did a little more research on the web. If he wanted to create such a setup for his own glasses, to protect them during shipping, for example, he'd have to create a detailed digital model of the glasses using some kind of computer-assisted design program, then deliver that model to a company that had blank foam blocks and a C&C machine or a laser cutter that could use the model to cut the exact shape of the glasses into the foam with very low tolerances. He shopped around a little, even made a couple of phone calls to talk to the representatives of several companies. If he had the digital model in hand, ready to go, the fastest he could hope to get the foam insert would be two weeks.

He looked into digital modeling. Computer-assisted design, or CAD, software could design just about anything. But the programs required a great deal of skill and artistic ability. Cam downloaded one of the leading apps just to try it out. He was an artist himself, often making pencil sketches when he had some downtime—which had been irritatingly hard to find lately—and he was more tech-savvy than most. Yet he couldn't make heads or tails of the CAD software. He downloaded another of the top apps, then a third. They were all similarly obtuse. CAD modeling was a specialized skill. Not the kind of thing any novice could pick up in a day and use to make a detailed rendering of a physical object.

And yet, the woman had stolen the glasses and returned them ten days later. In those ten days, she'd not only fabricated the foam, but she'd modeled the glasses, as well. And she'd hacked into them enough to override the greeting so that Cam heard her voice every time he put them on.

In fact, he'd been so unnerved the first time he put them on after getting them back that he hadn't worn them since. He'd tried more than once, had taken the glasses out, unfolded the earpieces, and held them in front of him, ready to put them on. But then he'd seen the woman's face in his mind, her green eyes glowing, her red hair flying like Medusa snakes around her head, and he'd chickened out every time. He didn't want to add her voice to his nightmares.

Somehow, this woman had stolen a piece of technology the world had never seen, hacked into it, understood the system well enough to overwrite part of it, then made a 3-D model of it and fabricated a foam case for it. Then she'd figured out Cam's real name, figured out where he lived, and delivered the glasses in the foam case to Cam's apartment without being seen. And she'd done it all within ten days.

Cam sat back in his chair so hard that the wood of the chair legs screeched against the tile floor. He let out a long, heavy sigh.

He'd met talented people before. Plenty of them, in all walks of life. He'd spent a lot of time with Marc and Mary Taylor, for example, two of his parents' closest friends, and the couple that they considered to be their mentors. They were like parents to his mother and father, like grandparents to Cam. And even at an advanced age—they were both in their seventies by the time Cam was old enough to remember them—they were some of the most talented individuals Cam had ever met, before or since.

Mary could pick any lock in the time it took to sneeze, and she could crack any safe in under thirty minutes. She could take apart any machine, tell you exactly how it worked, and reassemble it perfectly in the time it took you to pull your jaw back off the floor.

Marc was a genius at building rapport. It didn't seem like the kind of thing you could be a genius at, until you saw Marc work a bank full of nervous hostages. By the time Mary had the safes open and the bags loaded, Marc was sitting crisscross applesauce with the hostages on the floor of the lobby leading a game of Never Have I Ever, the entire group laughing and teasing each other like they were at a high school reunion instead of an active bank robbery. Once, at a credit union in Milwaukee, the security guard even radioed the police outside to divert them so that Marc and Mary could make a clean escape. If Marc had chosen politics or business, he'd have been a millionaire. Instead, he chose a life of crime and became a multi-millionaire.

But as talented as Mark and Mary and the dozens of other people Cam had met over the years were, he had never met anyone with the kind of skills this woman in black seemed to possess. Slipping into the DOJ building wasn't the hardest thing in the world. Cam had seen much tougher security in the private sector, and it had been a holiday, after all. But it was still a government building, requiring some skill to infiltrate. And the woman had done it with obvious ease. What's more, Cam hadn't even known she was there, even while he was wearing the Nestech glasses. That was a feat Cam still couldn't fathom.

And now this. Hacking the glasses, fabricating the foam, delivering the package to his doorstep. All in the blink of an eye. And for what? She didn't need to return them. Most people would have kept the glasses.

Cam sighed again and shook his head. Who was this woman, and what game was she playing with him?

The more he learned about her, it seemed, the less he understood.

26

AT LUNCH, a shawarma place two blocks from campus called Shaima's, the rich, heavy scent of garlic, roasted lamb, and French fries filled the air. Sarah made a joke about Motsu and the table erupted into laughter. Annie laughed so hard she choked on her bite of food. Reggie, still laughing with the others, patted and rubbed Annie's back until her coughing subsided, then gave her a quick side-hug before letting go. Annie nodded and smiled gratefully to her.

Sam watched it all, marveling at how quickly, how seamlessly Reggie had fit in with his group of friends. Their tight-knit group of five had become a tight-knit group of six, just like that. Competition or not, Reggie was a good person, warm, caring, smart, and funny. She fit right in, like she'd been there all along.

Once the laughter had died down, Reggie threw her napkin on her empty plate and scooped up her trash. "I've got to head to class," she said. "I'll see you all later." The others murmured their goodbyes. Reggie set a hand on Sam's arm. "My place tonight, right? Around five?"

Sam nodded. Reggie waved at the others and left.

Sam's head was ducked and tilted toward the arm Reggie had touched. His skin still tingled beneath his shirt where her

146

hand had been, and Sam couldn't help smiling. He wasn't even sure why. The way she touched him, talked to him so casually. The way she laughed with his friends. Something about it all just made him feel warm and happy inside.

"What. The. Fuck." Motsu grabbed both of Sam's shoulders and shook him with each word. Sam lifted his chin, tried to control his smile and adopt a neutral expression, but the look of incredulity on Motsu's face just made him smile even more. "You like her," said Motsu, his voice an astonished whisper. "She's your enemy, and now you like her."

"Enemies to lovers. It's like a good romance novel," said Jem. The others looked at him. "What?" he said. "I can read romance."

After a pause, Sam said, "I don't know what you're talking about." Motsu released his shoulders and sat back down. "And we're not lovers," he said to Jem. Sam looked around the table at the others. "I mean, of course I like her. She's great. Don't you all like her?"

"Of course we like her," said Jem. "But you *really* like her."

Sam shook his head, confused. "What do you mean? I like her just as much as I like all of you."

Jem laughed. "Sam, you and I used to hang out after class all the time. We've been friends for three years now."

"Right."

"But I've never been to your apartment. Not once."

Sam frowned. "That can't be true."

"No," said Jem, "it is."

"Well, I've never been to your place, either," said Sam. "Have I?"

"No, you haven't." Jem shook his head.

"We both like it that way, though, right?" Sam asked. "We like having a place that's just ours."

He looked around the table again. They were all looking at him and smiling like proud, indulgent parents watching their only child figure out one of life's more obvious lessons.

"No," said Jem, "it's just you." He held up his hands, palms out, and shook them. "And that's totally okay."

Sam looked at Annie. "You've been to Jem's place?"

Annie nodded.

Sam looked at Sarah. "You, too?"

"Of course," she replied.

"Even Motsu has been over," said Jem.

Motsu scoffed. "I practically lived on his couch last summer."

"Yeah," said Jem, "and I'm still finding Pop-Tart wrappers in the cushions."

Motsu shrugged and smiled his winning smile, the one that melted any heart. "Just a little memento of our time together."

Jem rolled his eyes, then looked at Sam again. "And I've been to Sarah's, to Annie's. You're the only one who never comes over," he said, "and never invites anyone to your place." He smiled wide. "But then Reggie Moon comes along and now she's coming over several times a week? And you're going to her place? And you're making dinner for each other?"

"Well," Sam said, "that's just because we happen to live in the same apartment complex. And we happen to be working on this project together. That's all."

"And I've barely seen you since you met Reggie," said Jem. "Outside of class and lunch, I haven't seen you at all."

"None of us have," said Sarah. She held up one hand as Sam opened his mouth to protest. "Not criticizing. Not begging for your attention. Just observing."

Sam pushed one hand through his hair and blew out a breath. "So what are you saying, that I'm spending too much time with her?"

"No, you idiot," said Sarah. "That's not what we're saying at all."

"And that's why we're saying it," said Annie.

"Et tu, Annie?" Sam shook his head.

"Because you'll never see it yourself," Annie finished.

"You'll never admit it to yourself," Jem added.

Sam threw his hands up in exasperation. "Admit what?"

Motsu clapped a heavy hand on one of Sam's shoulders. "You got it bad, brother."

"Got wha—"

Sam stopped himself mid-sentence. He looked around the table. The others were all staring pointedly at him, that parental patience again, waiting for him to put the last puzzle piece into place, to see the big picture.

Sam shook his head. He didn't want to fall for Reggie. He didn't need the distraction. Not now. Not when he was so close, when his time was running out. He needed to focus on his mother, on the AG, on Stratham and the woman in black.

And yet Reggie was the first person he thought of every morning. He'd get out of bed and think about getting coffee and then think about bringing some to Reggie. He'd think about seeing her open her apartment door, seeing the smile on her face, already knowing it was him standing there. The way her smile reached all the way to her gorgeous green eyes. He waited each morning to hear her voice for the first time, as if his day didn't start until he'd heard it. As if his heart didn't start beating until he heard her voice.

Oh, fuck. His friends were right. He had it bad for Reggie Moon.

"At least you have good taste," said Motsu. He squeezed Sam's shoulder. "Reggie is smoking hot."

"Thanks for your deep insight, Motsu," said Sarah.

"I..." Sam stammered. "I don't... I can't..."

"Why not?" said Annie. "You guys seem great together."

"She's clearly into you, too," said Sarah.

"What do you mean?" asked Sam.

"Are you fucking kidding me?" Sarah replied. "What do you mean, what do I mean? You're a grown-ass man, Sam. You know what I mean."

"She wouldn't be cooking dinner for you every other night if she wasn't interested," said Annie.

"We just always end up working together through dinner-time. It doesn't mean anything."

Annie shook her head. "No one does that," she said flatly. "Takeout. DoorDash. Go somewhere, maybe. But cooking? Several times a week? Uh-uh."

"I wish someone would cook for me," said Motsu.

"Yeah, good luck with that," said Annie.

Sam glanced up to see Sarah regarding Annie with surprise and a bit of pride.

"How do you feel about her?" asked Jem. "I mean, we've all told you what it looks like, but none of that really matters. What does it feel like for you?"

Sam furrowed his brow. "I guess I haven't really thought about it like that."

The table was silent for a long moment. Sam looked up and saw Sarah and Jem and Annie exchanging meaningful glances. Motsu just sat in his chair, arms folded, regarding Sam with a smirk.

"Well," said Jem quietly, "maybe you should."

And maybe he was right.

After another long pause, Motsu grabbed a handful of fries from Sam's plate and shoved them into his mouth. "I'm off to class," he said, his voice muffled by the fries as he pulled on his coat. He swallowed hard, then grinned at them all.

"Maybe I can convince Professor Smythe to cook me dinner tonight."

Sarah and Annie booed loudly and threw fries at Motsu. He opened his mouth and tried to catch them. Sam and Jem joined in, and the group devolved into laughter as Motsu fled in a shower of fried potatoes.

Shaima, the restaurant owner, a tall Israeli woman with a huge heart and a temper that would strike fear in the heart of a

Navy Seal, scowled at them from behind the counter. The four of them scrambled out of their seats and set about cleaning up the mess they'd made.

It seemed that Sam had a mess of his own on his hands. And he needed to figure out what to do about it.

27

SAM NOTICED a little buzz in his chest as he locked his apartment behind him and walked up the stairs and down the walkway to Reggie's apartment. The lights were just starting to flicker on over the walkways. The air was biting, the sky a dark grey. Another set of mid-winter storms was moving in, but as Sam approached Reggie's door, he felt a flush of heat and unzipped his jacket, flapped the sides to cool off.

When Reggie opened the door, her long, dark hair was tied into a messy bun, revealing the long curve of her slender neck, and her face was lit with a sexy, lazy smile. That little buzz in Sam's chest became a full-on swarm of bees. They dove from the hive in his chest straight into his stomach, flipped it and spun it so hard he thought he might pass out before he even made it inside.

Okay, so maybe he was starting to feel something for Reggie, something more than just friendship.

Reggie left the door open without a word, just that lazy smile, and padded barefoot down the hallway back to the living room. Sam tried hard not to focus on the way her leggings hugged her body, or the way her hips swayed as she walked. Tried not to notice the hourglass curve of her waist as she lifted her arms to fix her bun and the hem of her sweatshirt lifted with it, revealing a deep, shadowed furrow down the center of her strong, bare lower back.

No. No. He would not fall for another femme fatale. Reggie was his competition. She was a friend, at most. Nothing more. She could be nothing more. Cameron Hauk had stolen from places with security systems so advanced they made Fort Knox look like a Boy Scout camp, and he'd done so without making a noise and without breaking a sweat. Surely he had the willpower to resist one beautiful woman.

Though his past would suggest otherwise.

Reggie turned, her arms still fixing her hair. Her shirt was lifted over her midriff, revealing a flat, toned stomach. In the golden light from a lamp on a sideboard, her green eyes shone like jade.

"You coming?" she asked, then gave that sexy smile again, dropped her arms, and walked into the living room.

Sam gulped, took a deep breath, and stepped inside. He could do this.

He could do this.

Maybe if he kept saying it to himself, he'd eventually start to believe it.

Walking into Reggie's living room was like walking into another world, a world of light and color, of creativity and intelligence. The textures, the smells, the art. Every time Sam visited, he felt transported. Maybe it was the contrast with the grey skies and the dingy, slushy snowbanks of the city, but walking into Reggie's apartment lifted his spirits.

Not lifted. It elevated them. Sam felt elevated in Reggie's place, a buzz of a different kind. A high without the drugs.

He'd discovered over time that Reggie herself had made several of the pieces of art hanging on the walls. One was a colorful collage of news clippings, faded photographs, and bits of jewelry or metal all pasted together. When you looked closely at each piece, they told individual stories that hung loosely together. But when you stood back to take in the collage as a whole, a single image emerged that tied all the individual stories together.

Another piece was a two-foot by three-foot ink-on-paper drawing in the style of an old Japanese woodcut. The image was simple, a man in silhouette seen from behind. Rain falling against a lit background, water on the ground around his feet. His head turned to one side under his umbrella, a bare sliver of light revealing a hard-set mouth, a sharp nose, an eye cast down. A sparse drawing, but it was enough to evoke a deep melancholy in Sam, an ache that yawned within his chest. Every time he looked at it—at the darkness against the light, the slump in the shoulders, the downcast eye—he could feel the man's loss, his loneliness, his solitude and his pain. The image was so simple, just black lines against a taupe background, yet it opened a vein in Sam, a direct line to his own pain, his own frustration, his own sadness, and his fear.

It was gorgeous artwork. It made Sam want to run home and pick up his pencil and sketchbook. He'd been so busy lately, he hadn't made any art at all in weeks, since before the holiday. He always got a little jumpy when he went too long without sketching. The quiet scrape of pencil on sketch paper, the wordless place in his mind's eye, the shutting out of everything else in his life created a private place of repose, a place no one else could access. Sam could be himself there. He could relax there.

It had been too long since he'd visited that place. He planned to see his mother again the following weekend. Maybe he'd take the train up instead of driving. He could spend the time sketching, clearing his mind of all the worries about the AG and Stratham, and about the woman in black, and about school.

And about Reggie. He turned away from the drawing of the man in the rain. Reggie carried two giant steaming mugs from the kitchen and set Sam's on the coffee table, then sat in one of her armchairs, a pink microfiber chair that was all curves and cushions, tucking one leg underneath her and holding her mug in both hands, sipping carefully and relishing the taste.

"Hot cocoa," she said as Sam came over and flounced down into the warm embrace of Reggie's overstuffed yellow couch.

"Are there marshmallows?" he asked, leaning forward. The couch didn't want to let him go. Sam had to push against the couch back with one arm to bend forward far enough to peer into the mug.

"Homemade whipped cream," she said. Sam's eyebrows shot up in delight. He glanced at her and she held up one finger, her eyes shining, and added a single word. "Frozen."

"No shit," said Sam. He picked up the mug. A stark white iceberg of whipped cream floated on the top of the cocoa, the edge slowly melting, forming a light brown border in the near-black liquid. He took a sip. The iceberg floated toward him as he tilted the mug. The cold of the whipped cream countered the sting of the hot chocolate almost instantly, but with enough of a pause to give him a split-second of burning pain on his tongue, just enough so that the soothing cool of the whipped cream that followed brought even more pleasure to the sip.

And that was just the temperature. The cocoa itself was made from dark chocolate, rich and thick. The whipped cream was smooth and sweet. Both were clearly made by hand. Together, they made the perfect combination, each one tempering the other. If Sam had eaten a spoonful of the whipped cream, it would have been cloying. If he'd taken a sip of pure chocolate, it would have been bitter. But the combination of the two was magical. His taste buds lit up like Mardi Gras at night, partying down Bourbon Street with no thought of the dawn.

He and Reggie worked on their project for a while, though by this point, their work consisted mostly of talking and laughing. The project was already more or less complete. There were a few small details to clean up, a few more references to pull together, some fine-tuning on the text. But they both worked hard and worked quickly, by nature, and though they'd been meeting regularly for more than a month, the project had only taken two or three weeks to complete. At this point, they were meeting less for the sake of the project and more out of habit. Or out of friendship.

Or maybe more.

Sam shook the thought from his head.

"No?" Reggie laughed. "You're opposed to eating tonight?"

"What?" said Sam, startled. He glanced at a small clock Reggie had on her side table, a tiny wooden clock painted in antiqued turquoise, with an oversized oval face and stubby hands. The clock was beautiful and kept perfect time, but with the combination of a comically large face and ridiculously short hands, it seemed to be poking fun at itself. It even had two tiny wooden shutters on either side, so that you could fold the shutters closed and hide the face altogether, leaving what looked like just a turquoise wooden block on woodblock feet.

But the shutters were open now. Sam could see it was already almost nine o'clock. The mugs on the table were cold and crusted with dried dregs of cocoa and cream. They'd been talking and laughing for four hours already. It had passed in the blink of an eye.

"You shook your head," said Reggie. "Don't you want to have dinner?" She stood. "Actually, I don't even care if you do or not. I'm starving. I'll eat without you."

"No, of course." Sam felt color rushing to his cheeks. "Sorry. I was thinking about something else."

Reggie looked over her shoulder at him, that one eyebrow raised in her signature look of dubious appraisal. After a moment, she smiled. Sam felt the flush in his cheeks grow hotter.

"I won't ask what you were thinking about," she said.

Sam didn't reply, though he was grateful for her restraint. He went into the kitchen, where Reggie was already pulling ingredients out of the refrigerator. Sam gathered a cutting board and a knife, pulled a pot and a pan from a cupboard and set them on her cooktop. They had done this enough lately that they each knew their role. They had learned to work together, a well-oiled machine. A team.

It had been a long time since Sam had been a part of a team. Since his mother had gone to prison. Fifteen years since the last job he'd done when he wasn't completely on his own.

Too long.

He looked over at Reggie as she stood from the fridge with an armful of Swiss chard and carrots, all striated leaves and carrot stalks, and kicked the door shut behind her. He and Reggie could never really be a team unless Sam told her the truth.

Unless Cam told her the truth.

Reggie caught him staring, raised that eyebrow at him again, and smiled. Sam smiled back, took the carrots from her arms, and started chopping.

No. He would not jeopardize his plan until it had come to a conclusion, one way or another. Reggie was not his goal. His mother's freedom was his goal, and he wouldn't risk it for anything.

Not even for a beautiful, intelligent, dynamic woman like Reggie Moon.

They ate, a delicious parmesan tortellini tossed with sauteed carrots, chard, and fennel. They drank, a light and fruity Riesling. It was Friday night, so they opened another bottle and drank a little more. They made coffee, laced it with Irish whiskey, dimmed the lights and put on a movie. Reggie chose Out of Sight, a Soderbergh film with George Clooney as a suave bank robber and Jennifer Lopez as a sexy Federal Marshal. The irony was not lost on Sam. Laying there on the couch with

Reggie, watching a movie about a thief chased by a beautiful cop. They eventually fell in love, of course. Like that happens all the time in real life.

Sam couldn't figure out if Reggie had chosen the movie because it was a great film, a Soderbergh classic, of if she'd chosen it because it was a romance. He half-hoped, half-dreaded that it might be the latter. If Reggie showed any interest in him, Sam doubted he'd be able to resist.

He needn't have worried. Instead of focusing on the romance, Reggie immediately started cracking jokes, criticizing Clooney's plans. He got by mostly on charm and looks in his jobs, she said. *You'd be surprised about what you can get, if you ask for it the right way.* That was one of Clooney's lines.

And he was supposed to be some great bank robber. In the first scene, he impulsively robs a bank after getting insulted by a former prison cellmate. Walks in alone, takes advantage of his looks, his charm, and what he sees around him to con an innocent young female teller, all without using a gun. What if his charm didn't work? What if the tellers were all men?

Never happens in these movies, Sam pointed out. So sexist.

He totally winged it, relied on a random customer with an open briefcase to fool the teller. What if the customer closed the case? What if he left early?

Stupidly risky, Sam said.

No planning, Reggie added. No self-control. Any professional thief would be in jail within a year if that was the way they operated. If you can't control your own impulses, how the hell could you rob two hundred banks like Clooney's character supposedly did?

Sam swallowed hard. He was struggling with his own impulses.

They criticized J-Lo in similar fashion. How could a Federal Marshal be so stupid? Clooney breaks out of prison and immediately goes back to his known associates, his known haunts.

The feds should have been all over that, should have collared him within hours. But he slips through their fingers every time, and J-Lo is made to look like the smart one, held back by idiot superiors because she's a woman. Sexism is real, but then she falls in love with a suspect? Again, no self-control. Totally unprofessional, even if he was Clooney-hot. J-Lo would be forced to resign, for sure, if they ever got caught. And what does that say about women?

By the end of the movie, they were both hooting and hollering at the screen. It was a great movie, one Sam had seen many times, and he'd never ripped into it like that before. It might have been the wine or the whiskey. It might have been the late hour. Or it might have been the company. But Reggie was on a tear, and Sam couldn't remember the last time he'd laughed so hard for so long.

When the movie ended, neither one of them seemed ready for the night to end, so they put on another one, the first Lord of the Rings movie. Peter Jackson. Extended edition. It was already midnight and the movie was four hours long, but they put it on anyway.

Predictably, they fell asleep. Sam woke up around two AM, laying sideways on the couch, just as the fellowship was leaving Rivendell. Sideways-Frodo was asking sideways-Gandalf which way to Mordor.

He arched his neck to look over at Reggie. She had flopped down from her seat on the left side of the couch. Sam had done the same from the other side, so that their heads were together in the center. All he could see was the top of her head. He could smell her dark hair, shining in the light from the television. Even at two in the morning, it smelled like lavender. He wanted to close his eyes and inhale the smell, to breathe it in and inhabit it.

She was sleeping, right? He propped himself up on his elbow to see her face. Her eyes were closed. Two in the morning.

They'd both fallen asleep on the couch. He could take a little sniff. That wasn't creepy, was it?

He knew it was a little creepy, but he did it anyway. He lay his head back down close to the top of Reggie's head, closed his eyes, and pulled in a deep breath. He could smell the lavender, like purple clouds behind his eyes. But he wanted more.

He worked himself a little closer on the couch, then a little more. Reggie's hair tickled the tip of his nose. He could feel her heat against his face, like turning toward the sun. Sam felt all the muscles in his body relax, like he'd slipped into a warm bath or walked through the front door, finally home after a long day. He pulled in a deep, delicious breath, deep into his chest, his belly, let the breath, the heat, the lavender scent swirl through his mind and his body.

He wanted more. He wanted to press his face against her hair, to feel its silk against his cheek, to feel her heat against his skin. He wanted to put his arms around her, pull her close, feel her shape against his.

He felt himself stiffen. He wanted more than just that.

No. No, he didn't.

Or maybe he did, but he couldn't have it. Shouldn't have it.

But he could have one more breath.

Eyes still closed, he emptied his lungs completely, then took in a long, slow breath.

The heat had gone. The scent was still there, albeit fainter, but the air was cool. Sam frowned and opened his eyes.

And saw Reggie, propped up on one hand, watching him with a tiny smile on her face in the flickering light from the television screen.

"Were you... smelling me?" she said.

Sam popped up in an instant, straight-backed on his end of the couch, staring straight ahead at the TV screen. "What?" he said. "No..."

"You were smelling my hair, weren't you?" said Reggie.

"No, I wasn't." Sam rubbed the back of his neck and looked at the floor, at the kitchen, anywhere but at Reggie. He felt like a little kid again, nervous, caught staring at the pretty girl in class.

"Right," said Reggie. "You just happened to be breathing very deeply with your nose buried in my hair."

"I mean, I was *breathing*. My head may have been next to yours."

"I don't blame you," Reggie said. "I have amazing hair."

"I was asleep. I wasn't smelling your hair."

"Oh, so you don't think I have amazing hair?"

"No," Sam protested, "I do. Of course I do."

"And that it smells as amazing as it looks?"

"It does." The memory of a moment ago came back to him, dreamlike. "Totally. Like lavender. So amazing."

"So you were smelling it, then."

"Well, yeah. I-I mean, no, I wasn't. I mean, I was asleep. My head might have been—"

"Close to mine."

"Right." Sam nodded.

"And you smelled it in your sleep."

"Right." Sam was nodding vigorously now.

"And it smelled amazing."

"Exactly." Sam stopped nodding, caught himself. "I mean..."

"Like lavender."

Finally, he looked over at Reggie. She couldn't restrain herself any longer and busted out laughing.

She'd been fucking with him. The whole time.

"Your face," she said, her own face red with laughter. "Damn, I should have recorded it."

"Okay, okay," said Sam. He felt himself flush hot, and not with laughter. But he couldn't maintain his hurt feelings when Reggie was laughing like that. The sound was too beautiful, too joyous. It washed away the hurt. He laughed with her.

That had been close. Too close. Not just with Reggie

catching him smelling her hair, but with Sam's thoughts. He didn't want to fall for Reggie. Not now. Not until the job was done and his mother was free.

But as she switched off the TV and followed him to the door, as he put on his jacket and stepped outside, the icy air stinging his cozied skin, and as he turned and looked at Reggie leaning against the open door, her shining, lavender-scented hair swept to one side, framing her beautiful face before it draped over her shoulder, he could feel that same feeling in his chest, the same thing he'd felt on the couch a few minutes earlier.

He didn't want to fall for Reggie Moon. But he already had.

28

CAM'S MOTHER stared hard at him from across the visiting room table. It wasn't an angry stare, but Cam had never seen that particular look on her face before. It was part serious, part searching, part laughing, part crying, and a whole bunch of other things Cam couldn't even identify. The look was completely unnerving.

His mother's pale blue eyes scanned Cam's soul until he couldn't take the intensity any longer and looked away, flicked his eyes to the concrete floor, the flat grey walls and ceiling, the other tables in the room. There were seven round metal tables, each coated in orange plastic and bolted to the floor in the center of four coated metal benches, bolted in quarter arcs around the tables. All but one of the other tables was filled with inmates and their visitors. A full house today.

Cam glanced at the correctional officer standing guard in the corner of the room. His name was Officer Trunck, but Cam knew him as Dan. Dan smiled faintly and nodded back at Cam.

Cam's mother, Paulie Hauk, had made friends with all of the officers in Taconic Correctional Facility, practically on the first day she'd arrived fifteen years ago. She hadn't done it out of cunning or some scheme to curry favor. She was just that kind of person, the kind of person who sees others for who they are, people with fears and hopes and loves and worries. People aren't all good, she would say, but they're all human. And Paulie could always see the humanity in people.

So whenever Cam came to visit, which he did nearly every week, the officers greeted him like their own son, because he was Paulie's. And they all loved Paulie.

But Cam would be willing to bet she'd never given them the look she was giving him.

Cam dragged his eyes back to his mother, but avoided her continuing stare. Instead, he examined her hair. Her hair had always been salt-and-pepper, silver streaks amid jet-black, ever since he was a kid. Now, though, for the first time, there seemed to be more silver than black. It had only been a week since he'd visited. How could she have gone grey so fast? Or maybe he just hadn't noticed last time. He'd been distracted lately.

Cam frowned and examined her face. He saw lines where there had never been lines before, around her lips and at the corners of her eyes. And she seemed paler than usual. Her cheekbones had always been high and sharp, but now the cheeks below them seemed hollow, the shadows from her cheekbones in the fluorescent overhead lights a little darker, a little deeper than usual.

He had to get her out. His mother was a vivacious woman, younger than her years. But fifteen years in prison was a long time. She'd resisted the effects of her incarceration thus far, but maybe it was catching up to her now. She was aging. She would be fifty-six this year. He had to get her out.

Maybe that's why she was looking at him so weird. She was dying in this prison, losing weight and going grey, and Cam was sitting in front of her talking about some girl. She was pissed.

And he didn't blame her. He'd lost focus. He deserved her anger. He screwed up his courage and met her gaze, ready to face her ire, to get the tongue-lashing he deserved.

When he finally looked at her eyes, they had softened. The searing intensity had melted into eyes brimming with tears of joy. The lines around her eyes crinkled and bunched as the lines around her mouth spread into a wide smile. She lifted her hands by her ears, squeezed them into exultant fists, then released them, held them out toward Cam's cheeks, but pulled them back without touching him. Physical contact was not allowed in visitation areas, not even for favorite inmates like Paulie.

She clapped her hands instead and gave a little squeal of excitement. "What's her name?" she said, practically bouncing in her seat.

"Reggie," Cam said. "Reggie Moon. Short for Regina."

He couldn't help but smile back, both from seeing his mother's excitement and from relief that she wasn't angry at him after all. But he smiled from the feeling of Reggie's name on his lips, as well. Hell, he'd never even kissed her, never felt her soft, sensuous lips on his own, yet the feel of her name, the sound of it, was enough to send his heart pounding.

"What's she like?"

Cam reached toward his pocket, held his hand there and glanced at Dan, raising his eyebrows in silent question. Dan, like all the other guards, was a top-notch professional. He immediately saw Cam's movement.

Cam had been frisked before entering, as usual, and had cleared it with both Sue, the officer who'd let him into the visitation room, and with Dan to bring a sheet of paper inside to show to his mother. When he told them why, they both beamed like proud parents.

Dan nodded to Cam, but still watched him closely. The consummate professional.

Cam pulled the thick paper from his pocket, unfolded it, and laid it flat on the table for his mother to see. It was a sketch of Reggie that he'd drawn on the train as he was traveling up from

D.C. that morning. It had felt great to be drawing again. Like pulling up a warm blanket by the fire on a cold, snowy night. It had felt even better to be drawing Reggie, remembering every detail of her face, her hair, her long, sensual neck.

The result was a good likeness, if Cam did say so himself. But it still didn't capture Reggie's wit, her warmth, her sharp, observant mind. It captured a vague sense of her beauty, but it didn't capture even a fraction of who she was.

"Gorgeous," Paulie murmured as she leaned over the table and examined the sketch. She looked up at Cam. "But that's what she looks like." She smiled faintly. "I asked what she's like."

Cam shook his head. His eyes drifted toward the ceiling above his mother's right shoulder as he fell into his thoughts. What was Reggie like? How on earth could he describe her in just a few sentences? He would need days. Years. He could talk for the rest of his life and still not do justice to the woman who, despite his best efforts, had come to be more than just a friend to Cam.

He wasn't sure if Reggie felt the same way. Probably not. And even if she did, her feelings would undoubtedly change when she learned the truth about Sam Davis.

But Cam had to at least admit to himself that his feelings were real. The first and most important rule of playing a long con, of playing a role that wasn't yourself, was never to forget that you were playing a role. Even as you inhabited your alter ego completely, you had to maintain something, some small nugget of truth locked away in the back of your mind. Like a key that not only opened the door to your true self, but reminded you that your true self still existed. Cam could lie to the rest of the world as much as he liked, but he had to make sure never to lie to himself.

Or to the woman he loved. He'd seen how happy his parents were in all those years before his father died and his mother went to jail. Their relationship had been based on openness and honesty. He wanted the same for himself, whenever he found the right woman. He would not have a relationship based on lies. He wanted one based on love and mutual respect, just like his parents had.

Was Reggie the right woman? Was she the one, after all this time? Cam was in his thirties now. He'd fallen for a lot of women in his life, far too many, and far too easily. And he'd always been disappointed. Would Reggie be any different? Were his feelings for her any different than his feelings for the others? If so, he needed to come clean with her, before things went any further.

But what if she didn't feel the same way about him? She'd shown no real signs of romantic interest. Just friendship. Close friendship, sure, but friendship, nonetheless. If he told her everything, exposed his true self to her, told her about his mother and his plans and his past, she could expose him. If she didn't care about him the way he cared about her—or even if she did—she could turn him in to the police. Cam had covered his tracks. He was a professional, after all. If the police got involved, he wouldn't go to prison, but his plan to free his mother would be ruined.

No, it was too risky. Even if he was in love with Reggie—and he wasn't sure if he was or not, didn't really even know what the word meant—he couldn't tell her anything until after the plan was done, when he'd either freed his mother or failed in the attempt.

And if he failed with the Attorney General, he'd have more things to worry about than Reggie Moon.

"Cam," said his mother softly.

He shook himself from his thoughts. He'd forgotten what his mother had asked him. When he looked at her, she was smiling.

"Sorry," he said, frowning. "What was the question?"

His mother's smile grew even wider. She folded the drawing slowly and slid it back to Cam. "It doesn't matter, love," she said. "You just gave me all the answers I need."

Cam's frown deepened.

"I'm lying to her, Mom," he said. "It doesn't feel right."

"Then stop lying to her."

His eyes popped open and he shook his head. "I can't. It's too risky."

"Risky how?"

"What if she doesn't feel the same way? Or what if she doesn't agree with what..." He flicked his eye toward Dan again, in the corner. Dan was looking at one of the other inmates. Cam leaned closer to his mother and lowered his voice. "What if she objects to the plan? She could ruin the whole thing."

Paulie leaned back, pulled in her arms and let her hands drop into her lap. She stared down at them for a long moment. Cam could see the grey spreading in the roots of her hair. He had to get her out.

Paulie looked back up, her expression loving, but wistful.

"I've been in here a long time," she said softly.

Cam felt a stab of pain and guilt in his gut, like someone had shivved him.

"Fifteen years, three months, twenty-six days," his mother continued. "Since you were sixteen years old."

"I know, Mom," Cam swallowed hard. "I'm so sorry. I'm trying to—"

"I've missed so much of your life. Had to watch it from in here, hear about it when you visit."

The shiv in Cam's gut twisted.

"I've heard you tell me about so many young women." She looked up, raised an eyebrow at him. "There have been a lot of them, you know."

Cam laughed bitterly. "I know. Believe me."

Her kind smile returned and she looked back down at her hands in her lap. "I know you cared about each of them." Her voice grew softer, gentler. "And I know you want what your father and I had." Paulie looked up, leaned in toward Cam, her hands still in her lap. "I want that for you, too." Her mouth pressed into a hard line, the lips flushing white for a moment before she released them. "I wanted to teach you, to help you find that for yourself, if I could." She sat back again. "But it's hard to do that from in here."

The twisted shiv yanked from Cam's gut and he began to bleed all over the floor. He was failing his mother. And she was suffering in here. He had to get her out.

"But this time," Paulie said, a firmer tone to her voice, "this time is different. I can see it."

She was staring hard at Cam again.

"What do you mean?" he said.

"This girl. This woman. Reggie." Paulie nodded slowly. "There's something different about her."

"How do you know? You've never even met her."

"I know because there's something different about you. The way you look when you talk about her. The way you respond when I ask about her. Even the way you chose to draw her." She leaned in again, set her hands on the table, reaching toward Cam, even though she wasn't allowed to touch him. "You're in love, Cam," she said. "Not lust. Not infatuation. This time..." She tilted her head to one side, then the other, peering into Cam's eyes as if double-checking something. She nodded again. "This time, I think it could be real."

Cam gulped. His mother was right. She was saying what he could already feel in his bones, his muscles, his limbs. It scared him to death, but it felt right.

He'd never admitted as much to himself precisely because it scared him. And because it made so many other things so much more difficult.

"I don't know if she feels the same way or not," he said, his voice a hoarse whisper.

Paulie sat back and shrugged.

"That's not something you can control, love," she said. "But if you don't tell her, if you don't make it clear how you feel about her, she may never know. She might be feeling the same as you, in love, but afraid to act because she's afraid you don't feel the same way. Because she's as afraid of being hurt as you are.

"But someone has to be the first one to be brave. Love is about trust and vulnerability, and that takes courage." She tilted her head and smiled. "Do you love her enough to take that risk? Do you love her enough to be vulnerable with her, even if it means you could get hurt?"

Cam's pulse raced at the thought, both from fear at putting his heart at risk of being stomped into the dirt and from excitement at the possibility that Reggie might feel the same. The possibility, the hope it brought, was like sunshine. But then the dark clouds rolled back in.

"I won't risk the plan, Mom." He shook his head. "Not now. Not when we're so close to the end."

Paulie sighed. "Cam, I love you."

"I love you, too, Mom."

"I love you, and I want you to know how grateful I am for everything you've done for me."

Cam dipped his head. It was cruel that physical touch was not allowed during visits. He understood the rule. He would have the same rule if he were the warden. But it was no less cruel for being logical. He'd never wanted a hug from his mother more than that moment. Even just to hold her hand would have helped.

Paulie continued. "But the plan is not important to me."

Cam jerked his head up. Paulie's eyes were sad and kind.

"Don't say that," he said. "Don't give up hope."

Her eyes widened in surprise. "Hope? I've never given up hope. But my hopes aren't for myself." Those sad, kind eyes watered. She lay one hand over her heart, then extended it toward him. "They're for you, Cam." She folded her hands together on top of the table. "What's important to me," she continued, "is you."

Cam's mouth opened, then closed again. He stared down at those hands, hands that had held him, had supported him. The knuckles bulged a bit more than he remembered. The veins stood out a bit more. But they were still strong, the skin still smooth.

They formed into fists. Paulie rapped the table gently as she spoke.

"I would rather die in here," she said, "knowing that you'd found happiness, than spend the rest of my life on the outside knowing that it cost you a chance at real love. A chance to find the love I shared with your father."

"No, Mom." The thought of his mother dying in prison was more than Cam could bear. He dropped his head as tears welled in his eyes, brushed them back with his finger and sniffled his nose to keep it from running. "I won't let that happen."

"Won't let what happen, Cam? Won't let me die in here, or won't let yourself be happy?"

"I'll get you out of here, whatever it takes."

"It's not so bad here, love." Paulie looked around, gestured toward the other inmates in the visitation room. The ones who saw her smiled or nodded back. "I've made friends, good ones, with inmates and officers. There are good people here. My life isn't in danger, not like some other places I hear about. I get fed three times a day, have access to plenty of books. I get outside every day for exercise." She shrugged. "It's like living in a senior care facility, only without the fashion options."

She smiled again, but this time, its light did not reach her eyes.

"Tell her, Cam," she said. "Tell her everything. Be courageous. Take the risk. And let what happens, happen." Her smile fell, her eyes became distant and sad. "Love is worth it. If it's real, it's always worth it in the end."

She stood. Dan came around behind her, ready to escort her to the inmate's door.

"And bring her here sometime," Paulie said. "I'd like to see what she's like."

She kissed her fingers and blew them toward Cam. "I love you, son."

Cam stood. "I love you, too, Mom."

He held up his hand in a wave and watched her go through the inmate door, watched Dan pass her to Trina, another officer. Dan came back to the visitation area and Trina escorted Paulie down the hall and out of sight.

She did not look back.

"You okay, son?"

Cam turned to see Dan standing beside him, hands propped on his duty rig, his eyes observant but kind.

"Yeah," Cam replied, giving a weak smile. "Thanks, Dan. I'll be okay."

But as he wound his way through the other tables and out the visitors door, as he was frisked once again, then collected his wallet and phone and pulled on his jacket, he wasn't at all sure that what he'd said was true.

He wasn't okay. And he wasn't at all sure that he would be.

CELINA WATCHED Cameron exit the front door of the Taconic Correctional Facility and stand on the curb by the road, hands stuffed deep in his pockets, head bowed down to stare at the blackened slush piled in the gutter, slowly melting into grit, sludge, and water. The flat grey sky mirrored the dinginess of the snow, the dullness of the cracked concrete, the hapless severity of the chain-link fencing behind Cameron, and its crown of razor wire. Even the trees on the other side of the street, opposite the correctional facility, seemed listless, their leaves long dropped, their branches denuded, their bark as grey and faded as the sky.

Celina wasn't there in person, but she'd tracked Cameron all day, watching his movements with great interest. He had left early in the morning. Celina had tailed him downtown to Union Station. When he got on the Acela train, she switched to remote monitoring his cell signal on her phone using an app she'd built years ago for tracking people of interest.

She went back to her apartment and kicked back with some Julian Lage on the speakers and a strong double macchiato, and watched on her phone as he made his way through Baltimore,

Philadelphia, and Newark until he finally disembarked at Penn Station in New York. She thought maybe he'd knock around in the city for a while, give her more mysteries to unravel about the man.

But he surprised her again. He went straight from Penn Station to Grand Central, got on the Harlem line and rode it all the way north, out of the city, upstate to Bedford Hills. She had no idea, at that point, what he was doing. When he disembarked at Bedford Hills, he must have called an Uber, because his dot on her map moved fast from there, straight to the Taconic Correctional Facility.

She hacked their feeds. With all the physical security prisons have, you'd think they'd beef up their digital systems. Some of them were still running Windows Vista. The only vista that ancient OS provided was to Celina, letting her hack into every camera in the prison. She followed Cameron through security check after security check, watched him laugh and joke with the guards like they were old friends. She watched him give a bag of something to two of them. Looked like bags of candy.

He finally sat down to visit with an older woman for several hours. Dark hair streaked with grey, angular face. Beautiful, with eyes whose kindness Celina could see even through a camera hanging in a corner of the ceiling across the room.

The feed was video only, so Celina couldn't hear what they were saying, but they seemed close with each other. Cameron's mother? Celina looked closer. Yes, she could see a resemblance. The cut of the cheekbones, the curve of the jaw, the way her eyes softened when she spoke and sharpened while she listened.

While they talked, Celina checked the prisoner rolls, figuring it would be faster than running facial reco. She started with the obvious, looking for an inmate with the last name of Hauk, and there she was. Paulina Hauk, fifty-six years old, fifteen years into three consecutive twenty-year sentences for multiple bank robberies dating back to the late-1980s. Parole review set no earlier than forty years. Paulina had a ways to go yet.

So Cameron's mother was in prison, not quite halfway through her sentence. Celina was surprised she was at Taconic instead of a federal facility. Serial bank robbery was usually an FBI matter. She should have been in Waseca or Aliceville, or even Dublin. But maybe the judge felt bad for the long sentence and let her stay at Taconic. Closer to her son or something.

She filtered the visitor logs and scrolled through the results. Cameron Hauk had appeared like clockwork every Sunday for the last fifteen years. Without fail. Unbelievable. He sometimes came twice in a week. A momma's boy.

But where was the father? Paulina had seen no other visitors in fifteen years. Celina made a mental note to do more digging later.

She watched Cameron on the curb from the camera at the front door of the prison, watched his shoulders slump, curl in, his head bowed like he was trying to roll himself into the fetal position while he waited for his ride.

She couldn't hear what he'd talked about with his mother and Celina had never bothered to learn to read lips. He'd shown her something, a paper. It looked like some kind of drawing, but she couldn't make it out in the grainy video feed. She wished the world would hurry up and upgrade to high-def cameras everywhere, with color and sound. It would be a hell of a lot easier to snoop around that way.

Whatever the drawing had been, it couldn't be too important. Cameron had shown it to the guards to clear it with them before he brought it in to show his mother. Still, he'd gone to all that trouble, and that made Celina curious.

His Uber came, Cameron got inside, and Celina switched back to tracking him on her phone. Straight back to the train station, straight back to DC.

The man loved his mother. And clearly not just for free food and laundry service. Another surprise from Cameron Hauk. Maybe he adored his mother the way Celina had adored her father. That was something she could understand.

Now it was time for her to try to understand Paulina Hauk.

<h1 style="text-align:center">30</h1>

Cam jogged up the steps from the metro station, avoiding the slippery patches of pooled snowmelt on the tiled steps. The snow had come mid-morning, beautiful lilting snowflakes drifting down from a pale white sky. But then the sky had darkened, the wind had risen, and the lilting had become a pounding. Faces that had been tilted up to the sky now hunkered down between tucked shoulders. Smiles became grimaces. Meandering steps became purposeful strides as everyone rushed to get somewhere warm and dry.

The metro exit was covered by a long, wide quilt of windows that arced over the exit like the shell of a turtle. Before stepping out into the teeth of the snowstorm, Cam took a beat to readjust his jacket, tuck in his scarf, and pull his wool collar tight against his neck. In a plastic grocery bag under his arm, he was carrying the box from his apartment, the one left for him by the woman in black. He re-wrapped the plastic bag around it, making sure the cardboard box was protected from the wet, then tucked it back under his arm, shoving his hands deep into his coat pockets for warmth. He wished he'd thought to bring gloves and a hat, but he'd been too distracted, too frazzled when he left the apartment that morning, and he hadn't thought to check the weather.

It had been a hectic week for Cam. It was the middle of the semester, with midterm exams to take and papers to turn in. He'd gotten through it, but it had taken up all of his time and energy. He'd spent a full week doing nothing but going to class, then coming home to study and work.

He hadn't seen his friends. They'd all been just as busy as him. He hadn't even seen Reggie. Cam felt her absence like a wound that wouldn't heal, a constant ache that at times made it difficult for him to focus on what he was doing.

But he forced himself to push forward. He still hadn't thought through what he'd discussed with his mother. He hadn't slowed down long enough to really think about what she'd said. The midterms were a welcome distraction, and Cam may have thrown himself into his schoolwork with a little more intensity than it warranted, just to avoid revisiting his mother's advice.

But today was Saturday. Midterms were over, and he had no work to do. Sarah was hosting a party at her place. Cam hadn't decided yet if Sam Davis would make an appearance. He hadn't spoken to Reggie about it, either. He didn't know if she was planning to attend or if she wanted to get together for dinner, or both.

He hadn't heard from her at all since the night they'd watched movies until the wee hours over a week ago. The night she'd caught him smelling her hair. He tried not to read too much into her silence, but he couldn't help fearing that she was intentionally creating distance between them. He'd crossed a line. It was borderline creepy that he'd smelled her hair while she was sleeping, but then he'd been weird about it afterward. She'd tried to play it off, to laugh about it with him, but he'd persisted in his awkwardness. That only made it worse.

And then she'd ghosted him. She had been texting with him every day, but he'd gotten no calls or texts from her all week.

Granted, he hadn't reached out to her, either, and neither one of them had followed through with their morning routine of greeting each other with coffee and walking to class together. Mondays were usually the days when Reggie would come to Cam's door bearing two travel mugs filled with coffee. But Monday had come and gone with no knock, no coffee, no Reggie. Cam had waited and waited, waited so long he arrived at class ten minutes late and had to sit alone in the very back of the lecture hall.

It wasn't fair for him to blame Reggie. Cam was a grown man. He was perfectly capable of picking up his own phone and texting someone. He didn't need to pine away waiting for a text that never came.

But he was hoping he wouldn't have to do the work himself. If Reggie kept coming to him, Cam could be with her without having to think about whether or not he *wanted* to be with her. But if she didn't come, and Cam found himself missing Reggie, he'd have to make the effort to see her. And then he'd have to admit to himself that he wanted to see her. And then he'd have to think about how badly he really wanted to see her, and for how long, and everything that meant for his plan and his mother and—

Cam shook his head and pulled his phone from his pocket, checked again the directions to the craft store. He still didn't want to think about Reggie, and he had more important things to focus on. He was tracking down clues to the identity of the woman in black. She was a threat to his plan, just like Reggie would be. Anyone who knew the truth was a potential threat. And Cam wanted to know who he was dealing with. Intentional or not, the woman in black had left clues behind. One of them was the crepe paper on the box. And Cam had found a craft store that carried it.

The rhythm of his strides helped Cam to zone out as he walked, focusing only on avoiding other pedestrians and avoiding any slippery patches on the sidewalk. He pushed all other thoughts to the back of his mind and walked fast. By the time he arrived at the craft store ten minutes later, he had even worked up enough of a sweat to open his collar.

A bell over the door gave a thin tinkle as he stepped inside. The store ran straight ahead of Cam, a long, narrow space filled with tables and shelves lined with paints and paper and brushes and pens and all manner of art supplies. Cam spied materials for drafting and drawing, for framing and printmaking, for sculpting and all manner of painting, with oils and acrylics and gouache in racks beside easels and palettes and stands.

A thin, bald man wearing glasses with round black frames that were one-size too large for his face stood behind the register, pulling a thin brush across a canvas set on an H-frame easel. Over a black t-shirt and black jeans, he wore a brown canvas work apron, spattered and slashed with blue, black, and grey paint.

"You're brave," he said without looking up from his painting. "Didn't think I'd see any customers at all in this weather."

Cam unbuttoned his jacket, unwrapped his scarf, and stuffed it in his pocket, welcoming the cool air on his neck. He stepped up to the counter and glanced at the canvas. The painting was only half-finished, but it showed an elderly woman looking out a window, one wrinkled hand holding the other by the wrist, like she was a nurse taking her own pulse. The reflection in the window was of the same woman in her youth, holding one hand up in the same gesture, but held out as if for a suitor to kiss. The lines faded to white on the edges, unfinished. Even half-complete, it was beautiful work.

"I thought this was a craft store," said Cam.

The man arched an eyebrow and cast a glance at Cam that was acidic enough to strip the varnish from a coffee table, his brush still poised over his canvas.

"*Arts* and crafts," he said, then turned back to his painting. He muttered, "Brave, but not so bright."

Cam ground his teeth and ignored the barb.

"Do you sell construction paper here?"

"Not to anyone older than six." This time, the man didn't even bother to look around, didn't even pause his brushstroke.

Cam sighed. He'd already gotten off on the wrong foot somehow. He needed this guy to help him, and it didn't seem like he was so inclined at the moment.

"That's beautiful work," Cam said, trying to keep the irritation out of his voice. "I love the story in the image. Wistful, resonant. Lost youth, lost beauty. Lovely."

"I was thinking more about the wisdom gained with age," said the man. "Dropping the insecurities and superficiality of the young and realizing what's truly of value in life."

"Right, right," Cam stammered quickly. "Of course. I can see that. For sure. Beautiful. Profound, even."

The man sighed, set his brush down on the easel, and turned to Cam.

"You an art critic?"

"No."

"Then stop trying to sound like one and tell me what you need."

Cam was beginning to get some idea why the shop was empty, and it had nothing to do with the weather. He unwrapped the cardboard box from the plastic grocery bag and set it on the counter.

"Do you sell this kind of construction paper? This crepey black stuff on the outside of this box?"

The man rolled his eyes so hard that for a moment all Cam could see was the whites. He looked like he was undead. A snarky, undead craft store employee.

Sorry, a snarky, undead art *and* craft store employee

"That crepey black stuff," said the man, pulling the box toward him, "is 200gsm heavy crepe paper in midnight black."

He turned the box from side to side, examining it from all angles.

"This is good work," he muttered. "Did you make this?"

"What?" said Cam. "No. It—it was a gift."

"Whoever made this is really good. These cuts are precision. Exact."

"Cuts?" Cam leaned down to examine the box. "Isn't the paper just wrapped around the box?"

"If it were, you'd see wrinkles or folds on the sides and corners, places where the excess paper was taken up." He pointed to one corner, his animosity toward Cam lost in his appreciation for the work. "If this were folded, it'd be thicker here. But it's not."

Cam looked more closely. It just looked like black paper on a box corner to him. He looked back up at the man.

The man sighed and rolled his eyes again. The animosity was back. "Whoever did this took the time to cut off the excess before gluing it down. And they did it with precision cuts. They didn't use kitchen scissors and Scotch tape. They used an X-Acto knife, at least. Maybe even a Cricut and a CAD template." He turned the box back and forth on the counter, the derision in his expression fading once again to appreciation for the handiwork. "They knew what they were doing."

"Okay," said Cam. "But I'm trying to find the person who did this. Can you tell anything about them from the way they did it?"

"I thought you said it was a gift."

"An anonymous gift."

"Uh-huh." The man scanned Cam across the counter from waist to head, one eyebrow raised. "I can't imagine why they wouldn't want you to contact them."

"The box," Cam said, no longer bothering to hide his irritation. "What can you tell me?"

The man sighed again, but returned to surveying the box. He picked it up and peered at the bottom, examined the top.

"Like I said, whoever made this knew what they were doing. I can't say for sure, but it looks like they might have made the box itself, too."

"Like, made the cardboard?"

"Cut it and folded it from a larger sheet of cardboard." He turned the box in his hands. "This isn't an ordinary shoe box. The weight, the lines. These corners are too sharp, too crisp to be store-bought." He looked up at Cam. "This is a real gift. It might seem like just a box, but whoever made this is a skilled artisan. They took the time to make you something by hand." When Cam stared blankly back at the man, he shook his head and dropped his eyes to the box again. "Can't imagine why they bothered."

"What about the paper?" Cam said. "That wrinkly black paper." At the man's flash of irritation, Cam hastened to correct himself. "The heavy crepe paper. Is that unique? Do you sell that here?"

The man shrugged his shoulders. "We sell paper like that here." He pulled off the box top while he spoke. "Not exactly the same, but... Hang on."

He pulled the handwritten card out of the box, then reached beneath the counter and came back with a magnifying glass, a round glass on a black handle, straight from 221B Baker Street. He peered at the card, then bent with the glass to peer at the paper that covered the box.

"I don't know who your secret admirer is," he said, then straightened and stared at Cam, "but I know where they got their paper."

31

By the time Cam made it across town, the light was fading behind the thickening storm clouds and the snow was driving harder than ever. The temperature had to have dropped at least ten degrees. Cam's ears were red and numb and he couldn't feel the tip of his nose. But he was on a mission, and he was getting closer to finding an answer.

The address he'd gotten from the man at the arts and crafts shop led to an alley in one of the less reputable parts of town, a warehouse district populated mainly by drug addicts and their dealers, prostitutes and their pimps, and similar denizens of the dark. It also happened to be populated by a growing community of artists. There was undoubtedly some overlap between the groups.

Cam checked the address once more and stared at a grey metal door set into the side of a brick facade that had been tagged and re-tagged with graffiti so many times the wall looked like a kaleidoscope. He banged on the ice-cold door with the heel of his palm, readjusted the box in its plastic bag under his arm, then shoved his hand back into his coat pocket and waited.

No response.

He banged again, pocketed his hand once more to keep warm, and glanced nervously over his shoulder. A man emerged from a dark, abandoned warehouse across the alley, attracted by the banging. He looked burly and mean, wearing only a white tank top and dark jeans despite the cold, the muscles of his tattooed arms bulging as he wiped his hands on a towel.

Cam banged again, harder, and kept banging until the door jerked open at last.

"Alright, alright. Fuck."

The woman who opened the door would be pushing five feet in four-inch heels. Her dark hair was rolled into dreads dyed bright green at the roots and dark blue-purple at the tips, swept off of one side of her face and falling down to her shoulder on the other side. She wore an oversized grey sweatshirt that crossed her collarbones at an angle, exposing one shoulder. A tattoo of a flock of birds in flight rose up from beneath her sweatshirt to her bare shoulder. Wide hoop earrings bounced against her jaw as she eyed Cam from head to toe.

"Yeah?" she said, pulling the side of her sweatshirt over her shoulder, then wrapping her arms around herself against the cold. She glanced down at the box in the bag under Cam's arm.

"You Maggie?" said Cam, bouncing from foot to foot. The air in the alley had already been frigid, but as the sun had set, a wind had kicked up. It cut through Cam like a knife, chilling him to his heart.

The woman felt it, too. "Fuck," she said, pulling her arms tighter around her body, "come inside before my tits freeze off."

She stood on her tiptoes to see over Cam's shoulder and gave a quick lift of her chin before turning to climb the stairs. As Cam closed the door behind him, he saw the man across the alley go back inside.

Cam followed Maggie up a narrow staircase. The walls and

even the stairs themselves were covered in artwork. Unlike the brick walls outside, these paintings were coherent, all forming one consistent, progressive image from the bottom of the staircase to the top. As he climbed, it was as if Cam were walking through the painting, walking through time.

At the bottom of the stairs, groups of tiny black-speckled blue-grey eggs nestled in grass thickets amongst the roots of massive redwood trees. A few steps higher, the eggs cracked open to reveal tiny hatchlings, wet-feathered and squint-eyed, bulbous and open-mouthed. Their purple-red skin glistened through patchy white gossamer.

As he climbed further, the hatchlings grew stronger and bolder, yellow starbursts with yellow beaks, walking and squawking and finally taking tentative flight.

Toward the top of the staircase, the birds hunched in the tree branches, cawing at each other. They were mature now, though still young, and Cam could see they were hawks, with black backs and rust-brown legs.

At the very top of the staircase, the hawks soared above the canopy, their broad, strong wings spread against a cloudless blue sky, black feathers bright in the sun, a mantle of red-brown across their spread shoulders, a glint of experience and hard-won wisdom in their dark, searching eyes.

The story unfolded as Cam climbed, open-mouthed, admiring both the genius of the execution and the conception of the work itself. As he rose up the stairs, Cam felt as if he himself were hatching, progressing, unfolding from a tiny, fearful chick to a mature hawk capable of soaring anywhere in the world.

Ahead of him, as she reached the top, Maggie glanced over her shoulder, smiled faintly as Cam admired the work.

She led him through a doorway into her art studio, a single room that spanned the entire second floor of the warehouse, at least a hundred feet long and forty feet wide. Large windows set in the brick walls ran the length of the room on both sides, admitting a flood of natural light, dusky blue with the twilight and the dark cover of the snowstorm. The ceiling was exposed wood, blackened and spotted with years of neglect, the joists for the floor above them fanning overhead toward the back of the room. A wide beam ran its length down the center of the ceiling, supported at intervals by square wood posts, the only things that pierced the track of Cam's eye across the studio.

Cam could see why an artist would want to work there. It was a beautiful space, really, so long as you didn't think too much about the whole building collapsing at any moment.

The floor was solid concrete, a fact that did nothing to ease Cam's worries as he glanced at the rotting joists overhead, thinking about the weight of the concrete over their heads. Semicircles of paint splattered over years of use stained the floor at intervals, oriented around easels of various sizes and proportions. Rows of cans curled around the easels, each can dripped over its sides with a different color of paint.

Cam counted at least six different works of various sizes around the room, everything from a two-by-three watercolor in front of him to an eight-by-eight mixed-media piece beyond that and a massive ten-by-twenty canvas on the side, covered with black oil paint, the yellow eyes of some menacing, mystical creature just beginning to emerge from the darkness.

In the distance, at the back of the room, a circular pedestal held a large block of something grey and thick. It might have been clay or stone. Behind it was a computer workstation and a large metal enclosure, maybe a 3-D printer or a fabricator of some kind. Across from that, along the windows, was a broad washbasin, like a wide metal bathtub that stood on a low table.

Maggie wound her way through the various works with the relaxed ease of someone who had built the space organically and inhabited it every day. As Cam followed her, approaching the massive canvas, the smell of oil paint and turpentine grew stronger. He shallowed his breaths. The menacing eyes watched him as he passed.

Beyond the oil painting, as they approached the sculpture, dust tickled Cam's nostrils. Must be stone, then, not clay. Not the healthiest work environment. But then, no one ever said the life of an artist was easy. Cam glanced around the room again and spotted a variety of face masks strewn about the space. Maggie was no fool. She protected herself. Cam made sure to keep his mouth closed, to breathe lightly through his nostrils as much as possible.

"Do you work with other artists here?" he asked. "This is a lot of work."

"Just me," Maggie said without looking back at him. "I like to stay busy."

She led him to the sculpture, then turned right toward the windows. As he passed, Cam admired the work. The stone was one massive block. It must have weighed as much as an SUV. Cam wondered how on earth Maggie had gotten it up to the second floor. He also wondered uneasily whether the floor was strong enough to support it. His fears about an impending building collapse suddenly seemed more reasonable.

The sculpture itself was still in its infancy, barely started. The top quadrant of the block had been carved to reveal a woman's face and hair, one shoulder, and one arm. The arm was outstretched, with a hawk perched on the palm of her extended hand. The work was still rough, but already Cam could see the power in it, in the intensity on the woman's face and the oddly gentle relationship she had with the hawk. They were two independent souls, free to part at any time, but choosing to be together in that moment.

Cam realized he'd stopped to gawk. He turned to see Maggie standing by the washbasin, watching him as he took in her sculpture, that faint smile on her face again.

"Beautiful," Cam said, gesturing to the sculpture. "Already so powerful."

"Hmm," Maggie said, her eyes roving over the work. "I'm always torn, with stone sculpture. Do I leave it rough, let the power of the stone speak? Or do I shape it smooth, polish it, make it something beautiful, but in a less natural way?" She looked at Cam. "You an artist?"

"Sketches," Cam nodded. "Pencil on paper. Charcoal, sometimes. Nothing like this." He swept his arm to indicate the entire studio. "This is incredible."

"Hmm," she said again.

A woman of few words.

"What's that over there?" Cam gestured toward the computer workstation and enclosure in the back of the room.

Maggie glanced at it. "CNC machine," she said. "For precision cutting and fabrication."

"Oh yeah? What kind of materials can it cut?"

Maggie arrived at the table with the washbasin, stood between it and another table behind it that Cam hadn't seen from across the room. She squatted down below the washbasin. A series of shelves and a set of drawers were arrayed below the table, all overflowing with papers and tools and a chaotic mess of supplies.

"Wood, glass, plastic," she said while she rummaged through one of the shelves. "Some kinds of metal. Depends on how I set it up."

"How- How about foam?"

Maggie stopped rummaging, looked up at Cam, and grinned. "Yep. Foam, too."

Cam nodded, trying to seem nonchalant. The way Maggie raised her eyebrows and looked away, going back to her rummaging, he didn't think he pulled it off.

Cam looked up close at the washbasin for the first time. He could see now that it was much more than just a metal tub. The basin stood on the far side of the table, filled with about one foot of water chummed with torn paper dissolved into multi-colored fibers. A wide mesh screen in a wooden frame lay propped against the side of the tub.

On the near side of the table were more mesh screens in wooden frames, each propped on small blocks of wood above low plastic trays wet with dripped water, each covered in fibers in various stages of dryness. Each tray angled toward a hole in its center, a drain for the water. Cam imagined a pipe underneath to catch the drainage, or maybe a large bucket Maggie could use to recycle the water back into the tub.

On the screens themselves were fibers in a variety of colors and thicknesses and textures. Cam had learned the basics of making paper in an art class in high school. Dissolve paper fibers or other materials into a slurry, then dip the screen into it, pulling it up through the slurry to trap the fibers. Once you had the desired size and thickness, set the screen somewhere to dry or press the wet paper onto an absorbent surface.

Cam turned to look behind him. On the other table, several sheets of paper had been pressed onto pieces of felt or towels or squares of plywood and left to dry. There was even what looked like a tiny steam press, used for... well, Cam didn't know what Maggie used that for. Ironing the paper, maybe? Whatever the use, it was all fascinating, nonetheless.Closest to Cam, a heavy metal arm at least three feet long had been fastened to the side of the table, attached to some kind of hinge, with a long handle at one end. He grasped the handle and pulled the arm up. The sound was like a broadsword unsheathing. A blade attached to the handle caught a bit of stray light and gleamed like the teeth of an eager monster. An image flashed through Cam's mind of his own arm pinned to the table beneath that eager blade, the blade flashing down like a guillotine, his severed hand flopping to the concrete floor with a wet thud.

"Paper trimmer," said Maggie, looking up over her shoulder

at him. Cam jerked at the sound of her voice. "Careful," she said, smiling. "It's sharp."

Cam shuddered involuntarily at the gleam of her smile. He lowered the handle back into its sheath.

A series of wide, short shelves hung underneath both tables, filled with sheets of dried paper in all different colors, thicknesses, and textures. Cam bent to look at the shelves. With a flush of excitement, he spied some of the crepey black paper that the woman in black had used on the box. He pulled the corner of a sheet, felt it with his fingers. It was definitely the same stuff.

Maggie took a cream-colored envelope from a small drawer beside the shelves, stood and held it out to Cam. His name was handwritten on the front in black ink. The artistic strokes of the writing were the same as he'd seen on the card that came with the box.

Cam took the box from under his arm and set it on the washbasin table, the handles of the plastic bag slowly unfolding from their wrap. He took the envelope, felt the paper in his fingers. It was rough and uneven.

"How do you know this is for me?" he said.

Maggie just raised her eyebrows, a gesture that said she thought Cam might actually be an idiot, but was too polite to say it out loud.

Cam turned the envelope over in his hands. He looked more closely and saw flecks of blue and yellow and pink throughout.

"Did you make this paper?" he asked.

"Of course," Maggie replied. She gestured to the washbasin. "That's what all this is for."

"Never met anyone who made paper," he mumbled as he examined the envelope more closely.

"It's easy to do," Maggie said. "Most people can't be bothered."

"Most people don't even use paper anymore."

"That, too."

"What can you tell me about the woman who gave this to you?"

Maggie stared back at him. She wasn't going to tell him anything.

"Did she make this?" Cam asked.

He pulled the box from the plastic bag, held it out to Maggie.

Maggie took it, turned it in her hands, admiring the craftsmanship like it was a hand-carved antique wooden box from the Napoleonic era.

"It wouldn't surprise me if she did," said Maggie. "This is exquisite."

"It's a cardboard box," said Cam.

"And this," Maggie waved at her basin and screens, "is just paper." She sighed and went back to admiring the box. "Pat warned me about you when he called."

"Pat?" Cam thought for a moment. "The craft store guy?" Maggie nodded. So that's how she knew who he was. "What did Pat have to say?"

"Said you were coming," Maggie replied. "Said you were trying to find someone." She lifted her eyes to his and skewered him with her stare. "Said you were the kind of guy who couldn't see what was right in front of him."

Cam squared his shoulders. He wanted to protest that characterization, but lately, he had to admit there was some truth to it. He shook his head.

"Did she tell you to give this to me?" he asked, holding up the envelope. He gestured with it toward the box in Maggie's hands. "The woman who made that?"

Maggie nodded and smiled. "She said you'd probably come knocking, eventually. Said to give you that if you did."

"What if I didn't?"

Maggie shrugged.

Cam slid one finger under the flap of the envelope, glanced at Maggie, and hesitated for a moment, debating whether to open it in front of her or wait until he got home. Curiosity got the better of him. He pulled open the flap.

There was a card inside, made from the same card stock as the note in the box, but much larger. Cam pulled it out. Handwritten in the center were two words:

Getting closer

He flicked the card stock with his finger and looked up at Maggie. "Did you make this, too?"

She nodded and opened the steam press. A piece of card stock lay inside, similar to the one in Cam's hand.

Cam flipped the card over. On the back was a sketch in colored marker. A multi-colored strip, all pink and gold, like pulled taffy or ribbon candy, swooped and curled and arced in three dimensions across the page. The strip was chopped and torn on the edges, like an insect had been nibbling on it. Some of the tears and cuts jammed together were the ribbon curled over itself.

In the center, walking along the strip, was a caricature of a personified number three, with legs and arms and eyes and a mouth, whistling. It was wearing glasses. Nestech glasses. In one hand, it held a balloon that floated above it. Etched on the balloon, in black marker, it said *e-3*.

Cam stared at the image, flipped the card over, then back again. He examined the envelope. His name was on the front, but there was nothing else on the envelope, inside or out.

"Is this it?" he said, looking up at Maggie.

Maggie smiled. "That's it," she said, handing the box back to him. "Thanks for stopping by."

An envelope and a card, with a picture book drawing of the number three carrying a balloon down a pink-and-gold rainbow strip.

What the hell?

Cam put the new card and the envelope in the box, wrapped

the box in the bag again, walked the down the stairs and back out in the cold.

He thought back to the words on the card. *Getting closer*.

Maggie shut the door hard behind him. He heard the deadbolts snick shut. Three of them.

As he propped up his collar, secured the box under his arm, shoved his hands deep into his pockets, and hunched his shoulders against the wind, he suddenly felt like he was further away than ever from getting the answers he needed.

32

Cam sat on his futon couch in his apartment, staring straight ahead at nothing.

He had nothing in his hands. No laptop, no drink, not even his phone. He'd stowed the cardboard box, with its ribbon and now two cards with clues, with the Nestech glasses in the cabinet in the corner. The only light in the apartment came from above the stove in the kitchen, a tiny beacon, a distant lighthouse in the encroaching darkness of a gathering tempest.

He'd barely eaten that day, just a bite of toast and a cup of coffee before heading out to the craft store to search for the identity of the woman in black. He'd met two very interesting people, found another clue, but was no closer to solving that particular mystery.

Once he got home, he had nothing left to distract him from another mystery, a thought that had been stalking his mind as he went about his business. He'd kept the anxiety at bay by running around town, chasing leads. But once he got home, in the dark, the thought pounced on him. It held him down, squatted on his chest with a weight like a bull elephant holding an anvil.

And then it was her, legs straddling his torso, red hair cowling her face, one arm thrust against the ground beside his ear, the other pressing a loaded gun to the center of his forehead.

It was March 3rd.

The day in the clue on the back of the first card.

threee-three

He'd waited in dread all day for something to happen. He didn't know what it would be. Maybe the woman would kill him. Maybe she would reveal his true identity to his friends. Maybe she would out him to the school as a fraud, get him kicked out and doom his mother to yet more years in prison.

Or maybe she would simply appear, would show herself to him and end the mystery once and for all. They'd have a good laugh and be on their merry ways.

Cam didn't know what would happen, and that made the waiting even worse.

He'd come home from his day spent chasing clues and paced miserably around his apartment for a while. Sarah's party had started an hour earlier, but Cam didn't feel like pretending to be social.

After several hours of self-torment, though, he'd broken down and gone to the party simply for the diversion it would provide. To take his mind off his worrying.

It didn't work.

He stayed for an hour, spent the entire time propped in a corner with a drink in his hand that never touched his lips.

The party was packed. At least fifty people in Sarah's one-bedroom apartment. All of his friends were there. They cheered and hugged him and slapped him on the back when he arrived, but they were all drunk by then. Sensing his sour mood, they quickly dissolved back into the crowd to celebrate surviving their midterms with people who were better company.

All of his friends were there except one: Reggie. Jem told him she'd already come and gone. Cam had missed her by only twenty minutes or so. He wanted to ask Jem if she'd said anything about him, about Sam Davis. If she'd wondered where he was, where he'd been all week. But he resisted the urge.

He left without saying goodbye, left his unsipped drink on a table by the door and walked out into the cold. The snow had stopped. The plows had cleared the main arteries. Cam caught an Uber back to his apartment.

And now he was sitting in the half-dark, staring at nothing, waiting for whatever was going to come.

It was eleven-thirty on the night of March 3. Half an hour left for God-knows-what to come crashing down upon him.

He sat on the futon, hands gripping his knees, for another twenty-five minutes, unmoving, unseeing, then checked his watch and sat for three more. Just when his spirits started to pick up, when the tempest clouds thinned just a bit, when he allowed himself to think he might escape whatever wrath awaited him, that he might have misinterpreted the clue on the card, he heard a knock.

A knock on his door.

At 11:58PM on March 3, Cam heard a knock on his door.

His first thought was to check the video feed, to see who was out there. Was it the woman in black? Was she standing there holding a gun? Or had she left another package, maybe a bomb in a box this time?

No, that wasn't her style.

Cam had left his phone on its charger on the nightstand in his bedroom. His laptop sat across the room on his desk, powered down.

There was no point in waiting for the laptop to boot up, no point in wasting time going to the bedroom for his phone. Come what may, he would meet his fate head-on.

He stood, his hands suddenly slick with sweat. He wiped them on his pants as he walked to the front door, walked with the slow solemnity of a condemned man meeting the noose with his head held high.

He didn't bother looking through the peephole. The woman in black, an assassin with a gun, the Grim Reaper himself, Cam's fate would be what it would be.

He undid the locks. The doorknob was cold in his hand, slippery in the sweat that had already reformed. He gripped it tight, turned it. He closed his eyes, pulled in and held a long, slow breath, and opened the door.

"Hey, stranger," came a familiar voice, low and sultry. "Didja miss me?"

The voice soothed him like a balm to a raw wound. Cam opened his eyes to see Reggie standing on his doorstep, a magnum of champagne held by the neck in one hand, two champagne flutes held upside-down by their stems in the other.

"Missed you at the party," she said. She held up the bottle and the glasses. "Thought we could celebrate together." She looked over Cam's shoulder at his dark apartment. Her eyes gleamed with humor. "I don't want to interrupt your seance, though."

Cam glanced past Reggie, up and down the hallway. It was empty, the overhead lights bright and welcoming, the walkway dark with wet, but clear of snow.

His eyes came back to Reggie's. She raised her eyebrows, raised the bottle and glasses again and waggled them. Cam stepped back, held the door open for her, and released his held breath slowly, silently, as she entered. He checked his watch.

12:01AM.

Relief flooded into him, and with it a lightness and an energy he had missed all day without realizing it. The weight of the day sloughed from his shoulders, from his soul. And there in front of him was the woman he thought he might love—in that moment, he could finally admit it, if only to himself—holding two glasses and a massive bottle of champagne.

He flicked his hand and let the door swing shut with a resounding thump.

"Fuck yes," he said, locking the deadbolt and clapping his hands. "Let's celebrate."

33

When Cam crawled back to consciousness the next morning, his tongue felt furry and thick in his mouth, and he could feel every pounding beat of his heart like a hammer blow to his temples. The insides of his eyelids were an orange color bright enough to send stabs of pain deep into the back of his skull.

When he straightened one arm to lever himself upright, fluttering his eyes barely open, he immediately wished he were horizontal again. He bent his arm again and obliged his body's protests, flopping back down.

Against something soft. He cracked one eyelid, immediately closed it again as the light, now white instead of orange, seared his brain. But he'd seen his pillow, his bedsheets and comforter. He was lying in bed.

He prepared himself for another assault on his senses, cracked one eyelid again, and scanned his body. He lay on top of his covers in just his boxer briefs. He paid for that information with a pain like he'd just been lobotomized without anesthesia.

No, on second thought, that would have felt better.

Turns out splitting a magnum of champagne between two people isn't such a good idea after all. But it had been a hell of a fun night. What he could remember of it, anyway.

He and Reggie had drunk, they'd talked, and they'd laughed and laughed and laughed. Cam's stomach muscles were actually sore from laughing so much. Or was it from puking? He closed his eyes and rubbed the back of his neck, working out a crick that had formed while he slept. He ran his tongue around the inside of his mouth, worked up some saliva, and swallowed. No, Cam thought with near-certainty, there had been no puking. Just relief and release.

And what else?

What else had he done last night?

Or, more specifically, what else had he and Reggie done last night? Cam couldn't remember. If something had happened while he was drunk, if he'd done something he'd regret, or, worse, something he might not regret but couldn't even remember, he'd never be able to face Reggie again.

His eyes flew open this time. The stab of sunlight knocked him back for a moment, but he pushed past it. The stab of mortification that tore through him was worse. He propped himself up on one arm again and looked around the room.

His clothes were strewn in a line from the doorway to the bed. His clothes. Not Reggie's.

The bedcovers beside him were rumpled, but not turned down. Had nothing happened? Cam frowned. He couldn't decide if he was relieved or disappointed at the thought.

He squeezed his eyes shut again and flopped back down against his pillow, his left hand falling on the pillow beside him. Cam heard a soft crunch. He squeezed his hand gently. A piece of paper crumpled beneath it.

He slit his eyes open again. A note lay under his hand on the pillow, written on a piece of thick, textured paper torn from his sketch book. He rolled onto his back and held the note in the air an arm's length above him.

Your pantry is shit. Went to my place for food. Took your keys. Back soon. -R

Cam dropped his hands with the note to his chest and let out a long, heavy breath. She'd stayed, spent the night. He didn't know what may have happened, but whatever it was, she was coming back. She was still willing to hang out with him.

The relief was far greater than any disappointment.

With a great deal of difficulty, Cam swung himself out of bed. It had been a long time since gravity had felt quite so strong. He was usually very careful with alcohol. When you had secrets to keep, getting drunk was generally a bad idea.

Another shot of panic coursed through him. He couldn't remember what he'd done last night, but he also couldn't remember what he'd said. Had he said anything he'd regret? Forget about his feelings for Reggie. Drunken babbling about those would be embarrassing, but hardly catastrophic. But had he said anything about his mother? His plan? His real identity?

He folded the note and tossed it on the nightstand, pulled on his pants and his t-shirt from the floor. All the bending and the moving and the verticality threatened to bring his insides to the outside. Cam shuffled to the bathroom to splash cold water on his face. He swished a mouthful of mouthwash, then another, then gave up and brushed his teeth and his tongue again and again until the fur had been shaved down to his tastebuds.

In the living room, the remnants of the prior night's festivities remained. The two empty champagne flutes on the coffee table, the empty magnum bottle on its side on the floor. Two cups of coffee half-drunk, one of them in a puddle of spilled coffee, now dry, from when they'd decided at four AM it would be a good idea to wake themselves up so they could watch the sunrise. That was the last thing Cam could remember.

His phone was in his pants pocket. He checked the time. Still early, only 9AM.

He bent down for the empty bottle, squeezed his eyes against the sudden rush of blood and pain to his head. He straightened, waited for the swaying in his head to stop, and tucked the bottle under his arm, took both flutes in one hand and the coffee mugs in the other and brought them to the kitchen.

They hadn't eaten anything last night. Of course not. Cam had no food in the house. He'd been so focused all week on his schoolwork and his clue hunting and his worries about Reggie ignoring him, he hadn't bothered to shop for groceries.

Still, they'd drunk a whole magnum of champagne and hadn't eaten a damn thing. All that and less than five hours of sleep? No wonder Cam felt like reanimated roadkill.

He threw the bottle into the recycling bin, forced himself to fight through the throbbing in his head, rinse the glasses and mugs, and put them in the dishwasher. Penance for being an idiot the night before.

As a reward for the effort, and to bring himself some measure of relief, he pulled down a fresh cup and made himself a coffee. The smell of the double-shot as it poured from the Nespresso machine was like a warm blanket to a freezing man. He bent down and pulled in a deep breath of it, cupped his hands around the glass to better direct the smell. He wanted to shove his entire face under the spout, let the coffee pour straight down his throat. He wanted to crawl into the cup, sink beneath the liquid salvation like a hot bath and let it cleanse the hangover from him.

"Should I give you two a minute?" came Reggie's voice from behind him.

Cam heard the rustle of paper grocery bags and a thump as she set them down on the counter, then a clatter as she dropped his keys beside them. The coffee finished pouring. Cam resisted the urge to suck it down in one swallow. Instead, he held it in one hand, stood and turned and leaned calmly back against the counter, forcing himself to stand up straight and smile, ignoring the pounding behind his eyeballs.

"You're back," he said, managing a tone of breezy lightness that surprised himself. He sipped his coffee like any civilized person, not one reduced to his current sub-human state, and plastered a mild smile on his face. "I didn't even hear you leave."

Reggie raised one eyebrow at him and snorted.

"Kinda dark in here, isn't it?" she said.

She turned to the windows, watched him carefully as she opened the slats, angled them so the light pointed directly at his eyes. Cam tried to hide his wince as the light speared his skull.

"That's better." She walked back toward the grocery bags. "I went for some breakfast food for us." She peered inside the bags. "I got us some eggs and hash browns. And some bacon. The real kind, nice and thick and fatty."

She looked up from the grocery bags at Cam.

"Fatty bacon is the best," she said. "You know why?." A broad smile spread across her face. "The grease. You ever had eggs and hash browns cooked in real bacon grease? Sooo good. The potatoes soak up all that grease and get all crispy. Eggs, too. You practically have to pour out your plate when you're done eating. Or," she winked at him, "just tilt it to your lips and suck it all down."

Cam's stomach swirled. An acid tang appeared in the back of his throat. With effort, he kept his smile pleasant.

Reggie stalked toward him. "I got us some orange juice, too," she said. "Fresh. Tangy." She shrugged casually. "Some might say the acid in the juice doesn't sit well with all that grease, but I don't know. I kind of like it." She stalked even closer. "What do you think? Do you think orange juice mixes well with bacon grease and greasy fried potatoes and eggs fried in fatty bacon grease?"

Cam choked back down whatever object had just appeared on the back of his tongue. It was chunky. It burned as he swallowed it again. He brought his coffee cup to his mouth to hide his gagging.

"Hmm," he mumbled. He smelled the coffee right under his nose. Where before it had been a salvation, now the strong sharp smell pushed him closer to a line he didn't want to cross.

Reggie came closer still, just two steps from Cam. "I couldn't decide, though," she said. "So I picked up some tortillas, too." She stepped closer. "And some fresh salsa. Hot salsa." She shook her head and moaned. "I love a good breakfast burrito," she said, "smothered in fried cheese and hot salsa."

Cam belched into his mouth. It came with two more chunks.

"Then I thought, why choose? Why not mix it all up? Fry the tortilla in the bacon grease. Mix in the greasy bacon and the hash browns and the eggs and the cheese."

Cam closed his eyes, rested the coffee cup against his upper lip. The inside of his stomach was like an angry mob sharpening their pitchforks.

"Roll it all up right there in the pan, fry it up in the grease, slap it right down on the plate and smother it in hot, spicy salsa."

Cam's stomach churned. He groaned, trying to push the images from his mind.

Reggie stepped closer.

"Serve it up still dripping with a nice—"

She came closer.

"—big—"

Closer.

"—glass—"

Closer, her voice now a whisper in Cam's ear.

"—of fresh-squeezed orange juice."

Cam's stomach boiled and burned. The mob had lit their torches. His whole esophagus felt like a line of acid fire. He belched into his mouth, little bursts of flame. Each one brought more chunks to the back of his tongue, more chunks to re-swallow. How could there be chunks if he hadn't eaten anything? He focused on his breathing, pulled in a long, slow, cool breath. In through his nose, out through his nose. Again. And again.

He opened his eyes. Reggie was standing right in front of him, not one foot away, watching him closely, her green eyes shining, her mouth twisted in a devious grin.

He recovered his equilibrium, returned her stare with a cool stare of his own.

Her eyebrows raised. She backed off, nodding, impressed. She peered back into the grocery bags.

"Then I thought, 'Oh, that's right. I don't eat that garbage.' So I got us some fresh fruit, granola, and yogurt instead." She pulled the ingredients out of the bags and set them on the counter. "How does a yogurt parfait sound?"

Cam swallowed hard, managed a weak smile.

"That sounds great," he said.

"Good," said Reggie, grinning at him again, "because I did the shopping, so you're doing the cooking." She gestured to the fruit as she turned toward the living room. "Get chopping, party boy."

They sat at the table in his kitchen and ate their breakfast together. The yogurt soothed Cam's stomach and cooled the acid churning there. The granola soaked it up, and the fruit—strawberries, raspberries, and blueberries, fresh and clean on his tongue—gave him some much-needed nutrients. With a good breakfast and a gallon of cool water in his stomach, Cam recovered enough to feel mostly human again.

Reggie didn't reveal much about the prior evening, just laughed at Cam's oblique attempts to tease information out of her. After torturing him for a while, she did assure Cam that nothing untoward had happened. They'd both slept on top of the bed for a couple of hours. Cam had stripped himself down as he walked in there, but he'd passed out the instant his head hit the pillow, and Reggie hadn't been far behind.

She told him he'd drunk most of the bottle himself. Reggie had only had three glasses. She hadn't been counting, but Cam must have had eight or nine. Cam groaned at the thought and pressed his palm to his still-aching temples. Reggie just laughed.

"You were a gentleman," she said, "even when you were drunk." She smiled at him, not a teasing smile, but a genuine one.

Cam nodded. A knot untwisted in his chest. At least he could rest easy on that score. He hadn't done anything stupid. But had he said anything stupid?

"What did we talk about?" he asked.

"What do you mean?" said Reggie. Despite the open, innocent look on her face, the twinkle in her eye suggested she knew exactly what Cam meant. "We talked about a lot of things. Like we always do."

"Did I say anything... you hadn't heard before?"

"Like what?"

Cam shrugged. "I don't know. Just... anything."

Reggie laughed. "Let's see," she said, staring at the ceiling and thinking. "We talked about midterms, about the snow, about Sarah's party. We talked about Sarah and Jem and the others for a bit, about Motsu and Annie. We talked about movies and food, about your mother and graduation, talked about the project a little."

Cam chilled. "Wait, we talked about my moth—"

"Oh, and you said something about how your life had changed completely since you met me." She grinned at Cam. "For the better."

Cam's chill thawed in a rush of heat.

"Oh, really?" He laughed lightly, but suddenly felt uncomfortably warm, his cheeks flushed and burning. A sweat broke out on his forehead. He felt feverish. Delirious, even, his head spinning and tilting. He stood and managed to take a step to the window, cracked it a little and let the cold air cool his skin.

"Yep."

"That was nice of me to say," he mumbled.

"It was, actually," said Reggie.

"And what did you say in return?"

Reggie stood from her chair and came to the window. "It's thirty-five degrees outside," she said softly.

She shut the window slowly, deliberately, then turned to face

Cam head-on. Her eyes were bright and soft and stunningly beautiful, shining in the mid-morning sun like emeralds.

Cam's spinning head spun even more, but this time, it spun around those eyes. They became his focal point, his center.

"I said I felt the same way," she said.

She held his gaze.

"You did?" said Cam. He swallowed hard. "You do?"

The emotions swirling through him made him, for a moment, want to throw up again. Thankfully, that feeling swirled away, taking with it all vestiges of Cam's hangover. In that moment, standing with Reggie, the bright, clear sun streaming through the window, illuminating her face, her eyes, as if they glowed from within rather than without, as if the sun itself were but a reflection of the light within Reggie Moon, in that moment Cam felt alive from head to foot.

Reggie put her hand on Cam's cheek. Her skin was warm, soft, her hand strong and tender.

"I do," she said, softly.

Her eyes trailed from Cam's eyes to his lips. She brought her head closer, raised her eyes to his once more.

"I do," she said again.

This time, her voice was just a whisper.

34

As THEY KISSED, a great weight lifted from Cam's heart. The light streaming through the window, warm against his cheek, seemed to cleanse him, to strip him bare. All his doubt, all his resistance, all his self-denial disappeared in one blessed, sun-drenched instant. With one touch of Reggie's soft lips, with two words from her mouth—*I do*—the burden of worry lifted from Cam's heart.

But as that weight lifted from his heart, another weight, even heavier, pressed down upon his mind. That weight threatened to pull him away from her lips, away from the window, away from the one place he wanted to be more than any other in that moment: in Reggie's arms.

He had feelings for Reggie, real feelings. He couldn't deny that to himself any longer, and now he'd admitted it, at least in part, to Reggie.

And she returned those feelings. Incredibly, miraculously, she felt the same way.

But Reggie's feelings were based on a lie. Reggie cared for Sam Davis, not Cameron Hauk. Reggie cared for a hard-working, straight-laced top student in a criminology program.

Though they'd never discussed their career ambitions—an odd omission, Cam suddenly realized, given the wide range of topics they'd discussed together—Reggie cared for a man she probably assumed would find a career in law enforcement, someone who would carry on the noble tradition of defending America's laws against those who would seek to break them, to tear them down, to defile the rule of law that was the bedrock upon which America was built.

Cam sought no such thing. He had no intention of working in law enforcement, of course. Quite the opposite, he intended to continue actively working against law enforcement. But he still believed in the rule of law. If he got caught, he believed he should be punished accordingly. Those were the rules of the game.

Without laws, the world would be chaos. There were too many selfish assholes out there, people who cared about nothing and no one but themselves, people who would set the world on fire just to toast marshmallows over the flames.

People like Attorney General William Jenkins, in fact. People whose own ruthless ambition meant more to them than any rules, any laws, any society, any moral code. Cam would gladly use those people for his own purposes. He would use their arrogance, their selfishness. He would use their power—for so many people like that were powerful, and so many powerful people were like that—to secure his own freedom and that of his loved ones. That was also part of the game. But that didn't change Cam's reverence for the rules themselves. Without rules, how could there be a game at all?

But Cam knew that a criminal's appreciation of the law would not be enough to satisfy Reggie. Cameron Hauk was a criminal. An honest criminal, a noble criminal, or so he tried to be, but a criminal all the same. Someone like Reggie, someone who really was a hard-working top student seeking a career in law enforcement, would not fall for a criminal. It would be a deal-breaker.

And the longer Cam stalled in telling Reggie the truth, the deeper he let himself fall for her and her for him, the more he knew that weight would bear down upon his heart until it squeezed the very life out of him. And the more unfair it would be to Reggie in the end. He didn't want that. Not for himself, and not for Reggie.

But her lips were so warm, so soft against his. Her smile was so bright, and brought such a devious, playful, beautiful twinkle to her gorgeous green eyes. Cam wanted nothing more than to forget about that weight, forget about all of those complications and just enjoy each moment for what it was: time with a woman he was falling in love with.

That was the truth of it all. Cam was falling in love with Reggie, and he didn't want that feeling to end. He'd been searching for so long. He'd been with several women over the years. Smart women. Beautiful women. He'd fallen into bed with them and had fun with them for a few months or weeks or days, or in one case, just for a few hours. He'd thought himself in love every time, but every time it was mere infatuation.

This time, he knew it was different. He was different. Older, hopefully wiser. More cautious. He'd been with Reggie nearly every day for almost two months, doing nothing but talking. That is what had led to the feelings he had now. Not mere phys-ical attraction. Not lust. Friendship. He had gotten to know her, and she had gotten to know him, and they'd fallen in love.

Or he had, at least. And even if Reggie was in love with him, Cam knew she'd shun him the moment he told her the truth. He knew that she would never speak to him again after that moment. So he wanted to delay that moment as long as possible.

What's more, he knew that as soon as he admitted the truth to Reggie, his plan for his mother's freedom would be over. He could not expect her to keep his secret. It wouldn't be fair of him to even ask it of her. She would tell his friends. She would tell the school. The authorities would get involved, and Cam's plan would be shot to hell.

And so Cam couldn't tell Reggie the truth, even if he wanted to, until his mother was out of prison. It was selfish of him. It made him no better than assholes like Jenkins, using an innocent woman for his own ends. But he would not fail his mother.

Was that how men like Jenkins became who they were? One small, reasonable step toward moral greyness at a time? One compromise, one choice of the lesser of two evils after another, until they looked around one day and found themselves to be the greater evil?

This weight on his mind, this pain, this poison-tinged pleasure, was his own making, and he would have to bear it until the end.

But he knew he would bear it much longer than that. When all was said and done, Reggie might have a broken heart, but she would heal. She would go on to find another lover. Cam knew that his own heart would be shattered, and he knew that he would be the one holding the hammer. Every time the pieces began to reform, he would remember what he'd done to Reggie, and he would shatter his heart all over again.

And he would deserve that punishment.

There were rules, after all, and the rule against lying to someone you loved was one of the big ones.

Cam was used to doing what most people would consider the "wrong" thing, but that was based on a moral code created by the fat cats, the rich assholes in society, the ones who were writing the rules and then breaking them whenever it served their own purposes. Theft was supposed to be wrong, even if you were stealing from robber barons who didn't deserve the money, had obtained it through thievery of their own, and wouldn't even miss it when it was gone. That wasn't wrong in

Cam's book. That was rigged. That was the people in power trying to brainwash everyone else into accepting their power forever. It was wrong not to fight against any power that tried to rig the game.

But to deceive Reggie was truly wrong in any book. And Cam would pay a price. He would be punished. Deservedly so.

Until then, he would enjoy Reggie's company, her attention, her love. He didn't deserve that. And Reggie certainly didn't deserve the broken heart.

There was one other alternative. He could push her away. He should push her away.

But he knew himself, knew he wouldn't have the strength for that.

And he knew he didn't want that.

But he had to try. Pushing Reggie away now, before her feeling got any deeper, was the right thing to do. It was the right thing for her, and it was the right thing for Cam's mother.

And so he did.

He pushed her away, at the window.

Reggie's full lips were on his, soft and supple. They parted just slightly, just enough for her tongue to slip across his, to part his lips, then drive into his mouth. She gripped the back of Cam's head, pulled him hard against her mouth, driving her tongue deeper.

Cam slid his hands up the sides of her thighs, over the swell of her hips and into the hollow of her waist. He wrapped his hands around her there, felt the push and pull of her muscles as she moved, as she pressed herself against him, pressed her hips to his. He slid his hands to her tight, round ass, pulled her against him, felt her hips grind against his own, felt his own want, his own need rise to meet hers.

Then he slid his hands back to her waist and pushed her away.

Pushed her hips away from his.

Pushed her mouth away from his.

Pushed her away from him until they stood there, face to face in the sunlight streaming through the window, Reggie's chest rising and falling as quickly as his own. Her face glowed. Her emerald eyes shined.

But now her eyes shone with more than just reflected sun. Now, there was a fire there, too. A fire fueled by hunger.

She frowned when he pushed her away. Just for a moment, her eyes unfocused, turned inward, and she frowned. The fire in her eyes cooled.

And then those eyes focused on his again, and the fire in them flared to white-hot. Cam could see the hunger overwhelm her.

And his body responded, instinctive, automatic, overwhelming. His hunger lit an inferno within him that match the fire blazing inside Reggie.

Their bodies came back together.

Crashed back together.

The inferno consumed Cam, swept away all of his thoughts, his hesitation, burned the weight into ash.

He felt the heat from Reggie's fire in the way she pulled him to her, the way she devoured him.

They devoured each other.

The flames of their mutual hunger joined together, and burned everything down.

Cam pulled her hard against him. She wrapped her legs around his waist, clenched him tight with her thighs. She ran her hands through his hair, pulled his mouth hard against hers, explored him with her tongue.

Cam cupped her ass through her tights, felt it grip and relax in rhythm with her thighs against his sides, in rhythm with her hips bucking and rubbing. Cam held her, backed past the coffee table and futon. Reggie tugged his t-shirt up over his head, tossed it on the floor behind them, ran her hands over his chest and back, her heat against his bare skin.

He backed through the hallway, into the bedroom. Her touch drove him out of his mind. Every place her skin met his blazed with exquisite heat. Every touch made Cam want more, more. He wanted to have her, to consume her, to embody her. He wanted to be inside her, and wanted her inside him. He wanted far more than sex, more than a mere coupling. He wanted a joining, a melding.

They fell backward onto the bed, Reggie straddling his waist. She pressed her hands against his chest, pressed herself upright, then slowly, seductively, her green eyes watching him watch her, she peeled off her sweater.

She wore nothing underneath. Her long, dark hair swayed against her chest as she moved her hips against his. Cam ran his hands slowly up her torso, reveling in her smooth skin, in the ripples of muscle underneath. Up, up, slowly, softly, up to her full breasts, her nipples erect in the cool air. Reggie let her head fall back, hooked her feet inside his crotch and gripped his sides with her thighs and ground her hips against his. He ran his finger in a slow circle around one nipple, then again, then scraped his fingertip lightly across the top. Reggie gasped at the touch, arched back and thrust her hips forward. Cam moaned at the pressure, slid his hands down her bare back to grip her hips and thrust them once more, then again.

Reggie fell forward, still straddling him. She threw both arms out to either side of his head, held herself there over him.

Curtains of her dark hair encircled them. The light from the window glowed behind it, like they had entered a place only they could go, a place out of time and space.

In that place, nothing else mattered. Nothing else existed. No school. No attorney general. No prison. No false identities.

He reached up one hand, held it against her cheek.

In that place, there was no Sam Davis, no Cameron Hauk. There was only Reggie Moon.

He trailed that hand slowly over her skin.

In that place, Cam finally felt peace.

Reggie bent down, traced her lips over his jaw, his neck, his chest, his stomach. She undid the button of his pants.

And Cam felt much, much more than mere peace.

35

Celina stood at the window of her apartment and watched the snowfall sputter as she sipped her double espresso. She'd changed into loose lounge pants and a sweatshirt a size too large that hung over one bare shoulder. Soft, warm, and comfortable. She cradled her cup against her chest, feeling its warmth in her palms and through her shirt.

The sky outside was leaden and the air was crisp, but it was too warm for real snow. They say that March either comes in like a lion and goes out like a lamb, or it does the opposite. So far this year it was coming in like a lamb.

That meant, as the Disney pirates say, there be storms ahead.

Celina sighed. Some of those storms would be of her own design.

She sipped her coffee and sighed again, in pleasure this time. Nothing like a good, strong coffee.

Especially after sex.

Especially after good sex.

Celina smiled. Her body still tingled, the aftershocks of the orgasms she'd had.

She hadn't intended to sleep with Cameron. She meant to fuck *with* him, not to fuck him. But life has a plan of its own, sometimes. And sometimes Celina got herself into trouble by following along.

But hey, intuition is the part of you that's in tune with the plans of the universe, right? So if you follow your intuition and you wind up in the shit, then you're meant to be in the shit. Nothing wrong with a little shit here and there. Keeps things interesting.

And if there's one thing Celina had learned in the years since her father had died, there is no amount of shit in the universe that a tech billionaire's fortune can't wipe clean. If there is a god, she wipes her ass with hundred dolla bills, y'all.

But this wasn't that kind of shit. This wasn't just getting a judge to look the other way or getting a disgruntled employee to write a backdoor into some code. And this wasn't some random asshole in a bar when she was feeling horny one night.

This was Cameron Hauk.

Tall, sexy, mysterious Cameron Hauk.

Talk about life having a plan of its own. Three months ago, that name had meant nothing to her. And then Cameron had literally fallen into her lap. Or fallen under her lap, anyway. And he'd been wearing that Nestech prototype, the one that only five or six people in the world had ever even seen, let alone worn.

By itself, the prototype was enough to raise Celina's interest, but using it to sneak around the Department of Justice in the middle of the night during a holiday break? Celina had been intrigued. She'd gotten curious. Who wouldn't? She decided to figure out who this mystery man was. And she decided to fuck with him and have some fun in the process.

Then fate had decided to fuck with her, too. It turned out Cameron was at the same university as her, and in the same year, and he was top of the class. Like her, Cameron was using an alias. And his GPA—which he'd earned through hard work— was just a fraction of a point behind Celina's GPA—which she'd earned by faking her transcripts. Celina didn't plan that. She didn't even notice it when she was setting things up. It all just happened, as if according to plan. Life was practically forcing them together.

But Cameron didn't know that. He thought he was sleeping with Regina Moon, not Celina Maxwell.

But would he even care? I mean, it wasn't like he didn't enjoy himself. Celina knew how to make a man happy in bed. It wasn't fucking rocket science. Just make them think they're the best lover you've ever had, moan a lot when they twiddle around, and hope they last long enough for you to actually get off.

Only Cameron hadn't been like that. At all. Celina had taken plenty of lovers, but he hadn't been like any lover she'd ever had before.

Cameron had been slow and considerate. Curious, even. He took his time, explored her body, experimented with something —a flick of a finger or the touch of his tongue—and watched her for a reaction. He was totally focused on her, so much so that Celina had wanted to return the favor. Pleasuring him had actually given her pleasure in return. That had never happened to her before.

And the orgasms. Good god. Four of them, each one better than the last. No, not better. Different. Once with his fingers, then his tongue, then with him on top, and finally, the biggest and the best of them all, with Celina riding him. They went together that time, another first for Celina, and she was shocked at how much his climax enhanced her own orgasm.

Or maybe it was just because it was the fourth one, and because it was both clitoral and vaginal, where the previous orgasms had been either one or the other. Either way, it was a mind-blower.

And she'd been impressed that Cameron had lasted that long. They were at it for hours. Either the man was a part-time porn star—and he would make a damn good one—or he was naturally blessed with incredible stamina. Celina had spent too much time with him over the past two months to suspect the former. Cameron Hauk was just a stallion. Almost as good as a dildo.

Another aftershock rippled through her. She shuddered with the pleasure.

Maybe even better than a dildo.

Celina tossed back the last of her coffee and rinsed the glass in the sink. As the water sluiced over the glass and over her hands, she thought back to the buildup, to the previous night when she'd plied him with good champagne and watched him get drunk, watched and waited for him to say something about the Nestech glasses or about his mother or about the reason he was at the DOJ building that night. She was irritated that she hadn't been able to find any answers in her usual computer-based ways, so she'd fallen back on a tried-and-true method: get the man drunk and get him to talk.

She'd already run her usual battery of searches on the internet. The Nestech glasses had given her Cameron's real name, a welcome gift, as he'd done a remarkable job of building his alias and hiding his identity. But with his real name in hand, she'd been able to learn quite a bit in short order.

Cameron's father had been killed in an ironic twist of fate—the plan of the universe, again—and his mother had gone in for three counts of unarmed bank robbery. It was the unarmed part that impressed Celina the most. Any clod could point a gun, but from what Celina could tell from the court transcripts and FBI records she'd hacked, the Hauks pulled off brilliant, beautiful bank heists, clever and carefully planned, using charm, misdirection, intelligence, and pure cohones to get their loot.

And they never left any definitive evidence behind. Hundreds of FBI agents had tried and failed to solve the cases, until one clever FBI agent, a rare genius at her job, had pieced the story together over time. Even with her talents, the connections were tenuous, at best, but she knew she'd figured it out. She just couldn't prove it.

Until they had Paulie Hauk in custody. They'd been able to pin her to three robberies using DNA from strands of hair that had been found at the crime scenes, DNA that somehow had never found its way into their system prior to Paulie's arrest.

Some might call it horrible luck that Paulie had been caught at all. Celina called it tragic fate. But whatever the reason, even though Paulie had gone down for just three jobs, Celina was absolutely certain that the Hauks had pulled off more than that in their time. Probably more like a hundred times that many.

And their son was carrying on the family business in their absence. Maybe not robbing banks, exactly, but he was definitely up to something. No one sneaks around the Department of Justice building in the middle of the night on a holiday break dressed all in black and wearing prototype augmented-reality glasses without being up to something.

But what the fuck was it? Celina was one of the top five hackers in the world. And that was no brag. If she were bragging, she'd say she was the best. But objectively, she was in the top five, hands down. Yet with all her skill, she still hadn't been able to find out what Cameron was up to. She'd had to resort to meat-space tactics like getting him drunk. The people who weren't good enough to hack called it social engineering. Celina called it a pain in the ass.

And it hadn't even worked.

Proving Celina's feelings to be correct. Meat-space was unreliable. People were at once both completely predictable and entirely unpredictable. They were maddening. Celina did her best not to rely on people for anything important. They simply couldn't be trusted.

She set her coffee cup on the rack to dry and went back to the window, staring into the increasing greyness as the sun began to fade. The snow had given up for the moment, but maybe it would try again once the sun went down and the temperatures dropped. Her window gave a view onto the street below. She watched the streetlights blink on, the light first flickering, then becoming steady and strong. Between them and the glow from the traffic lights on the corner, the encroaching darkness took on a shifting tinge of yellow, green, and red.

Celina had deliberately stayed away from Cameron all of the last week to throw him off his routine. He'd gotten used to having her around. She'd insinuated herself into his life, made him reliant on her for food, for drink, for companionship. Being paired together for a class assignment was a gift from that hundred-dolla god up there, the plan of the universe again. But she would have found a way to get close to him, even without that gift.

And then she'd abandoned him. Cold turkey, no note. She wanted him to feel off-kilter, and the timing couldn't have been better. She'd caught him smelling her hair that one night—weird, but kinda cute, especially watching him get all flustered afterward—and then tracked him to the prison in New York where he visited his mother. And then it was time for midterms, a naturally stressful time.

Stress was the goal. If the hair-smelling incident was any indication, he seemed to be falling for her, as was the plan. By abandoning him then, he'd worry about whether or not he'd blown his chances. That would stress him out. Ghosting him whenever he texted or called would make it worse. And midterms would add even more stress.

She gave him a full week to wind himself up, enough time to let him marinate in stress and stew in worry, but not enough for him to get pissed off and say good riddance. Her plan was to corner him at Sarah's party, get him good and soused, then bring him home to interrogate him. The party hadn't worked out, so she'd gone to his apartment instead. Same difference.

He'd been wound up, all right, but not about midterms or

about her. He'd been wound up about something else. When he answered the door, he kept looking down the hallway like he was expecting a different person, someone he obviously feared.

It hadn't taken long for Celina to realize she was the one he feared. Not Reggie Moon, but the woman he'd met at the DOJ. The woman who'd left the box on his doorstep, who'd left a trail of clues for him to follow. A trail that, after all this time, he still hadn't been able to follow.

Celina shivered with a sudden chill. She wrapped her arms around herself and tried to rub some warmth into her body. She thought back to only a few hours earlier, when she and Cameron had been warming each other. She'd been hot then, sweat beading on both of them as they explored each other's bodies. She shivered again, not from the cold this time, but from the thrill of the memory.

He hadn't said much, even when he was blitzed. The man was a vault. But he had slurred something about March third and a woman in black, and that's when Celina knew she'd gotten to him. The box, the glasses, the clues. She was all up in his head, just like she'd wanted to be.

She'd broken men before using the exact same playbook. Prey on their fragile minds, take advantage of their childish egos. Men were easy. It took so much energy and ignorance to maintain the illusion that they were the masters of the universe that Celina could walk boldly in the shadows of their blind spots and go freely about her business. If the men ever opened their eyes, they'd see exactly what she was doing. But they never did. They were so busy fooling themselves into believing in their own invincibility, they failed to do anything useful, anything that would actually help them learn and grow.

She'd been called a man-hater in the past, usually by ex-lovers who wanted another fix and couldn't believe Celina would reject them. But Celina didn't hate men. Not at all. She just didn't have time for the coddling bullshit they required in order to coax them into doing anything useful.

No woman needs a man. Period. They may want one from time to time, but they don't *need* one. But most women don't know that. Society—run by men—works hard to convince them of the opposite, to convince them that men are necessary, that men are essential. Men are taught the same thing, which is why they strut around, preening their ignorance, believing that they are the top of the food chain.

But Celina knew better. That was the part that really pissed the men off. She knew she didn't need them, and they couldn't stomach that fact. That was a blow too close to home, too hard for them to rationalize away. It struck far too close to the quiet fears deep inside them. They couldn't ignore it.

And so they reacted in the way that fools and cowards always do, with anger and violence.

Celina knew how to defend herself. She was like Sean Connery in The Presidio. She could kill a man five different ways using only her right thumb. After her father's death, she'd made sure of that, made sure that if anyone ever came for her the way they'd come for her father, she'd be able to fight back.

For all that, no man had ever tried to hit her. She figured their self-preservation instincts held them back, even if only subconsciously. They'd done their best to bully her, to abuse her emotionally. But you can't hurt someone emotionally if they don't care what you think.

A few, seeing that, had threatened physical abuse. One had even come at her with a heavy stone bookend raised above his head, ready to strike. But something in her eyes had stopped him dead. He'd taken two menacing steps toward her, bookend raised high, anger in his eyes. Celina had seen him coming, and something had flooded her system. Not fear. Definitely not fear. Adrenaline, maybe, or just the thrill of a challenge. Whatever it was, it was fight, not flight. She was excited to fight that asshole. She was ready to kick some ass.

And he must have seen that in her eyes. He was just some tech bro pussy, anyway. Thought he was a big, strong man because his net worth ran to eight digits. Even Celina's bank account would have taken his down in a fight without breaking a sweat.

And when he looked at her face, he stopped cold in his tracks, arm still in the air. His eyes went wide and his face went slack and Celina would not have been surprised to learn he pissed his organic, microplastic-free, sustainable cotton pants. Without a word, he set the bookend carefully on her table and walked straight out of the house, never to return.

So no, no man had ever hit her. Thankfully so, for Celina would have killed the asshole, would have been tried for murder, would have mounted a credible case for self-defense, and because of the man-slanted sexism inherent in all levels of American officialdom, she would have been found guilty of involuntary manslaughter—for no mere woman could ever intentionally kill a man in hand-to-hand combat—and would have spent the next six to eleven years in a California prison.

Instead, she was standing at her window in Washington, D.C., watching the weather and thinking about another cup of coffee.

And thinking about Cameron Hauk.

She shivered again as a flush of heat washed through her. She hadn't meant to fuck Cameron, but she'd fuck him again. That's for damn sure. Again and again and again, if she could.

And maybe, at some point, she could get him to talk. He'd mentioned that woman in black. She could use that.

It was all she had, anyway.

She heard a knock on her door, checked through the peep-hole, then undid the locks and pulled it wide open. The gust of cool air did nothing to slow the heat that rushed through her.

Cameron was standing on her doorstep, barefoot and bare-chested, wearing only a loose pair of sweatpants. He leaned one muscular arm high on her doorjamb, a t-shirt clutched in his hand overhead.

Celina raked her eyes over his chest. He wasn't bulky. He was no meathead body-builder. Celina hated that. It was like squeezing a rock. No, Cameron's chest was lean and long, his muscles strong and well-defined. She let her gaze drift slowly down from his head to the sharp V running below his waistline, then slowly back up again.

Cameron's nipples were rock hard. She had no idea why he was standing there in the cold without a shirt, but she felt her own nipples tighten in anticipation of what was to come.

Round Two.

"You look cold," Celina said. "Come inside and we'll get you out of those pants."

36

CAM WOKE in his bed in the fading afternoon light. At first, he couldn't remember if the sex with Reggie had been real or just a dream.

If it was a dream, it was the best dream ever.

He sat up, looked around, and found another note on his pillow, again written on paper torn from his sketchbook, again written in Reggie's confident, artistic handwriting. The beauty of the strokes, the forward lean of the script, the way the words were arranged on the page. It was fitting that she'd used sketch paper to write it. The note itself was practically a work of art.

That should help your hangover. Talk soon. -R

Cam smiled. She was right about that. Best hangover cure ever. He stood and stretched, buck naked, and found that his lingering headache was gone completely and his stomach felt normal again.

He'd need to shower at some point, but for the moment, he just wanted to luxuriate in his own skin. His senses felt like they were alive for the first time in a long time. His skin tingled. He pulled on a pair of sweatpants, not bothering with underwear, and the feel of the soft fabric as it caressed his skin reminded him of Reggie's soft hands doing the same thing just a few hours ago. The thought made him hard again.

He smiled, shook his head, and pushed a hand through his hair. He had to get his mind out of the gutter. It was late on Sunday afternoon. He had things to do. A lot of things to do.

He pulled on a t-shirt. The same sensations overwhelmed him. The feel of the soft fabric sliding slowly over his chest made his nipples hard, too. He remembered the way Reggie kissed him, first on his lips, soft and slow and sensuous, then down his chest, lingering on his nipples for a moment, then trailing down, down, further down.

He was rock hard now. Everywhere.

Damn it. Focus, Cam. There's shit to do.

He couldn't even focus enough to remember what that shit was, exactly, so he let his body lead him via muscle memory. He went to the kitchen and made himself a cup of coffee. It was nearly sundown and he shouldn't be drinking coffee this late, but he needed the distraction. And maybe a cup of coffee would pull his head back on straight and give him the energy to focus.

He had plenty to focus on. Schoolwork, the Attorney General, the woman in black, his mother.

His mother. Reggie had said something about his mother, about how they'd talked about her the night before, when Cam was wasted. What had he told her?

Panic rose up in his chest, but then he eased it back again. Whatever it was must not have been too bad. Reggie didn't seem worried or upset by anything he'd said.

Quite the opposite.

Cam sipped his coffee and tried to keep his mind focused on something useful, but his thoughts kept drifting back over the last few hours. He was standing in the kitchen, looking out the window where Reggie had first kissed him. He remembered the feeling of her lips against his, the way her tongue had explored his mouth, searching and insistent. The way she'd pulled his head against hers, drove her hips against his again and again.

The kitchen was suddenly stuffy. The coffee was scalding on his tongue. Sweat formed on Cam's shoulders and the base of his neck beneath his t-shirt. He flapped the base of his shirt to cool himself off.

He ripped his eyes and his mind away from the window, looked toward the other room instead, toward the futon couch, the desk.

Toward the bedroom.

They'd walked through there, Cam walking backwards, Reggie's legs wrapped around his waist. The shirt he'd been wearing then was still on the ground where it had fallen when Reggie peeled it off of him. Then he'd felt her hands on his chest, on his skin.

He came out of his reverie and found he'd walked into the living room, unaware of his own movements. His hand was even touching his chest through his shirt, the way Reggie had touched him.

He tossed back the last of his coffee, set the glass on the table in front of the couch. Why the fuck was it so goddamn hot in here?

He checked the thermostat by the front door. It was set to sixty-seven degrees. He cranked it down to sixty.

He was practically burning. If he stayed inside any longer, he'd be a pile of ash on the ground.

He grabbed his keys and pulled open the front door. The cool air blasted against him, cooled the sweat on his brow, but only for a moment. His body was on fire.

He stepped outside, let the door shut behind him. He was barefoot, but couldn't feel the cold concrete on his soles. If there had been snow on the ground, Cam was sure his feet would have melted it in a heartbeat.

He paced back and forth in front of his door, hoping that moving through the chill air would cool him down. It didn't.

Maybe he needed to walk faster. He stopped pacing and strode quickly down the walkway. The air felt more like a breeze now, against his forehead. But it did nothing to cool him down.

He strode faster still. Maybe a higher floor would help. The air would be colder up there, the walkways more open to the wind.

He climbed up one flight, taking the stairs two at a time. The exertion made him even hotter. He got to the landing at the top and pulled his t-shirt over his head. The air against his exposed chest felt like a lover's hands caressing him. Reggie's hands. He moaned at the sudden relief, and at the memory.

And the sound of his own moaning made him hotter all over again.

Swearing under his breath, Cam strode even faster down the walkway, practically running now, the numbers on the doors flashing by him. Forty-nine. Forty-eight. Forty-seven. Forty-six.

Forty-five.

He jerked to a halt.

Forty-five. Reggie's door.

Cam was surprised to find himself winded, his bare chest heaving, his breath clouding before him as the overhead lights flickered on. He could smell the bite of impending snowfall in his nose. His pulse pounded in his ears.

He raised one hand high and leaned against Reggie's doorjamb, pulling in a deep breath through his nose, letting it out slowly through his mouth, trying to calm his breathing.

His chest stopped heaving, but his heart still raced.

He knocked on the door without even knowing he was doing it.

His heart raced faster.

He heard the click of the locks.

His heart raced even faster.

And then she was there. In the open doorway.

His heart stopped then. Stopped right in his chest.

And his breath? His breath was gone.

The sight of Reggie Moon took it away.

She stood in the doorway, still holding the doorknob. She wore an oversized sweatshirt that left her shoulder exposed. Her soft pants flowed down to her bare feet. Cam instantly imagined himself running his hands over her skin, over her shape beneath her soft pants, drawing her close to him, against him.

Her eyes widened just a bit, then just watched Cam. He fell into those limpid green pools, fell deep, stunned. Her eyes roamed over his body, from head to toe and back again. Cam's nipples hardened at the touch of her eye.

Those green eyes gleamed for a moment and the side of Reggie's lush lips twisted up.

"You look cold," she said. "Come inside and we'll get you out of those pants."

They only made it to the end of the hallway.

Then the kitchen.

Then the couch.

And the coffee table.

Then the bed.

Oh, the bed.

And then, later, the shower.

Cam couldn't lie to himself any longer. Didn't want to.

He was in love with Reggie Moon.

37

THEY SPENT the night together every night for almost two straight weeks, sometimes at Reggie's place, sometimes at Cam's. They spent nearly every moment of every day together, too, during that time. Breakfast, then class, then lunch, then the afternoon together—usually in bed—then dinner, a movie, and back to bed again.

It passed in a blink. It passed like a dream.

And then Cam remembered everything he'd been ignoring for two weeks. Two glorious weeks, but two weeks where he'd done nothing to help his mother. He hadn't even visited her, hadn't even thought about it. He burned with shame when that realization came upon him.

He'd already finished his schoolwork for the rest of the semester, but he still had to go to class and prepare for the exams. Yet he'd fallen behind over the last two weeks, skimping on his notes, texting Reggie instead of paying attention to his professors, even skipping classes to be with her. In three years, he'd never missed a lecture. In the last two weeks, he'd missed four. He still had to close the 0.003 point gap between his GPA and Reggie's, and missing class was not going to help.

For her part, Reggie never seemed to have to study or attend class. She didn't seem worried about anything at all. Exams didn't faze her. Projects, papers, even midterms hadn't seemed to stress her out. Cam didn't know how she could maintain such a high GPA with so little apparent effort. He knew Reggie was smart, but she must be some kind of genius.

And Cam had a lot more to worry about than just his school-work. He had a high-profile government official to blackmail, and he still needed to get into the DOJ to get the evidence he needed from Stratham's computer. Graduation was in two months. Time was running out. Cam would need to do that job soon.

It was Friday afternoon. Stratham should have come back from his west coast trip that morning. Cam would need to hack into the campaign servers again to check the most recent fundraising schedule, but he figured Stratham would only be in town for the next week or two, at most.

And Cam still needed time to plan. He was supposed to have been doing that for the last two weeks, but he'd let himself be distracted by Reggie. He couldn't afford to lose any more time.

As he and Reggie walked back to the apartment complex after lunch on Friday, Cam told her he had some things he needed to do that weekend. Reggie accepted the news without debate, said she had some things to catch up on, too. With a long, tender kiss that made Cam want nothing more than to change his mind and invite her inside, they split up at Cam's apartment and went their separate ways.

He went inside, shut the door, closed his eyes, and leaned back against it, his lips still tingling from where Reggie had nipped them playfully before walking away. That woman was an obsession for him. A drug. He couldn't seem to get enough of her. Just being away from her for thirty seconds left him with an ache low in his stomach, like an organ had been ripped from his body and left a gaping hole behind.

He shook his head. He was doing it again, falling too hard,

too fast. He had to pull himself back, had to keep himself focused. There would be time to pursue his relationship with Reggie after his mother was out of jail.

If Reggie still wanted him once he told her the truth.

That sobering thought was enough to bring Cam back down to earth. He pulled his laptop from his shoulder bag and sat down at the desk. Within ten minutes, he was inside the servers for the Jenkins campaign, searching for the latest schedule.

Fuck. Stratham was set to leave again a week from Sunday for a fundraiser in Florida. As if there was any chance Florida would go to a Democrat like Jenkins. But the Attorney General did have a reputation for being tough on crime, and he was a proud gun owner and a hunting enthusiast. Why anyone would take pleasure from hunting and killing an innocent animal was beyond Cam, but it seemed to play well in the red states.

Cam scanned the rest of the schedule. It was already mid-March. Stratham was in DC for one more week, then the trip to Florida, then a long tour of the southern states and up through the heartland to the Midwest before turning back toward the coast. He wasn't scheduled to be back in DC again until the morning of commencement day in two months, probably to collect money from whatever wealthy donors would be in attendance at the ceremony.

The dinner with Jenkins that was awarded to the top five students in the class traditionally occurred each year on the night before commencement. The valedictorian would then spend the morning of the day of commencement alone with Jenkins, leading up to the commencement ceremony in the afternoon. At the ceremony, the valedictorian would give their speech, introduce the Attorney General, and have a brief photo op on the graduation stage, after which Jenkins would speak to the graduating class and invariably laud the valedictorian for the many talents and abilities he'd seen in them during their time together that day.

Cam had to be that valedictorian. Once he had Jenkins alone, he could make a discreet, but persuasive, pitch to free his mother in exchange for keeping the incriminating information to himself. In order to pull that off convincingly, he had to have his evidence buttoned up, backed up, and ready to go by that morning. He needed access to Stratham's laptop for that.

Which meant he had one week left. It was the only remaining opportunity for him to gain the access he needed, unless he was willing to skip class to chase Stratham around the country and try to gain access somewhere else. But Cam didn't have time for that, didn't have time to research venues, study Stratham's habits on the road, or plan a location for the job.

He wanted more than one more week to plan another job at the DOJ, but at least he'd done some research already. He'd broken in once, knew the building and the security setup by heart. He just didn't know if they'd changed anything since then. And he didn't know Stratham's habits. He had one more week to learn what he could. It would have to be enough.

He was out of time.

He spent the rest of that night, through the night and deep into Saturday morning, digging through files in Jenkins' campaign servers, then hacking into the DOJ network and digging through files there. He had one eye out for campaign finance data, always, but didn't expect to find it on servers that were open to so many people. Still, you never know. Cam hoped for a gift to fall into his lap, but he didn't expect it.

Instead, he found what he did expect. Information. Within the campaign servers, he was looking for any information he could find about Stratham's routine. The man he'd met on a luxury yacht nine months earlier had seemed like the sort of man who liked a routine. Given as much travel as he did, he probably carried his routine with him. Indeed, Stratham never seemed to let go of his laptop. His routine probably revolved around that.

But did he need a cup of coffee at specific intervals? Did he need a certain lunch or snack at specific times? How often did he use the bathroom? Did he use a cleaning service? Did he have an IT person who maintained his computer? Anything and everything Cam could learn was potentially useful. And he didn't have much time, so he cast a wide net, reading every email, browsing every note and file written by Stratham's assistants and office staff.

He didn't learn much. Stratham drank coffee, black, and didn't seem to be precious about it. He'd drink any swill he could find. If his cup ran dry, he didn't run out for an immediate refill, but he'd get more when it was convenient.

Stratham drank liquor, mostly good whiskey, but never while working. He only drank in social situations, never alone, and never at campaign events. Cam could have sworn he remembered Stratham drinking something during that night on the luxury yacht, but maybe it had been club soda or Coca-Cola.

Stratham did tend to work late, often sending emails to his team at one or two in the morning. He didn't have a spouse or children. Didn't have a girlfriend. Didn't even have any friends, as far as Cam could tell. He was dedicated to his work, and he worked non-stop.

Fortunately, those late hours seemed to take place at the DOJ building fairly regularly. In fact, he seemed to be there every Tuesday and Friday when he was in town. Cam could tell from the IP addresses on the emails he sent that he was usually in the DOJ building until at least midnight on those days.

Cam hacked into the DOJ systems next, first checking the security roster and schedules to see if anything had changed. Aside from one daytime guard who had left for family reasons and been replaced, nothing seemed to have changed from the winter. The night guards were all the same.

He checked the camera feeds next, cycling through until he found the feed outside Stratham's office. Like most government offices, the DOJ was required to keep records of their security feeds for somewhere between thirty and ninety days. The DOJ kept theirs for ninety. Cam scrubbed back through all of that footage, looking for signs of Stratham.

Stratham had been away a lot of that time, but when he was there, it was always on Tuesday or Friday. In another window, he checked the camera feeds at the campaign office. Stratham was there the rest of the week, and often on Saturday, as well.

Wherever he was, he never left his laptop alone in the office, keeping it tucked under his arm, even when he was just going to the bathroom or to the break room for more coffee.

That was going to be a problem.

Tuesday and Friday seemed to be significant because Stratham always met with the Attorney General in the AG's expansive fifth floor office in the DOJ building on those days. They would usually meet at the end of the day, around six or seven, after Jenkins' other meetings were done. They'd some-times meet for hours, having dinner brought in for them. Cam switched to the fifth-floor camera outside Jenkins' office and scrubbed through the footage for those days. Sometimes one person or another would join them, but it seemed that most times those meetings were for just the two men, discussing their campaign strategies.

And discussing their nefarious tactics.

A flash of sunlight through the window blind caught Cam's eye and broke his concentration. He stretched back in his chair, his muscles screaming at him. They'd been stuck in one posi-tion, hunched over his laptop, for too long. The bones of his back and his neck cracked and popped as he twisted and turned and worked the tension out of them. He stood and paced around the desk to get the blood moving in his legs. He cracked one of the slats on the window blinds. Bright sunlight poured in, prac-tically blinding him, suddenly reminding Cam of how tired he was.

He checked the time. It was already ten in the morning. He'd been awake for more than twenty-four hours. His eyes seemed to drag shut of their own accord at the thought, and Cam barely made it to his bed before he crashed.

He woke four hours later, still fatigued, but feeling much better than he had been. After a quick shower and a double espresso, he was hunched over his laptop once again.

His stomach broke his focus the next time, growling so loud it sounded like a pond-full of frogs had moved into Cam's living room behind him. He checked the time in the corner of his computer. Almost 9pm, and he hadn't eaten since lunch the previous day.

He stood and pushed one hand through his hair. His mind was still swimming with the information he'd been sifting through on his computer. Emails and notes and camera feeds and schedules and drafts of speeches and pitches. He hadn't found any detailed records of contributions from major donors. There were records of all the small donors who gave money over the internet or in donations of less than a thousand dollars, but Cam wanted the big fish. The whales. The ones who gave hundreds of thousands or even millions. The ones who expected something in return.

Those were the ones candidates would die to have as contributors. Those were the ones they would kill for.

But he hadn't found anything useful on the servers. He was sure now that all the really sensitive information would be on Stratham's laptop. Nowhere else.

His stomach growled again, insistent. Just as Cam looked blankly toward his kitchen, wondering what food he might have left in his cupboards, he heard a knock on the door. He checked quickly through the peephole, then pulled the door open.

Reggie stood on the doorstep with a foil-covered baking dish in one hand and a plastic grocery bag full of something in the other.

"I know you said you needed some time to yourself this weekend," she said with a sheepish look that made Cam's heart leap into his throat, "but everyone has to eat, right?" She held up the baking dish and the bag.

Cam smiled at her. It's true that he needed time to work, but he'd done a lot of work already, and made good progress. And Reggie was right. He was starving. He had to eat. And he would have had to stop to make something for dinner, anyway. Why not spend that time with Reggie?

"Perfect timing," he said. "Come on in."

38

"YOU MADE AN ENTIRE LASAGNA?" asked Cam as he opened a bottle of Cabernet Sauvignon to breathe and set the table with glasses, silverware, and napkins.

"I had a lot of time on my hands," replied Reggie from the kitchen, where she was dishing up the food.

She must have, because the lasagna she made used four kinds of cheese, a homemade Bolognese sauce, and even fresh, homemade noodles. She had made a fennel orange salad with a homemade citrus vinaigrette and some garlic bread to go along with the lasagna. Though she'd added the butter, garlic, and cheese, she admitted she hadn't made the bread itself. She said it as if that admission was something shameful. Cam was still astounded by Reggie's long list of artistic talents, the culinary arts being just one of them.

They dug into the food in relative silence for a few minutes, both of them proving to be hungry at that late hour. When their plates were half-empty, Reggie asked, "How was your day? Did you get any work done?"

Cam wiped his mouth on his napkin and set it back in his lap. "Actually, yes. I didn't get much sleep," he grinned, "but I got a lot done."

"That's good." Reggie speared another forkful of salad. "What are you working on? That LCJ paper Jem was talking about yesterday?"

Cam shoved a forkful of lasagna in his mouth, more to give himself time to think than because he needed the food at that particular moment. He didn't like lying to Reggie. He didn't want to do it if he didn't have to. In fact, the longer he went on lying to her, the more pissed at him she would be when he finally did come clean with her.

But he couldn't risk telling her the truth until after graduation, after his mother was released. How deep would he have to dig his hole before then? Was there any way he could be with Reggie for the next two months and not lie to her face the whole time?

"No," he said, "just some other things I'm working on." He didn't want to lie to Reggie at all, so he wouldn't. Not unless he absolutely had to. He would fall back on bland vagaries and half-truths instead. It wasn't much better, but at least he wouldn't be lying. Not technically.

Though he wasn't sure that defense would be very useful when the time came to tell the truth.

Reggie chewed her mouthful of salad, looking at him thoughtfully and nodding.

"Were you looking for the woman in black?" she said as she loaded another forkful, her voice innocent as a lamb.

Cam nearly choked on the wine he was drinking. How did Reggie know about the woman in black?

Reggie smiled at him. "You mentioned something about a woman in black," she said. "The other night, when you were drunk."

"Did I?" Cam croaked. He wiped the table with his napkin, wiping up the droplets of wine he'd spit out. They stained the white napkin with a circle of dark red that expanded as the wine soaked into the fabric.

"You said you'd been trying to find her."

"Huh," said Cam. He stabbed at his lasagna, his fork coming up empty again and again. "What else did I say?"

"Weird stuff," said Reggie. "At first it was weird, anyway. You were talking about a box and a card and some clues."

"That is weird."

Reggie laughed. "Very funny." She shook her head at him and took a swallow of wine. "It all made sense once you showed me."

Cam had finally managed to load his fork with food, but now it froze halfway to his mouth. He swallowed hard, his mouth suddenly bone dry. He set his fork back down and drank a hasty sip of wine.

"Showed you what?"

"The box," said Reggie around a mouthful of lasagna. She looked at Cam as she chewed.

"I showed you a box?"

Reggie nodded, still chewing.

"What... kind of box?"

Reggie swallowed and frowned at him. "That cardboard shoe box," she said. "The one with the black crepe paper on the outside. Very pretty, actually. I love that kind of paper." She took a bite of garlic bread.

"I..." Cam swallowed, his tongue suddenly swollen in his mouth. "I showed you that?"

"Did you ever figure out that second clue?"

"Sec—" Cam's throat felt like it was closing off, like in another minute the room would grow dark and he would pass out. He closed his eyes. "Second clue?"

"You know, I was thinking about that ribbon."

"I showed you the second clue?" Cam had no memory of showing Reggie the box. "Did I show you the first clue?" Of course, he had no memory of a lot from that night, but he couldn't believe he would have done that, even if he was blacked out drunk. Why would he show Reggie the box? Why would he tell her about the woman in black?

"Those notches on the sides—" Reggie continued.

He must have shown her, though. How else would she know about it? Cam swore in that moment never to get drunk again. It was too risky. He'd never had a problem with it in the past, but that night had been... well, tense.

"—I think they might mean something—"

But that didn't matter. He could understand why he'd gotten drunk, but that didn't mean it was forgivable. He'd spilled a secret that night, one he preferred Reggie didn't know. It wasn't a crucial secret. It was an odd secret, but it didn't betray his mother or jeopardize his plan.

"—but I'd like to take another look, if that's alright."

At least he didn't think it did. What else had he told Reggie? Did he tell her how he'd met the woman in black? Did he tell her why he'd been in the DOJ building in the middle of the night during a holiday break? Did he show her the Nestech glasses? Also not a massive deal breaker, but those glasses would have opened up a whole new set of questions that Cam would prefer not to answer.

"Sam?"

And someone as smart as Reggie, someone with a nose for investigation, someone looking to make a career out of solving mysteries and catching criminals in their lies, would follow that lead like a dog following a juicy piece of rare steak.

"Sam."

"Huh?" Cam came back to the present moment with a start. Reggie was sitting across the table, holding a loaded fork resting on the plate, a look of concern and confusion on her face.

"Are you okay?" she asked. "I think I lost you there for a second."

Cam felt his face flush with heat. Reggie had been talking and he'd completely tuned her out, lost in his own thoughts.

"Sorry." He held up one hand and shook his head apologetically. "Sorry," he smiled wanly, "I haven't had much sleep. I think I zoned out for a second."

Reggie smiled, that mysterious, knowing gleam in her eye again. Someday, Cam hoped he'd know Reggie well enough to interpret that gleam. He never would, of course, but he could still hope.

"Maybe you should go to bed," said Reggie. "Maybe," she lifted the fork to her lips, "I should take you to bed."

She arched one eyebrow as she chewed, and Cam felt the heat from his face flush through his entire body. He felt a tightening in his core and a stiffening in his pants. He should resist. He still had a lot of work to do, and tomorrow was Sunday. He needed to visit his mother and apologize to her. He should finish his meal, thank Reggie and kiss her goodnight, then get a good night's sleep. Alone.

But Reggie had that gleam in her eye again, and this was one gleam that Cam already knew how to interpret. Her eyes alone were enough to set his heart galloping, but when she had that look in them, all the other parts of his body went racing through the paddock, too. He knew what he should do, but he also knew what he wanted to do.

He smiled at Reggie across the table. "Maybe you should," he said, sipping his wine.

Neither of them got much sleep that night, but what sleep Cam did get was deep and restful. He woke next to Reggie feeling energized, despite the early hour. They shared a cup of coffee together and parted ways, Reggie heading back to her apartment while Cam headed to the metro station.

He had told Reggie he had some errands to run that would take him all day, then some work to do that would take him all night. She nodded and kissed him goodbye without complaint or question, said she'd swing by with coffee on Monday morning to walk to class together.

Reggie trusted him. But she shouldn't, and her trust made Cam's deception all the more shameful. But as important as Reggie was to him, Cam's mother was more important. It had been too long since he'd visited her.

The train clacked and swayed. Seated beside the window, Cam could feel the cold outside through the glass, could see the snow-strewn fields glide by. Occasionally, a train would appear on the other track, headed in the opposite direction. The sound of its approach would build like the scream of a bitter ghost until it burst in a great whump as the trains met and passed, clattering and clacking, the blank faces of other riders drifting past as if in a dream or a daze. As the last car raced by, another whump would sound, reversed, a vacuum sucking the ghosts and the riders along with it, leaving nothing but empty fields strewn with snow in its wake.

Cam sketched as he rode. Images of Reggie asleep in bed in the morning sunlight, of her hair framing her face, neck arched as she straddled and rode him, of her eyes gleaming in the soft light across the dinner table.

His thoughts turned to what she'd said about the box and the clues and the ribbon. He wrote out the clues. *Threee-three. Getting closer.* He drew from memory the image from the second clue, the swoop and curl of the ribbon, the personified number three, whistling and walking, with the Nestech glasses and the balloon that said *e-3*. He sketched the ribbon. Reggie had said something about the notches. From just his memory, Cam couldn't recall much detail other than their approximate location.

He didn't think too hard about the clues. He just sketched them to pass the time and to seed his subconscious with the information. He let the words and images he sketched slide across his mind like the scenery slid across the window beside him.

When he got to the prison, his mother wasn't upset with

him. She didn't seem the least bit surprised to learn why he hadn't come the last two weeks. She smiled instead, her face glowing as she watched Cam and listened.

It was after nine PM by the time he got back to his apartment. He heated a plate of leftovers in the microwave and sat down at his desk to eat in front of his computer. He had a job to plan, and not much time left to do it. Friday night would be his last good chance to get the information he needed to free his mother.

Cam released a deep breath and set to work.

39

EVEN AFTER THE time it took to rent a car at the rental place near the apartment, Celina had still beaten Cameron to his mother's prison by a good hour. She wasn't a lead foot, but she liked to enjoy a drive, and she'd rented a Tesla Model 3. Those cars are fast. Not as fast as the pre-production Lucid Air Sapphire that was sitting in her garage in California, a $250k electric car that could go 0-60 in under three seconds with barely a whisper, but still fast enough for a hell of a fun drive up I-95 at ninety miles per hour on a bright, clear, crisp late-winter day.

She tracked Cameron's progress on her phone from the parking lot of a strip mall a block from the correctional facility. Celina still couldn't believe they built prisons in the middle of communities like that. In this case, the inmates at Taconic weren't very dangerous, but soon enough they'd be housing convicted murderers in the basement of luxury downtown high-rises just to maximize profits for the real estate developers.

She watched the map on her phone as the dot representing Cameron approached, then watched through her windshield as his Uber turned the corner and passed by. An hour later, she watched the whole thing again in reverse. Cameron took a five-hour train ride every weekend to spend one hour visiting with

247

his mother. That was love, the kind of love that made Celina respect Cameron even more. It was the kind of love she'd had for her father.

Before Stratham and Jenkins had murdered him.

Funny enough, she bore no ill will toward the goon who actually killed her father. She'd tracked him down, but he was just a contract killer. He was paid to do a job, and the job happened to be sticking a syringe full of poison in her father's neck. The goon had a wife, a little boy, and a two-bedroom house on a boring suburban street, with a Honda Civic in the driveway and a yard that he mowed every week. Just your average, everyday assassin for hire, struggling to make ends meet.

But Stratham and Jenkins knew what they had done. They were the ones that had called in the hit a year ago. They were the ones responsible, and she had the proof. Naturally, the fuckers would never go down for their crimes, no matter how much evidence Celina produced. Her family had been wealthy enough for long enough to know how the system really worked. They talk about the scales of justice, and people assume it means that justice is fair and balanced. But what they really mean is that the degree to which justice is applied is scaled to their net worth and their influence. The more wealth and influence, the less the justice system applies to you.

But, in this case, Celina would make sure that justice was served, nonetheless.

She waited until she saw the dot on her screen moving down the tracks back toward D.C. before she put the Tesla in gear and drove to the correctional facility herself.

She'd never been to a prison before and didn't know what to expect. It turned out to be much like in the movies, with the exception that the guards weren't bored-looking, shifty-eyed, cruel-faced cretins, although maybe they saved the hard-asses for the maximum security facilities. The guards Celina encountered were professional, attentive, and surprisingly personable.

And thorough. Jesus, were they thorough. Celina had left everything but her phone and her wallet in the car, just to make things simpler, but the guards still took their time searching her at each step through the facility. Every time she passed through a locked door, she underwent a search.

But it was always a female guard, and they were always respectful, informing her of where they would be placing their hands before they did it. And they placed their hands in some sensitive areas.

Celina could respect their attention to detail. It was when people got lax in their work, in their thinking, that things went sideways. Lack of attention to detail usually came down to a lack of imagination. These guards left nothing to the imagination.

Within reason, anyway. At least they didn't do a cavity search. Again, that was probably more of a max security thing.

The visitation room was empty when Celina was finally admitted. A dreary room, half prison yard, half elementary school cafeteria, with a concrete floor, a plaster ceiling, and windows that opened onto nothing but watchful guards. No view of the outside. Not even a skylight to let in the sun. The only seats were a handful of bolted-down steel tables and benches coated in some kind of plastic, chipped and scarred from decades of use and colored in jumpsuit orange. With that plastic in that color, it was like they wanted to make you barf, but still make it easy to clean up afterward.

"Only fifteen minutes left until visiting hours end," said the guard, a large, round woman with a hard face and kind eyes, as she held the door for Celina. She said it in a friendly, informative way, but a way that made it clear that in fifteen minutes exactly they would cut Celina off mid-sentence and drag her from the room, if need be.

Fortunately, they were quick to retrieve Cameron's mother. Celina had barely sat down on one of the benches, the cold of the steel seeping through the plastic into her ass, before she saw a woman come through the inmate door on the far side of the room.

Celina recognized Paulina Hauk from the pictures she'd pulled up when she hacked into the prison network. Medium height, thin, but not gaunt, with shoulder-length hair that was starting to look more silver than black, but still somehow made Paulie seem half her age. Or maybe that was her eyes, a pale blue that seemed to take in everything and find it all amusing as hell.

Paulina seemed confused as she came down the hallway, looking at the guard who escorted her like he'd made some kind of mistake. But when she stepped through the door to the visitation room and laid those pale eyes on Celina, she gave a wide smile that shined like sunlight, filling the room with a warmth and a feeling of love and peace that Celina had never experienced before. She could immediately see why Cameron was willing to spend so long on a train just to be with his mother. Aside from the obvious family connection, Celina could see in an instant that Paulina Hauk was a genuinely good person, one of those rare people that lifted up everyone around her.

"Mrs. Hauk," said Celina, holding out her hand, "I'm Celina Maxwell. Thank you for meeting with me."

"Call me Paulie, please." Paulie's smile didn't dim in the slightest when Celina introduced herself, but her eyes flashed with a wicked kind of merriment as she held her hand a foot from Celina's and made a handshake motion in the air.

Celina's eyes widened at first, but then she nodded her head and pulled back her hand, remembering that the guards had told her that she was not allowed to make any physical contact with the inmates. Paulie had been in prison for... what was it? Fifteen years? Fifteen years during which Cameron had seen her nearly every weekend and hadn't been allowed to touch her even once. That was punishment for both of them, bordering on cruel and unusual.

Paulie gestured graciously for Celina to sit and they both took a seat, the hard bench pressing painfully against Celina's pelvic bones, despite the plastic coating.

"I've seen your face before," said Paulie. She lowered her voice and leaned in. "Though the name that came with it was different." She winked at Celina.

Celina frowned. "You've seen my face?"

"My son likes to draw," Paulie said, smiling. "This Reggie Moon he talks about"—she glanced over Celina's shoulder at the guard standing in the corner—"bears a striking resemblance to you."

It took Celina only half a heartbeat to pick up on the meaning of the glance.

"Funny how that happens sometimes," she said. "There's even a word for it, I think."

"Doppelgänger," said Paulie.

"Doppelgänger," said Celina at the same moment.

They both smiled, and Celina felt welcome in a way she hadn't felt since the last time she'd seen her father.

"I know Reggie, actually," said Celina. "We're friends. Close friends."

"That must make for some interesting conversations at parties."

Celina laughed. "I could tell you some stories."

Paulie smiled.

"I'm here on Reggie's behalf, actually." Paulie raised her eyebrows in question. "She's been seeing your son for a few weeks."

"I heard about that."

"Things are getting... more serious."

"I heard about that, too," Paulie grinned. She spread her fingers on the table. "Let me guess. Reggie is worried about opening up to Cameron, right? Worried about... sharing sensitive information?"

"Yes," said Celina, stunned at the guess, "Exactly."

"Is she afraid she might get hurt?"

Celina winced. "More afraid she might hurt him."

Paulie sat back and smiled. Not the room-filling sun smile she'd worn earlier, but a thoughtful smile, her eyes staring deep into Celina's eyes as if they were cataloguing her soul's deepest secrets.

"It speaks highly of Reggie that she would be worried about that kind of thing so early in the relationship."

"I know she's come to care for your son." A lump came up in Celina's throat and her mouth was suddenly as dry as hot sand. She swallowed hard. "Quite a bit, actually."

Paulie tilted her head to one side.

"And Reggie didn't expect that to happen?"

"No," Celina replied, softly, "Fuck, not at all." She put her hand over her mouth. "I'm sorry," she said from behind her fingers. "I didn't mean to curse."

Paulie shrugged and looked around her. "It's a prison, dear. You saying fuck is not exactly a lockdown incident."

Celina snorted a quick laugh and nodded toward her hands in her lap.

Paulie regarded Celina with a faint, wistful smile. "You know, I remember when I met Cameron's father for the first time." She looked toward the corner of the ceiling, calculating. "Forty years ago, now." Her eyes faded into memory again, but her smile grew brighter. "I was sixteen. He was nineteen." She closed her eyes and shook her head. "He was so fucking hot." She laughed, the sound like the tones of a vibraphone, and opened her eyes again. They were bright, but Celina could see the moisture building in them. "And so mysterious."

Celina raised one eyebrow. Even after all this time, after fifteen years in prison, she could see how much passion Paulie still felt for her husband. It flooded through the air between them, so infectious Celina couldn't help but smile.

"How long did it take him to open up to you?"

Paulie laughed again, that same mellow, musical sound that somehow made Celina's heart swell in her chest with the love it conveyed.

"Well, he was mysterious before I met him, but he laid himself wide open the first night we met. Told me everything. Anything I wanted to know."

"Did he do that with everyone?" Celina couldn't even imagine doing that. Her life was one of deception, of secrets kept closely guarded so no one could use them against her, to hurt her.

"Nope," Paulie said. "Just me. Said I was like truth serum." Her eyes faded into the past again. "He had all sorts of crazy ideas about how to live a better life, a freer life. Outside the confines of modern society." Paulie nodded her head slowly at the memory. "I was the one who took time to open up. I didn't know what to believe about him. Didn't know if he was feeding me a line of bullshit just to get me in bed."

"Did it work?"

Paulie barked a quick laugh. "Honey, I was hooked from the moment Sam Hauk laid those gorgeous blue eyes on me."

Cameron's father's name was Sam. Huh. And if Sam's eyes were that gorgeous, between him and Paulie it was no wonder Cameron had those incredible ice-blue eyes of his.

"I didn't care what he said," Paulie continued. "I was more afraid *he* wouldn't want *me* if I told him what there was to know."

The guard in the corner moved to stand beside the table. Paulie glanced up at the clock. Celina turned to look for herself. Only one minute left. The time had flown by.

Paulie leaned forward, folding her arms under her chest.

"You want my advice? You tell Reggie that life is short. Shorter than you think." Her face clouded for a brief moment, then that wistful smile returned. "Don't waste it worrying and wondering. You never know when you'll have another chance. At anything. Be bold the first time. Be brave."

The guard laid a hand softly on her shoulder and Paulie stood. Celina stood with her.

"At least then," Paulie said, "no matter what happens, you know you did what you could."

Celina watched her turn and walk toward the inmate door, the guard close at her side. As the guard held the door open for Paulie, she looked back at Celina.

"And Celina?" Paulie said. "Come visit me again sometime."

Celina smiled and nodded. "I'd like that"

Paulie gave her that magical, life-giving sunlight smile once more. "Me, too," she said.

Celina watched Paulie's orange-suited back move out of sight down the hallway, then wandered out of the visitation room in a daze. The large, round guard held the door open for her as she approached.

"That the first time you met Paulie?" she said.

Celina looked at her, confused for a moment, lost in her thoughts.

"Um, yeah," she said. "I'm friends with her son."

"Just friends?" she asked, eyebrows raised in question.

Celina's shock at the question must have shown on her face.

"Sorry," she laughed. "None of my business. But Cameron comes here a lot," the guard said by way of explanation. "And we all love Paulie." She shrugged. "We've kind of adopted Cameron as our own."

Celina nodded. She wasn't sure how to respond to the guard's question, though. Did she maintain the Reggie Moon ruse? How much would the guard have heard of Celina's conversation with Paulie? She had to assume the guards had heard everything. It was a prison, after all. Privacy was one right that didn't exist here.

"He's seeing my best friend."

The guard nodded and locked the visitation room door as Celina gathered her phone and her wallet from the small locker she'd left them in. The guard moved ahead of her and opened the door that led toward the front desk.

As Celina passed, the guard said, "You tell your friend to take care of Cameron." Celina turned to look at her. "He's a keeper." She started to close the door, then pulled it open again. "And tell her if she hurts him"—her face took on a look that made Celina see why the woman was an effective correctional officer—"she'll have a whole prison full of officers to answer to."

Celina smiled and nodded through the cross-hatched glass window as the woman closed the door and locked it again. As another guard escorted her down a grey concrete hallway toward the front desk to sign out, she pulled some of the puzzle pieces together in her mind.

Cameron. Sam Davis. Paulie Hauk.

She didn't know what Cameron was planning, but he was devoted to his mother. And Celina could see why. After only fifteen minutes, Celina could see how special Paulie Hauk was. After all this time, Cameron must be frantic to get her out of prison. She knew she would be, if Paulie were her mother. Hell, she might start trying to get Paulie out even now, after one short meeting.

She signed out at the desk and followed yet another guard through the maze of prison hallways toward the front gate. How would she get Paulie out, if she were Cameron? After fifteen years, he must have tried a few things already. An old-fashioned prison break was a fool's gambit. Near impossible to pull off, and it left you constantly on the run. Unless you were willing to have plastic surgery to change your whole appearance, you were signing up for a short, stressful life. Even with the surgery, you couldn't change your DNA. If you got caught doing something, anything that would get you booked, they'd eventually put things together.

She nodded to the guard at the gate and stepped out the door into the open air. The sun squatted on the horizon, red like a forest fire behind the trees across the parking lot to the west. The scrape of her footsteps on the salted blacktop was the only sound in the still of the early evening.

Celina knew from the information she'd dug up that Cameron had gone to law school, which suggested he had tried the more conventional routes first, appealing through the court system, looking for angles and loopholes. Without getting his hands dirty working the unjust side of the justice system, that was a long-shot approach, too. Would Cameron have known that? Would he have known which judges to bribe, which official palms to grease? Did he have the financial resources to do it? Even if he had, Celina didn't think that path would have worked. He would have had to have done it before Paulie was convicted.

She got in the Tesla and sat behind the wheel, staring through the windshield as the flame of the sun slowly doused itself on the horizon line.

Cameron had gotten his law degree years ago, and it hadn't led to Paulie's release, so it must not have worked. Why, then, would he be getting a degree in criminology? The law degree was a long-shot, but it made some sense. A degree in criminology was about catching criminals. It would do nothing to help free his mother.

Could just be interested in criminology, pursuing the degree for his own benefit? It seemed unlikely. And why would he use a fake identity? There were no outstanding warrants under his real name. And a criminology degree would lend him an air of legitimacy, like he was a reformed criminal. It wasn't much, wouldn't get his mother out, but it wouldn't hurt his chances. If he got caught using a fake name, he'd be screwed.

And then there was the DOJ building. That's where Celina had first met Cameron, when he was sneaking around the DOJ building at night. What the hell could he possibly have been doing there? She was pretty sure he wasn't just checking out the architecture, trying to beat the tourist crowds.

And he'd had the Nestech glasses. Another mystery. She could see why he would have been wearing them that night. Celina had her own tech tools that she used on jobs, tools that not only let her see in the dark and monitor what was around her, but that hid her from cameras and other surveillance technology. And even from Dr. Nestrom's glasses, she'd been happy to discover when she tested it. But she still didn't know how Cameron had come to have the glasses at all. She might have to reach out to Kat or Brandon Nestrom to see what they knew about it. If they would even tell her. Corporate frenemies, and all that.

Celina sighed as she stepped on the brake and put the car into gear. The headlights came on, bright in the new dark, and swung through the parking lot like twin daggers.

More like prison searchlights. She laughed hollowly as she wound through what passed for rush hour traffic in the small town, working her way back toward the highway. She had a long drive ahead of her, and she wasn't looking forward to it like she had that morning.

She'd come all that way to meet Cameron's mother, to satisfy her own curiosity and to try to understand Cameron a little better. She'd met Paulie, and she was glad of it. More than curiosity, she'd liked Paulie Hauk. She had no doubt she'd be back again.

But when it came to understanding Cameron, she was just as in the dark as ever.

40

THERE WERE ONLY four weeks of class left, and Cam was glad he'd gotten his work done early. He would have no time that week for schoolwork.

His friends mostly left him to himself, busy with their own end-of-term crush. After the last four weeks of class, they'd have one week, called dead week, to study for finals, then one week during which finals were scheduled. And then they would be done. They'd have one more week to hang out, party, get their final grades, and, if all went well, to graduate.

Jem and the others were totally focused now. Even Motsu was working hard. And, somehow, he and Annie had become inseparable. According to Sarah, they spent all their time outside of class together, but nothing had happened between them. Yet. To both Sarah and Cam, that seemed out of character for Motsu. But he seemed genuinely happy, and Annie was practically floating.

"You okay, Sam?" Jem asked over his burger one day at lunch. It was just him and Sarah at the table with Cam. The others hadn't arrived yet.

"Yeah," Cam replied, scooting his stool closer to the high table with a metallic screech against the concrete floor. "Why?"

"I don't know." Jem narrowed his eyes. "Something about you seems... different, somehow."

Cam scoffed and bit into his burger.

"Do you see it, too?" Jem asked Sarah.

"Yep," she said, her mouth full of cheeseburger. "You're like a different person."

A chill raced down Cam's spine.

"What?" Cam said, wishing his voice wasn't wavering so much. He cleared his throat. "Don't be... what... what are you talking about?"

Jem stared at Cam, face scowled in thought, then snapped his fingers. "It's ever since you started up with Reggie," he said.

Sarah nodded in agreement.

"It's like you're a totally different person now." Jem grinned at him. "She's changed you, Sam."

The chill raced down Cam's spine again, this time for a different reason. He tried to stammer a reply, but his mind was suddenly racing in a thousand different directions at once.

He nearly jumped off of his stool when a hand clapped down on his shoulder.

"Who's changed him?" said Reggie, standing beside Cam, one arm draped over his shoulder.

Cam pulled in a breath, Reggie's lavender scent immediately calming him, and sighed in relief.

"You," said Jem. "You took our Sam Davis and made him into a totally different person."

"Molded him in my image," said Reggie, giving Cam a quick peck on the cheek. "Isn't that what women do?"

"Fuck yeah," said Sarah around another mouthful of burger. She wiped one hand on a napkin and held it up in the air. Reggie high-fived it with a loud smack.

"Pfshh," said Cam, waving one hand at Jem in dismissal. "Whatever. I'm still the same Sam Davis."

I am Sam Davis.

I am Sam Davis.

He'd gotten lax lately. Something about Reggie, all the time they were spending together, just the two of them. He was letting his guard down, losing focus. He'd even told her about the woman in black, for fuck's sake.

I am Sam Davis.

For eight more weeks, I am Sam Davis.

"Nope," said Jem. "You used to be Sam. Fucking. Davis." He chopped one hand up and down with each word and scrunched his face tight, like an angry drill sergeant. "Now, you're Sam fucking Davis." He held both hands in loose fists and swiveled his hips in his chair, biting his lower lip in a cringey nerd-dance.

Sarah said, "More like Sam. Fucking. Davis." She snarled one side of her lip and pumped her hands toward her thrusting hips with each word.

"Oh, really?" Reggie said with a grin. "What are you telling these guys when I'm not around, Sam?"

Elbow on the table, Sam smacked his forehead to his palm and peeked over both shoulders to see if anyone was watching. "You guys are fucking embarrassing, is what *you* are."

Reggie laughed at all of them, a loose, uninhibited laugh that Sam couldn't help but smile at. She took the stool next to his.

"Are we right or are we right?" Jem asked Reggie, holding his hands wide.

"Right about what?" said Annie, arriving with Motsu at her side.

"I recuse myself from this case," said Reggie.

"Sam's different," said Sarah around another bite. "Reggie's changed him."

"Totally," said Motsu, pulling up two stools from a neighboring table and holding one for Annie before sitting in the other. Sam and Sarah exchanged a quick glance and a smile. "Reggie has you whipped, my friend. Totally pus—"

"Don't say it," said Annie, Sarah, and Reggie in unison.

"Er," Motsu froze in place for a moment, then cleared his throat and straightened his posture. "I mean, she's whipped you into shape." He nodded over-earnestly. "I think you've changed for the better," he said.

The three women looked at each other, seeming to come to a tacit agreement.

"Acceptable recovery," said Reggie.

Sarah shrugged and nodded as she bit into a handful of fries.

"Best we can hope for, at this point," said Annie with a sigh.

Motsu widened his eyes at Jem and Sam. Jem just raised his eyebrows, but Sam grinned at Motsu. He'd never seen him like this before. Usually, he just rolled in and did his Motsu thing, self-centered and sexist, in a charming way, putting everything out there and not caring what anyone else thought. Maybe Motsu was the one who was starting to change. Maybe he was starting to grow up.

And if so, Sam would bet anything that Annie was the reason for it.

"Listen," said Sam, "I'm gonna be holed up this week, trying to get a handle on everything, so you're probably not going to see me much."

"Maybe you haven't changed after all," said Jem.

Sam gave him a curt, sarcastic smile.

"Doesn't matter," said Motsu, squeezing three packets of ketchup onto his burger wrapper and dragging some fries through it. "We're all going to be studying our asses off for the rest of term, anyway, right?"

He stuffed the fries in his mouth and looked up at them all while he chewed. The rest of the table just stared at him in silence, everyone but Annie and Reggie showing varying expressions of shock on their faces. Sam had never, not once in three years, heard Motsu say a single word about studying, let alone staying in to study. He was usually the one trying to get everyone else to blow off their work to go to a party or a bar downtown.

"What?" he said.

All eyes shifted from Motsu to Annie, who chewed her food quietly beside him. When the eyes fell on her, she just smiled sweetly and kept chewing.

"And you all think I'm the one who's changed?" muttered Sam.

Only problem was, they were right. Sam had changed. Since he'd been spending so much time with Reggie, he'd shown more Cam than Sam. He'd let his guard down, let his persona slip.

He was lucky that Jem was a good enough friend to say something. He didn't think he or any of the others suspected the truth. The truth was too crazy to even register as a possibility for them, he was sure. But there were others out there, Sam's professors, perhaps, with enough criminology experience for alarm bells to ring if Sam were to let his guard slip much further.

And that was the last thing he needed. He was in the home stretch with school. He had issues to resolve, the main one being the goddamn three-thousandths of a point gap he still had to make up with Reggie in their GPAs. But he could worry about that next week. For now, he had information to collect, and only one week to get it.

He and Reggie walked back to the apartment and said goodbye with a long, lingering kiss that almost weakened Cam's resolve. He wanted nothing more than to spend the afternoon in bed with her, the slant sun slowly drawing a finger of fading light across the bedcovers as he and Reggie lay naked beneath them, giving homework a whole new meaning.

Instead, Cam watched Reggie walk away, then shut the door, pushed the thought away, and set his mind to focus on his plan instead. He needed a double espresso and his laptop, in that order.

Coffee in hand, the rich scent alone sharpening his mind,

fighting off the stupor his lunch threatened, Cam sat at his desk, threw open his laptop, and set to work.

In his initial break-in at the DOJ, he had been hoping to find a desktop computer in Stratham's office that he could hack, or even a wireless keyboard where he could capture keystrokes. At the very least, he thought he might be able to sniff the DOJ network for a route into Stratham's laptop.

But he hadn't gotten far enough to have a look around Stratham's office, and after weeks of further research, he'd discovered that he wouldn't have found what he needed, anyway. Stratham used his laptop and only his laptop. He didn't connect to any networks, not even at the campaign office, using his cellphone as a hotspot whenever he needed to connect to the internet. He never used peripheral devices, and he backed everything up to a thumb drive he always kept in his front pants pocket.

Those were Cam's new targets. Either the laptop or, preferably, the thumb drive. The drive would be easier to transport and conceal, and it would likely take Stratham longer to notice that it was missing. But if Stratham always kept it in his pocket, how could Cam get to it?

He could pick Stratham's pocket easy enough. But Stratham had seen Cam before, on the yacht of the billionaire Russian arms dealer last summer. Cam had operated under an alias then, but Stratham would recognize Cam's face. Cam was sure of that. If he approached Stratham from the front, the job would be a thousand times more difficult.

And coming up behind Stratham would be tricky, too. People have an innate sense for when someone is sneaking up on them, unless they're distracted. If Cam could get Stratham into a crowd, he could pick his pocket easily. But Stratham was rarely in crowds, as far as Cam could tell. Unless he was at a fundraising event, Stratham tended to be a loner.

He could break into Stratham's house and steal it while he

was sleeping or showering. Cam did some quick research and found no private residence listed for Stratham. The only contact information listed for Stratham in Washington D.C. was the campaign office and his office at the DOJ building. Did the guy sleep at the fucking office? It wouldn't surprise Cam, actually. Stratham lived for the campaign, it seemed.

He checked hotel reservations and Air BnBs and came up similarly blank. Stratham could be using a fake name, but even his credit card charges showed nothing.

Fake name and a fake credit card? It was certainly possible, but Cam didn't have the time to figure it all out.

And without any address, he'd have to tail Stratham twenty-four hours a day to find out where he lived. Cam didn't have time for that bullshit, either.

However he was going to get that laptop or that thumb drive, it would have to happen at the DOJ building. And it would have to happen this Friday.

Stratham always met with Jenkins on Friday afternoons at the end of the work day, then usually stayed at work until well after midnight. He could try something at Jenkins' office, but Cam didn't know if there were guards or private security that he would have to contend with. He knew Jenkins had a security detail, so he supposed there would be something. That was a complication that Cam didn't want to worry about. Plus, he wouldn't want Jenkins to see his face prior to the graduation meeting. He couldn't wear a ski mask and just waltz into the office of the favored candidate for president.

Jenkins' office was out. If he was to get to Stratham in person, he'd have to do it in Stratham's office or while Stratham was walking to or from Jenkins' office.

Confronting Stratham directly would be a desperate tactic, a last resort among last resorts. More than likely, it would result in Cam's arrest before it would result in his getting the information he needed. Stratham would undoubtedly recognize Cam from the yacht trip the previous summer. The man had a mind for names and faces. It was one of the things that made him so good at his job. And that night on the yacht had been memorable. Not every cruise in the bay involves the murder of a billionaire Russian arms dealer. Even fewer involve its cover-up. And even if Cam wore a mask, Stratham would know his body type and shape, the way he moved. He wouldn't recognize them from the yacht, but those were still characteristics that Cam would rather not reveal.

He cursed himself for getting so distracted for the last several weeks. If he'd had more time, he might have been able to come up with some way to do this job. He might have learned more about Stratham's schedule or his habits. He could have found some hidden server somewhere, or an online backup he could copy.

But there was no point in worrying about what could have been. His parents had always taught him that. Plans inevitably failed at some point, and stewing over the failure just robbed yourself of precious time. Better to focus even more completely on the moment, to absorb whatever information and opportunity it presented to form a new plan to get from where you actually were to where you wanted to be.

And besides, Cam wouldn't trade the last few weeks for anything. Just thinking about Reggie sent a shiver of warmth up his spine and a flush of heat to much lower parts of his body.

He caught himself short at the thought. Wouldn't trade the last few weeks for anything? What about his mother's release? Would he trade it for that?

He thought back to what his mother had told him, that she'd rather spend her life in prison knowing Cam was outside with someone he loved than spend her life in freedom watching Cam be alone. She would want him to choose Reggie over herself.

But Cam would never do that. Couldn't even imagine it?
Could he?

He closed his eyes, took a deep breath, and shook the thought from his head. It was a moot point. Once Reggie learned the truth about his fake identity as Sam Davis, she would want nothing more to do with him. Ever. There was no point in thinking about a trade-off, because there would be nothing to trade.

No, Reggie was the best thing that had ever happened to Cam, but that relationship was doomed from the start. He would enjoy it as much as his increasing guilt would allow while he could, but his primary focus was still on freeing his mother.

He just had to figure out a way to get past Vernon Stratham and his fucking impenetrable security habits.

41

THE REST of the week passed far too quickly. By late Friday evening, Cam was near panic. He still had no plan for getting the laptop or the thumb drive from Stratham. He'd checked every angle, every scheme, every ruse he could think of and still came up empty. The only tactic that seemed remotely possible was one he despised: violence.

He could hold Stratham at gunpoint in his office at the DOJ and demand the thumb drive. Or, better yet, he could sneak up behind him with a plumber's wrench or a rag soaked in chloroform and knock him out, then steal the drive from his pocket while he was unconscious.

Cam didn't know enough about Stratham to know whether or not he had any experience with self-defense or hand-to-hand combat. That was part of the problem. Not enough time to do a proper job on the research. He hadn't seen any evidence in Stratham's past of military service, intelligence training, or anything other than a life spent in finance and computers. But lack of evidence was not the same as proof that something didn't exist.

And Cam himself was not exactly Jackie Chan when it came to dealing with others. His family abhorred violence. He'd never hit anyone in his life, or been hit, for that matter. He didn't carry weapons, not even fake ones. He never threatened innocent bystanders during a job. He'd barely even raised his voice.

Some criminals—maybe even most criminals—resort to a life of crime out of anger. They lack the skills to succeed, or they feel they've been betrayed by the system or short-changed by a society rigged against them. They're often correct in that feeling. The world is rigged in favor of the rich and the connected. That's why Cam and his family had no moral compunctions about robbing those kinds of people.

But for the Hauks, crime was a mental game. It was a puzzle, a challenge to find a way to get what they wanted from people who could afford to lose it, and to do it in a way that hurt no one (other than the rich victims, and then only in their balance sheet) and left no chance that the Hauks would be caught.

Conversely, the angry criminal used crime as much to exorcise their demons and release their pent-up aggression as for anything else. These are the criminals who pistol-whip the old lady in the teller's line at the bank the moment they walk in screaming about a hold-up. These are the ones who abuse women and threaten children. These are the ones who race down the sidewalk, twenty-dollar bills fluttering behind their hastily zipped shoulder bag, firing their guns at random over their shoulder at the cops.

These are the ones whose random over-the-shoulder gunshots kill innocent fathers who just happen to be standing on the sidewalk, with their wife and son in the car watching them die.

And now Cam was actually considering stooping to their level. It was the cardinal rule of engagement for the Hauk family: no one gets hurt. And yet here he was, trying to figure out how he could incapacitate Stratham and steal his thumb drive. As if Cam had any expertise in that approach whatsoever.

But there was no other way. His parents always said violence was a failure of imagination. Now Cam's time was up, and his imagination had failed. His mother's freedom was on the line. If he was ever going to break that family rule, this was a worthy time to do it.

The weather was in the low-fifties, warm for late winter at this time of night, near midnight. He dressed in his black jeans, long-sleeved black t-shirt, and high-collared black pullover, stuffed his black beanie in his back pocket, and sat on the futon couch to pull on his black socks and black sneakers. He didn't have a ski mask. Didn't own one. Never had. But he still had a rubber mask of Donald Trump from Halloween last year in his closet. That would work as well as anything. He stuffed that inside his belt and under his shirt. It pressed against the small of his back, the cold rubber irritating his skin, a reminder of his failure of imagination.

He slid the Nestech glasses into the chest pocket of his pullover and headed into the night.

Across the street to the northeast of the Department of Justice building is a luxury condominium and shopping area called Market Square. There is another Market Square one mile to the southwest that is actually a location for a recurring farmers market. Cam could never quite figure out the nomenclature for these places, but it was Washington, after all, and he gave up expecting it to make sense years ago. He was quite sure the rich investors in the luxury condos were spending a lot of money to differentiate their property from the lowly farmers market to the south. They deserved what they got for their lack of imagination.

Just as Cam deserved what he got for his own lack of imagination.

Skulking about in the shadows of the Department of Justice building near midnight is generally not a good idea. However, at midnight on a Friday night, especially late in March, when the weather was hinting at spring, it was much more acceptable to skulk if in reasonable proximity to a shopping district. Spending trumps security, after all.

Across from Market Square, straight east from the DOJ building, was a quiet little park outside the National Archives Museum, built around a small memorial dedicated to Franklin Delano Roosevelt. It was no more than a ring of shoulder-high shrubs, a few rows of flowers, and an inscribed marble block, but it brought a lovely moment of peace and beauty to a corner that was otherwise dominated by Washington monoliths and ostentatious wealth. More importantly for Cam's purposes, it afforded a sidewalk bench, set between tall bushy trees in the adjoined shadows of two streetlamps. From it, his back toward the shopping center, he could observe the DOJ building without risk of drawing attention to himself, prepare himself mentally for the job, attune his senses to the space, and choose his moment to act.

It was something of a ritual. His parents taught him that every space, every situation was a fluid, living thing. When you're a surgeon, you don't operate without connecting the monitors to the patient and seeing what the vital signs are like in the moments before you drag your scalpel through the first layers of skin and muscle and fat. When picking a pocket, you take some time to absorb and match the rhythms and movements of the mark.

Similarly, you don't start a job without first attuning yourself to the vital signs of the space. How many people are there? Are they relaxed or on edge? Every space has an energy, one that shifts and flows over the course of the day and night. What is the energy of the space? Is it slow or fast? Hot or cool? Gritty or smooth? There is no right or wrong, just different approaches to different conditions.

Cam was hoping for a slow, cool, smooth feel, with relaxed, happy guards inside. As he sat on the bench, the cold of the evening seeping into his bones through the wooden slats, he felt slowness, felt the relaxed happiness in the air. A Friday night with nice weather lent itself to that feeling. The shopping area was crowded and boisterous. That feeling would leak through into the surrounding buildings.

But as he sat, soaking everything in, slowing his breathing and his heartbeat, stilling his mind, Cam felt something beneath all of that. Beneath the slow, relaxed happiness was an edge, a bite, like the poise of a predator's jaw opened wide just before it clamped down on the neck of its unsuspecting prey. That feeling was colder, more brittle, mean and suspicious.

His parents would case job sites for months, visiting at various times of the day and night on various days of the week, trying to absorb the patterns of the energy of the space. Looking for ideal conditions, ideal energy. The comings and goings of employees, guards, regular customers or visitors. The impact of the news or the weather on the space. Their friends would laugh at them for this preparation, for this new-agey woo-woo shit. Until they realized that Cam's parents, in decades of work, had never been caught. Never even been suspected, that they knew about. Until fate dealt them that one bad hand, their record had been perfect.

And now here Cam was again, breaking more of the rules he'd been taught and had trained with since he was a kid. He hadn't studied the rhythms of the area, not since the prior winter. These kinds of things tend to change with the seasons. Tonight's conditions were not great. Too volatile. According to his training, he should walk away and wait for a better day.

But he didn't have time to wait. He had to act tonight, regardless of the conditions.

He checked his phone. 1AM. Time to go. He switched the phone off and slid it into his pocket.

The last thing he did was put on the Nestech glasses. At a casual glance, they looked like any other glasses, but Cam didn't want to risk calling attention to himself or to the glasses, so he waited until the last moment to put them on.

When he pressed the button on the arm of the glasses near the temple, the floating blue Nestech logo appeared in his view for a few seconds, then faded to reveal a white-on-blue outline of his surroundings, from the trees beside him to the marble FDR memorial in front of him to the DOJ building across the street beyond that. A moment later, the outline had faded and Cam was looking at the scene as if he were looking through a normal pair of clear eyeglass lenses, with the exception that he could see clearly in what would be shadows, could make out more detail in what would be bright lights. And he could read the inscriptions on the walls beside the doors of the DOJ building across the street, inscriptions that he'd normally need to be standing in front of to make out, but which were as legible from across the street at night as they would be under a magnifying glass at high noon. And he could see the identities and movements of every person around him, including every guard within the DOJ building. The people in his field of view looked as they normally would. Everyone else appeared as shadowy human shapes.

Cam had the same thought he had every single time he put the glasses on: this technology was absolutely amazing.

And then he heard the voice.

"Hello," it said, directly in front of him in his spatial field. Then the sound panned to each side. In his left ear, the voice whispered "Cameron Hauk". In his right ear, it whispered "Sam Davis".

The voice—her voice—was no less alluring today than it had been the first time he'd heard it, the day the woman in black had left them on his doorstep. Aside from that day, this was the first time Cam had worn the glasses since.

Her use of his alias and his real name didn't shock him anymore. He knew to expect it. But the voice still stirred him. He felt a stiffening in his core at just the sound of it. The voice was sultry, hot, intimate.

But there was something else about it. Something familiar.

After a moment, Cam laughed out loud, then covered his mouth and looked around to see if anyone had noticed. No one had.

The voice, the sultry intimacy. It reminded him of Reggie's voice. No wonder he'd felt himself stiffening. Just the thought of Reggie was enough to get him going. Something about the voice of the woman in black reminded Cam of Reggie. The intimacy of it, no doubt. Through the sound output of the glasses, the voice was whispering softly right into his ear. The only other person to do that lately was Reggie.

The thought of Reggie gave Cam a pang of guilt, but it also comforted him. He liked the thought that Reggie would be with him on this job, even if only in his mind.

The thought that the woman in black might be with him, too, made him clench his jaw. She'd hacked the glasses and put her voice into the startup routine. What else had she done? Was she using the glasses to track him right now? Was she hacked into the feed somehow, so she could see what Cam was seeing?

It didn't matter. He didn't know who the woman in black really was, but she'd been slinking around the DOJ building in the dark that night, just like him. She was unlikely to report him to the cops, even if she was watching him right then.

Cam waited for the light at the crosswalk and crossed the street calmly, slowly, hands relaxed in his pockets. Just another pedestrian out late on a Friday night. He kept his breathing deep and slow, slowed his movements to what seemed like a crawl. When we get nervous, our senses heighten and our sense of time speeds up. In order to seem normal and relaxed to a casual observer, it's helpful for us to move at what seems, from our perspective, to be a very slow speed. After factoring in the dilation effect of the anxiety, we wind up looking normal.

Cam stepped to the side of the sidewalk outside the DOJ building and stopped, his back to the street, his face hidden in shadow. He looked down at his hands like he was checking his phone, hoping no one would notice the lack of a screen glow in the night. When the Nestech glasses told him when the area was clear and no one was around to see him, he stepped calmly off the sidewalk, walked across the grounds to the DOJ building, and slipped into a hidden back entrance he'd hacked before his last job, hoping the hack hadn't been discovered and fixed.

It hadn't. He was inside the building. There was no turning back now.

For better or for worse, he had a job to do.

42

CAM SLIPPED EASILY through the dark halls of the Department of Justice building, his black sneakers making no noise in the hush of deep night, the polished marble floors on the third floor gleaming silver in the low after-hours lighting. He passed the bank of two elevators in silence, watching the movements of the security guards in the viewscreen of his Nestech glasses. Seven were on duty that night, two of them stationed in the surveillance room, another at the front desk, and four more making their rounds throughout the building. Among many other advantages the glasses afforded, Cam could move with more speed and ease knowing exactly where the guards were.

There were more people in the building that night than there had been the last time Cam had broken in. Then it had been a holiday, with most people at home celebrating with friends and family. Tonight was a normal work week. Even at one AM on a Friday, there was still a smattering of employees at their desks or in their offices, either the most dedicated workers or the loneliest of leftovers.

Fortunately, the cubicle farm around Stratham's office on the third floor was empty. Stratham himself was still with Jenkins in the Attorney General's office, probably working late to finalize plans before Stratham left for his two-month fundraising tour. Jenkins hadn't officially declared his candidacy for the presidency yet, but the pundits all expected it to be imminent. Could even happen during Jenkins' speech at Cam's graduation, for all Cam knew. Seemed as good a venue as any, and it would explain Stratham's extended absence. He would be lining up not just campaign donations, but political support for the Attorney General, as well.

The AG's office was on the fifth floor. In his glasses, Cam counted the shapes of eight private bodyguards stationed outside the double office doors and arrayed down the hallway near the elevators and the entrances to the stairwells. He could see the outline of another bodyguard inside the room, near the outlines of Stratham and Jenkins, helpfully labelled by the Nestech AI. With a tap of a button, he could even switch to the camera feeds from inside the office, could see the two men in high-resolution black-and-white video, sitting in high-backed leather armchairs, two crystal tumblers and a half-empty bottle of whiskey on the table between them. Stratham's laptop was open on the table, as well. If Stratham was true to form, he'd have his thumb drive in his pocket. If the office had had an audio feed, Cam could have used the glasses to tap into that, too. Maybe even record it to get the evidence he needed. But no such luck. He had only silent video, and so far, it showed nothing incriminating.

Cam had expected he'd have to wait once he got inside. He'd hoped that Stratham would be done with the AG by now and alone in his own office, but he knew there was a good chance that he wouldn't be. But Cam didn't want to risk missing Stratham altogether by waiting until even later in the evening. Better to be inside and early than outside and out of luck.

With all the security in place, there was no practical way for Cam to get into the AG's office. He would have to wait for

Stratham to come out, to get someplace where he would be alone and vulnerable.

No better place than Stratham's office itself. Stratham would eventually leave the Attorney General, and he'd likely go back to his office, to pack up his computer and grab his coat, if nothing else.

The third floor was a maze of office cubicles. Their high walls were covered in a fabric that had the texture of burlap and the smell of ancient must. They blocked any visibility across the room. You'd have to be seven feet tall to get an unobstructed view across the space. It was a good place to get lost.

Or to hide.

Cam wound his way through the labyrinth until he stood outside Stratham's office door. Stratham's keycard was in Cam's pocket. Once, it was central to Cam's plan. But now it had become a last resort.

The daytime guards at the DOJ were well-trained, but not well-armed. They carried radios and little else. They were meant to act as warnings and deterrents.

The nighttime guards were another matter. Most were former D.C. cops. They carried guns and batons and knew how to use them.

If Cam used the keycard to gain entry to the office, he would have only a few minutes before one of those security guards would come knocking. They'd see the keycard swipe on their systems, would know that Stratham was still with the AG, and would get suspicious.

That would not work out well for Cam.

And that was assuming the keycard was even still active. He'd lifted it from Stratham's bag nine months earlier. Stratham would have had to get a replacement keycard. It would have been standard practice to deactivate the old one at the same time.

Stratham was clever, though. He might have left it active as a trap, had the security team set up alerts for whenever the card was used, so that they could catch the thief. That's what Cam would have done.

On his first break-in, Cam was happy to trigger the alarms. He had planned to be in and out of Stratham's office before any guards could get there. But this was a different scenario, a different plan, and it required a different approach.

Cam could break into the office the old-fashioned way, but he hadn't had time to research any alarm systems that might have been placed on Stratham's door. It was a better play for Cam to wait and watch. Stratham was a workaholic. Cam was ninety percent sure that Stratham, even at this late hour, would come back to his office to work after he was done meeting with the AG. When he did, Cam would see his movements in his glasses. Cam could just sit and wait for Stratham to arrive, wait for him to unlock his office, attack him from behind, knock him out, and take what he needed from Stratham and from his office.

Cam waited in an office chair in the shadows inside a cubicle across the aisle from Stratham's office. He pulled on a pair of thin leather gloves he'd brought and stuffed his hands in the pockets of his pullover, fidgeting with the small syringe inside.

For the hundredth time that evening, Cam pulled the syringe from his pocket and checked to make sure it was ready. The cartridge of the syringe had two chambers, one filled with Benadryl, the other with a mixture of Haldol and Ativan. Unless Stratham had gained a hundred pounds since last August, the dosage should be plenty to sedate him for an hour or two.

The syringe was designed to be used one-handed. Cam would sneak up from behind as Stratham opened the office door. He'd jab Stratham in the side of the neck with the needle and press a button. The two chambers would mix together, and the resulting cocktail would empty into Stratham's neck muscle. It was quick, easy, non-lethal, and relatively painless. And a type of violence Cam thought he could handle.

Or so he hoped.

He didn't have to wait long to find out. Twenty minutes later, he saw movement in his glasses two floors above. Two bodyguards stayed by the fifth-floor elevator while the others fanned out down the building's two stairwells, with a bodyguard stopping on each floor, including the garage level.

A moment later, the Attorney General and Stratham exited the AG's office, accompanied by the last bodyguard. They'd be taking the elevator, apparently, and the AG's security team was making sure no would-be assailant would stop the ride to get on, sweeping the stairwells at the same time for good measure.

Cam felt adrenaline flood his bloodstream as he watched the figures of Jenkins and Stratham get on the elevator on the fifth floor, accompanied by the three bodyguards. His muscles tensed, and he focused again on his breathing to slow his mind, slow his movements, and steady his pounding heartbeat.

The elevator descended to the fourth floor.

Stratham would get off on Floor Three. He'd come down the hallway to either the north door or the south door. Either way, there were only two routes to his office. He'd either come across the room and straight down the aisle toward the windows, or he'd cut down to the windows earlier and walk parallel to them.

Didn't matter to Cam. As soon as Stratham arrived at his office door, while he was swiping his keycard with his back toward the cubicle across the aisle where Cam hid, Cam would act.

Cam watched in his glasses as the elevator passed the fourth floor and the bodyguard stationed there peeled off and went down the north stairwell.

The elevator kept moving, toward the third floor.

Cam's muscles tensed again as the elevator approached the third floor stop.

And kept on going.

Cam's slow, steady breaths hitched. Panic flashed over him and the back of his neck broke out in a cold, prickly sweat.

Stratham wasn't going to his office.

Fuck.

Cam was on his feet and moving before his thoughts could even form in his mind.

Where would Stratham be going? He must be going home. But how? He wouldn't walk, not at this hour. Would he catch a cab? Call an Uber? Would the AG's driver drop him off?

Cam had to get to Stratham before he got into whatever vehicle he was taking. Jenkins and his bodyguards either drop Stratham off at the ground floor or they'd take him all the way to the garage level below. Cam didn't know which it would be, but he bet that they'd take him to the garage.

It was a risk, an assumption, but a calculated one. Even if Stratham wound up having to ride back up one floor to catch a cab, they'd err on the side of the Attorney General's safety rather than Stratham's convenience.

Cam had to get to the garage before the elevator did.

He couldn't take the second of the two elevators in the building. It would be too slow, and too obvious. He had to take the stairs.

Only problem was, the AG's bodyguards were also using the stairs. The bodyguard on the third floor had already headed down the south stairwell.

Cam burst through the door into the third-floor hallway and forced himself to take a beat to examine the situation. He fell back on his parents' training. Plans always fell apart. Life always intervened. You had to stay calm, keep your mind open, and use what life was giving you instead of getting angry or anxious about the failure of the plan.

Easier said than done, but the Nestech glasses gave Cam a huge advantage. He watched the bodyguards on the stairs. The fourth-floor guard had taken the south stairwell from the fifth floor to the fourth, then taken the north stairwell down from there. The third-floor guard had done the opposite. He'd taken the north stairwell down from the fifth floor to the third, then taken the south stairwell down once the elevator passed.

That had to be their sweep pattern. Come down one stairwell to their station, then go down the opposite stairwell to the rendezvous point, probably the garage-level elevator stop. If the pattern held, the second-floor guard would take the north stair down to the ground floor and the ground-floor guard would take the south stair to the garage.

The elevator was currently between the third floor and the second floor.

Cam raced toward the north stairwell.

With the movement in his body and the focus in his mind, Cam felt his heart rate settle, his muscles loosen. It was always easier to be in motion than to sit and wait. Too much time to think when you were waiting. Action was easier.

His parents chided him often for feeling that way. They told him to be patient, to focus less on the outcome and more on the process.

Only this time, the outcome was all that mattered.

It took every ounce of self-control he had not to throw open the heavy wooden stairwell door and let it bang off the walls. But there was a bodyguard in the stairwell below him, soon to be two bodyguards.

This time, he did have to listen to his parents. He had to be patient. He had to be silent.

The bodyguard from the fourth floor was only half a flight below Cam on the stairs. If Cam had guessed right about their sweep pattern, the second-floor guard would soon join him. Both of them would be trying to beat the elevator to the garage floor. That worked in Cam's favor. With them moving quickly, Cam wouldn't have to worry about sneaking past them on the stairs.

He'd just have to worry about sneaking past all eight of them in the hallway on the garage level.

He forced himself to breathe, to slow his mind and his movements, to let his muscles relax. He stepped softly down the stairs, watching the guards move ahead of him in his glasses, keeping one eye on the elevator.

Fortunately, the bodyguards were quick and took their jobs seriously. They reached the garage level before the elevator had reached the ground floor.

As soon as he heard the garage-level door click shut, Cam sprinted, taking the stairs four at a time, practically jumping from landing to landing. He didn't care about the noise, at that point. He only cared about getting down to the garage before Stratham did.

As he raced, his mind flew through the contingencies. If the elevator dropped Jenkins off and Stratham rode back up, Cam could easily manage the stairs. He'd run back to the first floor and wait to see if Stratham got off. If he did, Cam could catch him there. If he didn't, if the elevator continued to the third floor, Cam could beat the elevator up, return to the original plan, and meet Stratham at his office.

But there was one more possibility, one that sent a shiver snaking up Cam's spine. What if Stratham rode with Jenkins? Cam would have to contend with the full squad of bodyguards to get to Stratham before he got in the car.

That would be disastrous.

That would require desperate measures.

As he reached the bottom of the stairwell and put one hand on the door handle, ready to go through, Cam watched the elevator descend from the first floor to the garage level. He asked himself if he was at the point where he would resort to desperate measures.

He thought of Jem, Sarah, Annie, and Motsu. If he exposed himself and failed, he would lose them all.

He thought of Reggie and realized that they were all lost to him already. The man they knew was a fiction. The real Cameron Hauk was an enemy to them. Sooner or later, they were going to find that out.

Then he thought of his mother, thought of her spending the rest of her life in prison, thought of her dying in prison.

He tightened his grip on the door handle, steeled his muscles for action. He put his other hand in his pocket and held the syringe, ready to strike.

At this point, he'd resort to anything to free his mother.

Even desperate measures.

43

Celina could not believe what she was seeing.

Cameron Hauk wasn't the only one with high-tech tools, and Dr. Christopher Nestrom, genius though he was, wasn't the only person capable of making AR glasses. Celina and her father had developed their own tech—contact lenses, not glasses—before he died, and Celina had perfected it in the years since.

Tonight, she'd been watching the drama in the Department of Justice building unfold from the safety of her own hidey-hole, an empty office on the first floor.

Did Cameron really think he could take on eight trained bodyguards in a narrow hallway by himself? She'd spent enough time with him over the last few months to know he didn't stand a chance. And that syringe in his pocket only had one dose. He'd need eight doses just to incapacitate the guards.

And a fucking grenade.

And probably a fucking machine gun.

And someone who knew how to use the fucking gun.

And someone who knew how to use the fucking grenade.

Honestly, the whole situation was ridiculous, and Cameron was too smart for this bullshit. The man wouldn't hurt a fly, and here he thought he could win in hand-to-hand combat with a squad of trained fucking ex-military bodyguards?

She quickened her steps toward the first-floor stairwell, pausing for a precious few seconds to let one of the DOJ security guards—ex-police, not ex-military, but only slightly less dangerous—pass by unawares, then slipped silently through the stairwell door.

She'd seen the components of the B52 cocktail in the medicine cabinet of Cameron's apartment the last time she'd been in there, the spring-loaded syringe sitting right beside it. Innocuous enough, she supposed, to an unsuspecting visitor, but not very subtle, in Celina's opinion, and a little sloppy. At least he was smart enough not to mix all three drugs together. The Haldol and the Benadryl tended to precipitate out of solution after a few minutes when mixed together. But still, Cameron should be more cautious than that.

Only he probably didn't think he had any reason to be cautious around Reggie Moon. Celina felt a pang of guilt at that thought. Cameron had to know the truth sooner or later, but Celina preferred that he figure it out on his own. Then, at least he'd have the satisfaction of solving a puzzle to take some of the sting out of the fact that Celina had been lying to him for months.

Of course, he'd been lying to her, too, so maybe it would be a wash in the end.

Or so Celina hoped.

Besides, to be fair, Celina had expected Cameron to solve her little riddle in a week or two. A month, max. Here they were going on four months and he still hadn't figured it out. She hadn't expected to have to keep the secret that long.

And then they'd hooked up.

And then they'd hooked up again. And again. And again.

And then Celina started to have feelings for Cameron. Real feelings.

Real-ish ones, at least.

She'd never had real feelings for a guy before, so she wasn't sure exactly what it was supposed to feel like.

But she was feeling shit for Cameron that she'd never felt before, so that was something, real or not.

And so what had started as just a little game to pass the time had blown up into this big secret between them. It was annoying. But who gave a fuck, really? She hadn't known Cameron when it started, and there just hadn't been a good time to come clean. No one's fault, so no reason to be upset about it.

And the fact that Cameron was doing the same thing to her was just tit for tat. Something else to laugh about. An irony that they could marvel at. Kismet. The mysterious workings of the universe bringing them together.

That pang of guilt she kept feeling deep in her chest was some kind of societal conditioning deep in her psyche, some bullshit about keeping secrets from loved ones. She wasn't keeping any secrets. She just hadn't told Cameron the truth yet. She wanted to give him a little more time to figure it out on his own.

Though he was taking so fucking long, it was looking like she'd have to give him some hints. She couldn't wait forever. At this rate, she'd be six feet under before he worked it out.

And if she didn't get to the bottom of the stairs before the idiot opened that door, Cameron would be the one who was six feet under, courtesy of eight bodyguards who wouldn't even break a sweat in the process.

In the view provided by her AR contact lenses, stereoscopically synced to project a single image onto the world in front of her, Celina watched the last of the five roving guards reach the basement level of the building. One stayed behind by the elevator doors in the narrow hall while the others fanned out through the garage to clear the area in advance of Jenkins' arrival. Jenkins, Stratham, and the three remaining guards were still in the elevator between the first floor and the basement floor.

As Celina darted across the cold marble floors of the first-floor foyer, past the ridiculously ornate aluminum elevator doors, it occurred to her that a timely bomb dropped down the elevator shaft at precisely that moment would serve her revenge quite nicely. She could take out Stratham and Jenkins in one quick, easy stroke.

But then they wouldn't know who had killed them, or why. That wasn't revenge. That was just murder. Celina wanted to see the moment of recognition in their eyes before she killed them. She wanted to see the pieces lock into place in their minds as they realized who she was, who her father was, and what they had done to deserve the death she was about to serve up. She wanted to see that flicker of understanding before she pulled the trigger or pushed the knife through their aorta. This was personal for her. A bomb would get the job done, but it wasn't personal enough.

She slid through the door to the north stairwell. She didn't need the augmentation of her lenses to see Cameron one floor below her. The safety lights in the stairwell reflected a thin line of grey across his black-clad shoulders. His right hand was in his pocket. The left hand held the door handle. He crouched, poised like a baby lion cub about to pounce toward a herd of stampeding wildebeest. Imagining great deeds in his head, but poised in reality to throw his life away.

At least some of the guards had dispersed. Cameron stood no better chance against four of Jenkins' goons than he did against eight, but at least it was a smaller number. Celina still wouldn't let him get that far, but it made him seem a hair less nutso.

But only a hair.

She heard the ding of the elevator's arrival through the walls as she rounded the landing above Cameron. Her lenses amplified the visuals in the darkness, brought detail out of the shadows that she wouldn't be able to see with her naked eye. It also provided an overlay with a heat signature and what vitals could be determined at a distance. She saw Cameron's body tense, saw his core temp rise and his heart rate spike, the pulse bulging his jugular increasing in speed.

He'd heard the ding of the elevator, too, was readying his body for action. The idiot was really going to go through with whatever immensely idiotic plan he had in his head.

Men. Always confusing stupidity with courage.

Halfway down the last set of stairs, moving with the cat-like silence she'd perfected over the years, Celina swung her legs over the rail and landed softly behind Cameron ten feet below. Before he could even straighten from his crouch, she held him around his chest from behind and slid her hand over Cameron's inside his pocket.

She bent her hand and his, angled them toward Cameron's body, pressed them forward, pressed hard against his flat, muscled stomach.

And pushed the button on the syringe.

44

In the half-heartbeat between when Cam awoke and when he opened his eyes, he felt a tingling pressure that swelled in his toes and feet, pushed up through his legs, picking up frightening pace, then raced through his core, crashed into his chest, and shot through the top of his skull with a force that stammered his heart and flung him upright in bed, his eyes open wide.

He immediately squeezed his eyes shut again as spears of daylight from the uncovered windows stabbed into his sluggish mind. He pressed the heels of his hands against his eye sockets, pushing away the afterglare, pushing back the... what? The headache? No, it wasn't quite like that. It was kind of like the hangover from a few weeks ago, but softer, fuzzier, less stale in his mouth and less acrid in his stomach.

His body felt fine. Good, even. Rested. But his mind felt off, like two identical images superimposed, with one shifted to the side by three pixels. Just enough to feel wrong, but not enough to make it obvious as to why.

What the fuck had happened? He tried to think back, tried to remember the previous evening, but his brain refused to call the memories to mind.

He slit his eyes, flapped back the bedcovers, and swung his

legs over the side. His phone thunked to the floor by his bare feet. Cam looked down at it, looked down at himself, his mind still fuddled. He was wearing a t-shirt and his boxer briefs, but he had no memory of getting undressed, of getting into bed.

He picked up his phone and checked the lock screen. Ten-thirty in the morning on Saturday. He'd slept late. The last thing he remembered was—

"Oh, good. You're up."

Cam turned to see Reggie standing in the doorway to the bedroom. He didn't remember having her over the night before, either. And when she got up in the morning after they'd spent the night together, she usually wore one of his t-shirts, worn long over her panties or over a pair of his sweatpants with the waistband folded and rolled tight. But today she was fully dressed in leggings and a sweater.

"You haven't been returning my texts, so I got worried and let myself in this morning. Hope that's okay."

That explained why Cam didn't remember spending the night with her. But he didn't remember giving her a set of keys, either.

"You were sleeping like a dead man," she said, coming to sit beside him on the bed. She rubbed his back gently. The heat of her hand through his t-shirt felt so good that Cam wanting nothing more than to lie back down, melt into that sensation, forget his confusion and just float in it forever.

"Yeah," said Cam, rubbing his eyes again, "I guess I must have been tired. I don't even remember last nig—"

Last night.

He stopped himself from reacting physically, externally, so that Reggie wouldn't notice anything wrong. But inside, both Cam's stomach and his mind churned.

Last night.

The memories came in a rush, like a fog blown away by a gust of wind.

The DOJ building. He'd been about to attack Stratham and Jenkins, about to burst through the door like a fucking action hero in a movie.

Like a fucking idiot.

And then he'd felt a restraining arm across his chest.

And a stab in his side.

"Must have been a hell of a party," said Reggie, patting his back softly and removing her hand. "Wish you'd invited me."

Cam felt a chill where Reggie's hand had been on his back.

He felt another chill in his heart.

The woman in black.

He'd felt the thin stab in his side, and then a cold, spreading sting as the drug had injected into his muscle. He'd fallen straight backwards, straight back into the arms of his assailant.

The woman in black.

He remembered staring up at her face, those green eyes the only feature visible behind her balaclava, floating like a Cheshire cat in the dark of the stairwell, a dark that was getting deeper as the edges of his vision narrowed with each heartbeat, as the tranquilizer pumped deeper into his system.

"How— how did you get in?" Cam's mouth was so dry, his tongue was sticking to the inside. He could barely form the words, which hardly mattered because he barely knew what he was saying. His body was sitting in the morning sunlight on the bed beside Reggie, but his mind was in that dark stairwell as the woman in black lay him gently in her lap.

He remembered reaching for a strand of the dark hair that curled over one shoulder, curled out from under her mask. The woman in black had red hair, but in his memory, it was dark. It must have been the shadows in the stairwell, or the encroaching haze of the drug, or both.

But there was no shadow on her eyes. As the drug-induced darkness irised down around them, those emerald eyes were as clear as daylight, the last thing he remembered seeing before everything went dark and quiet.

"You gave me your keys," said Reggie, an odd smile quirking the edge of her mouth on one side.

Cam looked at her, beside him on the bed, then jerked back for a quick moment.

Her eyes were so bright in the sunlight, and so green.

Emerald green.

Just like the woman in black.

The chill in his heart spread through him, like the spreading chill of the injection, but throughout his entire body.

His mind was playing tricks. She'd drugged him. She'd injected him with the syringe in his own pocket, knocked him out, either by design or by sheer luck.

No, it couldn't have been luck. She had to have known the syringe was in his pocket, had to have known what was in it, what it would do to Cam when she injected it. She'd put her hand into his pocket. Pressed the button on the syringe without looking. She was ready to catch him when he passed out. She knew about the syringe, knew it was an auto-injector, knew what was in it, and knew what it would do to him.

Once again, the woman in black seemed to know everything. But how?

Cam squeezed his eyes shut against the thought, against the memory. He shook his head to clear it, but still could see only those emerald green eyes, hovering above a bright white mezza-luna smile.

"Don't you remember?" said Reggie.

Cam opened his eyes again and looked at her. The quirk of her smile was gone as concern darkened her features. He remembered the night before now, everything up to the moment the drug knocked him out. But he still didn't remember giving Reggie his keys. Didn't seem like something he would do.

There must be some lingering effect from the drug. He still must not be one-hundred percent in his right mind.

Besides, it was too much for him to see Reggie looking that way, her expression a mix of fear and confusion. And to think that he was the cause of it, that she was concerned because of his behavior. He wouldn't let a drug-induced lapse of memory make things worse. He wouldn't let the woman in black mess up what he had with Reggie.

Cam would mess that up all on his own. But not today.

"No, right," said Cam, nodding. He slipped his hand around Reggie's side and pulled her in for a hug. "I remember. Of course."

The heat of her body wasn't enough to stave off the chill inside him. Those Cheshire eyes still hovered in his vision when he looked at Reggie. When he looked at her gorgeous face, at her stunning eyes, all he could see was the woman in black.

After a moment, Reggie pushed him gently back, concern still on her face. She could tell. Reggie was an incredibly intelligent, intuitive woman. She knew something was up with him. She didn't know what it was yet. The confusion layered beneath the concern told Cam that much. But she would figure it out eventually.

She looked him over, ran one hand down his arm and onto his leg. "Are you feeling okay?"

Cam definitely wasn't okay, but physically, he felt fine. Good, even.

And starving.

He nodded, took a deep breath through his nose, and noticed for the first time the smell of eggs and toast from the kitchen. His stomach growled loudly.

Reggie looked down at his belly and laughed. "I guess that means you're hungry." She stood and turned to him, hands on her hips. "Well, come on, then," she said. "While you were in here sleeping the day away, I was in the kitchen cooking breakfast."

Cam stepped around Reggie to take a pair of joggers from a drawer and pull them on.

"That's so domestic of you," he said with a grin.

As she passed on the way to the door, Reggie smacked him on the ass, hard enough to make Cam, half in his joggers, stumble forward.

"Don't get used to it," she said, then gave him a sultry look over her shoulder that made Cam want to sweep her off her feet and get back into bed for a little longer.

45

THE MOOD DIDN'T last long. Cam was glum all through breakfast. He'd pushed aside his thoughts about the woman in black, but he couldn't push aside his failure from the night before. He'd failed to get to Stratham, and he'd failed to get the information he needed to blackmail the Attorney General. Without proof, any claims he made would be indefensible, even if they were true. Cam would have to pretend he had the evidence. He wasn't at all sure he was that good an actor. Not in a situation with stakes that high.

Reggie did her best to pull him out of his funk, first with food, then with conversation, then with flirtation, but nothing could fill the empty pit in his stomach. He'd failed. After three years working on this plan, after fifteen years of failing with one plan after another, he'd failed his mother yet again. She was going to spend the rest of her life in prison, all because of him.

"I think I figured something out about that woman in black," said Reggie.

That caught Cam's attention.

"What?" he said, startled to hear Reggie talk about the woman in black. He looked across the table at her, and once again his mind reeled as the image of the woman in black's eyes hovered in front of Reggie's. Both such a startling green color. The similarity was remarkable. But then, Cam was still dealing with the shock of last night and the effect of the drugs on his mind. It was to be expected that there'd be some lingering cognitive overlap.

Wasn't it?

"Do you mind if I have a look at that ribbon one more time?"

Like with the apartment keys, Cam had no memory of showing the ribbon to Reggie, or mentioning the woman in black at all. Then he remembered that he'd said something that night he was wasted. Or, at least, he remembered the conversation when Reggie told him that he'd said something while he was wasted.

In his entire life, Cam had never lost consciousness, never blacked out, either from drink or drugs or assault. Yet now he'd done it twice in the last couple of months.

He was losing focus. And now he'd lost his chance the get the information he needed from Stratham. But if he could catch the woman in black, maybe she would have something he could use, some angle he could play.

They cleaned up quickly and sat on the futon couch. Cam pulled the box wrapped in black crepe paper from the cabinet in the corner and set it on the coffee table in front of them.

The fact that Reggie knew about the woman in black felt surreal to him. Here she was helping Cam solve this mystery, but she still knew nothing about his real identity. In her mind, she was sitting beside Sam Davis, looking at clues left on his doorstep at random by some mysterious woman dressed in black. She didn't know who Cam really was, didn't know about his mother, his plan, his escapades in the Department of Justice building.

If she did know, she wouldn't be sitting on the couch beside him. She'd be out the door and on her phone calling the cops.

"It's these notches here," said Reggie, taking the ribbon from the box and running it gently through her hands, stopping at each shape cut into the edges of the pink and gold material. "If they were at the ends of the ribbon, or even if they weren't so precisely cut, I wouldn't think much of them. But look at these shapes." She pointed to the sides of several notches. "They're cut perfectly clean and the angles are precise. That might not be so weird if they were all the same, but they're not. Each one is different."

"Okay," said Cam, his interest piqued enough to finally drag his thoughts away from his shame. "So what do you think it means?"

"That's what I've been trying to figure out since you showed it to me." Reggie slid the ribbon through her fingers until she held it with a notch in both hands. "Look at these two notches."

Cam bent closer, inspecting the cuts.

Realization hit him like a brick.

"They're opposites," he said. "Exact opposites."

"You're right," Reggie replied, excitement in her voice, "which means they probably—"

"They probably fit together." Cam took the ribbon from Reggie's hands. He held the first notch in his left hand, then slid the rest of the ribbon slowly through his right hand, moving from notch to notch, matching each one against the notch in his left. Only one was the exact opposite. Only one fit perfectly together with the notch he held.

He got some clear tape from a drawer and taped those two notches together, then repeated the process for the rest of the notches. In the end, there were three sets of perfect matches. Once he had them all fit together and taped, Cam lay the ribbon on the coffee table and pressed it flat.

The strands of gold that wove through the ribbon, which had coalesced into odd, seemingly abstract patterns, came together when the ribbon was folded this way. The looping, decorative strands formed words written in a flowing, handwritten style of script. The script was so ornate that the words were difficult to decipher, but Cam could see that they were definitely words.

A prickle of excitement shot up the back of his neck. He looked at Reggie, and she smiled back at him.

Cam had to peel back the tape and tweak the way the ribbon lay on the table, had to align the edges perfectly in order to make out the words. He started at one end, sliding the two sides of the ribbon back and forth and up and down until he could decipher them.

"You..."

Tweak.

"Are..."

Tweak.

"So..."

Tweak.

Cam squinted at the ribbon.

"...Cloge."

He sat up.

"You are so cloge?"

Reggie looked at him, then leaned forward. She examined the ribbon, then pointed to a letter. "I think that G is an S."

Cam looked again, then nodded. "You are so close." He turned to Reggie, eyes wide, excitement in his voice. "We're so close."

Reggie grinned back at him. Cam's heart hitched in his chest at the sight. Reggie's beauty still floored him.

"It looks like there's more," said Reggie, peering down at the ribbon again.

Cam pulled his attention back to the task. He shifted to the next portion of the ribbon, took off the tape and shifted and adjusted the two strands of ribbon to make out the words there.

"For... Ty...," he said. "Forty." He shifted his hands again. "Five."

He slid his hands over the rest of the ribbon, but the gold strands didn't form any more words after that.

Cam sat back on the couch, his hands limp in his lap. "Forty-five," he said. "You're getting close. Forty-five." He shook his head and sighed heavily. "Another fucking riddle."

The shame and despair he'd felt earlier rushed back tenfold. Not only had he failed his mother last night, now he was faced with yet another challenge from the woman in black, one that he had no clue how to solve.

"What's the matter?" asked Reggie.

Cam sighed again. How could he explain without telling her everything? Maybe now was the time to tell it, anyway. Might as well pile on all the bad news at once.

But he didn't think his heart could take it. After failing the night before, the thought of losing Reggie was bad enough. The reality of it right then might just destroy him for good.

"It's just riddle after riddle from this woman in black," he said to Reggie. "It took me forever to track down the second clue, but I haven't even figured out the first one yet. And now there's a third clue. I just..." He shook his head again, then rubbed his face with his hands. "I'm just tired, I guess."

"Look," said Reggie, shifting to the edge of the futon and turning to face Cam, "you may have another riddle to solve, but you've just solved one. That's progress."

Cam shrugged. It was a good try, but it didn't give him much comfort.

"Besides," Reggie continued, "this time around you've got an advantage."

Cam thought for a moment, then frowned.

"What advantage?"

Reggie reared back and put one hand on her chest in mock offense.

"Me, of course," she said, then grinned.

Even through the crush of his hopelessness, seeing that grin on Reggie's beautiful face, Cam couldn't help but grin back.

46

CELINA KNEW Cameron would be unconscious for a while. A B52 is no recreational drug cocktail. It's safe enough if the dosages are right, but it packs a punch.

She knew he'd be disoriented and hungry, too, when he woke up, which is why she'd picked the lock on his apartment and made him breakfast. She'd gaslighted him about it just to make things simpler. She didn't like lying to Cameron, but she didn't want to get into the uncomfortable questions part of the relationship just yet. She wanted Cameron to figure some things out on his own first.

And now, more than ever, she knew that was the right tack to take. The guy was a fucking mess. The B52 was one thing, but even after she was pretty sure the effects had worn off—after he'd woken up and gotten plenty of food in his system—he was still moping around like a kid who'd been punched by the school bully and had his lunch money stolen.

Celina still didn't know what the hell Cameron had been doing in the DOJ building, or what he'd been so willing to risk his fucking life for. It had to have something to do with his mother, but she had no clue why Cameron would throw his life away by fighting four trained bodyguards with just one syringe for a weapon.

But whatever it was, she'd fucked up his fucked-up plan, and now he was all fucked up about it.

And he was really fucking bad at figuring out puzzles. I mean, fuck. 3e-3 should have been enough. 0.003 in E notation. Not that fucking hard. He was so obsessed with his class ranking, Celina thought he would have seen that right away. She'd been worried that it was too easy, too obvious.

But even after all this time, he still wasn't getting it.

It had taken him forever to find Maggie at the art studio. Maggie said he'd asked about the CnC cutter, so he'd probably figured out that the foam, the crepe paper, and the card stock all came from there. Hopefully he'd figured that out, anyway. The man was a genius at a lot of things, but at some things he was slow as fuck to catch on.

All of that shit was just meant to lead him to the second clue, anyway. And the second clue was just meant to help him figure out the first one, and to figure out the ribbon. The first clue would tell him who she was. The ribbon would tell him where she lived.

And the second clue he'd found wasn't even the one Celina had first intended. The original second clue had been much more enigmatic. But it had taken Cameron so long to find it that Celina had swapped the original clue for a simpler one. A giant number three holding a balloon floating like an exponent with -3 written on it? Walking along a pink and gold ribbon that was all intertwined and held together by a bunch of notches cut into the sides? How much easier could it get? If he'd needed another clue, it was going to be a piece of card stock with "THE WOMAN IN BLACK IS REGGIE MOON" written on it. And Celina would have fucking delivered it herself, wearing her hunting blacks.

But she'd set all of that up before she'd gotten to know him. Getting to know him was definitely not part of the plan. She was just fucking with Cameron before, something to pass the time until she could get her face-to-face with Jenkins and Stratham. But now, there was something on the line. Something real.

I mean, she'd met his mother, for fuck's sake. She hadn't met anyone's mother before. And, worse, she'd liked his mother. A lot.

She and Cameron were playing this weird game with each other, and Celina wanted it to end as soon as possible. Normally, she loved to fuck with people. It gave her a thrill to see how far she could push it, how much people would believe. And she was always stunned by how gullible people were. They'd believe anything as long as it didn't challenge their worldview, as long as it didn't make them work harder, either mentally or physically. They'd rather believe some outlandish bullshit than challenge themselves or change their own minds. That was just human nature.

But Cameron wasn't that way. Celina could see that even before she got to know him.

Before she fell for him.

She didn't know quite what his plan was, but last night at the DOJ building, he'd been desperate enough to risk his own life for it. And when she didn't let that happen, it had thrown him into a funk. A bad one.

And now she had to pull him out of it somehow.

She'd start by helping him with the clues. Just a few nudges in the right direction, some encouragement, a few reminders along the way to keep him going. Once he figured that out, all the cloak-and-dagger false-identity bullshit would be out of the way and they could be straight with each other. She'd tell him who she really was, he'd tell her who he really was, she'd tell him she already knew who he was, he'd get pissed, they'd argue, they'd fuck, they'd laugh, and that would be that.

And then he'd tell her what he was trying to do, and she would help him do it. It had something to do with his mother, probably some way to get her out of prison. Even after meeting Paulie just the one time for only fifteen minutes, Celina was willing to help with that.

But they had to clear away all the bullshit first. There was enough complexity already without that shit getting in the way. And Celina couldn't just come clean with Cameron. Jack Nicholson was right. Men can't handle the truth. Not head-on. They were too fragile for that kind of shit.

And right now, Cameron was especially vulnerable. She'd come right out and tell him, if she had to, but only as a last resort.

Cameron needed a win. He needed to solve this puzzle on his own.

She'd help him, of course, but in the way women have worked for centuries: by letting him believe it was all his own doing.

47

Cam became obsessed with the woman in black.

There wasn't much else for him to do.

He'd hacked the servers at Jenkins' campaign office again and confirmed that Stratham had left town and wasn't expected back until graduation day. He'd finished his schoolwork for the semester weeks ago. He still had to close the 0.003 point GPA gap with Reggie, but without hacking into the school servers, which Cam still refused to do, he had no idea if the work he'd already turned in had closed that gap or not. He would have to wait to find out until the final grades were posted at the end of the term.

Cam had nothing to do but focus on solving the riddle of the woman in black.

Reggie was a welcome distraction, but even she seemed to have noticed his obsession and stopped trying to distract him from it, choosing instead to lean in and help him with it.

Which was just as well. The riddle consumed him day and night. He knew the answer was obvious. He could feel it in the back of his mind. But for some reason, he just couldn't focus enough to see it. It was like he was trying to read a book while wearing someone else's glasses. He knew the words were there, knew he could read them. But he couldn't focus clearly enough to make them out.

Cam rehearsed the clues in his mind, over and over. He'd taken to keeping the ribbon and the two pieces of card stock in his backpack when he left the house. When he was alone, he would hold them in his hands and stare at them until the words came off the page and seemed to swirl around him, or until he felt like he had entered the scene with the balloon and the walking number three. Until, in other words, he felt like he was losing his mind.

He didn't want to do this while sitting in class, didn't want to lose his mind while surrounded by people. But he couldn't stop thinking about the clues. So instead of taking notes, he would type the clues again and again on his laptop, earning him more than a few weird looks from Jem.

"Sam," Jem leaned over in class one day to whisper in Cam's ear, "if I see the words *all work and no play* on that screen, I'm calling the cops." He glanced down at the laptop, where Cam had copied and pasted the three clues at least twenty times on the same page in various fonts and sizes. "Or maybe the psych department."

At lunches, Cam would push his food around his plate and stare into space, the words of the clues floating before him. His hands held only his fork, but he could feel the texture of the card stock and the ribbon in his fingertips.

He was so preoccupied that the others started to ask if he was feeling okay. Both Jem and Sarah, separately, had pulled him aside to ask if the pressure of getting back to the top of the class rankings was weighing him down. Even Motsu had said something to him.

Thankfully, Reggie was there to run interference for him. She made excuses, told them she'd been keeping him up. Study-ing, she'd say with a wink. Or she'd grin and say she was doing her best to sabotage his attempts to unseat her from the top of the rankings. The others would laugh and the conversation would move on. But that only worked for the first couple of times. After that, the laughter was thinner, their concern heavier.

Cam knew he was acting irrationally. He had to figure this shit out. He had to move on with his life, find another plan to free his mother. All plans fail. That was his parents' favorite aphorism. It was practically a mantra. It wasn't the failure that was the problem, they would say. Failing to respond to the failure was the problem.

It was time for Cam to respond, and at the moment, figuring out the identity of the woman in black was his best option.

His only option. He didn't know if solving that riddle would help him free his mother or not, but he knew that he wouldn't be able to focus on anything else until he figured out the identity of the woman in black.

And figured out why the hell she was tormenting him.

He and Reggie went to Reggie's apartment after their last Theories of Punishment class. It was their last class of the semester. Their last class of the entire degree. Three years of work, done.

April was nearly over and the days were getting longer. Where in January Cam had been trudging home from the library or an afternoon class in the cold and the dark, now the sun was still slanting through the window shades at seven PM. Their heavy winter coats had weeks ago been replaced with fleece jackets, then thinner pullovers. Spring had arrived.

And graduation was only three weeks away.

Cam slung his backpack to the floor and sagged into Reggie's couch. After a moment, he pulled his laptop out of his bag, almost from pure habit, and stared at the screen in sullen silence while Reggie, mercifully, did all the work of preparing dinner.

He stared at the file he'd had open in their last class, a Word document with the clues typed out in landscape orientation in font large enough to fill the screen.

Three-three

Getting closer.

You're so close. Forty-five.

Three simple clues. Nine simple words.

They taunted Cam.

He could hear the voice of the woman in black, the same voice he'd heard when they'd first tumbled down the stairwell in the DOJ building. The same voice he heard when he started up the Nestech glasses. It whispered the clues to him, mocking him, the voice dripping with barely restrained laughter, growing louder and louder in his mind, the voice echoing, amplifying, spinning around and around.

Cam slapped the laptop shut. The echoes faded into silence. He could stare at the damn words forever and he still wouldn't make any more sense of them. He'd been doing it for weeks already with no progress. He'd stared at them so much on that damn laptop screen that they hung behind his eyes, the after-image of the text burned into his brain.

He needed to change the format. Mix it up. Shake up his mind by shaking up his process. He hadn't sketched in months, and right then his hands itched with an irrational need to hold a pencil to paper.

He stuffed his laptop back into his bag and pulled his spiral-bound sketch book from another pocket. A folded piece of sketch paper, scalloped teeth on one edge torn and bent, came out with it and fell to the floor. Cam picked it up, unfolded it.

It was the note Reggie had left on the pillow the first time they'd slept together. Cam had put it in his backpack. It was silly and sentimental. The note didn't even say anything romantic. It said his pantry was shit. But he liked to look at it sometimes, anyway, when he was away from her, when he was in one of the classes they didn't share or when he was alone in the library studying. He imagined that it smelled like her. It didn't, but he would hold the paper to his nose anyway. It brought back the memory of her scent. And something about the confident, artistic handwriting and the beauty of the line strokes combined with the imaginary scent to bring the image of Reggie immediately to his mind, every time.

Even then, while the echoes of the voice of the woman in black still tormented him in the subconscious recesses of his mind, the unexpected sight of the note brought a faint smile to his lips.

He folded the note again and slid it back into the pocket of his backpack. He opened the sketch book, but the pencil he kept inside was worn and dull. He'd meant to replace it the last time he used it, but had forgotten. The tip was rounded from use and the length so short Cam could barely hold it, let alone sketch with it.

Just another frustration to add to the list.

"Reggie, do you have any sketch pencils?" he asked. "I'll take a 2B, if you have it."

"Not my medium," Reggie called over her shoulder from the kitchen. Cam heard a sharp sizzle as Reggie dropped something into a pan on the stove. "But I've got some Copics in my art kit. There's a set of sketching grays in there you can use."

Cam didn't like to use ink. Too permanent. Plans fail. Plans change. The same was true of sketches. He liked to use pencil to give himself more flexibility.

Or maybe he just didn't have Reggie's confidence when it came to his art.

He thought about running down to his apartment to get a new pencil, but his body felt as heavy as his mind. The thought of even that much exertion felt overwhelming.

And sometimes you have to make do with what you've got. Today, that meant Copic markers.

He got off the couch and pulled Reggie's art kit from the

closet where she kept it. What she called a kit was more a collection of kits. Plastic bins and boxes containing everything from markers to acrylic paints to oil paints to Mod Podge and decoupage materials and cleaning supplies. Everything Reggie would need for the various media she liked to work in. It was all neatly arranged and labeled, sorted by application. One shelf for painting supplies, another for collage, another for ink drawing, and another for 3D design and sculpture, which Reggie said she had recently taken up.

Cam pulled out a box labelled "Copics", found the sketch grays, and selected several markers in varying shades, from light grey to dark. With just one pencil, especially a medium-soft one like a 2B, Cam could vary his hand pressure and pencil angle to produce a wide range of tones and textures. With ink markers, though, he had less flexibility. He needed several markers to give himself the range of just one sketching pencil. Yet another reason he preferred pencils to markers.

But today he was making do.

He closed up the box and set it back in place in the closet, then sat on the couch again, sketch book in his lap. He had nothing in mind to draw, nothing but the clues that hovered in his mind constantly, and he didn't want to draw those.

He let his eye drift over the room, seeking inspiration. He saw his legs crossed in front of him, one foot dangling in the air. The coffee table beyond that, his backpack hunched beside it.

He let his eye drift past that to the light falling through the window, let it drift over the walls, over Reggie's framed artwork, over the furniture, the decor, the blankets and the flower arrangements and the photographs. All beautiful. All engaging. But nothing caught his interest. Nothing sparked his creativity in that moment.

And finally, he let his eye settle on Reggie herself.

And he felt the spark, the touch of magic inside him that made him want to draw.

His eyes followed Reggie as she moved around the kitchen. The rich smell of garlic and sizzling chicken embraced the room, his mouth watering in anticipation of the meal.

He let his drawing hand move of its own accord, not even bothering to look down at the page. It was a technique called blind contour drawing, and it was supposed to help connect your senses of sight and touch, to deepen and broaden the shift from left brain analytical thinking to right brain creative thinking.

And that's exactly what Cam needed. He needed to get out of the left brain that was stewing over and over on the clues and shift into his right brain for a new perspective.

Most blind contour drawings don't produce useful images. But Cam had done this so many times, his hands knew the dimensions of the paper instinctively, knew the length of his own strokes without looking. He kept his gaze on Reggie and let his hand draw what he saw, let that touch of magic spread through him, let the feelings of peace and love that Reggie sparked in him push away, if only for a moment, the poison of his obsession with the woman in black.

Those feelings, that magic, grew and grew in him until, finally, they tipped the scale in their favor. He felt his chest soften, felt it relax and expand as the tension of the last month melted away. The riddles and the clues and the voice of the woman in black were still there in his mind, but they'd finally been pushed back into a corner. Cam knew it was only a respite, but it was a welcome one, and one he desperately needed.

He stopped his hand, let it rest limp against the page. He closed his eyes, pulled in a deep breath, and rolled his head in a long, languid circle, letting himself feel that peace, letting it suffuse his entire body and mind.

When he opened his eyes again and looked down at what he'd drawn, that peace shattered in an instant.

The strokes of the marker on the page looked strikingly familiar. Like he'd seen them before.

Like he'd seen them all day, every day for the last few weeks, haunting every moment of his life, both waking and sleeping.

The strokes he'd just drawn looked just like the strokes drawn in every clue from the woman in black.

48

BLIND CONTOUR DRAWING was intended to shift you from your analytical left brain into your creative right brain.

Cam had spent the last month or more caged in a left brain that was tying itself into tighter and tighter knots trying to figure out the clues left for him by the woman in black.

Once he shifted into his right brain, the clues suddenly seemed head-slap obvious.

The last wink of daylight flared through the blinds in the corner of his eye, then snuffed out to a glowing ember, slowly dying.

Cam glanced up at Reggie. She was still in the kitchen, focused on the final prep for their dinner. The rich smells of cooked meat and heated bread that had made his mouth water a moment before now only reminded him of the empty pit in his belly.

The lines in his sketchbook, the ones Cam had just drawn with Reggie's Copic marker. They were exactly like the lines in every clue he'd received from the woman in black.

He leaned forward on the couch and pulled from his backpack the two clues that were written on card stock, the two clues that had handwritten words and drawings on them.

On the first clue, the words *threee-three* were typed, but on the flip side, the woman in black had written the name *Cameron Hauk*.

The strokes matched the size and style of the strokes Cam had made with the Copic marker.

He pulled out the second clue. Handwritten on one side were the words *Getting closer*.

Same strokes.

He flipped the card to look at the drawing of the personified number three walking on the ribbon with the balloon in its hand.

Again, same strokes. Same style.

His left brain had been banging on the door to his thoughts. It finally burst through.

Okay, fine. They all had the same strokes. They were all written by the same person with the same kind of pen. Which happened to be the same kind of pen Cam had just used, had just borrowed from Reggie.

But Copic markers were very common. Millions of people used them all the time. Just because Reggie and the woman in black used the same very common pen didn't mean anything.

Cam looked back at his drawing, compared the strokes with the clues again.

Definitely the same marker.

But, then, he'd guessed that the first time he'd seen them, hadn't he? He'd guessed that they'd been written with some kind of art pen, something like a Copic.

He stood, walked to the wall where Reggie had framed a drawing of hers, ink-on-paper, of a man in the rain in silhouette from behind. A simple drawing. Sparse. Beautiful.

Cam compared it to the sketch of the number three with the balloon. Totally different subjects, totally different style, but the same media. The same ink on paper.

Both made with Copic markers, or something very similar.

Again, not that unusual.

But as Cam looked more closely, he saw telltale signs. Similar angles to the cross-hatching. Similar weights to the lines, similar patterns. The unconscious parts of the images, the shadows, the fills, the connecting lines. The parts that artists have done so many times in so many drawings over so many years, the parts that have become subconscious through repetition and mastery. These were the parts that showed the artist's hand. More than the signature in the corner of the work, these subconscious strokes showed who the artist truly was. Only a master who was consciously trying to hide would override these subconscious habits.

And Reggie had not.

The sketch on the clue in his hand matched the drawing framed on the wall.

They weren't just made by the same type of pen. They were made by the same hand.

By the same artist.

His left brain had no comeback to that.

Dazed, Cam sat down on the couch again, looked at his own sketch once more. He'd gotten very good at blind contour drawing over the years. It was one of his favorite warm-up techniques. When most people used that technique, the result was an artistic jumble, with no distinguishable forms within it. When Cam did it, the results were actually quite good.

In this case, the result looked like Reggie.

His right brain had used a Copic marker to draw a picture of Reggie without even looking.

Come on, his left brain scoffed, attempting to recover through sheer bravado. You can't really think there's some connection there. Last time you were sketching, you were sketching nothing but Reggie. All Reggie, all the time. This is no different. She was standing right in front of you.

The thoughts washed over Cam. He looked again at the

clues again. This time, he wasn't looking at the lines. He was looking at their meaning.

This time, from a new perspective.

Threee-three.

Two threes.

He set the second clue beside it, flipped so the image was facing up.

The image of a number three, holding a balloon, with a negative three written on it.

Two threes, again.

He looked once more at the first clue.

Why was the word "three" misspelled?

Had he noticed that before? He must have noticed that before. He'd looked at the clue a thousand times. Had typed it into his own laptop a hundred thousand times.

He dragged his backpack over, pulled out his laptop, and flipped it open to check the latest Word document he'd used to torment himself.

Three-three, it said.

Without the extra E.

Fucking hell.

He closed his laptop, let it slide off his lap and back into his backpack. He looked again at the image of the number three with the balloon. A balloon with a negative three.

Threee-three.

Threee -three.

He looked at the drawing. The balloon hovered just above the head of the personified number three.

Hovered there like an exponent.

3^{-3}.

He pulled out his phone, brought up the calculator. Three to the negative third was 0.37.

What the hell did that mean?

He looked back at the first clue.

Threee -three.

Three e -three.

Large numbers, when written out, are often expressed in scientific notation. Ten trillion, for example, would be 1×10^{13}.

Tools with single-line outputs, like calculators, can't show exponents, so they use E notation instead of scientific notation to express large numbers. Cam had learned about it during his computer science studies. Instead of 1×10^{13}, a modern calculator would display 1e13.

Threee-three.

Threee -three.

Three E -three.

3×10^{-3}.

Cam didn't need a calculator for that one. That number was all too familiar to him.

0.003.

The GPA point differential in the class rankings between Sam Davis and Reggie Moon.

Another thought occurred to Cam then.

Moving with the frantic slowness of a man in a nightmare, he reached into in backpack, pulled out the note Reggie had left for him the first time they'd slept together. He unfolded it in slow-motion, knowing already what it would show, what it would prove beyond reasonable doubt.

Not the same pen. She'd used his sketch pencil, not a Copic marker, to write the note.

But, the handwriting. The strokes were the same. Confident. Artistic. The same slant to the letters. The same size and proportionality. The same unconscious flourishes at the ends of the strokes.

Cam dragged his gaze from the papers in his lap to the kitchen. He felt a stinging pain all over his skin, like dragging himself naked over a bed of sharpened razor blades into a swimming pool full of salt. But he felt it from a distance, like it was happening to someone else. Like watching a surgeon slice with their scalpel across your stomach, watching the blood well from the wound in a thin, round line, but feeling nothing through a thick, gauzy shroud of anesthetic.

"I hope you're hungry," said Reggie as she came around the corner of the kitchen bar, two steaming plates of food in her hands.

The sound of her voice. How had Cam not noticed before? It was the same sound as the voice in the Nestech glasses. It was the sound of the voice that had haunted his dreams for so many nights before he and Reggie had gotten together.

And those eyes, those green eyes that narrowed at him now in confusion. The shock he'd felt weeks ago, the startling super-imposition of the eyes of the woman in black and Reggie's eyes, hadn't been a hangover from the drugs that had knocked him out. It was his subconscious trying to show him, trying to get him to see what should have been obvious. Trying to get him to see what had been right in front of him this whole time.

He'd been chasing the woman in black for months. But she'd been right in front of him the entire time.

In front of him. Beside him.

Beneath him. On top of him.

Reggie Moon was the woman in black.

She stood by the bar, the two steaming plates rock steady, dead level in her hands. The look of confusion hung in her eyes for only a moment.

Then it melted away.

As it did, everything about her seemed to shift. Her stance widened. Her posture loosened. The energy she put off became more alive, more feral. Even her face changed. Still just as beau-tiful, maybe even more so, but her features somehow seemed sharper, harder.

In the flick of a thought, she shifted from Reggie Moon to... whoever she was.

The plates in her hands bobbed just a bit as her shoulders sagged. The confusion on her face washed into relief.

"It's about fucking time," she said. She turned her back to Cam and set the plates down on the table in front of the bar. "Now let's eat. I'm fucking starving."

While her back was turned, Cam scooped up the clues in his right hand, crushing them in his fist, and grabbed his backpack with the other.

Without another word to Reggie—to the woman in black, whatever her real name was—he walked out the door into the night.

49

CELINA'S first thought when she saw the look on Cameron's face was that something was wrong. He looked like he'd just gotten an email that his mother had died, been shanked in prison or something. His color was grey, his mouth hung open, his eyes looked stricken, like he'd just watched his dog get hit by a car.

Her second thought was relief. She saw the clues in his lap, saw the phone in his hand, open to a calculator. He'd finally figured it out. Finally, after all this fucking time, they could be real with each other.

Her third thought, after she'd set their dinner on the table and straightened up again, only to find the couch empty, Cameron's stuff gone, and the door clicking shut on an empty hallway, was that maybe she'd miscalculated, that maybe he wouldn't react like she would. That maybe he would view the events of the last several months as less of a game and more of a... what? Betrayal? Sabotage? Cruel and deliberate manipulation? The realization struck her like a fist.

Her fourth thought was much simpler.

Fuck.

50

Cam never wanted to see Reggie Moon again.

Every time the thought ran through his mind, he scoffed at himself. Reggie Moon didn't exist. She was a fabrication. A deception. A figment of his imagination.

All the things he felt—the acid ache in his stomach, the hollow gnawing in his chest, the blank nothing when he stared into the dark in his bed at night—they were all fake. None of it was real. It was all a lie.

And he'd fallen for it, hook, line, and fillet knife. The great thief, the great con man, had fallen for the con himself. And then fooled himself for months, not seeing the clues for what they were. Reggie's greatest con was the one she probably didn't intend. She'd gotten Cam to con himself.

He was a fool. Always had been, when it came to women.

No more.

He refused to see Reggie Moon again. Fool me once. But Cam would not play the fool a second time.

Fortunately, classes were over. All that remained was dead week—a week of study—then final exams.

Then a week for the first-years and second-years to go home while the third-years stayed behind to relax and party.

Then graduation.

Where Reggie Moon—who didn't fucking exist—would receive top honors and gain a private audience with Attorney General William Jenkins.

The private audience Cam needed to free his mother from prison.

He didn't know how the rankings had shifted over the course of the semester, if at all. The school only posted the rankings at the end of each term. Cam could see his own grades and his own GPA, but he couldn't see Reggie's. His GPA had gone up from a 3.984 to a 3.992. Nearly perfect.

But Reggie—or whatever her name was—had started at a 3.987. Her GPA had probably gone up, too. There was no reason for Cam to believe otherwise. She was smart.

Smart enough to fool him.

Smart enough to hide her identity from a man who had hidden his own for three full years without even a hint of suspicion, even from his closest friends.

Unless Reggie stumbled on her finals, which was highly unlikely, she would take the top spot.

And Cam's mother would rot in prison.

After that night in Reggie's apartment when Cam had finally figured out the clues, he'd stormed back home. He'd been mad at Reggie, mad at himself, mad at the world. Reggie had knocked a few minutes later, but Cam ignored her.

And that was the pattern for days. He stayed in his apartment, and Reggie would knock. Endlessly. She would call through the door to him.

Cam would put his noise-cancelling headphones in, crank up heavy metal, EDM, music he despised, but that did a good job of blocking out ambient noise. He didn't want to hear her and he didn't want to see her. Every knock was like a hammer to his heart, but the sound of her voice hurt even more.

He didn't want to see her, but he'd still watch through his

front door camera. The first night, Reggie stood there for two full hours, knocking. The next day, she came back like clockwork every thirty minutes, starting at six AM, and knocked for five full minutes each time.

Then came the notes, slid under his door.

Written on the same card stock as the clues.

Written with the same Copic marker.

Cam didn't know if she was rubbing it in or trying him to make him angry enough to respond or just tormenting him for her own amusement.

He ignored them all, let the notes lie in a scatter in front of the door where they came to rest.

He ordered food. He watched Reggie—the woman in black, the goddamn woman in black—intercept the delivery man, watched her knock on his door herself.

He didn't bother to eat that night.

By the end of the week, she'd stopped coming. Taking a risk and assuming he could leave without seeing her, Cam met his friends for lunch that Thursday at Taberu. Reggie was not there.

They all sat around a table with their umeboshi onigiri. They'd finally put it on the actual menu. Cam was the only one who refused to order it. He ate chicken yakisoba instead. It tasted bitter. It tasted like salt. He pushed it away after one bite.

Jem said Reggie had called him, said he didn't even know she had his phone number. Cam snorted at that. Reggie knew a hell of a lot more than anyone suspected.

"What did you tell her?" Cam asked.

"The truth." Jem shrugged. "Nothing. I don't know anything, Sam, because you haven't told us anything."

"It's obvious you two are fighting," said Annie. She was picking at her food, too. She always got too tense to eat during finals.

"Yeah, man." Motsu had already finished his own food. He

pulled Cam's plate in front of him. "What did you do?" He dug into the noodles like he'd ordered them for himself.

"No, no, no," said Cam, leaning forward in his chair and wagging one finger at the others. "This one's not on me." He heard his own voice as if from a distance. Too loud, too sharp, too angry. Curious heads turned at tables nearby. But he couldn't hold himself back. "You want to know what happened, you ask her. This is her fault. Not mine." He punctuated his words with that same single finger, stabbing against the table hard enough to set their drinks swaying in their cups. "Not. Mine."

No one said anything then. They all just looked at each other with silent stares freighted with meaning.

Cam fell back against his chair hard enough to push it backward, the chair legs shrieking over the concrete floor. He hated himself for his outburst, hated himself even more for dumping on his friends. They didn't deserve to feel his anger.

Reggie did.

"We're here for you, Sam," said Sarah at last, quietly, "if you need to talk about it."

Cam did need to talk about it. But he couldn't talk to any of them.

There were only two people he could talk to. One of them was in prison, probably for the rest of her life, now, thanks to him.

And the other? He wasn't talking to her at all.

51

CAM ONLY HAD one in-person final, scheduled for the next day, the last day of exams. Unfortunately, the final was for Theories of Punishment, a class he shared with Reggie—the woman in black.

He and Jem walked in ten minutes early, but the small classroom was already mostly full. Cam tried to keep his head down, but couldn't stop himself from scanning the room. He let out the breath he'd been holding.

She wasn't there.

He and Jem took two seats in the center of the middle riser, surrounded by people. Cam chose his spot because there were no open seats around him. He kept his head down and focused on his desk as he pulled his supplies from his backpack. He set his pencils, his eraser, and his watch on his desk with meticulous attention, as if their arrangement would affect his grade.

Still, he knew when she entered the room. He didn't see her, didn't look up. But he could feel her. The air became charged. The hair on his bare arms raised. Despite the fact that he was wearing only a thin t-shirt and the windows of the room were open to the soft morning breeze, a trickle of sweat snaked down from his armpit, working and winding in fits and starts. Cam slapped his t-shirt against his side to stop it, to soak it into the fabric.

The professor distributed the finals by row, handing a stack of stapled packets to the person at seated at the end of each riser. When the stack finally came to him, Cam took one with relief and passed the stack to Jem on his left.

Finally, he could focus on something other than her.

The final was straightforward. Professor Riskin pushed her students hard during the semester, but she was no sadist, and she knew the importance of a clean transcript. Her final wasn't simple, but there were no gotchas, no questions designed to make the teacher feel smart and the students feel blindsided.

Cam finished well before the allotted time had expired, but he refused to get up until she was gone. He didn't want to feel her eyes on him, didn't want her to follow him down the hallway.

He waited and waited, checking and rechecking his answers, rolling his pencil between his fingers, listening to the tick of the second hand on the watch on his desk, each tick like the slice of a pendular knife, wounding him, merciless and interminable.

Finally, the shriek of a chair pushing back. He knew it was her without looking, knew she was watching him as she stood. He knew, somehow, that she'd finished just as early as him, had been waiting for him to move first, had decided to be the initiator.

He stared down at his pencil, listened to the rustle as she gathered her bag, slung it over her shoulder. His sense of hearing seemed heightened, but only in relation to her. He didn't notice the sounds of the breeze in the leaves outside the window or the chatter of the people outside. But the sounds of her movement filled his ears.

The clip of her steps on the risers, in rhythm with time's wounds.

Murmurs of thanks and good wishes exchanged with the professor.

The soft clap as Reggie lay her exam in the basket.

The fading click of her heels as she left the room.

Cam waited for sixty more cuts of the clock, then sixty more, then sixty times five before finally pushing back his own chair. He managed a sincere smile and a word of thanks for Professor Riskin. She wished him well, then turned her gaze back to the rest of the class, still heads-down over their exams.

Cam hovered his hand over the basket where he was to turn in his test. Reggie's exam lay below him.

He could tamper with it.

He could do it without Riskin knowing. It would only take a moment.

Just one answer, perhaps two, changed from correct to incorrect. The margin between their GPAs was so razor-thin, that would be enough to push him to the top.

He could do it. The opportunity lay right there in front of him, its tender neck exposed. Time suspended, the pendulum stopped at its apsis, ready for a killing stroke.

In a heartbeat, Cam could put himself ahead.

And then what? He'd gain his audience with Jenkins, but he still had no proof. The woman in black had taken away more than his pride, more than his position in the school rankings. She'd taken away his last chance to get the information he needed to stand before Jenkins with a compelling argument. The school rankings were meaningless without that.

And Cam didn't work this hard, didn't come all this way just to cheat in the end. He would do anything to free his mother, but his mother would not want him to stoop so low. She would be free, but Cam would not be able to endure the disappointment when she looked at him. The Hauk's were criminals, true. But they did their work with honor.

He would have to find another way.

He set his exam paper atop hers and left the room.

52

CELINA'S THROAT grew thick when she saw Cameron in the classroom. His dark hair, tousled in that absent-minded way that set her heart to hammering. His muscular arms bare, the sharp curves of his chest visible beneath his t-shirt as he moved. It felt like forever since she'd seen him, even longer since he'd laid those deep, brown eyes on her.

Longer still since they'd—

Celina's breath hitched, but she managed to keep her stride steady. The guy in the closest front-row seat, some jurisprudence dweeb who wanted to be Chief Justice one day or something, glanced up at the sound, gave her a thin, hopeful smile, then buried it at Celina's cold stare and focused back on his sweating and test anxiety.

Unlike that guy, Cameron wasn't looking at her. He was fucking around with his pencils, but Celina knew he was paying attention. She could feel his focus like his hand on her skin. She tingled from it, grew flushed and hot in her core. She wanted him, hungered for him. And she knew he hungered for her.

But if he wanted to play rough, she would play rougher.

The exam didn't matter. Celina only showed up in person to keep up appearances and deflect any suspicion. She'd need to do well enough for the professors not to be surprised when she became valedictorian, but she would hack into the school servers at the end of the week and adjust her grades, as needed, to ensure that outcome. She doubted that the professors would compare grades without probable cause, so she did just enough work and earned grades just high enough to make sure they wouldn't have any.

But the work still came easy to her, and the Theories of Punishment final was no exception. Riskin was a good professor and a cool lady. Celina had done her research, of course. Riskin had fought her share of battles in her career and won most of them handily. She had nothing to prove to a class full of students. The test was fair and well-written.

And despite the fact that Celina was setting her own grades, she still knew her shit. She wasn't there for the degree, but that didn't mean she couldn't learn.

The world was all about power. Money was one form of it. Thanks to her father, Celina had lots of that. But knowledge was another form of power, and Celina gained more wherever she could. Especially for a woman, she needed twice as much knowledge as the men she took down.

A man could be a complete idiot, but with the right connections, he could ride the rails of the patriarchy right into any position of power he chose. A woman had to work a hundred times harder to overcome that patriarchy, to overcome the sexual bias that made every man look at every woman a pocket pussy instead of a thinking, feeling human being, to overcome the physical bullshit that made too many people think women were the weaker sex, and on and on and on.

Being a woman was a disadvantage in a lot of ways. But it was an advantage in many more. Society did its best to train women to ignore those advantages—pain tolerance, patience, sexual power, empathy, determination—or even to think that to use them for their own benefit was somehow shameful. That was a particularly clever and pernicious piece of patriarchy that some unusually clever man had instituted long ago.

But if a woman was bright enough to see those advantages for what they were and bold enough to use them, she would find the reason why the patriarchy worked so hard for so long to keep women down: women were inherently more powerful than men.

That was one of the many things Celina knew. And she was always finding more proof and learning new ways to use that particular piece of knowledge to her benefit.

She and Cameron finished their exams at about the same time. Celina had planned to leave when he did, corner him outside, force him to talk to her, or at least let her talk to him, let her explain. But he was still playing hardball. She looked from the top row down over the sea of heads bent over their exam papers. He was just sitting there, twiddling his thumbs, waiting for her to leave. He wouldn't look at her, but she could feel his attention on her like standing before a raging bonfire, the heat of his attention blasting her in the face. Did he really think he was hiding it? Did he really think that she couldn't feel it?

Fuck all that bullshit. Celina had better things to do than sit in a classroom all morning and play mind games with a sulking child. Celina would check in from time to time to see if Cameron's head was out of his own ass yet. Right now, it still wasn't.

She said quiet goodbyes to Riskin, dropped her exam in the metal receiving basket. She didn't bother waiting in the hallway for Cameron. She knew he'd wait another five minutes, maybe ten, before he left.

She considered waiting outside for him, cornering him on the sidewalk. She didn't like wasting time, but she needed him to understand. And she needed to understand him, needed to know what the hell he thought he was doing in the DOJ building. She wasn't at all sure that cornering him in a public place was the best way to get that information, but he wasn't responding to her any other way.

No. Fuck that. And fuck him. She strode out the front door of the building, down the cracked concrete steps, and took off down the sidewalk, her long strides moving her fast enough to make the soft spring breeze feel like a driving storm.

She would keep hounding him, keep knocking on his door. Maybe she'd just break in again and wait for him to come home. She didn't want to piss him off even more, and that definitely would, but if he was going to be a dumbass, Celina would have to take matters into her own hands. She'd force him to talk to her.

She knew how to get information out of people. Some thought that torture was the best way. But a person in physical pain would say anything to get you to stop. No, if you wanted real information, you had to figure out what motivated the person. What were they most afraid of? Or, even better, what did they love the most in the world? If you knew that, you knew what clamps to twist to squeeze the information out of them.

Not that Celina wanted to torture Cameron. But she did want to force him to pull his head from his ass and talk to her like an adult. He just needed to know what it was that had him so pissed off. It couldn't possibly just be the fake identity thing. There was something else, something to do with his mother.

She stopped dead in her tracks on the sidewalk. A slow smile crept across her face.

She had a much better idea than knocking on Cameron's door or lying in wait in his apartment.

No, Celina didn't like to dick around like that. Knowledge is power, and she'd learned that when you needed information, the best way to get it was to go straight to the source.

53

CAM STEELED HIMSELF FOR CONFRONTATION, then felt an odd twang of disappointment when he left Riskin's classroom and didn't find Reggie waiting for him in the hallway.

Not Reggie. The woman in bla— Jesus, what the fuck was her real name?

Cam blew out an angry breath and squared his shoulders, shifting his backpack and setting it more firmly on his body.

She was probably waiting downstairs, or maybe outside.

He walked down the narrow marble staircase, keeping his head down, but scanning side to side looking for her as he emerged into the ground-floor hallway.

She wasn't there.

He went outside, walked slowly down the sidewalk toward the train station. Still no sign of her.

Maybe she wasn't waiting.

Maybe she'd given up.

The hollow gnawing in his chest opened to become a gaping pit in his stomach.

Maybe she was waiting to ambush him at his apartment. She had a key.

Or so she claimed. She could have just picked the lock.

He really should upgrade the locks on his door.

She didn't appear when he walked through the front gate of his apartment complex, didn't appear in the elevator or along the walkway to his place.

He unlocked his front door and swung it open with a flourish, stepping through with a long stride.

There was no one there, either.

This time, the disappointment was more than just a twang. The gaping pit in his stomach yawned wide, a dark, bottomless chasm. He teetered on its edge.

Damn it. No.

He reeled himself away from the chasm, threw his backpack on the couch hard enough for it to bounce off the back and land with a sickening thud on the floor, and stomped into the kitchen. He jerked an espresso glass from the shelf, slamming shut the cabinet door a little too hard. The sharp report of wood against wood was both a satisfying mirror to the anger he felt and a pointed proof of the grief that same anger was trying to hide.

Grief, like someone had died.

Grief, like he'd lost a loved one.

Cam grabbed the handle of the cabinet door and slammed it three more times in quick succession, three sharp reports like the pop-pop-pop of pistol fire.

Fuck this shit. Fuck her.

Cam shoved a capsule in the coffee machine and jabbed the button. With infuriating mechanical patience, the machine summoned the throaty whir it uttered whenever it started to brew. After an interminable moment, a thin stream of steaming coffee emerged from the spout.

And fell in a splatter onto the counter.

Cam swore, rushed to push the espresso cup under the spout, held it in midair so the bottom wouldn't get wet from resting in the spilled coffee.

He looked at the cup in his hand, a white ceramic cup perfectly sized for a double macchiato, his favorite drink.

Reggie had bought the cup for him, in a set of four.

He remembered the look on her face—half laughter, half defiance, all gorgeous—as she stood in the doorway that afternoon, shopping bags in both hands and hanging from her forearms, filled with the tools and supplies she said a *civilized* kitchen needed to have.

As he watched the espresso pour into the cup, Cam realized he'd been smiling. His anger melted with the smile, revealing a tired weight Cam didn't have the energy to carry any longer. He sighed, closed his eyes, shook his head slowly.

What the fuck was he doing? He was freezing out a woman he cared about. A woman he loved. And why?

Because she lied to him about her identity? He was doing the same to her.

Because she knew all along who he really was and didn't say anything?

Because she'd given him clues to her identity and it had taken him months to figure them out?

Because he'd felt like a fool when he finally did?

Oh.

Oh, no.

Oh, fuck no.

He wasn't that kind of man, was he? The kind of man who got angry and burned his own house down when a woman made him feel small and stupid? Or, more exactly, when he did something small and stupid and she called him on it?

No. He wasn't that kind of man. He'd never been that kind of man. He refused to be that kind of man. His parents had raised him better than that. That was not what was going on here.

Then what was it? What the fuck was he so angry about?

Yes, he felt like a fool. He felt like he should have figured out the identity of the woman in black much, much sooner.

And, yes, he felt like a fool in front of Reggie when he finally did figured it out.

He felt like a fool for not figuring out the clues.

He felt like a fool for spending so much time with someone who was not who they were pretending to be.

He felt like a fool for thinking that he'd fooled her with his own double identity.

Was that why he was angry? Because she was so much smarter than him?

No. None of that felt right. Those things were all true, but none felt like the core problem.

He searched deeper, thought back to that moment in her apartment when the truth had dawned on him. He'd held the clues in his lap, looked around the apartment, looked up at her, holding the steaming dinner plates...

And he didn't know who she was. He was in love with her, but he had no idea who she really was.

It was more than feeling foolish.

It felt like a betrayal.

His love was real, more real than anything he'd ever felt with a woman before. Even his mother had commented on how different he looked.

And he thought Reggie loved him the same way. Or, at least, he felt like they were on that path together.

But were those feelings part of her act? Was she that good of a con artist?

Or maybe Cam had done the same thing he always did, the thing he'd sworn never to do again. When it came to women, he had a nasty tendency to deceive himself, to trick himself into believing in some fairy tale romance like his parents had, when the reality was not that way. Not that way at all. Maybe all the love he felt being reciprocated by Reggie was just the reflection of the feelings he'd been projecting onto her.

But if that was the case, Cam had no right to be angry with anyone but himself.

In fact, that would just be one more reason on a long list of reasons to be angry with himself.

The coffee machine finished. Cam drank his espresso.

It tasted bitter.

He spent the next day, Saturday, puttering around his apartment, going out onto the walkway a lot more than usual. To check the weather. To stretch his legs. To adjust his front-door camera, shake the dirt from his welcome mat, and sweep the doorstep. He even propped the front door wide open for a while, throwing open his windows, too, and telling himself it was to let in the warm early-May breeze.

He had little else to do, so he cleaned his kitchen, his living room, and his bedroom. He rearranged his closet and the cabinet by the front door. He even washed his own windows, taking off the screens and reaching through to clean the outsides, though the apartment complex contracted a window washer to come every month for the same purpose.

When he finally ran out of chores, he had to admit to himself that he wasn't hanging around because his apartment needed a spring cleaning. He was hanging around, hoping that Reggie—whatever her name was—would come by.

She didn't.

As the light faded in the evening, he walked two blocks for a chicken parmesan sandwich from a place that he and Reggie both loved, got it to go and carried it all the way home before eating it.

Still no sign of Reggie.

He ate the sandwich alone, standing at his kitchen counter, staring at the crumbs as they dropped into his sink.

The next morning, early, he stopped by Reggie's apartment, screwed up his courage, and raised his fist to knock. He didn't need to swallow his pride. He'd already choked on that, gagged, and threw it back up in a wet lump on the floor. Talk about looking foolish. He refused to let that foolishness poison him again.

He rapped softly, slowly, apologetically on the door. He waited, then knocked again, louder, listening for footsteps, a voice, anything.

He heard nothing at all.

He knocked again, waited again, stood there and repeated the process for a full hour before finally he had to give up to catch the train to reach his mother before visiting hours ended.

His mother had been the wise one, of course. On each of the two Sundays since he'd figured out Reggie's identity, his mother had counseled him, encouraged him, pressed him, then urged him to talk to Reggie, hear her out. He wasn't the only one who'd been lied to, she reminded him in a voice soft enough for the guards not to hear and the recording devices not to pick up.

They didn't usually speak plainly in the visitation room. The US penal system didn't take kindly to visitors using visiting hours to plot ways to spring the inmates. But Cam had been in no state of mind for subtlety during those last few visits.

And no state of mind to listen to sage advice from a loving mother. He'd been distracted and short with her. Where he would normally stay for an hour or more, he spent five hours each way on the train those days and had only stayed with his mother for fifteen minutes each time, with most of those minutes spent fuming.

He'd been a fool in more than one way, that's for sure. But now he could see that. Better late than never, right? And if he could see his mistakes, he could try to fix them.

As the train swayed and rattled under him, as the farms, fields, and forests, freshly green and hopeful with new spring growth, sped by outside the window, Cam hoped for just a bit more wisdom from his mother.

He hoped she could help him figure out how to clean up the mess he'd made.

54

CELINA SPED south over the Delaware Memorial Bridge between New Jersey and Delaware, with the top down on her rented Mercedes SL55 roadster. She'd gone in for the SL63, but the rental company's website had lied and they didn't have it. The SL55 was a fine second choice. Hardtop convertible, big engine, plenty of acceleration, the SL55 ran around $150k. Celina wasn't a car aficionado, but she loved the feel of the leather steering wheel, warmed by the sun, under her fingers, the twelve-inch screen in the center console showing her route and giving all her diagnostics. And above all else, she loved the way the car pressed her back against the warm leather seats as it accelerated.

Celina go fast.

The air had been warm by the correctional facility up north in Bedford Hills. It was warmer this much further south, but at ninety-five miles per hour with the top down, everything was a cool breeze in summertime.

The bridge itself wasn't much to look at. Army green tuning forks served as support towers. Suspension cables hung in curtains that reminded Celina of the beaded drapes you'd find covering doorways in a smarmy frat house.

The overall feel of the bridge was government industrial, but as she drove between the drapes she could look out over the Delaware River for a splash of beauty. The whole scene was probably more beautiful at night, but with the sun high and bright overhead, the tint of Celina's sunglasses made the sky a startling deep blue. With only a wisp of cloud in the distance, Celina looked to the east. The lenses made the water seem as blue as the sky, and crystal clear. It gleamed with the promise of release into the open sea, and an easy, winding path to get there.

Celina's own path had definitely been winding thus far. What still lay ahead was unlikely to be easy, but it still had promise. If it didn't, or if the juice wasn't worth the squeeze, she would have dropped that bad citrus in a heartbeat. Or, more likely, she would have thrown it in Cam's face.

But Paulie had talked her off the ledge, had given her some sage advice. Part of it was from the perspective of an older woman with a lot more experience in dealing with men. Part of it was from a mother with a lot more perspective on her son.

And part of it was from a woman who had been in love, who had loved long and hard and very, very well for a long time, then had it ripped from her in the blink of an eye. She knew love, and she knew love lost, and those two experiences yield a perspective that puts the tempests of early relationships into a much different context.

Celina had driven all the way to New York hoping to get that context, and she had.

She'd checked the tracking on her phone before she'd left. She could see that Cam was on his way to get some of that same perspective for himself. Good. Maybe he was finally starting to pull his head out of his ass.

Paulie hadn't hesitated for a second before helping Celina to understand what was probably behind Cam's attitude the past couple of weeks. Some of it was the usual male pride bullshit, but Cam, she said, didn't suffer from too much of that.

That was a relief to Celina. If he was the kind of man who

couldn't stand the thought of a strong woman, maybe even one who was smarter, faster, stronger, and ballsier that he was, then Celina wasn't even going to bother talking to him again.

She'd known already that he wasn't really like that. She'd spent enough time with him to figure that much out. But it was still nice to get confirmation from Paulie.

Paulie clued her in on what was really driving Cam, and it lined up with Celina's suspicions. If Celina loved her mom like Cam loved Paulie, and she was in prison, Celina would be racked with guilt trying to get her out, too.

Of course, Celina definitely did not love her mother the way Cam loved Paulie. She didn't love her mother at all. And as far as prison went, if the world were truly just, her mom would be in there for life. But, the world being what it was, the opposite was true. Her mother was one of the ones writing the rules, not submitting to them.

But now Celina understood what was driving Cam. And she thought she understood his plan. Paulie couldn't speak too plainly in a room filled with guards and other inmates and their visitors, but she gave enough hints to confirm Celina's suspicions. Cam wanted to use his audience with Attorney General Jenkins to secure his mother's release. Paulie had used the word "appeal", but Celina suspected it would be more of a bargaining process than an appeal. A man like Jenkins didn't have a better nature to appeal to.

And with a man like him in a position like his, the only real way to bargain was to blackmail.

That meant Cam needed dirt, and he'd been snooping around the DOJ trying to get it.

That explained why he'd been so pissed off after Celina had given him a hard pass on his stupid plan to get himself killed by Jenkins' goons that night. And why he'd been so pissed to learn that it had been Reggie Moon who'd done it. That was his last hope for freeing his mother, the culmination of his whole three-year plan.

Which made no sense to Celina, by the way. Three years of school just to get a meeting with the AG? Cam was a masochist. Either that, or the man seriously needed better hacking skills. Celina wanted the same meeting, but she was swooping in halfway through the last semester with a fake transcript. Why the hell hadn't Cam done that? Would have saved himself a lot of time and money.

Just one more way was she was smarter and ballsier than him. Celina was fine with that. She was smarter and ballsier than most people. And she'd never get laid if she insisted on sleeping only with men who were as smart as she was. Cam came pretty close, nonetheless. Plus, he was distracted by trying to free his mother. As fond as she was of him now, Celina figured he'd be even more interesting without that burden hanging over his head.

As she sped off the bridge, the blue width of the Delaware River passing into her rear-view mirror, Celina settled into her decision. After only two visits, Celina had already come to love Paulie Hauk. Judging from the way the guards treated her, it seemed Paulie had that effect on people. Cam or no Cam, Celina wanted to get Paulie out of prison.

She loved Paulie, and despite the hissy fit he'd thrown for the last two weeks, she loved Cameron Hauk, too.

It felt weird to even think that word.

Love.

Celina had only ever loved one man, and that was her father. She'd been with dozens of guys, but hadn't cared about any of them.

Until Cam.

And now that she finally knew what the fuck he was trying to do, she had made her decision.

She was going to help him.

Celina glanced at the viewscreen in her console. 120 miles to home. The GPS said it would take her two and a half hours with traffic.

She smiled, gripped the warm leather steering wheel, and floored the accelerator.

She'd make it in ninety minutes.

55

CAM DRUMMED his fingers on the orange plastic-coated table in the visitation room at Taconic Correctional Facility, waiting for the guards to bring his mother out to see him. Several of the other tables were in use, with other inmates and their visitors laughing or talking in hushed whispers.

At one table, an inmate named Mazie, a friend of Cam's mother, was having what looked to be a very serious conversation with her visitor—a tall, thick woman wearing a denim shirt with the sleeves ripped off, her arms bare save for the tattoos covering every inch of skin, with straight brown hair down almost to her belt.

Normally, Mazie would give Cam a grin and a head nod when he saw her. This time, she was all business, talking in hissed whispers to her visitor. For her part, the visitor looked like she was about to commit the kind of act that would land her in a cell next to Mazie. Her face was the red of fresh blood, her hands coiled into meaty hocks on the table before her.

Cam waited quietly. It normally didn't take this long for the guards to bring his mother up. While he waited, he puzzled over a comment Sue, the correctional officer who'd let him in, had made. Cam had handed Sue a bag of horehound candy—her

345

favorite, and a traditional gift Cam had been bringing her for fifteen years, since his mother first entered prison. She'd thanked him, turned to unlock the door, then smiled back at him.

"Like Grand Central in here for Paulie today," she said. "Good to see her have so many visitors."

Cam had been too confused to do more than smile faintly back and thank Sue for letting him in. Now, as he drummed his fingers on the table, he worked the comment over in his mind.

What the hell did that mean? Who else had visited his mother? The only other person Cam had ever known to visit was her lawyer, but she hadn't been involved in the case for over ten years. Not since Cam had finished law school and passed the New York bar exam himself. Could there have been a new development in his mother's case somehow, one that Cam wasn't aware of?

Cam was so lost in his own thoughts that he didn't notice the inmate door opening or his mother being led in. She appeared suddenly, sitting at the table in front of him.

"You seem distracted today," said Paulie, pressing her hand against the table with thumb and two fingers extended, American Sign Language for *I love you*. Since all physical contact was forbidden in the visitation room, it had become their standard greeting. "Everything okay?"

His mother looked as beautiful as ever. At age fifty-six, she seemed to be getting younger with every passing year. Instead of making her seem older, the silver streaked throughout her jet-black hair somehow made her look younger and hipper. The deepening lines around her eyes and her mouth just enhanced the feelings of love and joy that she always projected.

But Cam could see the way that her skin was just a little more pale, her eyes just a touch more weary than they'd been. Only someone who'd known Paulie his whole life would be able to notice.

But it was those small details, the ones only Cam could see, that gnawed at his heart in the middle of the night when he couldn't sleep for wanting so desperately to free his mother from prison.

Even with a touch of weariness, though, Paulie's eyes were still the bright, stunning pale blue they had always been. Today, Cam noticed an extra twinkle in them, a bit of mischievousness in the way Paulie's mouth twisted at the corner as she waited for him to respond.

"Sue said you'd had a lot of visitors today," he said, pressing his own hand to the table in the *I love you* sign. "Who's been here besides me?"

That smile quirked a little higher at the corners as Paulie's eyes slid from Cam to Mazie at the table behind him, then back.

"Just a friend," said Paulie casually. "You're not the only visitor I've ever had, you know."

Her smile was kind, but Cam felt his cheeks burn red all the same.

"No, of course," he mumbled.

Paulie leaned forward conspiratorially, coming as close as she could without breaking the rules and making physical contact with Cam. She glanced over Cam's shoulder at Mazie.

"Mazie's asking her woman for a divorce," she whispered.

Cam frowned. "Didn't they just get married?"

"Today's their two-year anniversary," Paulie nodded.

"Why does Mazie want a divorce, then?"

"She's back with her ex, Chicky."

"The one she dumped to marry that one?" Cam jerked his head over his shoulder toward the pair.

Paulie shrugged. "Days are long and lonely in prison," she said, then gave a wicked grin. "And Mazie doesn't have a lot of patience," she said. She glanced again at Mazie and raised her eyebrows thoughtfully. "Or impulse control, for that matter." She brought her eyes back to Cam again. "Kind of why she's in here, I think."

Cam shook his head. "Sounds like a soap opera in here."

Paulie grinned. "You don't know the half of it. Way better than a soap opera." She leaned back again. "But enough about The Bold and the Incarcerated." Her face softened. "How are you holding up? Have you talked to Reggie yet?"

Cam sighed. "Her name's not Reggie," he mumbled.

Her mother's look was compassionate, but still disapproving. "Is that what really matters at this point?"

Cam pulled his hands off the table into his lap and looked down at them, shaking his head.

"I thought relationships were supposed to be based on trust and honesty," he said. His voice grew quiet. "Isn't that what you and Dad had?"

Paulie waited for a long moment, long enough for Cam to look up, then smiled sadly at him.

"I know you want what your dad and I had," she said. "I want it for you, too."

She held out her hand toward Cam on the table. She knew she couldn't hold Cam's hand, but Cam knew that the gesture meant she wished she could. He put his own fingertips on the edge of the table to return the feeling.

"What your dad and I had didn't start off the way it was when you were old enough to see it."

Cam looked up and frowned. Paulie laughed.

"That's right," she said. "Shocking, isn't it?"

She laughed again, a sound that made everyone left in the room turn to look, smiles unconsciously coming to their faces. The correctional officer in the corner, the inmates at the table behind Paulie. Cam glanced over his shoulder. Even Mazie and her increasingly red-faced soon-to-be ex-wife smiled a little. That was the secret superpower of Paulie Hauk.

"Your dad told me everything from the start," Paulie said, "but I didn't."

"What do you mean?"

"Your dad spilled his guts to me on our first date. Told me all his crackpot theories, his kooky ideas for the future, all his counter-culture notions." She smiled at the memory. "And that was something back then. Back then, in the town we grew up in, a guy could get himself locked up if he let his hair grow longer than his ears. What your dad said to me was practically sedition. And that was before he even thought about being a thief for a living."

Cam had heard the story plenty of times over the years. How being with his mother was like being drunk or high for his dad, but without any of the side effects or impairment. The only downside was that he couldn't control his tongue. He just said everything that popped into his head. Couldn't stop himself. Spilled all of his deepest, darkest secrets.

Including the fact that he was hopelessly, instantly, ass-over-tip in love with Paulie from the moment he first laid eyes on her.

"But you didn't lie to him," said Cam. "Did you?"

Paulie tilted her head from side to side in a vacillating gesture.

"No," she said, drawing out the word, "but I didn't exactly open up to him, either. Not for a long time."

"That's not the same thing."

"Isn't it?" Paulie sat back on her bench, her back straight, and crossed her arms over her chest, staring hard at Cam. "Reggie—"

She cut herself off, held up one hand to stop Cam just as his mouth opened. "I know that's not her name, but we'll just use it for now."

Cam closed his mouth again.

"Reggie came to your school for some reason of her own," Paulie continued, then gave Cam an even harder stare. "Just like you did."

She couldn't say more, not with officers and recording equipment listening in, but Cam knew exactly what she meant.

"She wasn't expecting to meet you any more than you were expecting to meet her." Paulie raised an eyebrow. "And neither one of you was expecting to fall in love."

Cameron folded his own arms over his chest and grumbled softly.

"You don't think she's in love with you?"

It was like his mother could read his mind. It had always been like that. He could never get away with anything as a kid. He didn't know if it was from so many years of working as a criminal, that his mother had gotten really good at reading people, or if it was a gift she'd always possessed. Or if it was simply because she was his mother.

"How can I know if she is or not?" Cam said.

"You could ask her."

"She's lied to me about so much other stuff," Cam said. "She'd probably just lie about that, too."

"No," Paulie shook her head. "I don't care how good a con artist she is, you can't lie about love. The only people who can lie about love is us," she leaned forward and pointed to her chest, "to ourselves. Reggie can put it out there that she loves you, but as long as you're not lying to yourself, you'll know if she's telling the truth."

Cam huffed out a long breath. "How do I know if I'm lying to myself?"

"That's a little harder to figure out," said his mother, "but what have we always taught you?"

Cam had been helping his parents in the family business since before he could walk or talk. Among many other things, they'd taught him how to read people, how to quickly earn their trust, and how to play a con. The number one rule in a con, when you're assuming a fake persona: go deep enough to make them believe it, but...

"Never forget who you really are," he muttered.

Cam dropped his hands to his lap, picked at his thumbnails.

The longer the con, the more difficult and important it was to follow that rule.

Paulie nodded. "Find your center again," she said. "You'll find yourself there."

Cam's mother was his center. A large part of it, at least. She kept him grounded in his truth. Even when they had to speak in code so the officers didn't know what they were planning, he could look into his mother's eyes and see himself, his real self, there.

Cam had been working the Sam Davis con for three long years. Had he forgotten who he really was?

He looked up, looked into his mother's eyes. That pale blue color. The infinite kindness. The deep love he always saw and felt. His mother's secret superpower worked on him, too. He'd always felt her love, had never questioned it for a moment, his whole life.

Looking into those eyes now, Cam felt an alignment within himself, an alignment he didn't know he'd lost.

"Talk to her," his mother said, softly.

Cam nodded.

After weeks of avoiding her, of avoiding all the issues that had suddenly appeared between them, and after weeks of avoiding his own true feelings, Cam was finally ready to talk to Reggie, face-to-face.

56

TALKING to Reggie face-to-face turned out to be easier said than done.

Cam went straight from the train station to Reggie's door when he got back from the prison, stood outside knocking for a full hour, but the door never opened.

Every day that week, he did the same, and got the same result. He considered picking the lock, but couldn't bring himself to violate her trust in that way. He considered mounting a camera outside her door, setting up a motion-sensitive alert on his phone so he would know immediately the next time she came home. But that, too, felt a bit too stalker-like for his taste. He wanted to apologize to Reggie, to get her to open up to him. Nothing says "I'm sorry, you can trust me" like unauthorized twenty-four-hour surveillance.

Graduation was coming up on Sunday, and final grades would be posted by Friday afternoon. Cam knew in his gut that Reggie would be valedictorian. After that, the dinner for the top five students would be Saturday night. As top student, Reggie would then spend Sunday morning with Attorney General Jenkins, and graduation would begin at 1pm.

Cam was hoping to talk to Reggie before then. He didn't

know how that conversation might go, but if he told Reggie what he was trying to do, maybe she could think of a way to help him. Maybe she could pressure the AG for him during their morning together.

It was a lot to ask, probably too much to ask, especially after only knowing Reggie for a few months, even more so after they hadn't spoken for weeks. But Cam had to try, for his mother's sake.

But he wouldn't get the chance if he couldn't find Reggie.

The week passed. Cam, Jem, Sarah, Annie, and Motsu attended various parties, some official events put on by the school, others wilder parties hosted by students. Cam went to as many as he could, looking for Reggie. Every time he saw his friends—at a party or otherwise—he questioned them about Reggie, but none of them had seen her, either.

Maybe she'd gone out of town. Technically, there was no need for her to walk at graduation. The diploma was awarded as soon as the requirements were met. Maybe Reggie had already moved on.

It occurred to Cam for the first time that, if that were the case, he had no idea what she might have moved on to. Reggie Wood was as much a fiction as Sam Davis. He had no idea what Reggie's real name was, had no idea why she used the alias or what her goal was for being at the school. He had no way to know if she might have accomplished that goal and moved on or abandoned it altogether, nor where she might go next.

Cam was completely in the dark, completely at Reggie's mercy. The only way he would see her again, at this point, was if she decided she wanted him to see her.

And maybe that was the way it should be. She'd tried to talk to him. For a full week, she'd tried hard to see him. And Cam had pushed her away. He'd closed the door and locked it tight. Why should he be surprised if she decided to walk away and let Cam go fuck himself?

The parties grew wilder and wilder as the week wore on, but Cam only grew more and more distracted. In the beginning of the week, he'd hold his obligatory drink and stand in a corner for an hour or two, chatting and laughing with his friends, but all the while looking out for Reggie to arrive. By the end of the week, he would simply arrive at the party and scour the location in search of Reggie. If she wasn't there, he'd leave. His friends all had instructions to text him immediately if they saw her anywhere.

And when he left, Cam would go home. He'd knock on Reggie's door for a while, then go back to his place and check the camera footage to see if she'd stopped by while he was out. He'd sit alone in his apartment for fifteen minutes or so, then knock on Reggie's door again and repeat the process.

It was pathetic, really, but it was all Cam could think to do. And seeing Reggie was all he could think about at all.

Early on Friday evening, while he was making himself a cup of coffee, already settled for the night in a t-shirt and loose shorts, the sun low and bright above the horizon through his kitchen window, his phone buzzed again and again on the counter. Cam's pulse immediately doubled. He set down the cup he'd been holding and lunged for his phone, thinking, hoping, praying it might be Reggie calling.

It wasn't.

Instead, there was a flurry of texts from his friends.

He unlocked the phone and went to his messages app, hoping the next best thing had happened and they'd spotted Reggie somewhere. He was already at the door, slipping on his shoes, when he read the first text.

Wrong again. They hadn't spotted Reggie.

But the final grades had been released. Along with the final list of the top five students in the class rankings.

Reggie was top of the class, as Cam had expected.

But he hadn't expected what his friends were telling him.

Not believing their texts, needing to see the results for himself, Cam pulled up the school website with the official top five rankings and zoomed in to the webpage to check the result for himself.

Even seeing it with his own eyes, he couldn't believe it.

Reggie was top of the class.

But so was he.

Both of them had a final GPA of 3.996.

A dead tie for first place.

57

CAM'S MIND couldn't process what his eyes were telling him. He zoomed in further on the webpage to check the numbers more closely, then zoomed out to check again, as if seeing them in miniature would make them more verifiable. Then he refreshed the page, thinking maybe they'd posted it in error, a copy-paste mistake.

The numbers didn't change.

He waited. It would take time for the administrative employees to realize their mistake. It was late in the day on Friday. They'd probably already gone home for the weekend. Maybe they were stuck on the metro feeling sick about their careless, but understandable, error. Cam would give them more time to get home, log back in, correct the error, and repost the list.

He went back to the kitchen to finish making his coffee, slugged it back, then made another, not because he needed it or even wanted it, but because it gave his hands and his mind something to do.

Unfortunately, it also made him even more antsy than he already was. He set a timer on his phone and forced himself to wait one full hour before checking the website again. He spent that hour pacing a groove in the floor between his living room and his kitchen. The sunlight through the window grew brighter and more slant as he paced, then faded from golden to grey, then to silver as the lights above the walkway outside came on.

Cam practically dove across the room when his timer went off. He refreshed the webpage once more, zoomed in and out again, checking and re-checking.

The results hadn't changed.

He and Reggie were still tied for first place.

It seemed impossible. Had this ever happened before? How would the school handle it? It seemed unlikely that the Attorney General Jenkins, busy as he was, would free up a second full morning so that both he and Reggie could have a private audience with him. Did that mean they would share that time on Sunday morning? Or would they each get half a morning alone with Jenkins?

In the end, though, it wouldn't matter. Whether shared or separate, Cam would have his private audience. He wouldn't have made his pitch in front of Jem and the others in a public space. That would implicate them and it would make it difficult for Jenkins to capitulate and still save face. Between Cam's friends, the security team, and the wait staff, there would be too many witnesses.

And Cam's friends had no idea what was really going on. Cam wanted to keep it that way. He wanted them to maintain plausible deniability if anything about Cam's plan was ever to blow back and cause problems.

But with Reggie, he had no qualms about it. He didn't want any harm to come to her, of course, but somehow he knew she would be able to handle it just fine. Whatever *it* might be.

He wanted to tell her everything, anyway. She was pulling the same fake identity con Cam was, so he figured she was more likely to be comfortable with it. And if they presented a united front with the AG, Jenkins would think of them as one entity and still be willing to give Cam what he was asking for.

Or so Cam hoped. He still had no proof to support his accusations.

But that was a different problem, one he'd figure out when he came to it.

For now, he'd been given a gift. A miracle. Some kind of mathematical grade point magic.

A thought drifted through his mind, and Cam frowned. He grabbed his phone again, pulled up his personal school portal, with all of his grades and his own final GPA on it.

His GPA said 3.996.

But he could have sworn it said something different just last week, something lower. The number he remembered was 3.992, not 3.996. Could he be misremembering? With as much as he focused on his GPA, those numbers were burned into his brain. But a lot had happened in the last week. Maybe his memory wasn't quite right this time.

He scanned the letter grades for his classes from that semester. They all seemed to be the same as before. But for a GPA difference that small, he'd need to dig into the numbers behind them in order to detect any changes. He shifted to his desk and opened his laptop. He'd be able to work more easily there.

Just as he logged into his school portal on his laptop, he heard a knock. Absent-minded, still trying to search his memory for the truth, he padded to the front door, barefoot, pulling one hand through his hair.

Something seemed off about the GPA thing, but he wasn't sure what it was. Then again, why overthink it? He got the result he was hoping for, right? Chalk it up to that GPA magic and let it go.

Still, it nagged at him in the back of his mind. Cam didn't

like loose ends, and he had learned through a great deal of experience to trust his instincts.

His mother had told him to find his center again. When you had found your center, you tuned in to your own instincts. You listened to that soft voice in your head when it spoke. Right now, that voice was telling him something didn't match up.

Cam pulled open the door and looked up.

The voice in his head went silent.

His mouth went dry.

His heart stopped beating.

And time seemed to stand perfectly still.

Something magical was happening that day. Cam was getting everything he wanted.

First the class rankings.

And now this.

Reggie Moon—the woman in black, Cam's nemesis, his lover, the woman of his dreams—was standing in his doorway.

58

CELINA MAXWELL WAS a woman of action. She had wealth. She had brains. She had balls bigger than any man she'd ever met. She knew what she wanted and she didn't take shit from anyone on her way to getting it.

And she certainly didn't stand on doorsteps flapping her mouth open and closed, at a total, utter loss for words.

Until that night.

It wasn't just the thin t-shirt that showed every line of Cameron's lean, muscular body, the body that made Celina want to rip his clothes off every time she saw it just so she could get a better look.

It wasn't just his eyes, those deep, clear eyes, brown with flecks of yellow and orange, that seemed to pull her into a vortex every time she looked into them.

It wasn't just his gaze, the feel of his eyes locked with hers, of his eyes touching her face and her hair, of his eyes caressing her body. That gaze that she'd craved, that touch she'd been denied for three full weeks.

It wasn't just those things. It was something else. Something about *him*. His smell or his energy or his heat. She didn't know what it was, but it was something about Cameron Hauk, or some combination of things, that had crept into her body, into her blood.

She was addicted to him now.

When he was gone, she felt it. She felt cranky. She felt unsettled in her own skin, like she was wearing clothes tailor made for someone almost Celina's size and shape, but not quite. The world didn't fit right, seemed a little colder, a little less clear.

She'd been living in that subtle hell for three weeks.

And now, finally, Cameron was standing in front of her, looking at her, keeping his wide eyes fixed on hers when she knew he wanted to set them free, when *she* wanted him to set them free to roam over her body with abandon.

His thick hair was tousled in that sexy professor way she loved. All she could think about was plunging her hands into it, tugging it down to pull his lips harder against hers, to drive her tongue deeper into his mouth.

She could see the sharp lines of his pectoral muscles beneath his t-shirt, could think of nothing but running her hands over them, drawing her tongue slowly over his nipples and down the groove of his chest.

He wore shorts that hung loose around his hips. All she could think about was slipping her hand across the ridges of his abdomen, beneath the loose waistband, teasing his cock until it swelled and stiffened and throbbed against her grip, until a bead of wetness formed at the tip, slicking the soft strokes of her fingers, and he begged her not to stop.

And with all those thoughts running through her head, with all the feelings those thoughts sent coursing through her body, Celina had momentarily lost the capability of speech. She stood in Cameron's doorway, opening and closing her mouth like a woman in a movie with the sound turned off.

He seemed as stunned as she was. He just stood stock still, eyes intense and fixed on hers. She could feel the heat from him, like she'd stepped from the warm late-spring evening air into a furnace, one that stoked the heat inside her, the heat at her core. She wanted to take him right there, in the doorway. She didn't care who walked by, who might see, as long as she could have him again, all of him, every aching inch of him.

But...

No.

Not yet.

She hadn't come here for sex.

She'd come here to do what Paulie had advised her to do.

She'd come here to tell Cameron the truth. To tell him everything.

She slid past him in the doorway. Their bodies brushed against each other. When they did, Celina felt an electricity arc between them that almost snapped her last thin thread of self-restraint and left her helpless to hold back her more passionate instincts.

Almost.

She sat on the very edge of the couch, hands balled into fists on her knees. Cameron was still at the door, but in her mind he sat beside her on the couch. His heat washed over her. His smell.

And Celina was on him, pushing him onto his back, swinging her leg up to straddle him, grinding her hips against his, his pelvic bone rubbing hard against her—

She stood, just as Cameron came around the other side of the coffee table and bent to sit on the couch. He jerked back to standing.

A shudder washed through Celina, brought beads of sweat to her forehead and her back. She paced toward the kitchen, spun on her heel, then paced back.

Focus. For fuck's sake, she had to fucking focus.

Cameron watched her, confusion on his face.

She spun on her heel and paced back to the kitchen again. She forced her balled fists to open. They sprung closed again. Again, she forced them to open.

Pacing back and forth, hands opening and closing.

She must look like a lunatic.

She felt like a lunatic, her mind battling against her body.

"Do you have—" she said, her throat parched, voice hoarse. "Can I—"

Fuck. She couldn't even manage to ask for a glass of fucking water.

She paced into the kitchen and got one for herself, letting the faucet run while she drained one glass, refilled it, then drained a second without even taking a breath. She hunched over the sink, panting, for a moment, then set her empty glass in the basin with a tinny clink, let the water run over her hands, and turned it off. She rubbed her wet hands over her face, squeezed her eyes shut and let the cool water damp the heat inside her.

One deep breath, then another, then a third.

She ripped a paper towel from the roll, patted her face dry, balled the wet towel in her fist, and threw it across the kitchen into the trash can in the corner.

She had control again.

For the moment.

She came around the corner from the kitchen to find Cameron still standing in the same spot in front of the couch, looking wider-eyed and more confused than ever.

Celina started to move toward the couch, felt the heat from Cameron flare the flame inside her, and stopped herself. She stepped back again, maintaining what seemed a safe distance.

Another deep breath, then one more.

"Your name is Cameron Hauk," she began.

Cameron's expression shifted from confusion to something Celina couldn't quite pinpoint, a mix between relief—maybe? —and anger—perhaps?—and a kind of determined resignation.

He opened his mouth to speak, but Celina held up a hand to

stop him. She needed to get through this before she lost focus again. Cameron nodded and sat down on the couch.

"My name," Celina said, remaining standing, "my real name" — the admission opened a panicked hole in her heart she hoped Cameron would be willing to close — "is Celina Maxwell."

She waited for a moment. Sometimes her name caused a reaction, sometimes it didn't.

Cameron frowned, his eyes unfocusing for a moment as he tried to place her name.

His eyebrows shot up. He looked up at her.

Here comes the reaction. Usually either some form of pity for her father's death or some kind of awe for her wealth and her father's technical achievements or some kind of anger, depending on the political leanings of the person doing the reacting.

Cameron didn't give her any of those reactions. His eyebrows shot up, his gaze met hers, and his eyes narrowed for a moment. Then his face settled into an expression of benign, calm interest.

No pity. No awe. No anger. No reaction at all.

That, for Celina, was even worse.

She wanted to question him, to dig away at that calm expression and figure out what was really going on in Cameron's mind.

But this wasn't about him. Not yet. This was about her telling him everything. This was about her laying herself bare before him in a way she'd never done with anyone before.

Celina didn't know if she could do that, but she could at least tell Cameron the truth. She owed him that much, at the very least.

"I came to Washington... for personal reasons." Celina pressed her lips together and huffed at herself. That wasn't good enough.

And saying all of this out loud was going to be harder than Celina thought.

"I came here to settle a score," she said.

Cameron settled back on the couch, crossed his legs at the knee, and folded his hands in his lap, that same look of calm interest on his face. This wasn't going to be easy, and he wasn't going to make it any easier.

Good. She deserved that.

"My father was a wealthy man, a tech entrepreneur."

She raised her eyebrows in question at Cameron, and he nodded slowly in return. Good. He knew the backstory on her father. She wouldn't have to rehash his Wikipedia page.

She could focus on the stuff that didn't make it to print.

"After he sold his company, he got interested in politics. He wasn't looking for more power. He already had too much, he said. He wanted to give back, to use his wealth to make things better for the people who didn't have money, but who had brains and talent and who needed an opportunity, like he'd been given."

She paced back and forth in front of the coffee table. The movement helped her to keep the story flowing when her mind was screaming at her louder and louder to stop, to stop spilling her secrets.

And it helped her forget that Cameron was sitting there listening to her, to forget that he might listen to her whole story, then stand and tell her to get the fuck out of his apartment and his life, forever.

"My father met Bill Jenkins, then just a promising young California politician running for his second term in the House. My father backed him in that race, then lobbied President Hill to appoint Jenkins as Attorney General when the last AG, Mark Romer, died. My father was one of Jenkins' biggest supporters."

Her voice grew quieter.

"My father thought of Jenkins almost as a son."

Celina bore no ill will for that, toward her father or toward Jenkins. She was an only child, but she'd never for a moment felt like her father would have preferred a son or any of that kind of bullshit. Jenkins was like a son to her father, but not to fill any hole in their family or in his hopes for his family. Her father just liked Jenkins. He believed in him and in the causes he supported, the ideas he espoused, both in public and in private.

She glanced up at Cameron, hoping he wouldn't follow that stereotypical storyline in his mind. He wore the same expression of calm interest he'd been wearing since he sat down. Calm, interested, and entirely inscrutable. Celina couldn't tell if he was waiting for her to finish so he could throw her into bed or so he could throw her out the door.

She knew which one she wanted. No question. She wanted him to peel his shirt off, slowly, then take her—

No.

Stop.

Focus.

Deep breath.

She averted her eyes from Cameron and went back to pacing.

She told him about the start of Jenkins' presidential ambitions shortly after Hill's re-election, about her father's increasing involvement in the campaign. When she mentioned Vernon Stratham, she caught a glimmer of emotion behind that facade of calm interest on Cameron's face. She didn't know exactly what it was, but Cameron had been after Stratham for something.

Cameron's calm expression didn't change as she told him about her father's increasing concerns with the campaign, specifically with the finance arm, with Stratham. He didn't like the kind of donors Stratham was courting, didn't think the financial benefit was worth the risk of consorting with donors of more questionable character, no matter how rich and powerful they were. Stratham argued that if they didn't secure those donors for their campaign, the competition would secure them for theirs.

She told him about the night a year ago when her father had found something, something big, and had confronted Stratham. He told Stratham he'd be taking it to Jenkins the next night, but he wanted to give Stratham the benefit of the doubt, a chance to explain himself.

Cameron's expression didn't change until she told him about the next afternoon when she'd found her father dead in his study, slumped over his desk. The coroner's final report ruled the cause of death to be a heart attack. Her father had just seen his doctor three weeks earlier. Clean bill of health. No history of heart disease. His blood pressure, his stress levels, and his cholesterol were all low, his arteries were clear, and he had the cardio capacity of a man half his age. There was no way her father had died from a heart attack.

Cameron got up then, came around the table and stood before her. The look on his face wasn't pity. It wasn't even sympathy. It was something deeper.

It was empathy.

He'd been there before, himself. He'd watched his own father die on the street. She'd seen the articles when she'd first researched who Cameron was. It was one thing that made her interested in finding out more about him. Something they had in common.

Cameron didn't reach out to her, didn't hold her hand or take her in his arms, didn't shush her and tell her it would all be okay. He just stood before her, arms loose at his sides, with that look of empathy in his eyes, like he was living through that moment with Celina, the moment she walked into her father's study.

In that moment, Celina didn't need his touch, didn't need false promises for the future. She needed to feel like someone knew what she felt. So few people could possibly understand.

Cameron did.

She knew it from her research. But after seeing that look in her eyes, she knew it in her heart.

That confirmation was all she needed. The rest of the story poured out of her, like a river jammed by debris that finally breaks loose after a heavy rainstorm.

She told him about hacking the coroner's office, finding the tox panel from her father's autopsy. He'd been poisoned. The tox report had been buried, ignored.

She told him about tracing the poison to a specific lab, then to a specific contract killer. She followed the money back to a billionaire Russian arms dealer named Minsk, through him to various shell companies, then eventually back to one man.

Vernon Stratham.

"I'm going to kill him, Cameron," she said. "I'm going to kill him with my own hands. And when I do, I'm going to make sure he knows why."

She didn't look at him when she said it, didn't want to see whether or not his eyes lost their empathy.

"But I'm going to tell Jenkins everything first, make sure Stratham loses every single thing he cares about. His job, his money, his reputation."

She balled her hands into fists again, feeling her skin tighten, hearing her knuckles crack.

"I'll make sure Jenkins disavows him publicly. I'll make sure Jenkins personally heads up the prosecution to put Stratham in jail, make him pay fines that will wipe him out completely."

She clenched her jaw so tight she thought her teeth would shatter.

"He took what mattered most to me. I'll take everything he has." She let out a deep, slow, controlled breath. "And then I'll come for him."

She looked at Cameron then. There was pain in his eyes, but the empathy was still there. If he chose to leave her, so be it. She wasn't going to hold back from him any longer. She loved him, and Paulie was right. When you love someone, you tell them the truth. All of it.

And you hope they keep on loving you.

But she didn't expect it. She lied to him. He'd fallen in love with someone she wasn't, with a persona that was the opposite of herself in many ways. Reggie Moon was a diligent student and a brilliant criminologist, dedicated to a life in pursuit of justice, stopping the bad guys. Celina Maxwell was a lying hacker hell-bent on murder and revenge. She was the bad guy. If things were reversed, Celina would probably walk away.

Cameron didn't.

He stepped forward, took her hand in his. He brought them slowly to his lips and kissed them, slowly, gently. The touch of his lips sent bolts of lightning coursing through Celina's body. He looked up at her, those beautiful brown eyes full of more than just empathy.

In them, she saw love.

Even after everything she'd just told him.

Love.

When he kissed her hand again, slid the fingertips of his other hand lightly up her bare forearm, she saw more than just love in his eyes. A blast of heat came from him that nearly knocked Celina to her knees.

"Cameron," she whispered. His name passed her lips without thought, as natural as breath.

The control she'd felt earlier, the control she'd struggled to maintain, burned immediately to embers in the wave of heat coming from him, the same heat that blazed in her.

"Shhh," Cameron said. He ran his hand up her arm, across her shoulder, leaving a blazing trail of sparks beneath her skin.

"Celina," he said as he slid his hand behind her neck. Her own name had never sounded so sexy before.

He slipped his fingers into her hair, cupped her head in his hand, bent it gently up toward his. He stepped closer. Their bodies arched toward each other, her breasts barely touching his chest through the fabric of their shirts, but still sending lightning bolts through her body.

Celina's mind burned away like her control, seared white-hot in the raging heat between them, leaving nothing behind but pure sensation.

And desire.

She ran her hands around his waist, slipped them under his shirt, felt the hot, smooth skin in the sharp ridge in the small of his back. She pulled his hips tight against hers. Her body ached for him, to wrap her legs around his waist, burn away the clothing between them and fuck, forever and ever.

A small smiled played at Cameron's lips. Celina wanted to devour them. She craned her head forward. He pulled back, teasing her, that smile growing.

Celina growled like a feral animal. She wanted.

Those lips smiled more, then dropped. She saw the heat blaze in his eyes, and the fire in her burned all of her.

"Call me Cam," he whispered before he finally bent his lips to meet hers.

And the world burned away, too.

59

THEY HADN'T FINALLY CLOSED their eyes until the first rays of sunlight were already peeking through the blinds. The shadows they cast over Reggie's—Celina's—gorgeous body, lying on the bed beside him, immediately brought Cam back to attention. Even after a full night—a very full night—of activity, just having her beside him made him ready for more. And Celina was more than happy to accommodate.

And then, later, they'd both flopped to their backs, exhausted and happy. The bed sheets had long ago been pulled out and kicked to the ground, so they passed out on top of the bare mattress, legs entwined, hands cradling each other's damp-haired head, naked bodies slick with sweat slowly cooling in the morning air.

So Cam wasn't surprised to wake and find out it was already well after noon.

He was surprised to find that Celina wasn't there.

He sat up in bed and called her name.

Celina. It still felt odd on his tongue. Odd, but exciting.

He heard no response, just the quiet of his apartment. A brief stab of fear and doubt shot through him as he rubbed the sleep from his eyes, but then he had a thought. He opened his eyes and looked at the pillow next to his.

A note.

Written on paper torn from his sketchbook.

Cam smiled and picked it up. It was written in the confident, artistic handwriting he now knew belonged to Celina Maxwell, aka. Reggie Moon, aka. the woman in black. Where just a few weeks before, that same handwriting would have filled him with shame and anger, it now filled him with... what? Joy? Hope?

Love?

All of those.

Or the beginnings of all of those, at least.

He read the note.

Something to take care of. See you at dinner tonight. -C

She'd used a C, not an R, to sign her note.

He smiled, the foolish, slap-happy smile of a man in love.

In his mind and in his heart, Cam felt as though he stood at a border between two worlds. A beautiful, old-growth forest was behind him, filled with ancient trees that rose hundreds of feet into the sky, teeming with all manner of life, but cast into half-darkness by the canopy, the sightlines limited by staggered trunks of thick trees.

Before him stretched a wide-open field of hip-height barley, swaying in a soft wind, endless blue sky arcing overhead, eye roving as far as energy and interest could take it. He'd emerged from one intriguing, mysterious, beautiful world only to find a whole new world ahead of him, even bigger and more wonderful.

And tonight, he would dine with Celina Maxwell, not Reggie Moon.

No, tonight he would dine with both Celina Maxwell *and* Reggie Moon. Just like Sam Davis was a part of Cameron Hauk in some way, so too would Reggie Moon be a part of Celina Maxwell in some way. It had to be so.

And now Cam could take his time figuring out how.

He lay back down on the bed and stretched his body long and slow. He stretched his arms above his head, luxuriating in the energy that he felt from having used his body, mind, and heart to their fullest, then having slept long and deep.

A thought drifted through the lazy light of contentment in his mind.

Tonight, he would dine with Reggie Moon, not Celina Maxwell.

What the hell did that mean? Tonight he would dine with both Celina and Reg—

He shot back up in bed.

Dinner.

See you at dinner tonight.

Tonight was the dinner with Jem, Sarah, Annie, Reggie—

And the Attorney General.

Cam rolled to a seated position on the side of his bed, grabbed his phone from his nightstand, ripping out the charging cable as he did, and frantically searched through his email. He found a message from the school addressed to all of the top five students, detailing the plans for the dinner tonight.

7pm at La Pomme du Serpent, 8th Street SE. Semi-formal attire expected.

He checked the clock on his phone. It was 2pm.

He flopped backward on the bed and heaved a sigh of relief, his heart pounding hard enough to make the skin on his chest quiver with each beat.

Five hours. He still had time.

But not much.

First things first. He pulled his suit and dress shoes from his closet and checked them to be sure they were appropriate. The suit, tie, and dress shirt were still in the dry-cleaning bag from the last time he'd worn it, so he was okay there. He would look the part tonight.

He pulled sweatpants and a t-shirt over his naked body and brushed his teeth. He'd shower and shave later before he got dressed for dinner.

Tonight was a group dinner, anyway. For Cam, that meant it was mainly a reconnaissance mission, and a time to let Jem, Sarah, and Annie impress Attorney General Jenkins, let them try to gain a powerful contact and advance their own careers. Cam's real mission would be the following morning during the private meeting with Jenkins.

But would it even be private? How would the school and the AG handle the tie at the top of the class rankings?

Cam set a cup of coffee brewing and grabbed his phone. The bite of the coffee's scent woke him even before he'd had a sip.

Not that he needed the caffeine jolt. After seeing Celina last night, then seeing even more of her all night, and then finally, after three long years, starting the final stage of his latest plan to free his mother, he was getting more and more keyed up with every passing minute.

He found another email, this one from the AG's office, and read through it as he sipped his espresso. There was a lot of language in there about protocols for meeting the AG. No recording devices, no weapons, no cameras, and so on. Cell phones would be surrendered at the door, to be returned at the end of the dinner. Both a group photo and a photo of each participant alone with the Attorney General would be taken by a photographer contracted for the purpose and sent to the participants on a later date in 2x3, 4x6, and 8x10 glossy format, as well as a digital copy of both photos. The digital copies would be watermarked and trackable. If any photo were to be found online, it would be traced back to its owner. Any significant alterations of the photographs or negative characterizations of the meeting posted online would result in punitive action, as warranted and at the discretion of the Attorney General's office. Etcetera, etcetera. Blah, blah, blah.

Cam snorted. He could circumvent the watermark and the tracing with his eyes closed, which meant that Celina would have it circumvented before they'd even delivered the file. Hell, she'd probably figure out how to have the trace point right back to the AG himself.

But all the toothless warnings and precautions were par for the course for someone about to announce a bid for president. The slightest slip, the tiniest hint of a scandal could derail the Jenkins for President train before it left the station. The last thing they wanted was a photoshopped image floating around the internet of a smiling Jenkins with his arm around a half-naked underage college girl.

Although, with AI the way it was, Cam could make twenty versions of that image before he finished his coffee. It was a brand new world, and Cam was glad he wasn't the one running for office in it.

But the laundry list of rules did tell Cam one thing: The Jenkins campaign was very concerned about his image and his reputation. Jenkins knew the first rule of campaigning: control the message. He wouldn't let a gratis grad school photo op interfere.

That concern played into Cam's hands. The last thing Jenkins would want would be a leak about his campaign finance manager running a covert operation to assassinate political opponents. Not that any candidate would want that, but as the top cop in the country, Jenkins, in particular, would be damaged by an allegation of criminal activity—murderous activity—within his own campaign.

Of course, Stratham was smart about it. His targets would never be as high-profile as a competing candidate. That would be too obvious. But lower-profile targets were fair game. Enough to clean up messes, maybe put pressure on other candidates, but nothing that would make the top story in a news cycle. Staff members, maybe. Family members, perhaps.

Arms-dealing billionaires? Definitely.

And, apparently, major donors who had learned too much.

Cam had no proof, had nothing but what he'd seen with his own eyes on a yacht last summer and what Celina had told him last night. But that would have to be enough.

He scanned the rest of the email, but it was just more rules and procedures. Nothing concrete about when and where and who would join them.

He checked his email again, found another email from the school, this time addressed only to Sam Davis and Reggie Moon. The two of them were to report to the front desk of the Department of Justice building at 7:30am tomorrow to spend the morning with Jenkins. A brief itinerary showed that, beginning at 8am sharp, they would take a one-hour private tour of the building with Jenkins before spending two and a half hours in the AG's office. At 11:30am they would have an early lunch, then leave together in the AG's motorcade at 12:30 to arrive at the school in time for the graduation ceremony scheduled to start at 1pm.

He and Celina would be together the whole time. That was good. They could work together.

But Cam needed to fill her in on his plan. And he needed to know the details of her plan so they could coordinate.

Tonight. After dinner. That was the only time they would have, anyway. They'd come back home, and he'd tell her everything.

Everything she didn't already know, at least.

60

EIGHT HOURS after their last sexcapade, Celina's body still tingled all over. Fuck, it felt good to fuck Cameron again. It had only been three weeks, but it had felt like forever.

They'd made up for it last night. Three weeks of sex in twelve hours. She'd barely gotten two hours of sleep, but it had been worth it.

She smiled at the thought as she strode down the sun-dappled sidewalk in the warm afternoon breeze, then smiled even more as another jolt of pleasure ran through her. After-shocks. She'd been getting them all day.

Aside from that—or maybe because of that—her muscles felt loose and languid. She was more relaxed than she'd been in weeks. Her energy was high, her thoughts were clear, and her mind was firing on all cylinders.

She was ready.

Fuck, was she glad to have Cameron back again.

Cam.

Call me Cam, he'd whispered right before her mind exploded in a twelve-hour drug-free ecstasy trip that her thighs were still quivering from.

Jolt.

Jolt.

Shock.

Zing.

Her smile became a shit-eating grin.

Fuck, it was good to have Cam back.

A gust kicked up, rustling the garment bag slung over her shoulder. She couldn't wait to see Cam's face when he saw her in that dress tonight. A sheer black off-the-shoulder number with a hip cutout, it sexy while still being elegant. But in the right light, you could see right through it to the short skirt and busty top underneath. She had a cream-colored silk cashmere stole to use as a cover-up and make the outfit more business appropriate, but she'd make sure to find a moment to take it off and give Cam the full view. She knew it would be enough to make Cam's thoughts anything but business appropriate.

As far as Celina was concerned, the more inappropriate his thoughts, the better.

Shit. She shook her head. It was going to be hard to keep her focus tonight. Maybe it would be better for her to wear a pantsuit or a burlap sack or something. She had to be on her toes from the jump. She didn't know how Jenkins would react when he saw her.

She knew he'd react, but she didn't know how.

Could go any of a number of different ways. Celina had to be prepared for all of them.

He wouldn't make a scene. Not in the restaurant. He was too good a politician for that. If he could manage to hide his surprise at seeing her, she'd know that he'd gotten even better at controlling his emotions than he used to be.

After the initial shock, he wouldn't act right away. He'd let the dinner play out. He'd play the adored leader, aw shucks about his power, more interested in giving back and helping the next generation come up. It wasn't an act. It was all true.

But it wasn't all.

William Jenkins had twice the ambition of anyone running against him, ten times the intellect, and twenty times the cunning. He was handsome, he was idealistic, he was smart. And he'd studied at the feet of her father. Her dad had known how to weave a story that had Silicon Valley venture capitalists falling over themselves to give him their money, and he'd taught those same skills to Jenkins. Right up until he was murdered.

But how much did Jenkins know? She'd never been able to find the answer to that question. Every line of inquiry, every hack, every trace, every mark led to a dead end.

A soon-to-be dead end named Vernon Stratham.

But there'd been no hint that Jenkins himself knew anything about her father's death. His tears had seemed real enough at the funeral. His speech had been moving, the performance heartfelt. But any politician worth his salt could deliver a tear-jerker at a fucking funeral.

And lack of evidence was not the same as exoneration. She needed to see Jenkins face-to-face, when he wasn't expecting it. Unless he'd leveled up to the stratosphere, she'd know from the moment of recognition in his eyes how much he knew.

And then it could go anywhere.

He would play dumb through dinner and go along with the Reggie Moon thing. But would he try to say something, maybe during the photos? He could pull her aside at some point, by the bathrooms, perhaps.

He couldn't invite her to stay alone after dinner. That'd be a bad look. But he could have his goons pick her up on her way home. How would he handle Cam or the others if she walked in a group or shared a cab?

And when they did finally meet, would he play the long-lost friend, the almost-brother? Would he act bewildered about her alias, or would he laugh it off? Same old Celina, he could say, always up to something.

Or maybe he'd go the route Celina was hoping for. He'd drop

the politician act. He'd forgo the niceties and go straight to the pay-off, the bribes, or the threats.

And then she'd have him. Dead to rights.

She shifted the garment bag to the other shoulder, the dress billowing out behind her as a well-timed gust kicked up. She kicked aside some seed pods that had fallen on the sidewalk from a copse of trees whose branches reached over a stone wall. Her boots scuffed as she kicked the pods aside like a little kid stomping puddles in a yellow slicker and hat after a rainstorm.

She gave a loud sigh that blew away with the wind. She wasn't hoping for the threats. Not really. She had liked Jenkins when she'd known him before. And her father had believed in him with all his heart. Her father had loved him. For her father's sake, Celina wanted Jenkins to earn that love, to live up to the image her father had had of him.

That's what she was hoping for.

She just wasn't expecting it.

61

CAM HAD HOPED to ride to dinner with Celina so they could start discussing their plans for the following day, but she said she was still taking care of some things and would have to meet him at the restaurant. In fact, she said, she'd probably be a few minutes late, so please give her apologies to the Attorney General.

Cam had never been to the restaurant before, but he'd heard of it. La Pomme du Serpent was a high-end French restaurant that was booked out for a full year, but which somehow always seemed to have a table available for celebrities and high-ranking Washington power brokers. In Cam's experience, most of those kinds of places seemed to be more interested in the flavor of the month than the flavor of their food, but La Pomme was supposed to be one of the rare examples where the food actually lived up to the stratospheric prices.

And of course, the heir apparent to the most powerful office in the world could snap his fingers and get a private room with a table for six. As Cam got out of his Uber, straightened his jacket and tie, and shot his cuffs on the sidewalk under the soft glow of the lights above the restaurant entryway, he wondered if Jenkins would be paying for dinner himself or if the US taxpayers would be footing the bill. A prix fixe menu at $435 per person was hardly an efficient use of federal funds.

The lobby of the restaurant was a mixture of royal European elegance and nightclub chic. The carpet was thick, patterned in gold, forest green, and red the color of dried blood, as if the restaurant were subtly invoking the tableau of the serfs whose bloody toil in verdant fields earned their ancient lieges the gold the nobles used to fund their opulent lifestyles. Shell-backed couches and high-backed chairs with carved wooden arms and feet were bedecked in the same rich colors. Renaissance paintings—Titian, or maybe Giorgione, something from the Venetian school—hung in gilt frames beneath soft lamps on the wall and finished the feel of having stepped into the drawing room of a seventeenth-century French royal.

But the lighting was dark, moody, the kind of lighting you'd see in the private rooms of an upscale club, where the patrons wouldn't want their faces too easily seen as they indulged their less-than-savory nocturnal vices. The ceiling seemed to be very high, but its true height was lost in shadow. Cam couldn't tell it if it was real or just a clever illusion.

The only light that was remotely bright came from two lonely spotlights above a long, chest-high marble host station. With a high front that hid the computer screens and keyboards behind, it resembled the reception desk of a high-end hotel more than the front desk of a swanky restaurant.

There were two hosts behind the station. Their skin tone and bone structure gave them both a vaguely exotic vibe, and both bore an air of disdainful suffering suitable to the decor and the overall mood of the place. One was a tall, lean young man with dark curly hair and a wispy growth around his chin, impeccably dressed in a suit that looked tailor-made and far more expensive than a restaurant host should be able to afford. The other was an even taller, leaner woman, with a sharp, angular face, iron-straight blonde hair, and glittering gold earrings that dangled down the length of her long neck to her bare shoulders. Whenever she moved in the glow of the spotlight, her lithe body sparkled beneath a subtly sequined dress, as if she bore beautiful black scales instead of skin.

Jem, Sarah, and Annie were already in the lobby when Cam walked in. A burly security guard stood beside them, arms clasped in front, ignoring the others and looking off toward the doors to the main dining area. His expression was a mix of boredom and intensity, as if he had been waiting for someone to arrive for over an hour and was only now starting to get mildly irritated. With his shaved head, black suit, and long black tie, he looked straight out of central casting, even down to the squiggly tan cord leading to his earpiece.

"Still haven't found Reggie?" asked Jem when Cam approached.

Cam felt a grin split his face wide.

Annie laughed.

"If I had to guess," said Sarah, "I'd say he found her."

"We found each other," said Cam. "Several times." His grin widened even more.

"TMI, Sam," said Annie, holding up a hand.

"Yeah, TMI, Sam," echoed Jem, then stage whispered, "Tell me everything later."

"If you're back together, then why isn't she with you?" asked Sarah.

"She had some errands to run this afternoon and got hung up," Cam said. "She's running a few minutes late, said we should start without her."

"Ah, the privilege of the elite," said Jem. "When you're top of the class, the whole world waits for you."

The security guard must have been eavesdropping. He murmured something Cam couldn't make out, pressed his finger to his earpiece, nodded once, then motioned for the group to follow him.

"I'm top of the class, too," said Cam as they filed after the guard.

Jem slid his arm around Cam's shoulder. "Are you though?" They trailed the guard down a narrow hallway to the side of the lobby. "Or did she just not have enough time to pass you by?"

Cam's voice was indignant. "I caught up to her."

The others laughed, the sound deadened by the thick, old-world wood paneling that lined the hallway. The restaurant's sumptuous elegance didn't stop at the lobby walls. Cam's dress shoes sank into the thick carpet with every step. The recessed spotlights in the ceiling gave him the feeling of walking down a dark sidewalk at night, moving from streetlamp to streetlamp. If it weren't for the air of old money about the place, he would have half-expected to find a drunk homeless man passed out along the baseboards.

The hallway led to a set of wooden double doors. On each door was carved the face of a fierce-looking old man, long hair billowing around his disembodied head, eyebrows slashing toward the bridge of his nose, mouth contorted into a furious rictus. The face looked like an angry, vengeful, murderous king from a Shakespeare play.

Between the dim light, the lush appointments, the medieval imagery, and the way the sumptuous carpeting swallowed every stray noise, Cam was starting to wonder if Washington's elite came to La Pomme du Serpent for dinner or for ritual sacrifices.

The security guard swung the knocker on one of the doors. Cam didn't hear anyone respond from beyond the doors, but the guard must have heard something in his earpiece because he took the handles of both doors and swung them outward with a butler-like flourish that would have made Jeeves proud. He stood to one side, motioned for them to enter, and resumed his bored, hands-clasped stance against the door as they passed.

The room itself was a large rectangle, with no alcoves or antechambers, but the appointments elevated the space to regal status. This ceiling was visible, and was at least twenty feet high, coffered and carved with cherubs floating around central suns, each square tinged with a green patina and inlaid with gold filigree. Ear-high wainscoting lined walls painted in an elegant, muted copper color. Recessed spotlights ran around the perimeter, while a huge, crystal chandelier lit the middle of the room. Extending at least ten feet down from the ceiling, it consisted of three large crystalline spheres stacked on a central axis and ringed by nine smaller spheres spiraling around them in a helical pattern. The piece was stunning, and gave the impression, like so much of the restaurant, of a central royalty surrounded and served by a lesser population.

A large fireplace was set in the middle of the opposite wall, with narrow wooden doors on either side. There was no fire, but the andiron was stacked with logs, and a dim light hidden in the hearth cast a warm glow on them, cleverly giving the subconscious impression of flame without the heat that would have been uncomfortable this late in spring.

A thick stone mantle hung above the fireplace, with a large rectangular mirror above it. In the mirror, Cam saw the guard close the double doors they had entered. The guard stayed on outside, probably to stand watch. For some reason, Cam had the unsettling feeling that he'd just been sealed in, like the concubines of the pharaohs of old, sealed alive into the dead ruler's burial chamber.

The chandelier hung above a round table set in the center of the room. The table had to have been at least ten feet in diameter, yet only six chairs were spaced around it. The chairs had very high backs with ornate wood carvings along the crest, splat, and rails. They looked old and heavy, more like thrones than dinner chairs. Though the table was covered in a thick white tablecloth and set for an elegant multi-course dinner, the setup felt more like the Round Table of Camelot, or perhaps the kind of table used by the titans of industry in the early 1920s to smoke cigars, drink whiskey, and divide the plunder of the industrial age among them.

Three security guards were stationed around the room, all dressed exactly like the guard outside, all staring into space with the same disinterested expressions, hands clasped before them. Cam and the others stood uncertainly between the door and the table, not sure if they should seat themselves or wait for instruction.

Fortunately, they didn't have to wait long. The Attorney General emerged from one of the doors beside the fireplace, followed by a server in a black jacket and tie, a crisp, white apron strapped around his waist. The server took a position beside the fireplace while the Attorney General strode toward them, hands spread wide in greeting, million-dollar smile filling the room with its dazzling glow.

A wave of emotion swept over Cam, as if the Attorney General's appearance were the detonation of a nuclear blast. He felt a mixture of awe and admiration, and an abashed sense of recognition. Though there were four of them there, Cam felt like the AG saw him, individually and completely, and that he was not worthy of the attention.

All that and the man hadn't even said a word yet. Damn, that was the power of a natural-born politician. He'd heard people talk about others in the past, people like Bill Clinton or Tony Blair, the kind who could make you feel like you and he were the only people on the planet.

But now he was witnessing the effect first-hand. And it was impressive.

"Welcome, my friends," said the AG, coming around the table to join them, "and congratulations on your academic achievements. Very impressive indeed."

Jenkins was handsome in the way of powerful middle-aged men with chiseled jaws and a full head of dark hair just starting to grey. But to see him in person, to see that lean, smooth appearance and feel that astonishing charisma at the same time raised him to another level entirely, a level normally reserved for A-list movie stars. Cam could see exactly why Jenkins was the presumptive winner for the presidency.

Jenkins approached Annie first, then Sarah, smiling wide and staring deep into each of their eyes as he shook their hands warmly. Both of them melted at his touch like ice cream on a hot sidewalk, their cheeks burning red. Sarah didn't even like men, but she still seemed to quiver just from being that close to Jenkins.

"And thank you for joining me for dinner tonight." He moved on to Jem. Same smile, same gaze, same melting effect. "It's a real honor for me to meet the top students each year. A little tradition I like to keep," he said. He clasped Jem's shoulder and leaned toward him, like two old friends sharing a little secret. "Helps keep me young, you know?"

The way Jem's laugh skittered from his mouth like a nervous schoolboy, Cam thought Jem might have just fallen in love.

Jenkins took Cam's hand next. The smile was dazzling, the gaze arresting. Cam had the advantage of having just watched Jenkins give the star treatment to his three friends, but he could still feel the impact.

Jenkins' grip was firm, but not hard. His hand was warm and soft and dry, but not pampered or overly manicured. There was just enough hint of callous there to imply that Jenkins had known physical labor at some point in his life. Cam didn't know if that was true or not, didn't know how he managed to keep his hands calibrated so carefully to give that impression. But that was the impression that immediately came to Cam's mind, subconsciously. It was a remarkable feat of social engineering. Yet another reason why Jenkins was so highly touted. He could appeal to both the wealthy elite and the common man. And their orgasm-starved wives.

"Sam Davis," Cam said, pumping Jenkins' arm once and returning his smile. "It's a pleasure to meet you, sir."

"Mr. Davis," said Jenkins, his smile shifting slightly, becoming a bit more genuine. "I've heard a lot about you. We're looking forward to great things from you in the future." The broader smile came back as Jenkins turned to the full group again. "From all of you."

He surveyed them for a moment, then frowned slightly, made a show of counting them.

"I count four of you." He glanced at one of his guards in the corner. "Aren't we expecting five?"

"Reggie Moon, sir," said Cam, "our valedictorian. She's running a few minutes late. She asked me to give you her sincere apologies."

"Co-valedictorian, from what I understand," said Jenkins, clasping Cam on the shoulder. "An exact tie, for the first time in school history. Congratulations to you on that, as well. A great achievement. Hard-earned, I'm sure."

"Thank you, sir," said Cam.

"Well, it's too bad Ms. Moon couldn't be here from the start. I hope she arrives soon." Jenkins gestured toward the table. "But let's take our seats, shall we? Has anyone dined here before?"

They all murmured no while they moved toward the table and selected seats.

"Well, you're in for a rare treat. Chef Barbier is the finest French chef in the world. Grew up in France, studied at the feet of the masters, and came here to America in his late forties to bring fine French cuisine to our poor deprived nation." He grinned wide as he chose a chair with his back toward the fireplace, facing the double doors, and lay his napkin on his lap. "And while I disagree with his assessment of our cuisine, we're certainly better off for having him."

Sarah and Annie took seats on either side of Jenkins, with Jem beside Sarah and Cam beside Annie. When she arrived,

Celina would have the seat on Cam's left, directly opposite Jenkins. She would be the furthest away, but she'd have the best sight line. Trade-offs, Cam supposed.

As soon as they took their seats, the server disappeared into the back, only to return a moment later with a small army of other servers, similarly dressed in jackets, ties, and aprons. They handed out hot towels to clean their hands, filled tiny glasses with no more than a swallow or two of some kind of white wine, and set before each of them a large plate with a small bite of food in the center. It looked like a spring roll cut in half, split down the center, and filled with melon and cheese.

"An amuse-bouche to begin," announced the head server in a sultry basso voice as his army retreated through the door. "Black radish, smoked salmon, and fromage frais, paired with an Andalusian Vino de la Frontera." He bowed from the waist. "Please enjoy."

"Thank you, Simon," said Jenkins, inclining his head. He lifted his tiny glass in toast. The others did the same.

"To all of you," he said. "Once again, congratulations on your remarkable academic achievements, and thank you for allowing me to spend some time with you this evening. Cheers."

They all lifted their glasses and murmured in return. Cam watched Jenkins carefully from across the table, looking for any break in his act. Was he just a skilled actor, or was he really as charming as he seemed? He didn't need to waste his wattage on four young grad school kids, most of whom were obviously besotted with him already.

Cam decided to spend that evening studying Jenkins closely. He needed to look for an advantage, anyway, some opening in Jenkins' character that Cam could exploit to pressure him to release his mother. But, now that he'd finally met Jenkins in person, he was more curious about the man than ever. Was he the real deal? Or was he just another smarmy politician who could wheel out the charm when he needed it, then fall back to his normal power-hungry avarice when the cameras were off?

Cam watched as Jenkins lifted his glass to Jem, Sarah, and Annie, then directed his gaze to Cam. He bowed his head slightly and lifted his glass with what seemed to be a knowing look in his eyes. Cam reminded himself that, though he wasn't the president yet, this man had a lot of power. Probably almost as much as the current president, if not more. And power meant information. It was possible that he already knew who Cam really was. Now that he was so close to the end, Cam had to play the game carefully. He had to assume Jenkins knew almost everything.

And he had to study Jenkins to figure out what he didn't know yet. That hole in his knowledge would be Cam's opportunity.

He nodded back to the Attorney General from across the table and they both brought the tiny glasses to their lips. Cam sipped his wine. It was chilled and bone dry, and delicate, almost fragile on his tongue. Delicious.

As he sipped, Cam heard the door open behind him. He watched Jenkins' eyes flick up as he brought his glass away from his lips.

And, just for a moment, Cam saw Jenkins' eyes widen in surprise.

Surprise and... something else. Something Cam couldn't quite identify.

The mirror above the fireplace was set too high for Cam to see who had come in, but he figured it had to be Celina. He set his glass down and turned in his seat.

Immediately, he could see exactly what made the Attorney General's eyes grow wide.

Celina stood one step inside the doorway, hips tilted, a small clutch in one hand.

She looked absolutely drop-dead gorgeous.

62

CELINA GOT the attention she was hoping for when she walked into the private dining room a little more than fashionably late. And, more importantly, she got a reaction from Jenkins.

Her eyes found his face a millisecond after she walked in, caught the moment when his eyes swung over his wineglass from Cam toward her. And in that moment, she saw his eyes shift from a practiced look of conversational openness to a genuine look of surprise, then shock, as Jenkins first saw her, then recognized her.

And then, wisely, he looked down at his lap as he took his napkin in his hand and pushed back his chair. By the time he stood again, his face was composed, his eyes reset to the look of sparkling interest that Celina had watched him spend so many hours perfecting in front of the mirror, putting Celina's father's teaching to work.

Everyone thinks the eyes are the mirror of the soul, her father would say, but they're wrong. The eyes are the mirror of the mind. Like any great actor, a great politician learns to control his thoughts. That, in turn, controls his eyes. And the eyes are what evoke emotion in the people.

Control your thoughts, he would say, and you can control how people feel about you.

Jenkins had mastered that art. Which was why Celina felt a spark of triumph that she'd managed to break through that mastery, even if only for a brief instant. That breakthrough meant Jenkins was still human. And that meant Celina could still get to him.

She'd seen surprise in his eyes, then shock, but she hadn't seen guilt or anger. To her own surprise, she felt relieved at that, a tightness in her stomach easing just a bit.

But lack of evidence was not proof of innocence. It was possible he'd looked down before the guilt and anger came through. She'd have to watch him closely for the rest of the evening.

"You must be Ms. Moon," said Jenkins as he set his napkin on his chair and came around the table, hand extended in greeting. "I'm so glad you could come."

Even though he hadn't been able to keep that flicker of emotion from his eyes, Jenkins had definitely leveled up since the last time Celina had seen him. Charisma poured out of him, and he pulled off the handsome politician look as well as anyone Celina had ever seen. Tall, trim, strong, distinguished. No other candidate stood a chance. It would be eight years of President Jenkins, without a doubt.

Unless Celina took him down first.

"Thank you for having me," said Celina, plating a smooth smile on her face, adding a touch of star-struck breathlessness to her voice. Jenkins wasn't the only one who'd leveled up. "I'm so sorry for being late."

"Not at all." Jenkins took her hand, covered it with both of his. For a moment, his back was turned to the others, his eyes visible only to Celina. She thought she saw something flicker through them, some promise that they would talk soon.

Or maybe Celina imagined it.

"Please sit down." Jenkins gestured to the empty seat. "Your timing is perfect. We've just started."

Celina glanced at Cam as she moved to sit, smiled at the stunned look on his face as he drank in the sight of her. The chairs were too far apart for her to put her hand on his leg, but she brushed her fingers across his neck and teased the hair at his nape as she passed. She could see the heat enter his eyes as he watched her, felt a heat within her respond instantly, her entire body suddenly heightened in sensation. She could feel the sheer fabric of her dress as it shifted over every inch of her shoulders, her waist, her thighs as she sat. Every movement was like the sweep of Cam's fingers, like the soft touch of his lips against her skin.

A wave of pleasure swept through her body. She shuddered involuntarily.

Fuck, it was good to have Cam back.

She pulled her mind back to focus as she spread her napkin over her lap. While Jenkins continued the conversation, questioning Sarah about her plans, Celina surveyed the space. The room—the entire choice of restaurant—was designed to impress and intimidate whoever wasn't paying for the dinner. Jenkins was far too good to rely on such cheap tricks, but it never hurt to set them working for you, even if you didn't need them.

Still, the decor seemed out of character for the Bill Jenkins Celina remembered. Too bourgeois. Too stuffy. Too old and heavy. And way too dripping with money. This was the kind of location that would be low-hanging fruit for a left-wing challenger in the campaign. He'd show pictures of Jenkins dining with a bunch of fat cat billionaires and claim he was out of touch with the common people, that he would use his power to enrich himself and his already wealthy friends.

Maybe that's why Jenkins chose this location for a dinner with a bunch of poor graduate students. He could claim he was trying to give them a taste of something more, to inspire the next generation of blah blah blah.

Whatever it was, Celina knew there would be a reason. Bill Jenkins didn't do anything on a whim. That was another lesson he'd learned from Celina's father. He would have chosen this restaurant for some purpose that played into his broader plan.

More power to him. From the gaping schoolgirl looks on their faces as Jenkins kept the conversation moving, Sarah, Annie, and Jem seemed impressed. But Celina figured Jenkins was preaching to the choir with those three, like the lead singer of a boy band stopping for lunch with the eighth-graders at an all-girls boarding school. All shrieking and fainting, with nary a critical thought between them.

She glanced at Cam. Though his face was composed into an expression of polite interest, she could tell he wasn't enrapt by Jenkins the way the others were. Instead, he seemed to be studying Jenkins, reading him. He disguised it well. If she didn't know him the way she did, she doubted she would have caught on to it. He was good. As good as her or Jenkins at controlling himself, at playing the part when he needed to.

Dinner went on without much fuss. The food was pretentious and delicious, the portions as small as the prices were high. The conversation was easy, flowing, and congenial. Jenkins played along with the Reggie Moon alter-ego. Why he would do so, Celina didn't know. If he'd called her out, it wouldn't have mattered. Cam already knew, and he was the most important person in the room for her. But Celina had developed a genuine liking for Sarah, Annie, and Jem, and she would prefer to break the news to them in private and on her own terms.

The door to the left of the fireplace led down a short, narrow hallway to the restrooms. At one point, Celina had excused herself. When she came back out of the ladies' room, she found Jenkins coming through the doorway to use the men's room. As they passed, Jenkins stopped, glanced back toward the doorway, and waited for the door to close before speaking.

"It's good to see you again," he said, his voice low.

"Is it?"

Jenkins' brow furrowed. "Of course it is. I tried calling for weeks. I came by. I texted. You never answered."

Celina watched his eyes carefully. The dim lighting in the hallway cast them in shadow. She shifted her position, stepping toward the doorway, forcing Jenkins to turn his body to face her. In so doing, she turned him so that the light was shining on his face, while putting her own face in shadow.

Gamesmanship.

"It was a busy time," she said with a shrug. "I had a lot of questions that needed answering."

His eyes flickered, but only with genuine confusion and hurt. No fear. No guilt. No defensiveness.

"What kind of questions?" he asked.

Celina didn't bother trying to keep her own confusion from her eyes. Was he really playing that coy with her? He couldn't possibly think she'd believe he didn't know that her father had been murdered. His own fucking campaign had ordered the hit. She was insulted that he'd think she was that naïve.

"You know what fucking questions."

His head rocked back like she'd slapped him. His eyes showed sincere pain.

"What are you talk—"

The door opened, light from the dining room knifing across the hallway. Immediately, Jenkins plastered a look of pleasant amusement on his face and nodded to Celina.

"I'm glad you're enjoying it," he said, flashing that presidential smile. "Please excuse me. I'll rejoin you all shortly." He disappeared into the men's room.

Celina turned to see Cam coming down the hallway toward her.

"Everything okay?" Cam asked.

Celina sighed in frustration. Everything she'd seen thus far suggested one of two possibilities. One possibility was that Jenkins had reached a whole new plane of mastery, one in which he could let his act slip just enough to suggest that he wasn't able to control his emotions, all while controlling them completely. It would require superhuman control. Jenkins was one of the best Celina had ever seen, but no one could be that good. They were all still human.

That meant the other possibility had to be true, that Jenkins truly didn't know anything about her father's murder. That Stratham had organized the whole thing and kept Jenkins completely in the dark. Celina had heard politicians use the I didn't know defense a hundred times over the years, and she'd always figured it was total bullshit. How could they not know what was happening within their own campaign?

But maybe it wasn't always total bullshit. For most of those asshole hacks—Nixon, Reagan, Clinton, Trump—it probably had been, but for Jenkins, she didn't think so. He was good, but so was Celina. And her gut was telling her that Jenkins was innocent.

Either she was right, or Jenkins had become a world-class liar. If so, kudos to him. If he could fool Celina like this, he deserved the win.

"Yeah," she said to Cam, putting a hand softly on his chest. "Everything's fine."

He put his hands on her waist, pulled her in for a soft, gentle kiss.

"That's some dress," he said into her ear in a low, husky voice that instantly sent Celina's heart rate soaring. "I can't wait to see what you look like out of it."

Celina laughed quietly, then pulled Cam's earlobe into her mouth, sucked it hard and bit it. She pulled her head back, stretched his captive earlobe toward her while she put both hands on Cam's muscular ass and pulled his hips tight against hers. She could feel his cock grow hard against her.

Cam groaned.

Celina released his earlobe and smacked him on the ass. She smiled over her shoulder as she walked through the door to the dining room, letting her hips sway as she felt him watching, and left him in the hallway looking delightfully uncomfortable.

63

It took everything Cam had to stay focused on Jenkins after Celina had first walked in to the dining room. Later, after she'd teased him in the hallway to the bathroom, he gave up trying altogether. He barely heard a word of conversation after that, even the words he said himself.

Amid all the talk, the procession of food was endless. Soup, appetizer, salad, main course, palate cleanser, another main course, each one announced by the head waiter like they were at Buckingham Palace and the queen of England was about to walk in.

After still more food—a cheese course and dessert—the coffee came, and Cam thought he was finally free. And then they brought out one more dessert. He would call the meal excessive, but the portions were so small that the entire pageant added up to the same amount of food as a burrito plate at Los Bandidos. It was culinary community theater at Broadway prices.

When everything was finally said and done, Jenkins surprised Cam by escorting them all out the front door. Cam would have thought Jenkins would say his goodbyes and slip out the back the way he'd come in.

He thought that until they actually went out the front door, that is.

Even though Jenkins' security team swept ahead of them, they didn't disperse the small gaggle of reporters out front snapping pictures. Judging from the way Jenkins slid into the photo op, keeping himself square in the center of the group while taking care not to put his arm around anyone or even touch any of them intentionally, Cam figured it was a setup. Someone in the campaign had probably tipped off the press so they'd be waiting outside. Jenkins apologized to Cam and the others with well-feigned humility, but never let that superstar smile waver one bit while the shutters were clicking.

The cameras and reporters dissipated once their rides pulled up. Jenkins had his two black Cadillacs SUVs, while the others had called Ubers. Jem, Sarah, and Annie got into one Uber and pulled away, their faces still flush with the excitement of the evening.

Cam held the door of the other car for Celina, but before she could get in, Jenkins touched her on the elbow and pulled her around the corner into the mouth of an alley on the side of the building. Cam started toward them, but a security guard blocked the way, keeping his hands crossed at his belt buckle and his meaty face as bored and neutral as ever. He wasn't threatening Cam, but it was clear he wasn't going to let Cam get by him, either. For the first time, Cam noticed the slight bulge under each of the man's armpits. Jenkins' security detail was not fucking around.

Cam retreated to the open car door and waited, watching Celina and Jenkins from a distance. Jenkins seemed to be entreating Celina, while she seemed to be playing coy. Cam had seen that look many times before, and Jenkins met the same fate Cam had every time. His body language finally admitted defeat as Celina said something to him and walked toward Cam. Jenkins just watched from the alley as she took Cam's hand as he helped her into the car. With a glance toward both Jenkins and the guard, he shut the door behind her, then walked around the other side of the car and joined her in the back seat. To his credit, Jenkins looked more disappointed than angry.

"What was that all about?" Cam asked once the car had pulled away from the curb.

"I'll tell you later," she said with a nod toward the driver.

Unwilling to talk openly in front of an Uber driver? Seemed like an unusual amount of paranoia for Celina. He thought back to the other time he'd seen Celina and Jenkins speaking alone, in the bathroom hallway. Cam had interrupted them, but if they'd been talking about something personal, Jenkins had played it off well. The conversation had seemed pretty innocuous to Cam when he walked in. But Jenkins was a pro. Maybe they'd been talking the way he'd just seen them on the sidewalk. Maybe he'd interrupted something more heated than it had seemed.

Cam knew Jenkins and Celina had a long history. Maybe Jenkins had threatened her. Seemed unlikely, but it was possible.

God help the man, if he did. Cam would put his money on Celina every time.

But Jenkins had power, and people in power had many levers they could use to threaten and intimidate. It would be easy enough for them to pay off an Uber driver for information. Or send one of their own, posing as a driver.

Cam was all too aware of Jenkins' power. His plan required him to tiptoe right through the middle of that particular minefield.

Tomorrow morning, in fact.

They passed the ride in silence. Questions and concerns piled up in Cam's brain, about Celina and about tomorrow, but neither of them spoke until they were safely inside Celina's apartment with the door locked and an Ornette Coleman album playing softly on the stereo.

"Okay," Cam said as he sat on her couch. "Spill."

Celina stood before him. She heaved a deep sigh and crossed her arms over her chest.

"I don't think Jenkins killed my father," she said.

"I thought you said you had proof."

"I have proof that Stratham ordered the hit, but nothing that ties directly to Jenkins. I was hoping that when I surprised him, his expression might give something away." Her lips pressed tight. "It didn't."

Cam took a moment to process that information.

"So you think he's completely in the dark? Stratham is his campaign finance manager."

"I know it seems ridiculous," said Celina, pushing her hands through her hair. She jerked out the pins that had held her hair up and snapped them one by one into a bowl on the table beside her. "But I know him, Cam. I watched him. All night."

She snapped the last pin into the bowl, tilted her head back, and shook it as she combed her fingers through her loose hair. It fell down over her shoulders as she sighed once more, once more crossing her arms over her chest.

As hard as it was for Cam to believe that Jenkins knew nothing about something that big, he could see that Celina was convinced. And it was her father that had been killed. It would have been a hundred times harder for her to believe that Jenkins was innocent. If she was convinced, so was Cam.

"Okay," he said slowly. "So Jenkins didn't know."

Celina shook her head in disbelief. "Jenkins didn't know."

Cam stood.

"Fine," he said. "Jenkins might be innocent, but his campaign isn't."

He came around the table to stand before Celina. He stood

close, ran his hands down her arms, felt the heat coming off of her.

"We can still use that," he said.

Celina huffed again and looked away.

"What's wrong? Why do you seem so frustrated?"

She took a long moment before looking back at Cam, pain in her shimmering eyes.

"My father loved Bill Jenkins," she said. "I loved him, too. He was like a big brother to me. Until..."

Until she thought he'd murdered her father. Cam didn't need her to finish the sentence for him.

"So this is good news, then," he said. "Isn't it? Your big brother is innocent."

"Yeah, but now he's a fucking idiot."

Cam shrugged. "Aren't all men?" he said. Celina darted a suspicious glance at him. "Especially politicians?" She rolled her eyes. "At least he's an innocent idiot. That's more than you can say about most of them."

Celina's laugh was a bitter one, but it was still a laugh. Celina's dress had a sheer fabric overlay that crossed over her hip, leaving one side exposed. Cam slid his hands under the fabric, slid them over her warm, smooth skin, and pulled her against him.

In a quick gesture, she wrapped her arms around him, lay her head against his chest, and melted into his embrace with a vulnerability Cam hadn't felt from her before. He pulled her tighter, pressed a long kiss into her hair.

"We've got him all to ourselves tomorrow," he said quietly, "and we've got an advantage."

Celina lifted her head and nodded. One swipe of her hands over her cheeks and she was back to business, her eyes still shimmering, but now steely and focused.

"He doesn't know who you are," she said.

"And he doesn't know what you know."

Celina nodded. "Alright," she said. "We need a plan."

Something about the look in her eye and the strength in her voice made Cam stiffen. The air was suddenly redolent with her scent. His fingers sparked with the feel of her warm skin. The movement of her hips against his as she shifted her weight brought heat rushing through his entire body in an instant, pushed all other thoughts aside.

"We need something else first," he said.

His eyes fell to her lips. Those full, irresistible lips.

This time, Celina's laugh was light and genuine. She pressed her hand against his chest, held her arm straight to hold him back. Locked in his embrace, this just bent her torso backward and thrust her hips harder against his.

"Plan first," she said.

Cam ran one finger down the arm that was firm against his chest, slid it over the back of her restraining hand, up the V between two of her fingers, then rolled his hand under hers, took her hand and brought it slowly to his lips.

She let him do it. Her fingers curled over his.

He kissed her knuckles gently once, then again, then ran his lips softly, a whisper, over her fingers, staring at Celina as he did, falling into those endless green eyes.

Her eyes softened, then became unfocused. The tip of her tongue slid slowly across her lips. They glistened in the light.

"Okay," she said, swallowing hard, her voice a husky rasp. "Plan second."

64

THEY DID MAKE A PLAN.

But not second.

Not third or fourth, either.

And not that night.

They made a plan, but not until the dark, small hours of the next morning, as they lay spent in Celina's bed, her sheets a mad, tangled symphony around them, their limbs intertwined. Celina's ragged breathing gradually calmed as the light through the window slats from the lamps on the walkway outside glinted off their sweat as it cooled on their bare skin.

Fuck, it was good.

And though they'd only dozed for an hour or two, she and Cam were both up early and ready to go. They arrived at 7:15am at the Department of Justice building, fifteen minutes before they were due.

Jenkins arrived right on time at 8am for their tour. He had his game face on again, his eyes showing no recognition of Celina beyond the amount appropriate for a graduate student he'd just met the prior evening.

The president of their university was with him when he

walked out of the elevator and down the hallway to greet them at the front desk. Their heels clicked in rhythm against the marble floor, his custom-made Italian leather dress shoes and her stolid black leather block pumps.

President Foster would claim she was just doing her job, keeping a major benefactor happy by giving him private face time with the head of the school. Only in this case, it was Foster who was receiving the favor. She was practically beaming with an unearned sense of self-importance for having gotten her thirty minutes with the future President of the United States. A minor association for her to trot out at dinner parties amid a show of false modesty.

To Celina's irritation, Foster stayed with them through the tour, which ran longer than planned thanks to her constant questions and endless sucking up. Celina could tell that Jenkins, too, was losing patience with her, though he hid it deep beneath years and years of experience in suffering fools. He'd already had that talent when her father had found him. Since then, Jenkins had polished it to a shine.

Finally, they arrived at Jenkins' office and Jenkins said his goodbyes to President Foster, pointedly nodding his head toward one of his security guards, who stepped forward to escort her back to the lobby. Once the elevator doors had closed behind them, he sighed and smiled at Celina and Cam.

"We're running a bit behind schedule," he said, checking his watch. "I'm very sorry about that, but now you'll have my undivided attention."

He turned toward the double doors to his office. A guard held one open for them, and Celina and Cam followed Jenkins dutifully inside.

"In fact," said Jenkins with a smile, "I can make it up to you."

He led them down a short, claustrophobic hallway, past a small vestibule only big enough for an assistant's desk, and into his office. After the low ceiling of the hallway, the feeling of expansion was dramatic. The large rectangular room had ceilings at least twenty feet high, lined on two walls with windows almost as tall. A sweep of the space showed Celina that the decor was a mix of the traditional and the tastefully modern, with a lot of dark wood, a lot of old books, and the occasional touch of chamfered aluminum or brushed nickel on lamps, computers, and screens.

Though she'd never been there, from her research and surveillance work Celina was already very familiar with the layout. They'd entered in the southeast corner of the room beside the east wall of windows. In the southwest corner, an antique mahogany desk was flanked by gold-fringed US flags on tall poles, a framed picture of the current president on the west wall behind it. To its side, in the northwest corner, another doorway led to a private bathroom. In the center of the room, directly across from the long wall of windows on the north side of the room, three tasteful white couches rested atop a thick Persian rug in front of a cold fireplace set into the south wall, a large portrait from the 1800s of some big-nosed white guy with funky hair and rouged cheeks hanging above the mantle. Where there were no windows, the walls were covered in rich, dark, polished wood.

The room was expansive and impressive, giving the feel of power, ease, and opulence without ostentation. Though it was the historic office of the Attorney General of the United States, Jenkins had managed to decorate it in such a way that it felt presidential without presumption. Anyone who walked in there would subconsciously feel a little bit like they were in the Oval Office. It was the perfect decor for the perfect candidate.

Another one of her father's teachings. Let your surroundings speak for you. Subtly, but powerfully.

"Not only will you be able to ask me anything you like about what I do," Jenkins said, gesturing for them to sit on the couches, "but I'll let you in on a not so well-kept secret."

He smiled, standing in front of the fireplace while Celina and Cam sat, taking center stage before them.

"At the graduation ceremony today, I'll be officially announcing my candidacy for President of the United States." He clasped his hands meekly behind his back and looked down at his shoes, but Celina could feel the pride swell from him.

And she felt it swell from herself, too.

Damn it.

She was proud of the fucker. She didn't want to be. Bill was a good guy, an almost-brother to her, but he was a politician. Politicians were a smarmy bunch, even the best of them.

But her father had had high hopes for him, and fuck if she didn't still have them, too.

She just hoped Candidate William Jenkins didn't let her down.

"In addition to your career goals, you may have political aspirations of your own," Jenkins continued. "No shame in that, whatsoever. It's a wonderful thing to want to serve your country however you can.

"You can ask me anything you like, not just about my own career in the law, but my career in politics, as well, both past, present, and," he smiled modestly, endearingly, "hopefully, future. Including the campaign I'm about to announce."

He clapped his hands together.

"To that end, and to help field your questions, I've asked my campaign finance chairperson to join us, as well."

He held out one hand toward the short hallway from which they'd entered.

Celina felt the hair on her neck stand up, felt her skin crawl, tasted bitter bile in the back of her throat before she even looked over.

She knew who she would see.

She wasn't wrong.

She shot to her feet, hands balled into fists, her body quivering as rage coursed through her at the sight of Vernon Stratham walking calmly across the room to join them.

65

Cam's first thought when he saw Vernon Stratham enter the Attorney General's swanky office was for Celina. She had exploded off of the couch like a bullet from a muzzle. As Cam rose slowly beside her, he could see her shaking, her muscles clenched. He'd never seen her like that before. It was probably all she could do not to leap across the room and throttle Stratham where he stood.

Cam's second thought was much simpler. It was this:

Oh.

Shit.

"Vernon Stratham," said Jenkins warmly as Stratham approached, "I'd like you to meet our top graduates for this year. Two of them, in fact. For the first time ever. A dead heat."

"Is that right?"

Stratham's voice was as smooth as Cam remembered from the yacht where he'd met him the previous summer. As smooth and just as dry. Stratham was a professional schmoozer, outstanding at his job. But you can't fake compassion. Stratham's voice landed at professionally pleasant, instead. Smooth, and dry as bones bleached in the desert sun.

Stratham's appearance, too, was much the same as Cam

remembered. Instead of a tuxedo, he wore a dark grey business suit, light grey shirt, and dusky blue tie. Otherwise, he looked exactly the same. Same expensive fabrics. Same tailored fit. Same impeccable attention to detail, with cuffs one inch below his jacket on both arms, his tie knot perfectly centered and symmetrical. As before, the bald dome of Stratham's head was as shiny as his shoes in the light from the tall windows, the hair encircling it cut close and neatly trimmed.

"May I introduce Ms. Reggie Moon?" Jenkins gestured to indicate Celina. Stratham bowed slightly at the waist and extended his hand. Cam could see the muscles in Celina's jaw flexing as she hesitated for only a moment, then shook it.

Jenkins' gesture swung toward Cam.

"And this gentleman is—"

"Ah, yes," said Stratham, "of course."

The look on his face was first a flash of recognition, then a frown of puzzlement.

"—Mr. Sam Davis," Jenkins finished.

Stratham's frown of puzzlement morphed into arched eyebrows of amused suspicion.

Jenkins' ears caught up with his mouth as he processed what Stratham had said.

"Do you and Sam know each other, Vernon?" he asked.

Stratham reached out his hand. Cam shook it. Stratham's skin was soft, his grip solid and easy. But his stare bored into Cam like steel rods.

"My mistake," he said to Jenkins without breaking that stare. "You look very much like someone I once met, Mr. Davis."

Cam forced a relaxed smile to his face.

"I must have one of those faces."

He kept his muscles loose, his voice friendly. But his heart was hammering in his chest.

Stratham had met Cam before, but he hadn't known the name Cameron Hauk or even the name Sam Davis. Cam had used the name Paul Baker on that job, posing as a wealthy investor attending a political fundraiser. The job had gone to shit almost from the off, ending with multiple murders, including an attempted murder arranged by Stratham himself. Cam had been looking for dirt on Jenkins and had barely made it off the yacht without handcuffs and a police escort. No dirt, and no proof of Stratham's machinations.

And Stratham had seen right through the Paul Baker ruse. He hadn't known who Cam was, but he'd known he wasn't who he claimed to be.

That explained his stare. Cam wondered how much Stratham knew about Celina and her connection with Jenkins. If Jenkins really was innocent of her father's murder, he'd have no reason to hide his connection to her family. And Stratham seemed to know everything about everyone. Cam recalled the donor spreadsheet Stratham had kept on the yacht. It was his job, he'd said, to know every donor's greatest desires. And their greatest fears. Both were equally useful when it came to campaign finances.

If he knew that much about his donors, he must know at least as much about his candidate. And that meant he knew all about Celina.

If so, he hid it very well. There was no hint in his eyes or in his demeanor to suggest that he knew Reggie Moon was a fake identity.

But there was also no reaction to the daggers Celina was staring at him, nor the cold frost that had filled the room as soon as he'd walked in. Cam could feel it, and he could tell from the glances Jenkins kept darting Celina's way that Jenkins felt it, too.

Stratham was too smart, too savvy not to pick up on those vibes. He was a master manipulator.

No, he knew. Cam had to assume that Stratham knew everything.

And now he knew that both Celina and Cam were on to him.

And if Celina was right and Jenkins didn't know that Stratham was a killer, Stratham had to be feeling pretty uneasy.

An experienced killer—whether you pull the trigger or sign the check, a killer is a killer—with his career on the line, the presidency at stake, and his back against the wall?

That made Stratham as dangerous. A cornered predator.

Jenkins tried to keep the conversation moving, but between Celina's sudden deep-freeze and her one-word answers, he looked more uncomfortable than Cam had ever seen him.

"Vernon," he said, putting his arm around both Cam and Stratham and turning them toward the door, "why don't we divide and conquer? Would you please take Mr. Davis down to your office, show him what you do, and answer any questions he may have about the campaign?"

He steered them to the exit and stopped.

"I'll do the same with Ms. Moon. Let's meet back here in, say," he checked his watch, "twenty minutes?"

Stratham turned toward Cam. His slow smile sent a shiver down Cam's spine. The predatory look in his eye froze his heart.

"Twenty minutes," he said, his voice as smooth as a glass knife, "should be more than enough time for Mr... Davis... and I to get acquainted."

Jenkins smiled, nodded toward Cam, and turned back toward Celina. Stratham gripped Cam's shoulder with one firm hand, held the other out toward the hallway, indicating the way for Cam to walk.

Cam forced himself to breathe deep and steady as he moved ahead of Stratham.

The prey, strolling calmly before the predator.

66

CELINA STALKED toward the long row of windows in Jenkins' office. She stared out at the monotony of the facade of the FBI building. Row after row of stacked windows, each one perfectly square and symmetrical. Literal fucking square holes. No room there for round pegs. That was why they were so fucking easy to fool.

The thought should have made her laugh. Instead, it just made her angrier.

"What the hell has gotten into you?"

She whirled at the tone in Jenkins' voice, ready to rip his head off, but when she saw the confusion on his face, the concern in his eyes, her anger softened.

"That man," she stabbed her finger toward the door that Stratham had just walked out, "killed my father."

Jenkins' eyes widened for a fraction of a moment, then narrowed as his brow furrowed.

"What are you talking about?" Jenkins shook his head. "That man is my campaign finance chair, not an assassin." He scoffed. "The only thing Stratham could kill is an IRS audit."

"He didn't kill him with his own hands, Bill," said Celina.

Jenkins' face brightened when she used his first name. "But he ordered the hit."

Jenkins scoffed again, turned and waved a hand toward Celina.

"You've always had an active imagination," he said, taking a seat on one of the couches and gesturing for Celina to sit in the other. "It's one of your many strengths."

Celina's boiling blood chilled. Another fucking man telling another fucking woman that she was being fucking hysterical. The year was 2023, but it might as well be fucking 1923 or 1823 or 1723 or 1623 and on and on through history. She wanted to explode on Jenkins now, rip his misogynistic fucking face off. But she knew that wouldn't help anything, or anyone.

That wouldn't help Cam.

Celina stalked to the couches, but she didn't sit.

"You remember how Dad died?"

Jenkins' face fell.

"A heart attack," he said. "In his office."

"Did he seem ill to you, before then?"

Jenkins sighed. "These things happen without warning, Celina."

"Did he ever have the slightest issue with his heart?"

"How would I—"

"He didn't. No arrhythmia. Perfect cholesterol. Healthy diet. And no family history of anything but long lives and peaceful deaths."

Celina stepped closer to Jenkins. He leaned back slightly as she did.

"Did my father seem obese to you?"

Jenkins frowned.

"Overweight, even?"

"No," Jenkins admitted, "but Celina—"

"He was in better shape that I am. His doctor said as much at his last checkup." She held three fingers in Jenkins' face. "Three weeks before he died."

"What does that prove? Doctors make mistakes."

"It doesn't prove anything." Celina smiled ruefully and paced before the hearth. "No, I had to dig for the proof. And it wasn't easy. Stratham is good."

"Wait." Jenkins shook his head. "Are you saying you have proof that Vernon Stratham hired an assassin to kill Perry?"

She finally had his fucking attention.

She walked Jenkins through the trail of evidence, from the buried tox panel at the coroner's office to the identity of the contract killer all the way through the Russian arms dealer and the shell companies, with the entire chain of evidence leading back to one man.

Vernon Stratham.

Jenkins' face looked whiter than the couch he was sitting on.

"You have all of this? Documented?"

Celina nodded. "And verified." She pulled a thumb drive from her pocket, held it up.

"Show me."

Celina plugged the drive into the computer on Jenkins' desk, typed in a password to decrypt it, then stood back for Jenkins to see. He scrolled through the documents, the color returning slowly to his face, his expression shifting from one of shock to one of stony determination. A powerful man, deceived by a trusted lieutenant.

When he'd skimmed through all of it, he sat back in his chair, crossed his legs at the knee, and folded his hands in his lap. He seemed perfectly at ease, save for the rapid tapping of his thumb against the knuckle of his other hand.

"I'll need to keep this," he said. Without waiting for a response, he leaned forward and pulled the thumb drive from the port on the computer and tucked it in his pocket.

"That's my only copy," Celina said.

She held out her hand.

Jenkins shook his head.

"I'm sorry, Celina, but I can't put you at risk like that."

"Put *me* at risk? You mean save your own skin, right?"

"This information would ruin me."

"Exactly."

"In the wrong hands, without full context, the insinuation would end my career." Jenkins pushed back from his desk, stepped toward the windows and stood gazing out at the street below, at the FBI building across the way. "Even with the full context, it would still destroy any chance I had for the presidency. My opponents would claim I was incompetent, not knowing my own campaign finance chairperson was a murderer."

"No shit, Bill." She strode to stand beside him. Her voice softened. "Why do you think I'm here?"

She held out her hand once more.

"If you have this proof in your possession and my opponents find out, they'll come after you."

"I can handle myself."

"I would have said the same thing about your father."

She laughed. "You think Senator fucking Deacon is going to order a hit on me just to get you out of the race?"

She heard her own words as she said them.

Fuck.

She hadn't really thought of that. That blue-blood asshole would totally do it. He'd order the hit as he wiped his mouth between his rare filet mignon and the cheese course. Were they all as ruthless as Stratham?

Jenkins must have seen the look on her face. He turned to her, put a hand on each of her shoulders.

"Are you sure this is the only copy?"

Celina sighed. She nodded.

Without another word, Jenkins strode to the picture of the

president on the wall behind his desk, removed it to reveal a wall safe. He opened it with his fingerprint. Inside, Celina could see several sheafs of papers, a thin box made of red leather, and something that glittered gold in the light. Jenkins set the thumb drive inside, shut the door again, and replaced the picture.

"What are you going to do?" Celina asked.

Jenkins sighed, his shoulders slumping as he shoved his hands deep into his pockets, his face darkened with dismay.

"I'm going to have to have a chat with my campaign finance chairperson."

His brow furrowed, and he looked up at Celina.

"Is this the reason you're doing all this..." He made a circling gesture with one hand. "All this whatever this is with the school and everything?"

Celina twisted her mouth in a wry smile.

"You're not an easy man to get a private meeting with."

"All you had to do was call."

Celina's wry smile fell. If she'd called, she wouldn't have gotten the information she needed. If she'd called, Jenkins would have had a warning that she was coming, and Celina would have lost the element of surprise, and all the information it had given her.

"I'll remember that," she said, replacing her wry smile with a warmer one, "for next time. For now, though, we have another problem."

Jenkins looked confused. "What's that?"

Celina headed toward the door.

"You just sent my boyfriend downstairs alone with a killer."

67

Self-defense was not Cam's specialty.

Neither was self-offense.

As he and Stratham strode down the marble hallway together past Jenkins' phalanx of security guards, rode the elevator down one floor, then made their way along the main hall and through the cubicle maze toward Stratham's office, Cam tried to channel his inner Celina.

What would she be thinking right now? She might try to take Stratham out while they walked, use surprise to her advantage and jab him in the face with a sharp elbow or kick him in the nuts when he wasn't expecting it. Or maybe she'd wait until she was in his office so she could gather more evidence, then take him out with a stapler to the head or smash him with the door until he passed out.

Cam was more inclined to just run away. Stratham was thin and wiry, but he was a good twenty years older than Cam. Cam could probably outrun him, right?

But no.

Cam thought about his mother sitting in jail. Celina said she had enough proof to pressure Jenkins to free his mother, but what if something went wrong? It wouldn't hurt to have more proof, and just a few weeks ago, Cam had been willing to throw himself at six trained guards to get to the thumb drive that was probably in Stratham's pocket right now. And here they were, just the two of them.

No. This was an opportunity, and Cam had to seize it. Stratham had ordered a hit on Devin Minsk. He'd ordered a hit on Celina's father. But had he ever killed anyone himself? Had he even been in a fight? There was a big difference between hiring a killer and doing the killing with your own hands. There may not be much difference in the mind, but there was a difference in the body.

Stratham was a glorified accountant. What had Paloma Minsk called him on the yacht? A mathmagician. Stratham's skills were in spreadsheets, not switchblades. Digits, not daggers. Finance, not fistfights.

Cam was no Jackie Chan, either, but at least it would be a fair fight between two people with no training whatsoever. And if Cam could gain the element of surprise...

Stratham opened his office door with his keycard, the lock making a loud click in the otherwise completely silent room. Stratham turned the door handle, but stood there holding the door closed, considering the keycard in his hand.

"I wondered when you would use this," he mused. "The one you stole, that is. And I wondered why. No amount of digging turned up anything about a Paul Baker. And Minsk being Minsk, there were no cameras on the yacht that I could use for facial recognition. You've remained a mystery all these months."

He turned to Cam and smiled, a genuine smile that Cam actually found charming.

"And now, here you are. A chance to have all the mysteries revealed."

He entered the office and held the door for Cam, gesturing to a seat in front of Stratham's desk.

"You're assuming I'll tell you anything," Cam said as he stepped inside.

He didn't sit yet. As Stratham turned his back toward him to close the door and walk around the desk, Cam saw his chance to take him, to choke him from behind or swing a foot between his legs or bash him in the head with the laptop sitting on the desk.

Cam sighed. He wasn't going to do any of those things.

Stratham shrugged as he gestured for Cam to sit, then unbuttoned his suit coat and sat down himself.

"Doesn't matter now," he said. He pointed over his shoulder toward the ceiling. Cam glanced up to see a black glass semisphere bulging from the corner. "I've got your face on a dozen cameras. I have another alias—Sam Davis, was it?. And your attendance at the school. It's enough."

Cam was sure it wouldn't be. He'd taken great pains to make sure it wouldn't be.

But, then again, no one was ever truly secure any more. It was impossible to hide now. But you could still make it more trouble than it was worth to do the work to uncover the identity.

Nonetheless, with enough tenacity and enough access to enough sources, Stratham could connect him to his apartment, trace his movements, track him to his mother's prison, and then he'd know. If he had the access, and if he was tenacious.

Cam watched Stratham set his laptop carefully to the side of his desk and straighten two fountain pens that had shifted slightly off of parallel.

Stratham would be tenacious.

And Jenkins would have the access.

Stratham could figure out who Cam really was, but Stratham didn't know how much Cam knew about him. That was Cam's advantage.

His only advantage, at the moment.

Stratham sat back in his chair and folded his hands over his stomach. He smiled cordially, as if he were interviewing his favorite nephew for a job he had already decided to give him.

"What were you doing on Devin Minsk's yacht?" he asked.

"Looking for information," Cam replied.

"What kind of information?"

Cam saw no point in being coy now.

"The kind I could use to pressure the Attorney General to free my mother from prison."

Stratham's eyebrows shot up, and Cam felt a thrill. It felt good to surprise a man who prided himself on knowing everything.

"Who is your mother?"

Cam smiled grimly. "You wouldn't know her."

Stratham gave a soft laugh and nodded slowly.

"Why is she in prison?"

Cam's grin faded.

"A cruel twist of fate," he said softly.

"Life, I assume?"

"As good as."

"Where?"

"Taconic Correctional Facility, Bedford Hills, New York."

Stratham frowned. "That's not a federal prison. It's not under the Attorney General's jurisdiction."

"He's a powerful man."

"And you think whatever information you have would be sufficient to... incentivize the Attorney General to jump through whatever hoops are needed to secure your mother's release?"

"That was the plan, yes."

"And how is that working out for you so far?" Stratham smiled and tented his fingers before his lips.

Cam smiled back. "I'm here, aren't I?"

Stratham kept the smile on his face, but leaned forward and set his elbows on the desk. He made a fist with one hand, covered it with the other, bored into Cam's skull with that steel-rod gaze again. The combination of the fist, the gaze, and the smile was incredibly unnerving. Cam felt the skin on the back of his neck prickle, but forced himself not to squirm in his seat, forced himself to keep his own smile steady and his own gaze level and locked on Stratham's.

After what seemed like hours of this staring contest, Stratham's smile widened. He stood and moved to the small window of his office, a window with an impressive view through tan vinyl blinds of the cubicle wall across the narrow walkway outside his door.

"Yes," he said, fingering the plastic rod connected to the cheap louvers, "you are here."

He twisted the blinds shut and turned back toward Cam. Cam felt the skin on his neck prickle even more, a drop of sweat tracing down his side under his suit coat and his dress shirt.

Cam's smile faded. Stratham's, seeing it, widened even more.

A predator smelling fear in his prey.

"Let's have a little chat, shall we?" Stratham said through his toothy smile. "Man to man."

68

CELINA DIDN'T BOTHER to wait for the elevator. She took the stairs down to Stratham's office, Jenkins close behind her.

She didn't know what to expect when she got there. Would Cam be bloodied and beaten? Jenkins' guards had all still been standing in the hallway when they emerged from his office. But maybe Stratham had his own guards. Or maybe he enjoyed getting his hands dirty. Some of those sadistic fucks enjoyed bloodying their own knuckles once in a while. The crunch of bone on bone, the hot gout of blood from a nose as it crumpled, the split of a cheek beneath their fist made them feel powerful and alive.

Celina knew the feeling. The difference was, when she swung her fists, the person whose nose she crumpled deserved it.

But Stratham didn't seem like the type. Those hands of his hadn't seen a day of physical labor in his entire life. Stratham was too genteel for the dirty work. And like all rich, powerful people, he hired others to do the messy jobs while he maintained his manicured fingernails and plausible deniability.

But that didn't mean Cam wasn't in danger.

Celina took the stairs two at a time, Jenkins struggling to

keep up behind her. She burst out of the stairwell door, rounded the corner and into the cubicle farm at a trot, winding her way toward Stratham's office using the mental map she'd memorized from the last time she'd been in the building.

The last time Cam nearly got himself killed. He seemed to have a real knack for it.

Celina's heart hammered when she saw that the blinds were closed over the window to Stratham's office. Her feet flew over the threadbare carpet.

There was a keycard scanner on the door, but Celina didn't break stride.

She put her shoulder to the door. It snapped open, splinters flying from where the lock had shattered the wood.

It was a cheap door, thin and hollow. It flew open in a blur, banged against the wall like a bomb blast and ricocheted back, shuddering.

Cam was sitting in a chair across from her, in front of Stratham. Stratham leaned casually against his desk, one leg draped over the corner, his elbow on his thigh.

They both flew to a standing position at Celina's intrusion.

"Please do come in," said Stratham with dry calm, once he'd collected himself. "I'm sorry, I didn't hear you knocking."

"Jesus, Celina," said Jenkins, breathless, when he came up behind her. "That's government property, you know."

"Take it out of my taxes," she said.

She looked at Cam, who stood wide-eyed beside Stratham. He seemed to be intact. No blood on his face or his shirt. His hand had been in his pocket. When he drew it out, Celina noticed that all of his fingers were present and unbroken.

He seemed totally fine.

Her heart rate began to slow again, at last.

"I just didn't want to miss out on the discussion down here," she said

Stratham arched an eyebrow, casting a quick glance at Jenkins, who stood behind her in the open doorway.

"Mr... Davis, here," said Stratham, "was just telling me why he decided to pursue a degree in criminology. It's a fascinating story, Attorney General. You'll want to hear it yourself."

Jenkins looked from Stratham to Cam, then to Celina, disbelief and incomprehension on his face.

"I.. uh... okay, that sounds... intriguing." He looked at Cam again. "Perhaps we'd be more comfortable back in my office, though?"

Celina spiked Stratham with a stare, suddenly seeing an opportunity.

"I'll stay here," she said, "with your campaign finance chairperson."

She sneered at Stratham as she thought of all the ways she could torture him before she pitched him down the elevator shaft.

"No!" shouted Cam and Jenkins at the same time.

"No way," Jenkins continued, giving Cam an odd stare before he swung his eyes back to Celina. "I'd much rather you come with us, Ms. Moon. You, too, Vernon."

They filed out of the room and down the hall to the elevator, grouping themselves two by two, with Jenkins and Stratham ahead. Celina lagged behind with Cam.

"Are you alright?" she hissed at him.

"I'm fine," he said, "but I'm glad you barged in when you did."

"What did you tell him?"

"He knows me from another job," Cam said. "A con from last summer. I went by Paul Baker that time."

"What did you tell him?"

"Figured he'd already caught me out, so I told him about my mother. I told him I have information and I want Jenkins to get her out."

"Did you tell him what the information was?"

"No."

Celina nodded. "What did he say?"

They caught up to the others before Cam could answer. The elevator dinged and they all entered, making the short trip up one floor in awkward silence. Celina gripped Cam's elbow and held him back for a moment, letting Stratham and Jenkins exit the elevator ahead of them.

"What did Stratham say when you told him?" she asked Cam.

"He was trying to talk me into keeping it away from Jenkins. He wanted me to let him handle everything."

"But he didn't push you to tell him what information you had?"

"No. He asked once. I told him it was information that would ruin Jenkins' chances for the presidency. He didn't ask again."

Celina's grip tightened on Cam's elbow as they moved even more slowly down the hall toward Jenkins' office.

"He wanted to keep you quiet until he could have you killed," she said.

"I figured," Cam replied. "How did it go with Jenkins? Did you tell him about Stratham?"

"I did. I even showed him the evidence."

Cam's eyebrows shot up. "And?"

"He fucking took it. Locked it in a wall safe behind his desk."

They couldn't walk any slower, and they had run out of hallway. Jenkins stood in the doorway to his office, a welcoming smile on his face.

"Lunch is already here," he said. "Mr. Davis," he clapped Cam on the shoulder and steered him down the short hallway into the office, "you can tell us your story while we eat."

69

This was it.

The last stage in Cam's long plan.

If he was going to free his mother, this was when and where it would happen.

On cushy white couches under high ceilings, a clear golden mid-day light streaming through the tall windows, with a plate of baked tarragon chicken and steamed green beans balanced on his thighs.

Not exactly how Cam had pictured it for all these years.

But he'd take it however he could get it.

He and Celina sat on opposite couches, with Jenkins and Stratham seated together on the couch between. They all ate from plates held in their laps or crouched forward over the coffee table in the center.

An inelegant way to eat lunch, but no doubt deemed sufficient for a couple of dewy-eyed college students.

Cam took a long, slow breath in through his nose and let it silently out through his mouth.

Then, he began.

"My name is Cameron Hauk."

427

He waited a long beat, savoring the slight widening of Stratham's eyes.

Jenkins was less guarded. He stopped mid-chew, his brow furrowing. Celina had told him about Stratham, but hadn't said anything about Cam.

"My mother, Paulina Hauk, was sentenced to three consecutive twenty-year sentences for bank theft. She's been incarcerated in Taconic Correctional Facility in New York for the last fifteen years."

Jenkins finished chewing, swallowed, and took a drink of water from his glass.

"And you used an alias... why?" he said. "Because you thought your mother's situation would jeopardize your career in law enforcement?"

"I used an alias because I didn't want anyone to know who I was," said Cam. "My intention was to meet you, sir. In private. And I didn't want anything to interfere with that plan."

"You paid for and completed a three-year degree in criminology," said Stratham, his voice slow and dripping with disbelief, "working hard to earn top marks in your class, all so you could gain a private audience with the Attorney General?"

Cam glanced at Stratham, then back to Jenkins. "You're not an easy man to be alone with."

Jenkins frowned, his eyes losing focus for a moment. When his attention returned, the air of the welcoming host was gone. His eyes were pure political calculation. When they stared at Cam, he felt like Jenkins was probing his very soul.

"Okay, Mr. Hauk," he said. "You've got me alone." He glanced at Stratham. "For the most part. And you've got my attention. What is it you've waited all this time to say to me?"

Cam had expected to be nervous. When he'd pictured this moment—and he'd pictured it hundreds of times, maybe thousands—he'd assumed his palms would be sweaty, his throat would be dry, his voice would be wavering. He'd assumed he would have to fall back on his training as a con man to push past all of those feelings and speak with confidence and conviction.

None of that turned out to be true.

In that moment, sitting in the private office of the man who would soon be the most powerful person in the free world, Cam felt completely at ease.

"Your campaign is dirty, Mr. Attorney General." He watched Jenkins glance at Celina, who merely shrugged, before those eyes swung back to Cam. "It's rotten, sir. From the inside."

Cam kept his eyes on Jenkins, resisted the urge to look at Stratham, and was impressed that Jenkins didn't look at Stratham either. Celina said she'd told him everything. Most people's eyes in that situation would have at least feinted toward Stratham, their involuntary actions revealing their instinctive thoughts. Jenkins had better control than most.

"That's a very serious accusation, Mr. Hauk," Jenkins said, his voice steady and smooth as glass. "I suppose now you're expecting me to arrange your mother's release in exchange for your silence on this matter?"

"That's exactly what I'm expecting."

"As a top criminology student, I'm sure you're aware of the laws regarding the blackmail of a government employee." His stare, somehow, became even more intense. "And the penalties."

"Blackmail?" Cam shrugged. "That's one way to think of this, sir."

Jenkins raised his eyebrows. "Is there another?"

Cam smiled. Jenkins' stare wavered a touch in surprise.

"There's always another way to think about things."

"And how would you think about this," said Jenkins, "if you were me?"

"I believe in you, Mr. Attorney General," said Cam. "I'm a voter, and I think you're the best candidate. I've learned something, something big, something that would ruin your plans of ever becoming president."

"So you've said."

"As a concerned supporter, I'm bringing this to your attention before the information falls into," Cam shrugged, "less
sympathetic hands."

"And you believe it would fall into those hands?"

"It's a big internet, and I'm just a private citizen. I don't have
the resources to prevent a hack or a leak."

"Right." Jenkins laughed once, mirthlessly. "And freeing your
mother? How would that not be seen as a quid pro quo?"

"I'm sure she's already on a list of cases for your review." Cam
had added it several days ago, backdated to make it seem like it
had been there for years. "You happen to meet with me, a
helpful citizen, and hearing my name somehow rings a bell.
That leads you to double-check your list and see my mother's
name. If you happen to look into my mother's case then and
there, realize the injustice of it, and choose to right that particular wrong, how could that be construed as anything but
circumstance and happy coincidence?"

Jenkins laughed for real that time, a perfunctory bark.

"Believe me, Mr. Hauk, that could and would be construed in
any number of ways by my opponents, if they were to find out."

Cam leveled his gaze at Jenkins.

"But none of those ways would be nearly as damning as the
information I have."

Jenkins' smile faded. "You have proof?" He glanced at Celina,
then back to Cam.

Slowly, Cam pulled a thumb drive from his pocket.

Celina gasped in surprise.

Stratham's expression, which had been shifting between
sardonic and professionally neutral up to that moment, darkened. He patted his pockets. His darkened face then reddened
with fury.

That made Cam smile a bit.

When Celina had busted into Stratham's office, when Cam

and Stratham had shot to their feet, Cam had used the distraction to lift the thumb drive from Stratham's pocket.

The first active skill his parents had taught him was how to pick a pocket. It required a combination of distraction and dexterity. He started when he was seven years old, taking advantage of the fact that most people, especially men, completely ignore small children. They don't even see them.

Between the ages of seven and twelve, he'd lifted countless items, from diamonds and documents to wallets and wristwatches. His proudest lift was a sunny day in a crowded St. Mark's Square in Venice. He stole the cash from a wealthy-looking American tourist's theft-proof travel pack, even while it was tucked safely beneath the man's shirt. Five hundred euros.

A few minutes later, when he saw the man's wife and two smiling young kids join him further down the street, Cam had felt bad. He and his family stole from the rich, not from happy young families. Cam did the whole job again in reverse and put the money back, minus a small processing fee, of course. The man hadn't felt a thing.

But nothing he'd lifted in the past had ever been as valuable as the hard drive in his hand in that moment. In that moment, he held in his hand the key to his mother's freedom.

He didn't know what was on the hard drive. Not exactly. He hadn't had time to look at it. But he knew it was the backup of Stratham's laptop.

And judging from the murderous look on Stratham's face, Cam knew he had something good.

70

Celina was impressed. Somehow, Cam had managed to get the data he'd been wanting all this time. Either that, or he was putting on a hell of a bluff.

And Stratham was obviously pissed as fuck.

Good. That fucker deserved what he got. And if Celina got him alone, he'd get a lot more than just red in the face. She'd kill him. Right there in the office of the Attorney General of the United States, if she had to. What better place to serve true justice?

At that moment, though, they had a good old-fashioned showdown between Cam and Jenkins.

Cam was on the couch across from Celina, holding the thumb drive. Jenkins sat on the couch to her left, looking thoughtfully at Cam. Sitting next to Jenkins, Stratham was getting redder and redder. It looked like his head was exploding in slow-motion.

Now that was something Celina would pay to see.

"What's on that drive, Mr. Hauk?" Jenkins' voice was cool and calm. He was on familiar ground now, negotiating with an adversary for political favors. He'd not only trained for that, he'd done it a million times.

"Data," said Cam. "Records of contributions to your campaign. Some of them are from, let's say, unsavory characters."

"Not a great look," said Jenkins, "but not unusual. And hardly a campaign killer."

"Maybe not. But since you mentioned killing, I think you'd find that some of those unsavory characters actually are killers."

Jenkins smiled. "Again, not great, but not unusual. A president is president for all citizens."

"You're the Attorney General, so you'll know the answer to this question," said Cam, smiling as he threw Jenkins' earlier barb right back at him. "Does the president have blanket immunity? Is the president above the law?"

Jenkins' smile fell. "No one is above the law."

"Oh." Cam's voice was easy and light, as if they were discussing their lunch. "Well, then some of the records on here *will* be unusual. And definitely not great."

Jenkins' eyes narrowed to slits. "Why?"

"There are more than just inbound contributions in these records, sir. There are outbound payments from your campaign, as well. Payments to some of those unsavory characters. For some very unsavory deeds."

Jenkins paused. When he spoke, his words were careful, measured.

"If my campaign is as unsavory as you suggest," he said, "why would you think we wouldn't just incapacitate you and take the evidence?"

Cam gave Jenkins his best imitation of the *you can't possibly be that naïve* look. It had to be a bluff. He hadn't said anything to Celina about any evidence before. Bluff or not, Cam had to sell it with everything he had.

"This isn't the only copy, sir," he said with a slight smile. "And there are emails and file transfers to several prominent political journalists set to trigger in—" he checked his watch, "twenty-seven minutes, unless I cancel them first. Washington Post, New York Times, CNN. Oh, and Fox News." He smiled lightly. "They'll have a field day." Cam shrugged. "You could... What was your word? Incapacitate?... You could incapacitate me, if you like, but you'll only be hurting yourself."

Celina swung her gaze from Cam to Stratham, who was obviously murdering Cam in a thousand ways in his mind, then watched Jenkins. He was stone-faced, processing what Cam was saying, evaluating Cam's demeanor, his body language. Interpreting all the information available to him in that moment, weighing the consequences of various courses of action. Celina could practically hear the gears cranking in Jenkins' brilliant political mind.

Jenkins stared hard at Cam for a long moment, swung an accusatory glance toward Stratham, then sat back against the couch, his jaw set. Celina could feel the anger coming from him, could see it flashing in his eyes.

She'd seen him annoyed. She'd seen him frustrated. She'd seen him distraught. But for the first time, she was seeing William Jenkins when he'd been crossed.

It was a sobering thing to watch. Celina pitied anyone who wound up on Jenkins' bad side.

"Vernon," Jenkins said, his teeth clenched, "would you please give us the room?"

Stratham's eyes flew wide open. "Bill, you can't—"

"Vernon." Jenkins gave him a stare that would melt steel.

Celina couldn't help grinning when she saw it, and she had to correct her previous thought. Right then, it looked like Stratham was on Jenkins' bad side. And Celina didn't have one ounce of pity for him.

Stratham composed himself and stood, buttoned his jacket, and left the room with a slow, somber stride. Jenkins waited until they heard the click of the outer door being shut before he continued.

"Celina," he started, then paused to look at Cam. Seeing that Cam didn't react to his use of her real name, he sniffed once and nodded to himself, then faced her again. "I thought you said there was only one copy of that evidence."

Celina felt no joy at the question. Earlier, Jenkins had said he wanted the thumb drive so he could protect her. As if she needed protecting. She'd known then it was bullshit, but it was sweet-smelling bullshit, at least. She was disappointed to see him dropping the act so quickly.

"It's not the same evidence, Bill," she said. "Looks like your right-hand man is an even bigger asshole than I thought."

Jenkins swore softly, staring at the floor, then closed his eyes and pulled in a long, deep breath. When he opened his eyes again, the anger was gone. Just like that. It had been radiating from him a second earlier, and then it was all fucking sunshine and democracy again.

"Well played, Mr. Hauk," he said. He stood and buttoned his suit coat, then held out his hand.

Cam stood, stared at Jenkins' open hand for a moment, then shook it.

Jenkins winced, then turned it into a wry smile.

"The thumb drive, Mr. Hauk," he said. "If you don't mind."

"Oh, I do mind," Cam replied. He slid the thumb drive back into his pocket and clasped his hands calmly in front of him.

Jenkins curled his hands into fists, so tight Celina could hear his knuckles crackle.

She leaned back and spread both arms on the back of the couch, grinning.

She'd never wanted Cameron Hauk more.

71

Cam knew it was a risk. He was so close to getting everything he'd been wanting, not just for the last three years, but for the last fifteen. Since he'd watched the prison guards lead his mother through those fucking iron doors into Taconic.

And here he stood, before the man who could make it all happen, telling him no.

"You'll get the thumb drive," Cam said to Jenkins. "You have my word. But not until my mother is free and back home with a clear record."

"Your word?" said Jenkins. "You mean the word of a criminal? A criminal, I might add, who comes from a long line of criminals?"

"The line's not that long," Cam said with a wry grin. "My family business is just getting started."

His parents were the first criminals in his family. Before that, his lineage was full of lawyers and shopkeepers and corporate drones on both sides. Respectable (boring) people in respectable (boring) professions.

Cam had no intention of living that kind of life. And if he ever had kids, he would teach them the same way his parents had taught him, then let them make their own choices.

Jerkins was not amused. "Your word doesn't mean much to me."

Cam's grin disappeared, and his face grew serious. He'd heard people say in the past that jobs, cons—hell, even life itself —came down to a series of individual moments. This was one of those moments. This was *the* moment. He needed Jenkins to trust him, or the deal would never work.

He stared hard at Jenkins.

"My word is solid," he said, with every ounce of conviction his body and his mind could muster. "If I give it, I mean it. I may be a criminal, but I'm an honest one."

It wasn't much of a speech, but it was sincere. Cam's parents had taught him a lot of things, and living by his word was one of them. Honor among thieves. Without honor, without a solid moral code, they would become nothing more than thugs. Villains.

Cam glanced at Celina. She was biased, of course, but she seemed impressed with the speech.

It looked like Jenkins was, too. He clearly didn't like it, but it looked like he believed it. And after Cam's threats of contacting the press, he believed he didn't have much of a choice.

Seeing Cam's glance, Jenkins looked at Celina, who locked eyes with him and nodded. That seemed to confirm something in Jenkins' mind. Cam's chest filled with a bubbling brightness at the shift in Jenkins' attitude.

"What about you, Mr. Jenkins?" Cam said, working to keep his voice calm and level. "You'll have to hold up your end of the bargain. The word of a politician generally doesn't mean much, either."

"It'll take some time," Jenkins said, ignoring Cam's dig, then held up a hand as Cam began to protest. "Not weeks or months. Hours, certainly. Maybe days." Jenkins pressed his lips together and nodded grimly. "But you'll see your mother soon." He locked eyes with Cam. "You have *my* word on that."

Cam nodded. He knew something like this didn't happen with the snap of a finger. He'd expected to wait, especially since his mother was in a state prison, not a federal one, thanks to some legal fine print and the peculiarities of her case. He'd been expecting the process to take weeks. Hours or days was a welcome surprise, and that bubbling brightness in his chest grew even stronger.

Cam patted the thumb drive in his pocket.

"Until then," he said, "I'll keep this safe. And private."

"See that you do," said Jenkins, his voice as sharp as a blade, as hard as a sledgehammer, "or you and your mother will both be in jail for the rest of your lives. Traffic ticket, IRS audit. Hell, if you so much as jaywalk, I'll lock you both up and weld the goddamn cell door shut."

The look in his eyes let Cam know he meant every word that he said.

Cam nodded, then looked at Celina. That bubbling brightness broke into a tide of feeling, welling within him as he held her gorgeous gaze. Relief and joy and exhaustion and disbelief, all threatening to overwhelm him in that moment.

He forced the feelings down as best he could. He didn't want to celebrate—or break down—in front of Jenkins. There was still work to be done, promises to be kept. The gears of government were rusty and brittle, and no politician could be trusted, no matter what they said. Cam would believe it was done when he could finally touch his mother again, when he could pull her into a long-overdue hug.

But he was there. He'd made it to the end. After all this time, his plan was complete. He held those feelings at bay as best he could, but he knew he wouldn't be able to hold them back for long.

"Well, Mr. Attorney General," he said, swallowing the bubble of giddy enthusiasm in the back of his throat as he spoke, "I'd like to thank you for a lovely and productive morning. But now, we'd best be off." He nodded toward a clock on the wall. "We all have a graduation to get to."

Jenkins checked his watch and grumbled something. They walked out the door. Stratham was pacing in the hallway. As he fell into step beside the Attorney General, speaking with him in hushed, angry whispers, Cam slipped his hand into Celina's, intertwined his fingers with hers.

They trailed behind Jenkins and Stratham. Celina leaned her head toward Cam.

"Can I kill that fucker now?" she whispered. Her breath was hot in Cam's ear, sending a thrill through his body.

"I wish you wouldn't."

"Maim him?"

"Probably not the best idea."

"Okay," she sighed, "just a subtle disfigurement, then."

"I think Attorney General Jenkins will take care of Stratham for you."

Celina mumbled a reply that Cam couldn't make out. But he could guess from her tone the gist of it.

He smiled. He felt light in his chest, lighter than he'd felt in years. He felt light enough to lift off the ground and float toward the high, sky-lit ceiling above.

As they strode down the wide marble-floored hallway, Cam took the time to admire the murals on the walls, the statues in nooks along the way, the ornate marquetry on the pilasters. As the elevator doors opened, he took pleasure in the glint of the sunlight off the aluminum pattern inlaid on the doors.

Cam was about to enter a new world, one where he didn't have to pretend anymore, didn't have to worry anymore. He could live his life, with his mother at his side.

And Celina, too, he hoped.

As they rode down the elevator in silence, he and Celina in front, Jenkins and Stratham behind them, two of Jenkins' guards on either side, Cam looked to his side at Celina. She looked back, held his gaze.

So incredibly beautiful. So incredibly smart.

He heard the elevator dinged softly as they reached the first floor. The doors opened, spilling natural light on Celina's gorgeous face. She glowed as if from within.

Before they stepped off the elevator, Celina took a half-step backward and drove her elbow hard into Stratham's sternum. His breath left him in a whoosh, followed by a guttural groan. Stratham doubled over and fell to a knee, clutching his chest.

Celina smiled, a bright, sunny smile, hooked her arm in Cam's, and led them both off the elevator.

So beautiful, so smart.

And so incredibly dangerous.

Cam couldn't wait to see what they got into next.

72

THREE WEEKS LATER

Cameron Hauk carried two steaming glasses of double espresso from the kitchen through a pair of wide, sliding glass double doors onto a stone tile deck. It was early and the fog that blanketed the bay each night hadn't yet been kicked off by the day.

On Cam's right, the twin spires of the Golden Gate bridge were just visible poking above the fog bank, glowing bright orange as if they'd been heated by the touch of the morning sun. A beacon through the grey fog.

At ground level, the air was still chilly and the breeze from the sea dropped the temperature further to a cool fifty-two degrees.

Perfect.

There were six wide, cushioned Adirondack chairs arranged around a dormant fire pit on the tiled deck, oriented to look through a glass-walled railing and out over the low cliffside and across the endless tableau of the Pacific ocean. The view was stunning.

As Cam approached the chairs from behind, an even more

stunning sight came into view, one that stopped Cam's heart, then made it leap into the middle of his throat.

It had been two weeks since Paulie had come home, and Cam still had that same reaction every time he saw her. Sitting in front of the fire reading a book. Standing in the kitchen watching Celina prepare dinner. Walking barefoot in the hallway, stopping to experience the feel of the plush carpet beneath her toes. Every time he came upon his mother, Cam's heart stopped with surprise, then leapt with joy.

He hoped that reaction never went away.

This time, it was her dark hair shot through with silver that caught him first. It tufted in a bunch over the back of the chair cushion, stray strands blowing in the breeze like a weather vane, reaching back toward Cam. He stepped quickly toward her, the stone tiles frigid against his bare soles, still holding onto the cold of the night.

"Should have worn slippers," he muttered as he handed one cup to his mother, then slid into the chair beside her. He sat cross-legged in the chair, tucking his bare feet under his thighs for warmth. His knees jutted out beneath the chair's wide arms.

His mother took the cup with a broad smile that sent another happy shiver through Cam's body. She closed her eyes and sipped slowly, the steam from the coffee wafting up over her nose, her forehead, and away behind her on the breeze.

She let out a soft moan. "I hope I never forget how good this tastes," she said. She cradled the warm cup in her hands and opened her eyes, looking out across the ocean. "Or how beautiful this looks."

She leaned her head back against the chair cushion, turned it to look at Cam, and held out her hand. Cam reached across the space between their chairs to take his mother's hand in his. Despite fifteen years in a prison cell, her skin was as soft and warm as he remembered. Holding her hand was like laying your head down on your pillow at night after a long day. Easy, welcome, instantly relaxing.

"Thank you, Cam," she said.

She'd said it at least twenty times a day for the last two weeks, since that moment in the parking lot outside Taconic Correctional Facility, a continent's width away, when Cam and Celina had watched the iron door swing open and a line of guards pour out. One by one, they gave Paulie a hug goodbye. It was like the receiving line at a wedding, only in reverse. Every one of the guards came out to wish Paulie well. Cam was some distance away, but it looked like one or two of them even had tears in their eyes.

And then it was Cam's turn. He'd visited nearly every week for fifteen years, and in all that time, he'd never been allowed to touch his own mother. He couldn't squeeze her hand, he couldn't kiss her cheek, he couldn't give her a hug.

So when she came up to him in that parking lot, when she took both of his hands in hers, when he leaned in to kiss her cheek, then wrapped her small, thin body in his arms, the last bit of his tension, of the anxiety that Cam had held in his heart for fifteen years, finally released in a gush of soundless tears that streamed down Cam's cheeks, under his chin, and into his mother's salt-and-pepper hair.

As he sat in the Adirondack chair and held his mother's hand on the deck of Celina's San Francisco home, he felt those tears close at hand again, as they had been since that day at the prison. Since that day in Jenkins' office, really.

"Oh sure, your mom gets out of prison and I'm left to make my own coffee for the rest of my life. I see how it is."

Paulie didn't turn, but laughed out loud, three shimmering notes that made Cam's heart stop and leap again. He turned his head to see Celina standing in the doorway, hands on her hips. She strode forward, sat on the arm of Cam's chair, plucked his cup from his hand, and sipped it.

"That's okay," she said, leaning down to give Cam a kiss on his forehead. "I'll just take yours."

Cam wrapped his now-free hand around Celina's waist. She leaned in, her side against his head. He could feel the warmth of her, could smell her lavender scent.

He released his mother's hand to wrap both of his arms around Celina and pull her closer. He pressed his face against her, felt the swell of her breast, the firm swale of her abs. He pulled a deep breath, drawing deep that lavender scent, pulling into him, into every cell of him.

They'd made love not an hour ago, and Cam already wanted more. He couldn't get enough of that woman, Celina Maxwell.

He craned his neck and drew his eye up along her figure to her gorgeous face. She arched one eyebrow at him and the edge of her lips quirked upward. Cam grinned back.

He sat there on the deck, his mother beside him, Celina in his arms, looking out over the wide, grey sea. Gentle swells rolled in lines toward shore. He could hear them crash against the rocks below and roll in over the beach. Cam couldn't see them break, but he could see the white foam, the shattered wave floating back out to sea to reform and return.

The rhythm of the sounds and the swells lulled him. He held Celina even closer, let her warmth and that rhythm embrace him.

He reached out to take his mother's hand again. He squeezed it once. She squeezed back, then let it go. She sipped her coffee again, again released a soft moan of pleasure.

A single shaft of light broke through the fog and peered down at a single spot in the ocean, as if the heavens were searching for something.

Cam wasn't searching any more. He'd finally found every-thing that mattered.

<h1 style="text-align:center">73</h1>

CELINA FINISHED her double espresso just as the fog rolled back enough to reveal the Golden Gate bridge in all its weird orange glory. It used to be the perfect symbol for San Francisco, back when the city was a beacon for gay pride, alternative lifestyles, and hippies tripping on acid.

Now, San Francisco was a beacon for rich, entitled, white male tech bros who think they're smarter than everyone else just because they were lucky enough to get rich in an overheated, under-regulated tech market. And the bridge was still just weird and orange.

Beautiful, though. Celina went into the kitchen to make two more espressos, another for her and a replacement for Cam. She wasn't a total asshole. She'd stolen his drink, she'd make him another.

In the future, though, she did expect a hot cup of coffee waiting for her once in a while. She was no one's waitress.

And she knew she'd get it. Cam was that rarest of creatures: a good man. He was smart, but not arrogant. Bold, but not cocky. Driven, but not obsessive. Celina started the first coffee and looked out the window at the two of them sitting on the deck,

Cam holding his mother's hand between the chairs again. He wasn't a mamma's boy, but he loved his mother dearly.

Not that Celina would blame him if he were a momma's boy. Paulie Hauk was an incredible woman. Celina had gathered that much the first time she'd met with her in the prison. Now that she was able to spend real time with her for the last two weeks, out in the free world, Celina was even more convinced. At fifty-six, Paulina Hauk had the energy of a thirty-year-old, the wisdom of a ninety-year-old, the curiosity of a three-year-old, and the spunk of a sixteen-year-old. And all of it was wrapped up in a package of effortless beauty, welcoming peacefulness, and compassionate grace.

If Celina had a mother like that, she'd bust her ass to get her out of jail, too.

With her actual mother, though just as beautiful, graceful, energetic, and spunky as Paulie, Celina would rather see her behind bars than outside them.

It would never happen. Power is rarely punished. And when it is, the punishment never lasts long.

The Nespresso machine whirred to a stop on the first coffee. Celina swapped cups and pushed the button for the second coffee.

She was glad that the house had people in it again. For months after her father's death, Celina had isolated herself, first in grief, then in rage, then in cold determination to find the truth.

Eventually, that determination had led her to Cam and Paulie. A blessing.

So far, it hadn't led to any justice, though. Bill Jenkins, as expected, had announced his presidential campaign from the podium on the graduation stage. Since then, there'd been a flurry of press and TV spots and a tour of campaign stops around the country. Celina had watched the videos carefully. No sign of Stratham anywhere.

But no news of his demotion, either, let alone an investigation or arrest.

Celina thought about the morning of graduation day. She'd been close enough to Stratham. She could have killed him. Easily. Maybe she should have. There was no doubt he deserved it. But something had stopped her.

Not something. Someone.

Cam didn't like violence. He was no fucking good at it, that much was clear. But he was morally opposed to it, as well. And so was Paulie. They hadn't come out and said it quite so plainly, but it was obvious in everything they did. The way they planned their jobs, the way they prepared, the way they carried themselves. No defensiveness, no aggression.

When she'd gone to D.C. at the start of the year, Celina had fully intended to put Stratham—and Jenkins—in a body bag. She knew how to do it. She'd never killed anyone before, but she knew how to do it, and she knew how to get away with it.

But she knew that if she did, she'd lose Cam. Call it intuition, but something told her that was a red line for Cam.

Celina didn't know where she and Cam would end up, but she wasn't ready to cross any red lines just yet.

As he'd promised, Cam had brought the thumb drive to Jenkins once his mother had been freed. He'd made a show of deleting all other copies, emails, texts, etcetera. Enough to satisfy Jenkins and his supposed computer expert.

Of course Cam and Celina had kept a copy, along with another copy of the data Jenkins had taken from Celina. In the modern world, information was cheap, and computer storage was even cheaper. If Jenkins really believed he controlled that data, he was a fool. And Celina knew that Bill Jenkins was no fool.

But an agreement had been reached, and both sides were honoring it.

So far.

But if Stratham didn't get what he deserved, and soon, Celina would be forced to take matters into her own hands.

Hands which, after three weeks of idleness, were itching to fucking do something again.

The machine finished the second cup. Celina took one to Cam, then sat on the other side of Paulie to enjoy her own coffee.

The beautiful Pacific Ocean. The beautiful bridge. The beautiful view from the beautiful, secluded deck of her father's house. Now Celina's house.

Celina didn't give a shit about any of it. She was not built to sit around watching the fog roll in and out. She needed to work.

She glanced at Paulie, sitting beside her with her eyes closed. Paulie must have felt her gaze. She turned her head toward Celina.

A slow smile crept across Paulie's face as she regarded Celina. She winked.

As if on cue, the fog rolled back just enough for the full sun to emerge from behind it, bathing all three of them in warm light.

Celina grinned back at Paulie.

She'd just had a wonderful idea.

74

THE WARMTH of the sun seeped into Paulie's face and through her entire body. It felt even better after the delicious chill of the air in the morning. She closed her eyes and listened to the waves crashing and the seagulls squawking. Let the sounds flow through her. She drew in a deep, slow breath through her nose, smelled the fish and the seaweed, tasted the salt air on the back of her tongue.

She was a part of all this. She was a part of life. Whether in a prison cell in New York or on a deck overlooking the ocean in California, she was a part of the life around her.

She did miss her friends from prison, but given the choice, she preferred the deck in California.

She heard Celina deliver a coffee to Cam with a murmur and a kiss, then heard the chair cushions rustle as Celina sat down on Paulie's other side.

Her kids.

She was surrounded by her kids.

Celina wasn't her kid, but she already thought of her that way. Why not? Didn't hurt anyone. Paulie didn't know what would happen between Celina and Cam, but she knew they were in love. She knew they were good for each other. That much was obvious. Lots of things could get in the way, and lots of things would try over the years. But they were good for each other, and if they made sure to remember that simple fact, they might have a long, happy life together.

Like her and her Sam. A long, happy life that ended way too soon. She could choose to be bitter about the way Sam had been taken from her. A stray gunshot. The irony of cruel fate.

But bitterness wouldn't bring Sam back. And it would ruin the memory of him and their love.

Paulie could feel the same kind of love between Cam and Celina. It flowed through her now. Quiet, small, vulnerable, like the sounds of the waves and the heat of the sun. All it took to stop them was a closed door or an opened umbrella. But the love was there, and like the ocean and the sun, it would be there whenever the kids chose to open themselves to it.

Paulie felt Celina looking at her, turned her head and opened her eyes.

Cam was a hell of an artist, though he still wouldn't admit it to himself. But even he couldn't capture Celina's beauty. She was gorgeous. Long, dark hair that shimmered like the sea in the sunlight. Clear emerald eyes that blazed with fire as she squinted into the sun. A well-proportioned face with high cheekbones, full eyebrows, and a mouth with a scalloped upper lip and a plump bottom lip. She had the kind of looks that would stop traffic.

But it was the intelligence in those eyes that had first caught Paulie's attention. From the moment she'd met Celina, before they'd even spoken, Paulie could see that this woman had strength and smarts to match her looks.

Cam would have to rise to that challenge. He'd been so focused for so long on getting Paulie out of prison that he'd lost himself a bit. It hurt Paulie to see it. She would rather have died behind bars than watched him lose touch with the things that made Cam who he was. His sensitivity, his creativity, his confidence, and his ability to see and accept what was in front of him without judgment.

He'd lost some of that confidence over the years. Paulie had seen it slowly erode with every visit, with every year that passed where he still hadn't found a way to get her out. She was grateful for his efforts, but she'd never asked him to get her out. She wanted him to live his life. Live and love and tell her all about it. That's all.

But he'd done it, in the end. He'd sprung her. And he'd found love, too.

The sun lit Celina's beautiful face and made it glow like a beacon on a dark night. As Paulie watched, a thought came into Celina's eyes, a thought that lit her face even more, brought it to vivid life. Whatever that thought was, Paulie could tell it would be an interesting one.

Good.

Paulie had done a lot of jobs in her life, first with her husband and their crew, then with Cam along for the ride. They'd had a lot of great times together. If she never pulled another job, Paulie could live the rest of her life and die happy.

But what the hell? As long as she was free, she might as well have some fun.

Right?

75

THE SUN CAME out and Cam immediately started to feel hot. Even the cool breeze off the sea wasn't enough to cool him down. And the fresh coffee Celina had brought him didn't help. He felt sweat break out all over. When he wiped his hand over his forehead, it came back wet and shining. Time to head inside.

And maybe he could convince Celina to come along.

He felt himself start to stiffen at the thought.

Damn, he had it bad.

And that was good.

He smiled, tossed back the last sip of his espresso, and stood from the chair. When he turned toward Celina, she was looking at his mother.

She had a dangerous look in her eye.

Celina slid her gaze to Cam, snaring him with her gorgeous green eyes. He let himself be snared, happily.

Would he ever be able to resist those eyes? Would he ever want to?

Beside Celina, his mother turned her gaze to him, too.

Holy shit.

Her eyes had the same dangerous look as Celina's.

Good lord. Out of prison for only two weeks and already she had that look?

Cam shook his head at them, then turned his head toward the sea, toward the sun, to hide the smile that crept over his face.

Didn't matter. He couldn't hide it. The smile became a wide grin.

He turned back to them.

"Well?" he said to Celina. "Let's hear the plan."

Now that his mother was free, Cam didn't know what direction his life would take next. But from the looks on the faces of the two women in front of him, he could tell it was going to be a wild ride.

ACKNOWLEDGMENTS

As always, my love and thanks to Holly. Without your support, my love, none of this would be possible.

ABOUT THE AUTHOR

Kevin Robert Aldrich lives in California and is the author of several mystery and romance novels:

If you love a twisting, pulse-pounding mystery, you'll love the Cameron Hauk series: Eyes in the Dark, Key Witness, Scale of Justice, and Tête A Tête.

If you love heart-pounding romantic suspense, you'll love Bare Trap and Flames of Freedom.

If you like vampires, witches, and forbidden love, get a copy of Spellbound now.

And if you love powerful contemporary romance, try Racing Hearts and Ollie & Alli today.

NEWSLETTER SIGN-UP

To learn more about Kevin Robert Aldrich and stay up-to-date with all of his stories and novels, please visit his website:

www.kevinrobertaldrich.com

To be automatically notified of every new release, sign up for the Kevin Robert Aldrich newsletter at the website above.